THE COLOUR WAS RED

THE COLOUR WAS RED

Alan Shelley

Book Guild Publishing
Sussex, England

First published in Great Britain in 2008 by
The Book Guild Ltd
Pavilion View
19 New Road
Brighton, BN1 1UF

Typesetting in Baskerville by
SetSystems Ltd, Saffron Walden, Essex

Printed in Great Britain by
CPI Antony Rowe

A catalogue record for this book is available from the British Library

ISBN 978 1 84624 247 2

For Joey

Author's Acknowledgements

I am grateful to the following for permission to reproduce extracts in this book: from *A Subaltern's Love Song*, Copyright John Betjeman, by permission of the estate of John Betjeman; from *A Simple Lust* by Dennis Brutus (reprinted by permission of Pearson Education); *The General* by Siegfried Sassoon, Copyright Siegfried Sassoon, by kind permission of the Estate of George Sassoon and, in the USA, *The General* from *Collected Poems of Siegfried Sassoon* by Siegfried Sassoon, copyright 1918, 1920 by E P Dutton. Copyright 1936, 1946, 1947, 1948 by Siegfried Sassoon. Used by permission of Viking Penguin, a division of Penguin Group (USA) Inc.

I am indebted to Rupert Furneaux for his book, *Massacre at Amritsar*, which provided valuable factual information about this incident in 1919. The book was published in 1963 by George Allen and Unwin Ltd.

Chapter One

Matthew

As he lay awake, straining to hear above the drone of the air-conditioner, he thought he could hardly hold the British Council responsible for his predicament. Nevertheless, they were the reason why he had come to Lagos in the first place and but for them Nigeria, and its unhappy progression from colony to anarchy, would not have been the backdrop for the last dozen or so years of his life. Or should the blame belong to his father—to the intense and extraordinary concept of loyalty to friends and colleagues that Matthew had inherited? He turned to face his sleeping wife as he imagined the sound of the vehicle that would be turning into the driveway of his house containing members of the Nigerian army or the police force—or both—who had come to arrest him. In the warm and slightly humid darkness, despite the best that a second-hand Carrier could do, his imagination ran rife. After returning from the disquieting interview with the Security Services at Dodan Barracks he had discussed with Isobel, in an exhibition of what was a disturbing example of British phlegm, what she should do if he was to be taken into custody. Disturbing because the current tensions in the country meant that no common-sense assessment was possible as to what might happen to him if the powers that be decided to act. They talked in a matter-of-fact sort of way, hiding the panic they both felt, about the British High Commission being her first point of call, but they agreed she should also contact Rotimi—if he himself was not in custody. They did not voice the obvious: quitting the country should have been at the top of their agenda—but it was not. They were reluctant to contemplate this; their lives were in Nigeria, his business was in Nigeria and, even more decisively, they did not want to quit because of a threat that might never materialise. Were his actions as well known in the State Security Services as he thought they might be, and even if they were in the picture, would they bother with him? Did they have the efficiency to understand what role he had played, however relatively minor, in Nigeria's recent politics?

What he did know for sure was that the Nigerian authorities could act quite irrationally and it was this thought that, under his apparent composure, agitated his brain into an insomnia of outright terror. He tried to comfort himself with the familiar notion that in the small hours of the night the brain can inflame a spark of anxiety into a forest fire of fear, but the warm air and calmness emanating from his sleeping wife, and her gentle, high-pitched night-time breathing, only added to the feeling that this platitude was not working for him. His fevered imagination galloped through totally irrational images of the Chateau d'If and Devil's Island (he had recently finished reading *Papillon*) to be replaced by the equally forbidding, although more realistic, tales he had heard of conditions in the Lagos prison at Kirikiri. If they could lock up the Yoruba Wole Soyinka, their foremost man of letters, what might they do in the case of an Englishman who had been so passionately sympathetic to the Ibo cause? He had little faith at three o'clock in the morning in the concept of diplomatic immunity or any notion that his white skin might give him some protection. He turned over onto his right side, away from Isobel, and gave an involuntary shudder as he recalled Simon's Angolan/Portuguese relations who had had one of their number incarcerated in an offshore jail where the cell was invaded by two or more feet of water at every high tide. This image fed into the pictures he had seen on Nigerian TV of people involved in previous coups being taken to a local beach to be shot under public gaze. Hordes had flocked to this truly gruesome spectacle that soon became known as 'The Bar Beach Show'.

As Matthew dozed he thought about the short political history of the country since Independence. Isobel had worked for Sir Abubakar Tafawa Balawa, the first Prime Minister of the new Nigeria. She had respected him, like many others inside and outside the country, even though the writing of history would no doubt show that he was more under the thumb of the Sardauna of Sokoto than previously thought and doubts could be raised as to whether he had truly supported the concept of 'one Nigeria', or had always favoured a takeover by the North long before the Biafran case. After all, words from the speech he made as a

Northern member in 1947 were subsequently to assume the status of a mantra.

'We do not want, Sir, our Southern neighbours to interfere in our development . . . I should like to make it clear to you that if the British quitted Nigeria now at this stage the Northern people would continue their interrupted conquest to the sea.'

However, under him there had been a year or two of optimism and it had seemed as if the new democracy was going to work—but it was not to be. Unrest began in the Western Region and this led to the first coup of 1966 when many of the major political leaders, including the Prime Minister, were assassinated. At the time, the impact of this coup on the populace was muted, illustrated, Matthew thought, by the manner in which he had discovered there had been a military takeover. By that date he and Peter had set up their business, operating from an office on Broad Street. When they arrived there on that Saturday morning they found the telephone was dead, so Peter sent their messenger, Christopher, to the telephone exchange in Tinubu Square where he found the building guarded by soldiers. The irony was not lost on Matthew when he thought of how, a few years later, telephones in Lagos had virtually ceased working altogether without any intervention by the military. The January 1966 coup seemed to establish the norm for future uprisings in that the new leaders decided they must first obtain control of telephones and radio stations—particularly the latter, where all broadcasting was suspended and replaced by martial music of the most stirring kind. On the occasion of a subsequent military coup d'état Matthew had guessed, on his way to work one morning, what had happened from the output available from the radio in his car.

The next military intervention in July 1966 was predominantly anti-Ibo and, as he recalled those days of horror in Kano, led to the slaughter of thousands of Easterners in the North of the country where many had lived for generations. This in turn led to the act of secession when, on 30th May 1967, Emeka Ojukwu proclaimed the new Republic of Biafra resulting in a terrifying civil war where up to one million Nigerians lost their lives—and in which Matthew was to become involved.

His reverie was interrupted as he heard, more than once, the hiss of tyres on the wet road alongside his property but so far there had been no sign of anyone stopping. He drifted into sleep only to wake up with a start. Another car—or was it a lorry? Had it come to a halt? He passed the night in this fashion, with the result that when Herbert brought the tea at seven o'clock he was fast asleep.

He sat at the breakfast table and gazed blankly through the water-streaked French windows as he presented to the servants his usual quiet morning demeanour. Isobel and the children were still upstairs and unless Herbert had some new anecdote to recount, breakfast was normally taken in silence. Today was no exception. The *Daily Times* lay open to his right, but he was not reading as he re-staged, in truncated form, his night-time imaginings. He followed his paw-paw with the usual morning paludrine tablet and as he swallowed this vital prophylactic he could not help—despite the deep-seated anxiety he had been rehearsing throughout the night—recalling the connection between this small white tablet and Isobel; and if his mind had considered last night's sleeplessness to be a rehearsal of what might be to come, there was a further link. They had met during the rehearsal for a review he was producing for the British Council with the trivial title of *The Paludrine Show.* One of the objectives of the British Council was to promote 'Britishness', although whether his revue managed to follow this principle was a moot point. He could not help smiling as he wondered, not for the first time, what message had been conveyed in the sketch where, at a typical middle-class dinner party, a partially naked maid walked onto the stage bearing the first course and delivered the message, 'Madam said I should serve the salad undressed.' Salad was hardly at the top of the Nigerian menu and the relationship between a bowl of lettuce and dressing would have been totally lost on any audience of locals visiting the Council to imbibe some British culture. He found little comfort in these fruitless musings as he finished his tea and picked up his briefcase. He ignored the umbrella proffered by Herbert and ran to his car, dodging the rain as best he could. His driver Kadejo was his usual taciturn self. It was the 10th of January 1970.

Matthew Cresswell's ancestors had been small-scale tenant farmers in Leicestershire for many generations but at the turn of the century his grandfather, by hard work and some good fortune, had prospered. As a result John Cresswell had been able to extend the family farm-holdings by freehold purchases and send his only son,

Charles, to Uppingham School. The change in fortunes had not so affected the other child of the household, Charles' older sister Edith, who was to play an important role in his life and that of his family.

She had been born a year before Queen Victoria's Diamond Jubilee, when the British Empire was at its zenith and the Queen's Navy reigned supreme over the oceans. The sense of quiet pride, a by-product of the possession of such Empire that was bred in many Britons, particularly those of the middle classes, was imbibed by Edith at her mother's breast; but she was away playing in the fields of her father's farm before any curdling began with the Boer War, one of her country's first significant upsets. She might have seen, parading through Market Harborough, the scarlet tunics of the soldiers of the Leicestershire Regiment, destined to be involved in the defence of Ladysmith, but that, and the Empire as a whole, were utterly detached from her rural upbringing. The family, of yeoman stock, went to church every Sunday—Anglican of course—but they all worked long hours on the farm on the other six days. Edith attended the village school, walking the two miles there and the two miles back every day in all weathers. Her formal education was completed by the age of fourteen whereupon she became a full-time assistant to her mother, rather than part-time as hitherto. Her brother was to go away to a superior boys' school but she did not feel deprived. She was a girl and that was her lot in life. She met the sons of farmers who tilled the acres adjoining the Cresswell holdings at church, at ploughing matches and at the local dances. She was destined to become a farmer's wife—until all changed during the summer of 1914. It was the first cricket match of the season. The usual fixture with Kibworth Beaucham had been postponed and a game arranged with the Nottingham Wanderers, a team that played all over the East Midlands. Edith had graduated from any responsibility for providing refreshments for the players and was now the team's scorer. She was pleased to be amongst the action, as she called it. She was fond of cricket, but rebelled at the thought of becoming the 'lady in charge of the cucumber sandwiches'. The visitors batted first. When their innings was completed a mild altercation began between the opposing scorers over the destiny of the first boundary scored. Was it a leg-bye or did it come from the bat? The umpires were out of range, enjoying the home-made scones, and so, as the debate became more heated, the scorers turned to the Nottingham opener; was it off his bat or his pad? He could not remember but what he was sure of was his admiration for this spirited eighteen-year-old girl who was standing her ground as if at Rorke's Drift. He was Anthony Shelton, an infrequent player for the Wanderers, and just about to join up with the Sherwood Foresters. He sided with Edith and so they got married. Not that day, but in 1916 when her future husband had been given a training job at Regimental Headquarters after being gassed during the Second Battle of Ypres. For the first two years of the war Edith found time during her duties on the farm to write to Tony at the front and to read, and re-read, his replies. She was meticulous in keeping copies of her letters (eighty years later her nephew was able to arrange for the private publication of this correspondence at a time of acute interest in World War One).

After the war, Tony went back into the family lace business in Nottingham. The newly married couple occupied a variety of rented and regimental properties until the purchase of the Old Vicarage at Stanton in 1920 that was to become a home for succeeding generations of the Cresswells, until Adele sold it in 1991. Just before the war, the diocese had decided that the vicarage was too big and too expensive, so it had been sold and the rector allocated a new house built precisely for that purpose. The former parsonage was soon re-titled the Old Vicarage and so it remained. It stood in four acres, a handsome three-storey brick and slate building constructed around 1860. There were stables, a small lodge cottage and six bedrooms in the main house. 'Much too big for us,' said Edith, but Tony thought it befitted his prestige as an up-and-coming industrialist. Unfortunately, none of the extra bedrooms was ever occupied by their own children. It may have been the chlorine in Flanders, but the reasons for the couple's absence of progeny were never known. The house therefore became a refuge for Edith's brother and his family, which seemed to fill the gap.

Neither Tony nor Edith could understand why Charles decided to remain in the army after 1918. In particular Tony, with his experience behind him, tried hard and long to persuade Charles of the folly of his ways and promised to find him a place in the Shelton family firm but to no avail. The Old Vicarage became Charles' base for the whole time he was in India and a full-time home for his children, and eventually his wife, when they returned to the UK in the 1940s.

Matthew had also attended Uppingham School and left with sufficient academic credentials to be offered a provisional place at Nottingham University, to be taken up after completing his period of National Service, compulsory at that time. He had never envisaged having a military career like his father, but he accepted his posting to the Education Corp with a mixture of resignation in the face of the inevitable and curiosity to see how he would adapt to army life. In the event, his career as a man of arms—or a manipulator of chalk—was cut short when a second medical check determined that he had a heart murmur which rendered him unfit for duty. Whether his medical records became mixed up with those of another soldier he could not tell but routine medicals in later life revealed no defects of this nature.

The twelve weeks he spent at the basic training camp were a big shock. The first five years of his life had been spent in India and after that he had been loved and cared for at the Old Vicarage. Boarding school should have prepared him for army life, but then basic training for a National Serviceman in the 1950s was not exactly 'army life'. For Matthew it was a period of near torture. Uppingham School had cured him of homesickness but after the first two days at Catterick he wanted to escape back to Leicestershire and the comforts of his mother and Aunt Edith. He had been worried beforehand about basic training but the actuality of life as a squaddie was beyond anything he could have envisaged. At the village school he had sat side-by-side with the sons and daughters of farm labourers, the local road sweeper and even the village drunk, but he had never met anyone from the Gorbals of Glasgow or the Liverpool docks. Matthew tried to explain to his sister.

'In many ways I find them refreshing, they are so vital—crude, but full of life and energy. They hate the army but they don't articulate this very well because they are all too busy talking about sex, day and night.'

Jenny interposed that he must have been at a considerable disadvantage during such discussions but Matthew ignored this.

'It's their language. Not just the accents but the constant use of swear words. These chaps swear between syllables. Never heard anything like it.'

Jenny revelled in this. 'You mean like, dinner-fucking-time.'

'No, between syllables, though I can't remember any examples at the moment.'

'Let me try. "Break-fucking-fast".'

Edith and their mother chose that moment to enter the room and Jenny had the grace to look embarrassed. Matthew went on.

'And the lance corporals! They have one stripe. They are just one rank above us but their power is omnipotent. You can do nothing about it. Their word is law. Many of them are regular soldiers who could not find a job in Civvy Street. Very limited intelligence but somehow they all seem to have been injected with an army serum that produces the most vituperative language you have ever heard. They are masters of the art of the insult. In its mildest form, most of us are constantly referred to as "'orrible little men". I know there needs to be discipline but this is ridiculous. Are we going to be more effective at killing the enemy because the toe-caps of our boots are so shiny you can see your face in them? We have to clean the soles as well. Madness. They have us changing clothes dozens of times each day, from PT kit into best uniform and back again—ad infinitum. As we change they bellow at us, "Last man through the door is on a charge." For pity's sake, somebody has to be last.'

'Thank goodness you escaped,' said Adele.

'Well, I suppose once I had been posted to a regular unit it would have been easier. Everyone said the Education Corp was a cushy number, but I think I shall still have nightmares for years to come about that basic training.'

'Might have made a man of you,' opined Jenny, 'but I doubt it.'

'I wonder if in the future I shall feel I've missed out—but at least now I can get on with my life and go to the university straight away, all thanks to the medics.'

'Oh yes, your exciting life. What are you going to do when university is over? Get a nice steady job as a bank clerk, I suppose.'

Matthew ignored her.

'Surprising that they discharged me because one of the standard jokes is that at the medical examination two doctors are used: one looks in your left ear and the other in the right and if they cannot see each other, you are fit for service.'

'What nonsense,' said Edith.

'Funnily enough, I have never felt so fit in my life. I was fairly active at school but by the end of basic training all of us were in tip-top order I can tell you. So I got that out of it and one other thing—the humour. Another medical story. When asked to read the letters on the sight chart, the recruit pretends he cannot even see a chart and so, improbably, he is declared unfit and released. On his way home the delighted fraudster stops off at the pictures. When the lights go up he is horrified to find the doctor who examined him in the next seat. Quick as a flash he turns to his neighbour and says, "Can you tell me what time this bus gets to Southampton?" I suppose it was being confined together as we were that spawned this somewhat grotesque sense of fun. Last story, I promise. Soldiers come back from the NAAFI, some beer taken. One of their number is already in bed, fast asleep. The revellers wake and ask if he wants to buy a submarine. After they have gone to sleep, the victim wakes them one by one to ask what colour is the submarine.'

His premature departure from such frolics meant that he was able to take up his place at university before his twentieth birthday whence he emerged with a 2.2 in Modern History. What career, he thought, does this fit me for? Am I to finish up in Barclays Bank as Jenny predicted? This question was answered rather quickly by an advertisement in *The Guardian* for applications for junior posts with the British Council at various overseas locations. Without giving the matter too much thought, he applied and, after a day spent at the Council's head office in London, was offered a position in Nigeria at a salary of £950 per annum plus an overseas allowance of £295.

Matthew and his twin sister, Jenny, were fond of each other but they were widely different in nature; as Aunt Edith was not slow to declare, daughter followed mother and son the father. Their father had been a calm introspective man, tolerant of weakness in others but of a steely nature when his own principles were at stake. These principles were most often displayed when it came to supporting friends and colleagues; the ethos of friendship was extraordinarily strong in his character. His introversion stood in stark contrast to that of his Anglo-Indian second wife, and mother of the twins. Adele had left India in 1943 and since then she and Edith and Tony, until his death in 1955, had lived together in great harmony.

Adele was vivacious and easygoing, as was her daughter who found little difficulty in coming out on top in any contest with her quietly-mannered brother. Although Matthew was unsure of the details, it was clear that his sister was not short of male company, a fact which added to the fun she had at her brother's expense on the subject of the girls in his life. In this campaign she found the perfect Greek chorus in the shape of their mother and their aunt.

After Jenny had finished telling them about the party of last night, and whom she had accompanied to that event, she would point her finger at Matthew and, with a lilt in her voice, ask why he had not been there. Matthew would usually reply by saying that he had not been invited, but Jenny's question was only an excuse for the three ladies to feign concern for his amatory future.

'Surely there must be some girl at the University who will take pity on you. We are all looking to you to perpetuate the Cresswell name. What about the girl you visited Sherwood Forest with? Now that was a really romantic setting if you like.'

'She married one of the junior lecturers at Nottingham.'

'So, you let her get away. What's the matter with you? You're semi-civilised and not bad looking, even if you do wear specs, but I suppose if you are as reticent with them as you are with us, they will inevitably finish up calling you "four eyes".'

'What's it to you? At least I'm not a flirt.'

'Oh, Matthew,' said his mother, 'that's a little unfair. Jenny's like me. She enjoys having a good time, while you only seem to be interested in books.'

'Make your eyesight worse, all that reading,' was Aunt Edith's contribution. 'Get out in the fresh air. Play some golf.'

'Yes,' returned Jenny. 'There are lots of lady members at Worksop. You might find your true love in the rough on the fourteenth, or are you going to be bunkered for the rest of your life. It's those awful glasses—they make you look like a bookie's clerk.'

In the 1950s, men's spectacles were invariably of the horn-rimmed type and these, on Matthew, projected a serious manner which in his case was generally appropriate. He tended to frown more than most but his sense of humour was well-developed and invariably spontaneous. He did not have the sense of mischief exhibited by his sister but he was not always the butt of her jokes. After one particularly sarcastic outburst from her he gained his revenge by hiding one of her favourite evening shoes in the kitchen refrigerator. After she had wrecked the order of her wardrobe and made the staircase of the house ring with her cries of anguish, Matthew had been quietly delighted to be able to deliver the *coup de grâce* by persuading Jenny to get herself a cold drink to calm her nerves. When she discovered it, she threw the shoe at his head, but missed.

Matthew was essentially shy but he had inherited a dash of his mother's charm and made friends easily. He had not told the family about Joan. In his last year at university, one of his closest friends had persuaded him to play tennis on the public courts situated just off University Boulevard. Neither was very skilled at the game but this did not prevent them from enjoying several sets of mixed doubles with two girls they had met at the courts. The one Matthew partnered worked in a Boots shop at Goose Gate in the centre of the city. It was Jesse Boot's first shop and known as Branch No. 1. Matthew pointed out to her how appropriate this was since the same Jesse Boot had been largely responsible for the foundation of Nottingham University: he had donated the land upon which it was built and £50,000. However, when she told him her name was Joan it was not the history of the university that occupied his mind but Betjeman's subaltern.

What strenuous singles we played after tea,
We in the tournament—you against me!

Love-thirty, love-forty, oh weakness of joy,
The speed of a swallow, the grace of a boy,
With carefullest carelessness, gaily you won,
I am weak from your loveliness, Joan Hunter-Dunn.

In the poet's case, the tennis players become engaged but for Matthew and his lady 'of blazer and shorts' this was not to be. Both of them enjoyed the friendship but neither thought it might end in marriage. During the spring before his finals, he frequently took a bus into town where they met outside the shop before an evening at the cinema, or a decorous pub crawl, but their bouts of amorous behaviour tended to be limited to warm goodnight kisses outside her house in Beeston. If these were more protracted than usual and the last bus had gone, the long walk back to the university tended to dim the pleasure of the encounter. He never met her parents but on one occasion, when they were away, the goodnights were said on a rexine-covered settee in the sitting-room of their house. Matthew missed the bus that night by a considerable margin.

After university he returned to the Old Vicarage. Jenny was about to begin the Law Society course to qualify as a solicitor, but their mother was pleased to have them for the moment both under the same roof at the same time—where they could begin again to quiz Matthew about his love life. But their pleasure at this prospect was short-lived when he announced to the family over breakfast: 'Oh, you can forget all about that. I'm going to Nigeria.'

The forthright Edith was the first to respond.

'Good heavens, Matthew! I thought you would have had enough of foreign climes as a boy. Why did you not apply to the civil service? On the other hand, I'm sure a place could be found for you in the family firm. I shall call Edwards immediately after breakfast. You can commute to Nottingham every day and stay here and keep the ladies company until you get married—if that should ever happen.'

As Matthew grimaced, his mother took up another tack.

'Not a very healthy place, West Africa. Pity you couldn't find a job in Nairobi. I have quite a few Indian friends there.'

Matthew failed to respond, whereupon Jenny looked up from her boiled egg and, with a smile on her face, asked if she could come with him.

'I'd quite like to meet up with a big black man.'

At this Edith tried to imitate Lady Bracknell, but with limited success as Matthew finished his breakfast and informed his family he had accepted an offer from the British Council and would be leaving for Lagos in four weeks' time.

His new life in Nigeria began on the aeroplane which flew him, in the autumn of 1958, through the night—destination Lagos. The Stratocruiser Matthew found himself aboard carried fewer than one hundred passengers who could avail themselves of a downstairs bar area and it was here that Matthew met two people who were to have some involvement in his Nigerian adventure. They were Frank Jones, who worked for the British American Tobacco Company and was about to join their sister company in Nigeria, and Raymond Habib, a Lebanese businessman.

As Matthew negotiated the circular stair down to the lounge, he was greeted by words of welcome from its sole occupant, an olive skinned man who seemed to be comfortably ensconced, if the level in the glass of gin and tonic he was cradling was a reasonable indicator.

'Good, you found your way down then—great asset this for air travel.'

The speaker was slight of build with black, naturally wavy hair and the features of a man of Middle Eastern origin.

'What will you drink? I'm Raymond Habib and this is the third time I have enjoyed the delights of the Stratocruiser.'

'First time for me,' Matthew replied. 'In fact, except for the journey by sea from India to England in 1939, this is just about my only excursion away from England. Certainly it is my first experience of long-distance air travel.'

'What are you going to do in Nigeria?' asked Habib.

Before he could answer they were joined by another passenger who ordered a beer before he sat down next to Matthew.

'Well,' he said, taking up the last question, 'what exciting career have you put yourself down for in the "White Man's Grave"? My old boss, who was in West Africa before the war, never tired of repeating,

Beware, beware the bite of Benin.
Few come out, but many go in.

By the way, I'm Frank Jones; joining the Nigerian Tobacco Company.'

Matthew, rather diffidently, said he was going to work for the British Council in Lagos and when they asked what exactly the Council did he gave them the benefit of his limited knowledge.

'When I applied for the job I was totally ignorant of the purpose and history of the Council so I did some research. In the early 1930s the British Government realised there was a need for an organisation to promote British culture and education in other countries in a similar way to what was being done by France, Germany and Italy. An organisation was set up which, in 1936, became the British Council. In the early days its work included support for British societies and English schools in other countries, providing assistance for English teachers and libraries and promoting lecture tours, music performances, art exhibitions, etc. The first direct overseas representation was in Egypt in 1938, followed by Portugal, Poland and Romania later that year. During the war activities were restricted but after 1945 these were expanded to the rest of Europe and then, during the 1950s, there was an expansion of activity to the developing countries of Africa and Asia.'

He noticed that the interest of his fellow drinkers was waning under this barrage of detail.

'After that boring explanation,' said Matthew hurriedly, 'let me order you another drink.'

Frank Jones' response was, 'I assume I'll be stationed in Lagos—at least for my first tour. We must keep in touch.'

Habib said he knew a number of people who worked for the Tobacco Company, whom he had met either socially or through business. He then went on to explain that his family had been in Nigeria for generations, that he was primarily concerned with property development on their behalf and had, in fact, recently put to Frank's new employers a proposal to build a block of flats for their expatriate staff in Ikoyi. As they were both newcomers, he began to tell them something about their new home and the Nigerian people.

'Lagos is one of the most vibrant cities in the world—all things to all men. It is noisy, dirty and smelly but on the whole it exhibits, twenty-four hours a day, a sense of opportunity and good humour. The locals can be devious and charming at the same time with no apparent effort. Let me tell you a story. I found my driver was cheating me over the cost of petrol. In collusion with the pump attendant, he would obtain a receipt for ten gallons when, based on the miles the car had done, there was no room in the petrol tank for such an amount of fuel. When I taxed him on this he replied, "Ah, Master must savvy, this is an old motor and when car get old, petrol tank de expand." You have to congratulate them on their ingenuity!'

He explained that, although in Nigeria there were scores of languages and dialects, English was the *lingua franca* but most of the Nigerian workers employed a form of Pidgin English, as shown by the driver's reply. As a further instance he told a story of the marriage banns being announced by a priest to a mainly Nigerian congregation.

'This is the first calling of the banns of marriage of Esther Okolo and Peter Okafor. If anyone know any reason why dese two people no dun marry, make them come see Father for office, one time.'

The young men laughed at this but it was not clear whether they fully understood this example of the vernacular. They had both done some preliminary research into the history and politics of Nigeria but it was valuable to have information direct from Habib.

'At the moment, the boss-man is the Governor-General, representing the Queen of course, but with considerable administrative powers. He virtually rules the country through a civil service where most of the senior posts are occupied by Brits. There are also a number of long-established trading companies of British origin, while most of the banking is controlled by the likes of Barclays and others. In the main, we Lebanese fit into all of this in the form of small traders or transporters. Nigerians, in simple terms, are divided into the Christian south, the Yorubas in the west and the Ibos in the east with the Muslim north, mainly Hausa and Fulani. It is said that if representatives of the three main Nigerian tribes were sitting under a coconut tree, the Yoruba would see it as his right that the coconut would fall for him, while the Hausa would pray to Allah that he should be the lucky one, but the Ibo would climb the tree and take the fruit for himself.'

As more passengers entered the Stratocruiser bar Matthew thought what an ideal venue this was for those travelling on their own to meet and drink in a convivial atmosphere. Jones and Matthew talked together of what they envisaged Nigeria would offer them. What would their domestic arrangements be? Would they find the climate trying? And what about girls? Habib's contribution to this conversation was to tell them of the opportunities available for bright young men, how varied the social life was for expatriates and how they would, on the whole, find the Nigerian people easy-going and affable. Without directly revealing any sense of excitement, Matthew could not help feeling that he was displaying an air of sophisticated satisfaction at the situation he now found himself in, drinking Heineken 20,000 feet above the Sahara desert. What was he going to find?

The tranquillity of the cocoon provided by BOAC was very quickly shattered as the passengers were disgorged into the humid and hectic atmosphere of the Ikeja Airport at Lagos. This comprised a collection of single-storey buildings, clearly the result of piecemeal development, of varied design and construction mainly with heavily stained corrugated asbestos roofs. When the aircraft had stopped at Kano the passengers had been greeted by a blast from some local musical instrument—a form of elongated horn or trumpet—delivered by a splendidly costumed Hausa man, but Lagos airport was altogether more mundane. There was noise, but this was created by the human voice as the airport staff, porters, baggage handlers and the other flotsam and jetsam that airports seem to attract, shouted at each other at the tops of their voices. Matthew was quickly being introduced to the 'noise of Nigeria'. The constituents of this clamour were many and varied—motor horns, loudspeakers, the grinding of gears and the judder of diesel engines—but above all else, it was speech. As Matthew was to discover the conversation of two or three Nigerians met together, either by chance or arrangement, was capable of competing with the noise of Piccadilly Circus at rush-hour or King's Cross Station with steam-trains standing at every platform. The racket at the airport was accompanied by the high-pitched squeaking arising from several hundred little yellow birds that inhabited two gaunt trees adjoining the arrivals hall. As Matthew was to discover, these were the ubiquitous weaver birds. After the comparatively peaceful milieu of university life—and Aunt Edith's Leicestershire countryside—he felt like an underwater swimmer emerging from the calm and even-tempered depths to find a force ten gale in full spate above the surface. Then there was the humidity. As he reached for his suitcase his clothes were already damp, worsening as the sweat from his face dripped down the front of his new Army and Navy Stores' bush jacket. However, the heat was the real shock. The plane had arrived at nine o'clock in the morning but by now the sun was shining with a glare and a ferocity that took his breath away. Was this the sun, he thought, that on his country's Empire never set?

In 1957 the other major British West African colony, Ghana, had achieved independence and now Nigeria was scheduled to follow the same course—on 1 October 1960. Approaching independence also changed many other existing structures. For instance, the Nigerian Railway, which had been administered by the Ministry of Transport, was now to be converted into a statutory corporation and would become the Nigerian Railway Corporation. They had their headquarters at Ebute Metta, a suburb of Lagos, where in the Railway Compound were the offices, engine sheds and housing for senior railway staff. Before Matthew arrived, the British Council had been able to rent from the Railway a block of flats in the compound and this is where he was to be accommodated.

Raymond Habib had described Lagos as one of the liveliest cities in the world and, as Matthew became familiar with this astonishing town, he could only agree with that description. He would not forget the early impression of his new home gained during the first car journey from Yaba—where he initially stayed with his British Council superior, Maurice Green—onto Lagos Island, followed by a visit to the Railway Compound.

At first glance it appeared that everyone on view from Green's car was selling something, even though there were few, if any, buyers. On the streets of London, newspaper vendors were a regular sight, together with the occasional stall selling hot drinks or roasted chestnuts, but on the thoroughfares of Lagos, major and minor, everything was for sale. Goods were displayed at roadside shacks or on the arms of individual pedestrian traders who attacked every car on the road like a warm-hearted swarm of bees. The variety on offer was astonishing. On that first trip Matthew was offered sunglasses, a full set of kitchen tools, tubes of toothpaste, a variety of plastic cups, packets of detergent, an assortment of photograph albums and scores of different newspapers and magazines. Despite little interest being shown in their wares, all the sellers approached the would-be customers with a humorous aggression that delighted Matthew. Their enthusiasm was infectious and he suddenly felt perfectly at ease with the mass of Nigeria that surrounded the car whenever progress was at a snail's-pace; traffic was heavy and the roads were narrow. The apparent absence of trade was compensated for by an exchange of uninterrupted conversation, or exhortation, delivered at great speed and maximum volume. The 'Nigerian noise' again. Whatever were they shouting and how did one manage to hear what the other was saying over the general cacophony, to which was added an orchestration of car horns? There was no car driver in Lagos who did not use his horn as regularly as the accelerator pedal. It was certainly different from the High Street at Market Harborough, or even Oxford Street in London. The noise was deafening but no-one seemed to mind. Nor did the mass of people seem conscious of the noxious smell that rose from the open drains. These were vitally necessary during the heavy rainy season but for most of the year they became a convenient spot to ease both bowels and bladder and a depository for orange peel and other detritus of every description. At Victoria Street there were conventional shops, more like those to be found in a European city, but even here goods for sale overflowed onto the thoroughfare and business was transacted on the pavements rather than inside. Most of these emporia sold cloth and the proprietors were mainly Lebanese.

The traffic was dense; cars, cycles, buses and lorries all trying to beat the 'go slow', as it was called. Vehicles carrying passengers were dangerously overloaded. In addition to the people crammed inside there was a further army of travellers hanging precariously to the exterior of the motors. Each type of transport had its own special name: the larger buses were the 'molue' and the smaller the 'danfo'. The drivers were fearless in their quest for passengers and their determination to overtake anyone who impeded their breakneck progress. One variety of transport was nicknamed 'bole-kaja', which in Yoruba means 'come on down, let's fight'. In view of the antics of the drivers of these vehicles, Matthew thought it most apt.

Maurice Green had an anecdote about a Nigerian policeman trying to control such traffic. He approached a car snarled up in the congestion and peered at the driver, a nervous looking white man who was clearly new to the Lagos scene.

'You, what colour am I?' Confronted by this black and sweaty visage close up to his own face, the driver thought it would be more polite to say that he was of a brown colour.

'No,' said the policeman. He raised his large hand and showed it, palm forward, to the hesitant driver. 'When it is like this, it is red.' He then demonstrated a beckoning motion. 'And when it is like this, it is green.'

Matthew was to discover that Maurice Green had little sense of humour and it was difficult to know whether he considered this story amusing or simply an illustration of the stupidity of all Nigerians.

The contrast as the wide-eyed Matthew was driven into the Railway Compound was extraordinary. The streets of Ebute Metta that adjoined the one main entrance into the compound displayed a similar scene to Lagos Island, although in this area Matthew noticed some enterprises other than sale points—the vulcaniser for instance. No-one seemed to repair their own bicycle punctures in this country, that was a job for the vulcaniser, and when Matthew commented on this, Green told him that when a new bicycle is purchased it must be taken to the cycle man or vulcaniser to be taken apart and put back together again before the first ride. Matthew wondered how such a tradition had arisen but, he reflected, it did provide work for someone in a country where jobs were hard to come by. The sellers of oranges and underwear were prominent at the official entrance to the Railway Compound, but once inside the change was dramatic. Green's car no longer needed to avoid the massive potholes to be found on many of the streets of Lagos and its suburbs; the roads now being traversed were well maintained and the adjoining storm drains clean and relatively sweet smelling. The buildings closest to the main entrance, the offices of the Nigerian Railway Corporation, had been put up in the early twentieth century but they were well maintained and after the squalor Matthew had observed that morning, quite attractive in appearance with jalousies at most windows, propped open by well-worn poles that glinted in the strong sunlight. After a brief visit to the residential area, where many of the properties were detached houses standing in large gardens full of mature trees, Matthew was shown the block of four flats the British Council had rented where he was destined to begin his Lagos life. The next stop was the EB Club—Green was a member—where the sense of the old colonial was there for all to see. It may not have had the style of the clubs in Bombay to which he had been taken as a boy, but the purpose was the same: a haven where the white man could isolate himself from the native *hoi polloi.* The single-storey building was a hotchpotch of constructions: a well-stocked bar at the front adjoined a billiard room and behind these facilities was a modest ballroom with a highly polished wood-block floor. The French windows from this room overlooked the golf course where, it was pointed out to Matthew, the greens were not green at all, but rather 'browns'. It was difficult to maintain grass of the necessary quality in this climate and the devised alternative was oiled sand that was, at regular intervals, smoothed over by the myriad groundsmen to provide a tolerable putting surface. Matthew relished the 'difference' as he thought how unlike all this was to the Market Place at Uppingham or the golf course at Worksop.

During Matthew Cresswell's early years in Lagos, membership of a club featured strongly in his social life, as it did for most young expatriates all over Nigeria and throughout the Empire. The EB Club, like others scattered throughout the colony—as it still was—did not have rules precluding the indigenous population from membership but at that time few Nigerians were interested. After Independence that began to change but for Matthew in 1958 the club became an essential ingredient in the pursuit of leisure and the making of friends. He played tennis there, enjoyed the weekly open-air cinema shows and drank at the bar. Very soon he was familiar with nearly all the members. Many years later, when an established businessman, he joined the Metropolitan Club, founded much later in an attempt to replicate a London gentlemen's club. In the early days this club was established with an equal number of Nigerian members and non-Nigerians. It did not achieve its objective of becoming a West Coast Athenaeum but membership carried considerable prestige. Matthew was a committee member for a year or two and was intrigued to discover that one custom which had travelled well was the rule that one 'black ball' was all that was needed to prevent a membership proposal being agreed—except that for the Metropolitan Club, the balls were not black and white but red and green. Like the policeman: red for no, green for go.

He was somewhat surprised to find that the flat he had been allocated in the Railway Compound for his sole use so early in his career was well appointed, with two bedrooms, and he was even more surprised to discover that he was to have his own servant, already ensconced in the servant's quarters attached to the flats. Matthew found it hard to reconcile his spacious living accommodation with the one room allocated to Sampson but, as he was to learn, this modest space was far superior to anything his servant would have had in his home village. There had been servants at home in India but as he had left the country of his birth at the age of five his memories were limited. He could remember the ayah who had been with the family from his birth but now, as an adult, he was in daily contact with his own personal servant. In later years he realised that this relationship had an impact on his future life in Nigeria: the easy rapport established with his steward was extended and enriched in the case of his Nigerian colleagues at the British Council, leading as it did to the business and political partnership with Peter Okonkwo and, even more importantly, a deep friendship. Sampson was of stocky build with chubby fingers that revealed nails bitten down to the quick. Like most domestic servants he was an Ibo from Eastern Nigeria. His garb was the ubiquitous khaki shirt and shorts starched to such a degree that Matthew wondered if the knife-edged creases might inflict any permanent damage were his flesh and Sampson's clothes ever to meet. Like most of his peers, Sampson was usually barefooted. He was what was known as a 'yellow man', meaning that his chocolate hue was of the milkiest variety, but his most noticeable feature was his smile. This was much in evidence as he began to acquaint Matthew with the minutiae of domestic life for expatriates in Nigeria.

'Massa put clothes for laundry basket and I go wash and iron and next morning lay out what you go wear for office.'

Observing Sampson's attire, Matthew responded, 'Fine, but not too much starch, please.'

'And when come home from office, I pass bath.'

'You do what?'

'I go make bath full of hot water for you.'

Matthew did not comment further. Was he going to be deprived of the right to turn on a tap? Sampson then produced from his trouser pocket a small, slightly creased, notebook.

'You give me one pound and I go buy chop for market, and when done finish, you look book and give me more money.'

'Interesting,' said Matthew. 'What do you buy?'

'Everything, sah—and then go cook mighty fine chop.'

'You mean you do the cleaning of the flat, the washing and ironing, the turning on of bath taps, going to the market and then cook my meals—you are busy. What can you cook?'

'Very busy, Massa. Cook everything. Fish and chips, roast beef and Yorkshire pud, Auntie Queen Elizabeth pudding and tomato sandwiches—and on Saturday, very fine curry with all de gages.'

Matthew was to discover that gages were the various side dishes, such as ground coconut, stinkfish and other spices added to the West African curry which differed substantially from that of India.

The Saturday lunchtime curry was an honoured ritual. Whether at the club, or as guest or host at a private house, the white men in West Africa assembled at noon to drink large quantities of ice-cold beer before tackling the curry, usually chicken. The plates were dampened by a sprinkling of Lea and Perrins or Tabasco sauce followed by the rice and the stew in carefully ordered proportions. To this mixture was added the gages—all manner of fruit, dried and fresh coconut, stinkfish, onions and fried plantains topped off by a liberal dose of sherry or gin peppers. These were made using the strongest of red peppers which were carefully inserted into an appropriate bottle and then topped up with gin or sherry. The mixture would serve for many months until the pickling liquid became nearly too strong for human consumption. It was often said that if left for years spontaneous combustion would occur. Before the days of universal air-conditioning, all diners brought their own towels to the feast in order to soak up the perspiration engendered by this culinary agony. Desserts were rarely served and, as soon as the meal was over, all and sundry went home to sleep. The only cure for the feeling that came on about eight o'clock in the evening was to hurry down to the club for a medicinal cold Star.

As the weeks went by Matthew began to appreciate more and more the qualities in Sampson, particularly his ingenuity—and that of his ilk. Most of the flats occupied by expatriates in Lagos, and elsewhere in the country, were of the same basic design. There were two per floor, usually in three-storey blocks, where the kitchen of each flat gave out onto a single rear staircase used by the servants—in other words, adjoining kitchens were instantly accessible, one from another. One morning, Sampson regaled Matthew with the story of a near-disastrous dinner party that had taken place in the next-door block. After the soup plates had been cleared, the nervous wife—this was her first dinner party since arriving in the country—was nearly brought to tears as the steward entered with the leg of pork she had so carefully prepared only for him to trip and deposit the joint, crackling and all, on the plastic tile floor adjoining the dining table. Quick as a flash her servant had the meat back on the plate and returned to the kitchen to reappear with a cloth to wipe the grease from the floor and with a cheery, 'No worry, Madam, wait small,' he returned to the kitchen. The guests and their hosts tried to ignore the incident but the conversation around the table became a little strained. Five minutes later the servant reappeared with a wide grin on his face bearing a large roast chicken with all the trimmings. No-one said a word and this extraordinary event was treated as if nothing untoward had happened. After the guests had gone Sylvia, the fledgling hostess, asked the servant how he had managed to substitute chicken for pork at such short notice. Was it a miracle? The proud maestro explained that the pork was not damaged. A quick rubdown with a damp cloth was all that was necessary and, as fortune would have it, there was a dinner party in the next-door flat where chicken was to have been the main course. The two servants met together and a mutual exchange was quickly agreed. Sylvia thought it best not to enquire from her neighbour how she had been able to explain to her husband that the anticipated chicken had transformed itself into a leg of pork.

Some of the buildings in the Railway Compound had their origins in the early years of the century but Matthew's office was of much more recent provenance. The headquarters of the British Council was on Lagos Island but Matthew was posted to a new complex at Yaba—a northern suburb of the capital—that had been completed only two years before his arrival. The new British Council building was of a striking octagonal design and, although small, was utilised as a library and teaching centre. Matthew had been met at the airport by Maurice Green, who was in charge of the Yaba centre, but it was not until they were together on his first day at the centre that Matthew realised the stark disparity in their temperaments. Green showed him around the building.

'We're lucky to have these purpose-built premises, although whether our clientele appreciate it is another thing.'

'Yes, it is very nice and light. Gives a good impression,' responded Matthew. 'I believe you want me to look after the library. I shall enjoy that, I'm fond of books.'

'Indeed, but your major concern will be to try and make sure nothing is stolen. This lot would pinch anything that's not nailed down.'

'Well, I suppose they don't have much. The people I see on the streets appear to be pretty poverty-stricken and I believe if I hadn't seen conditions just as bad in India I would have reacted more strongly.'

'Yes, I saw from your papers you had an Indian background. Not that it is a place I aspire to visit, any more than I really wanted to come to Lagos. I'd applied for Rio but landed up here.'

'I see, but there must be enormous scope to do good here and, from what I am told, Nigerian parents are desperate to find some sort of education for their children.'

'No doubt, but you won't have heard the story told me by the local agent for Quink ink. According to him more ink is used in Nigeria than in England, where clearly the quantum of education provided is many times more than in this country. The explanation for this anomaly is that many Nigerian mothers believe that a spoonful of ink given to each child with breakfast advances their learning capacity. I know it is nonsense, but it is an indication of the type of people we have to deal with.'

Matthew cringed. Was this just a piece of amusing fantasy or were Green's anti-Nigerian sentiments being displayed to the full. He was only a few years older than Matthew, but in manner and demeanour he could easily have been taken for his father. Matthew smiled privately at this thought when he pictured how very unlike, in every way, Green was from his soldier-father. Charles Cresswell was a very rare breed. After spending most of his life in India he still treated all men and women as equals—but this could not be said for Mr Green. Matthew soon decided that the typical British Council type was someone half civil servant and half parish priest but he kept these views to himself, particularly with regard to Green, because he quickly learned that this somewhat superficial definition would need to be revised to cover his superior's case. Although he went to some lengths not to show it, Green actively despised the Nigerians. To him they were shiftless and deceitful—and unwashed. On one occasion Matthew tried to explain that in many parts of the world the locals complained that it was the white-man who had a noxious smell, but Green dismissed such a notion out of hand. After two years in the country he had failed to find any redeeming features in any of them and this disgusted Matthew who had felt at home with the Nigerians from the very beginning.

In addition to one other expatriate in charge of training courses, Brian Christie, the other personnel at intermediate level were three Nigerians, whose status was somewhat unclear but who were designated as 'Managers (Probationary)'. Matthew soon became close friends with the Ibo member of this trio, Peter Okonkwo. He was of even lighter complexion than Sampson with a natural aura of ease and culture that Matthew found refreshing compared with Maurice Green. He had not yet travelled outside the country of his birth, but he wore his degree in English from Ibadan University with a quiet confidence that greatly impressed Matthew. He was a member of an eminent Eastern family, his father being a local chief and wealthy businessman. When Matthew came across *Things Fall Apart*, he quizzed his friend about the fact that he had the same surname as Achebe's unfortunate hero, to which he responded that this was like asking why so many fictional characters in the Western canon were called Smith. He cited *1984*. In the early months Matthew tried, in his introspective way, to understand the characteristics of the Nigerians—how they differed from Occidentals—and to measure his findings against what he found within Peter's personality. He had not forgotten how simplistically Raymond Habib had described the three main tribes, but Matthew soon began to realise that it was much more complex than that. War between Britain and France in West Africa had been avoided by an agreement in 1898 that established the borders of Nigeria which at the time was mainly composed of a series of trading operations—and a mixture of very different peoples. The Yorubas in the west had a long history of well-developed kingdoms and established traditions. In the eastern part of the new country there were many tribes, the predominant one being the Ibo. Between these southern territories and the Moslem north was an area known as the Middle Belt peopled mainly by pagans. The southern people were on the whole Christians, largely Roman Catholic in the east. In view of this history, was there such a thing as 'a Nigerian'? How many of the citizens of this diverse country were Ibo or Yoruba first and Nigerian second? As Matthew was to discover, when this question was asked in earnest, attempting to find an answer resulted in a bitter clash where Nigerians fought Nigerians—or did they? Was the Biafran conflict a civil war? Was this an example of fellow countryman fighting fellow countryman? In the misery of the American Civil War the divide was clear but they were one people, or a least as much as those of the United States can ever be said to be one people. More pertinent for Matthew's analysis was the conflagration at the partition of India. Until 1947 they had been Indians together who then killed each other in the name of their faith; but, thought Matthew, was it any different in Northern Ireland? He was by nature a positive, even optimistic, man and he thought of the centuries it took for the congruent strains in the British heritage to be melded to form the Britain of today. So, in time, could Nigeria become a united country? Peter had always felt this way but the events about to unfold were going to shake that faith to its foundations. However, for the time being, and in the calm before the storm, the affinity between these two young men grew stronger and by 1959 their warm friendship was one of the most important elements in Matthew's life—until he met Isobel.

Isobel Ramsey had been living in the town of Uppingham when Matthew was at school there. When they met in Nigeria they wondered at this but concluded that fate had decided their paths should not cross while on the red soil of Rutland because how much more romantic to travel over three thousand miles to find each other. At the end of Matthew's first year in Nigeria someone had suggested it might be amusing to use the open space within the British Council building to stage some sort of entertainment. Foolishly, Matthew had let it be known within his circle that he had dabbled in amateur dramatics at university and, before he knew what was happening, he found himself cast as the director of what, after many false starts, became a 'topical review' entitled *The Paludrine Show.* Revues, as epitomised by the work of the two Hermiones, Gingold and Baddeley—and perhaps peaking with *Beyond the Fringe*—have today almost disappeared from the London stage, but in the 1950s they were popular attractions. Most of the material for *The Paludrine Show* was provided by Stan Freeman, the Railway's PR manager who was an extrovert character with an even more volatile wife who was said to have been a chorus girl in years gone by. Matthew was relieved at this; he was only the director and if the thing was a total flop he need not take all the blame. In any case, he thought to himself, I would never be able to write such banal rubbish. He tackled his task with care and enthusiasm but soon found his role as director a thankless one as friends, and friends of friends, who had promised their unwavering support, developed the most irritating habit of joining the company but turning up to only one rehearsal in three. These rehearsals were held at the hall of a school in the Railway Compound and it was at one of these, six weeks before curtain-up, that Matthew's old friend, Frank Jones of the Nigerian Tobacco Company, made an appearance.

Matthew looked around the ill-lit school hall and felt depression bearing down on his shoulders as he observed the sparse company. Where were the others? Why had he ever agreed to do this when he could now be sitting in the bar at the EB Club drinking a cold Star? Those present were talking together but with little spirit. They could see for themselves that there were not enough of them present to form even a half-decent chorus line, when they were joined by a posse of new faces with Frank Jones in the van.

'Hi, Matt! We've come to put you out of your misery. I've got the showbiz talent of Lagos here.'

His friend had brought with him three other NTC fellows, whom Matthew had met before, together with three girls, all strangers to him.

'Now this is Mary, the lanky one is Barbara and this bundle of joy is Isobel. She's a real star and you need look no further for your leading lady.'

At this Isobel punched Frank in the stomach, which stopped him before he could make any more remarks. Matthew thought, 'Oh my God! This lot look more trouble than they're worth.'

'Now see here' he announced, 'I have been trying to put this ridiculous show together for weeks, and as soon as I get the thing cast, half of the rabble drop out—so everyone here tonight, if you are not prepared to see the thing through to the end please let me know and leave the room immediately.'

No-one had the nerve to respond in the negative, so Frank Jones and all his accomplices found themselves committed. Isobel told Matthew afterwards that she had accepted Frank's invitation to accompany him to what he described as 'Matt's fiasco—it will be a bit of a laugh', but now she found herself on the same stage as the man with whom she was destined to spend the rest of her life.

Matthew had certainly noticed Isobel but as she seemed to be more than close to Frank, he decided to treat her as a 'rather jolly girl', who might be an asset to the diverse cast he had at his disposal. For her part, she had registered Matthew as a 'nice chap', but had assumed he was married since she observed, at future rehearsals, that he arrived and left with another female member of the cast. This was the wife of one of Matthew's friends who worked for the Railway; Matthew was simply a chauffeur. There was, therefore, an element of confusion on both sides but this was soon dispelled. Matthew quickly discovered that Frank Jones was deeply involved with another girl and, equally speedily, Isobel learned that Matthew was unmarried.

After three performances of *The Paludrine Show* at the British Council Centre, Matthew was prevailed upon by the committee of the EB Club to take the show on tour—for one night only—and perform at their famous New Year's Eve party. In Matthew's regular letter to his mother he described this occasion.

> Sorry to hear the winter has been so severe. Even after all these years, I suppose it is at this season you long to be back in India, even though I know the pilgrimage to Kohima was less than successful. From what I read Independence has brought little benefit to the people, be they Hindu or Muslim, but perhaps you could accept that for a few weeks of sunshine and some real Indian food. Perhaps one day we can all go back for a holiday, Jenny, you and me. In her last letter she told me Joe was back in South Africa and now married. As a result of meeting him she seems much exercised about apartheid and I can understand that. There are really no frictions over the colour of one's skin in Nigeria. They know Independence is on the way and most of the white people get on very well with the locals. In due course we will all be leaving. Not that any of us really want to settle here—climate and other reasons. We are settled into 'occupations', not into 'land'. I appreciate that the Afrikaner has nowhere to go to. South Africa is their home, but I just can't see that justifies the way the black South African is treated.
>
> I have some real news for you in this letter. Instead of boring you with the in-fighting that goes on at the Council, or repeating the sayings of Sampson, I have to tell you that I

have met a rather nice girl—and I can hear you all saying 'and about time too'. What you will find amazing is that she comes from Uppingham and was living there all the time I was at school. Do you think there is a happy portent about such a coincidence? She came to Nigeria about eighteen months ago, employed by the Colonial Office to work in Government as a secretary-typist, and spent some time in the Cameroons during her first tour. This is her second tour. You know I told you I had been landed with the job of producing some sort of a show that the Council, in the pursuit of 'Britishness', could use to display the best of British culture—but more about that later. Well, halfway through the planned rehearsals she appeared, brought by Frank—you know, my friend at NTC. By the way, her name is Isobel. We got on well together from the start although she thought at first I was a married man—ha ha.

Just before Christmas she told me at one of the rehearsals that some friends of hers from the Cameroons were visiting and as I seemed to be a bit of 'a man about town', would I take her and them for a tour of the Lagos nightspots. I must have told her that Peter and I do frequent them occasionally, although I had the good sense not to tell her of my first experience at the Lido—which I might recount to you one day. So what do you think about that! She asks me out—what a Lothario. Yes, and I can hear you and Aunt Edith saying 'That doesn't fit with our recollections of Matthew.' Whatever, we had a good time. The couple from the Cameroons—not yet exactly a couple—were Susan, who worked with Isobel as a secretary typist, and Richard who is a DO. As an old colonial yourself, and I am quickly following in your footsteps, you will know that DO stands for 'District Officer'. Sensible nomenclature I suppose; he is the officer in charge of a district. In colonial parlance his boss is a Senior District Officer and above him is the 'Resident'. Where does that come from I wonder? But then no more quaint than the boss man at the time of the Indian Mutiny, 'The Collector'. I suppose he collected the taxes? One of the trading companies here, John Holts of Liverpool, call their up-country offices 'Ventures' and they are run by 'Venture Managers'. I wonder how far they are allowed to 'venture'. I suppose when the firm was first set up it was a 'venture'. The original John Holt came to West Africa and traded from a hulk in the Calabar River about a hundred years ago. By the way, are you in the picture with regard to the Cameroons? After the First World War that country was taken from Germany and divided down the middle. Typical Imperial arrogance. The western half came to us and the other bit went to France. The Western Cameroons is administered by the Colonial Office as a Trust Territory and Susan works for the senior man, the Commissioner (another title!), who lives in a Schloss, courtesy of the Germans. What a mix-up Africa is.

But I digress. With Isobel things came to a head on New Year's Eve. I may have mentioned the EB Club in the Railway Compound. Well, traditionally their New Year's Eve party is the place to be as the year ends—the Governor General usually attends—and Len Sherman, who is on the committee at the club, asked if we would do an extra performance of our review for this New Year's Eve do. By the way it is called *The Paludrine Show*—a ridiculous title. Everyone was happy to oblige and I think it went down well but after the show Isobel and I found ourselves partnered off by the rest of the thespians with the result that during the early hours of the New Year I was driving her back to her flat in Ikoyi. I have seen her twice since then and we seem to have hit it off. She laughs a lot but has a bit of a temper when upset about something. I fear I might be too placid and unexciting for her, but watch this space.

I promised to include something about British culture. I fear that the Council in Lagos is not altogether successful in disseminating this. Our customers, at least some of them, enjoy the library and of course anything that might lead to them studying in the UK but really they have their own culture and, despite what Maurice Green might think, I don't see our mission to thrust Shakespeare *et al* down their throats. I suppose it was this view that resulted in the show I was putting together being more 'a piece of amusement' for the expatriates rather than the locals. We did try to introduce some topical pieces—one for instance where the office messenger becomes the boss and the white man is totally lost as he tries to undertake the messenger's duties—but most of the other stuff was, sorry to say, rather trite. However, we did manage to incur the censure of the local Roman Catholic Church over a slightly risqué sketch. Set in Hollywood, an extra keeps being left out of the shooting as a director calls out, 'Too late—too late.' This is boringly repeated a few times until the denouement when the director goes home to find the extra in bed with his wife. From under the sheets the extra bellows out, 'Too late, too late.' Sorry to bore you with this trivia but as you can see I am staging only the best of British! Peter thought the whole thing a waste of time, but he did come to one performance and I'm sure I saw some signs of amusement decorate his face.

Do give my love to Aunt Edith. Is she still striking dread into the members of the local WI? Will keep you informed on the Isobel front.

Matthew assumed he would marry one day and have a family but the absence to date of any serious relationship with the female of the species had not given him any real concern. He recalled how even on the aeroplane flying into Lagos he and Frank had wondered what girls they might meet in their new home, a topic that was also spasmodically raised with Brian Christie, but he was enjoying his new life in Lagos too much to give this subject a lot of thought—until Isobel came on the scene.

There had been the Resident Engineer's daughter, and her friend, but for him and Brian this was an incident to laugh over rather than regret. General Pullman, late of the Royal Engineers and the Indian Railways, was responsible for reporting to the Government on railway accidents. It was not a taxing job. He lived in the Railway Compound and was an habitué of the club golf course. Like his father, Matthew was keen on cricket and he had not been in Lagos long before he and Len Sherman, equally keen, decided that the EB Club should attempt to form a cricket side. There were some opponents they could challenge, such as the Ikeja Club close to the airport that had a team, as did one of the research institutes based in Yaba. The committee of the club approved the suggestion. The golf course did not attract many members and it was thought that, for the younger set, some further sporting activity, in addition to tennis, would be an advantage. Where to play? Len, who was even more strongly in favour of this idea than Matthew, suggested a concrete strip should be laid in the centre of the golf course. All cricket pitches in Lagos were of matting on concrete. The committee agreed and decided that the new cricket team should have the sole right to the golf course every other Sunday. Unfortunately, General Pullman did not agree. Despite being in a minority of one, if he felt like a round of golf on that Sunday he would appear and strike his small white ball as straight as he could, ignoring any danger to the cricketers, or any danger to himself as a result of a somewhat larger ball, a red one. As he was not a busy man, he could indulge his sport during weekdays, so his Sunday adventures were fairly few. Nevertheless Matthew Cresswell was not a favourite of his.

The General had an unmarried daughter living with him temporarily and she had a female friend visiting for a month or so. This was long enough for Matthew and Brian Christie to become friendly with the two girls, even though Brian thought that while the General's daughter looked like a horse her friend sounded like one. Matthew's relationship was not improved with the General, nor the daughter for that matter, when, returning her to the front door after a few beers, he managed to drive his car over her father's favourite patch of canna lilies and detach a thriving bougainvillaea plant from the patio wall.

The position was now very different—Isobel was firmly centre stage. She occupied a flat in Ikoyi, the premier residential district of Lagos, similar to the one Matthew had and he soon became a regular visitor at No. 6 Rumens Road. She was very good company and he enjoyed getting to know her better. Until she came to Nigeria at the age of twenty-three she had never been away from home. When asked why she chose to go to Nigeria she would say that she intended to travel and see the world but in the event she was to spend more than two decades in West Africa. Matthew was interested to find that Isobel had travelled to school every day by train, as had his sister Jenny, and Isobel would regale him with amusing stories of that journey, including how she was sometimes allowed in the cab of the engine and acted as the fireman and shovelled coal. She also recalled how she managed to break a window in the carriage while demonstrating the hook shot using one of the boys' cricket bats.

Another of her stories concerned someone Matthew knew well, his old headmaster at Uppingham. Before her African adventure,

Isobel had worked as a secretary in a local firm and her office was close to the High Street. From there she had seen one of the Uppingham schoolboys misbehaving. When someone complained to the school, the Headmaster came to Isobel's office to see if she could identify the culprit. It soon became apparent to her that the Head was attempting to suggest that the miscreant had been a town boy and not one of his. His first question was: 'Miss Ramsey, this boy you saw, he wasn't a gentleman, was he?' Isobel's reply was, 'How do you know?' This greatly amused Matthew who had thought the Headmaster at the time to be something of a snob. It prompted him to tell Isobel that the last love of his life had been a shop girl and that his grandfather had been little more than a farm labourer. These remarks made no impact on Isobel who had little regard for the nuances of class. She mixed as easily with Governors-General and Prime Ministers as she did with her house steward. Nothing seemed to faze her. On one occasion she left the keys in the lock to the office safe where the secret files were kept. Realising this she arranged to be at the office early in the morning so as to hide her transgression. The keys were not there, but the Permanent Secretary was. He had beaten her to it. She was, as she described it, severely ticked off. On another occasion she committed the cardinal sin of writing a minute in a file in the red ink reserved for comments by the Governor-General and when he saw someone had had the effrontery to use his colour, circled her comments in the file, in red of course, and wrote: 'Who is this Miss Ramsey?' But she survived. She was proud of the fact that she had worked with the first Nigerian Prime Minister, Sir Abubakar Tafawa Balawa, a man she greatly admired, and was delighted when it was he who presented the gifts the department had purchased to celebrate her wedding. The decanter and sherry glasses had pride of place on their sideboard for many years to come.

She had a wide circle of friends, both within Government and the commercial world, including a number of Swiss men who worked for the United Trading Company and one or two from the Lebanese community. She enjoyed her job but as she had not until then ever been away from home she clearly meant to make up for lost time on the social front by sampling the recreational life on offer, which was somewhat different from the milieu of an English market town. She was not a traditional beauty, inclining to plumpness, with fine hair bordering on the ginger. Her eyes were her best physical feature. They were wide and round and, thought Matthew, of an inquisitive nature, but it was her irrepressible sparkle that was her principal attraction. She had a perfectly natural gaiety which endeared her to so many people, male and female. To the latter, she was rarely seen as a rival while the male section of her circle enjoyed her company for the bubble of laughter which seemed to contain her. Matthew, of course, saw deeper than that, and soon discovered that the reverse side of this hit record could be a very discordant tune indeed. Nonetheless, he was soon irretrievably in love, but Isobel appeared not to be as attracted to him in the same way. This led to sharp disagreements when they would often suspend contact with each other for days, but it was always Matthew who relented first. After a short telephone conversation, he presented himself at her flat—Saturday lunchtime.

There was a perfunctory hug and Matthew suggested they go to the Ikoyi Rest House for a curry lunch. Isobel shrugged her shoulders, which were mostly bare because she was wearing the blue spotted dress he liked so much. He wondered if she had chosen that by accident or, as he hoped, because he was coming to see her. She fetched him a Star beer from the fridge—her steward was off at the weekend—and sat across the room and looked at him with those eyes of hers. Her face was expressionless and she said nothing. He drank copiously and frowned. Suddenly she started to her feet, said 'bloody fool' and launched herself at him like a ballistic missile. She folded her arms round his neck, spilling beer over his shorts, and turned her face towards him to be kissed. She had forgiven him. He replaced his spectacles, which had become detached from his nose by the force of her onslaught, and hugged her to him. As he drove back to the Railway Compound later that night he repeated to himself, 'She has forgiven me' but then, while crossing Carter Bridge, he woke from his lovesickness to ask, 'What for?' It did not matter. He had asked her to marry him—but he was not sure what her answer had been.

In the 1960s, Nigeria was still a fully paid-up member of the group of countries which formed 'The White Man's Grave' with the result that leave entitlements for expatriates were extremely generous. Government employees were expected to serve tours of fifteen to eighteen months, but at the end of such periods of duty they were granted one week's paid leave for every month of service.

In addition, if the travel back to the UK was by the Elder Dempster mail boats that took thirteen days to sail from Lagos to Liverpool, the leave period did not commence until the Liver Building was in sight. Alternatively, for those people who chose to travel by air, an extra week was added, each way, to compensate for the twenty-six days they might have enjoyed on the high seas. This meant that after an eighteen-month tour a Government employee who decided to enjoy the delights of the *MV Apapa* or the *MV Auriol* could be away from their post for a period of nearly half of a year. Matthew was due for leave in the March following the eventful New Year's Eve party. Isobel's tour did not end until November and when Matthew left for the UK he was still unsure whether they were engaged or not. Isobel joked that if they were to get married—and it would need to be in the UK or her mother would never forgive her—it would not be possible until 1976 because their leaves would not coincide until then. However, while Matthew was in the UK, he discovered a valuable ally in the pursuit of the indecisive Isobel—her mother.

Isobel warmly encouraged Matthew to visit her family of mother, father and much younger sister during his leave and he did so—more than once. He was cordially welcomed and their open friendliness resulted in his quickly telling them that he wanted Isobel to marry him. He also told them of the prevarication he had encountered. This did not surprise her mother and, although Matthew could not recall whether the suggestion had been hers or his, the week before he was due to return to Nigeria both of them went shopping for an engagement ring. This did the trick. Isobel could not withstand the dual onslaught and within days of his return the ring was on her finger and Matthew felt as though his real life was about to begin.

While he spent most of his spare time with her, the friendship with Peter Okonkwo deepened and on a number of occasions Matthew and Isobel, together with Peter and his girlfriend Dorothy, enjoyed the night-life of Lagos together. Matthew recalled his introduction to this—although he had not yet told Isobel of the experience—which had occurred during his first weeks in the country. Immediately after he was settled into his own flat, Brian Christie had introduced him to the Lido. The Lido was in Yaba and, although

Brian lived nearby, they went in his car. At first sight Matthew was not impressed. They had arrived at what seemed to be a more noxious slum than any he had yet encountered in Lagos. The two men had some trouble in reaching the entrance to the club as outside, alongside the evil-smelling storm drains, were hundreds of people trying to sell something—or someone—to those attempting to gain admittance. Eventually, they forced their way through and Brian paid the modest entrance fee. This so-called nightclub consisted of a patch of concreted yard enclosed by an unpainted wall topped with barbed wire. It was surrounded by a variety of shops and other business premises, constructed in the main of corrugated iron. A crude, partly covered bandstand occupied one corner; otherwise the club's open space was largely taken up with ranks of metal tables and chairs. The area was illuminated by the harsh glow of fluorescent strip lights hung precariously on a series of bamboo poles. Before either of them could take a mouthful of the beer they had ordered they were joined at their table by three women demanding a drink, or a dance, preferably both. Next to the bandstand was a minuscule area free of tables where a number of white men were attempting to emulate their black partners in the dancing of the highlife. Brian explained that this music had originated in Ghana but was very popular in Southern Nigeria. It was, he said, supposed to mark the hope and expectation of the people at the end of colonial rule.

Matthew was interested but could hardly hear what was being said over the noise of the enthusiastic band. His first reaction was that they could keep the dancing but he found the music exhilarating, fresh and new to his ears. The girl closest to Matthew held his arm and looked at him with rounded eyes.

'Honey, why you no dance with me?'

'No thanks, I want to listen to the music. What is the name of the band?'

'King Vidor and his Lagosians. What of drink?'

Matthew ordered beer for the girls. He thought the one who had set her sights on him looked a little like Louis Armstrong. In her case, however, the full lips, set in a face so flat it had virtually no cheeks, were heavily painted in a carmine that glowed phosphorescent under the club lights. The music continued and Brian danced with all of the trio in turn while Matthew tried to conduct some sort of conversation with the two who were left in his company. She of the cherry lips said her name was Mary and that she was a seamstress. As if to prove this, she re-tied the gaily coloured wrapper around her ample body and protruding breasts, which action seemed to Matthew to release into the atmosphere a perfume comprising an equal measure of body odour and moth balls. She wore a matching head-tie and when Matthew asked how the girls managed to keep their headgear in place when dancing, Mary removed hers to demonstrate the tying technique. This revealed a scalp the hair of which was as short as his, except for two extensions about the ears—a pair of flying plaits, he thought. When not dancing with Brian, or any of the other white predators, Mary sat as close to Matthew as the uncomfortable metal chairs would permit, short of sitting on his lap. It is said that animals can always sense if a man is in fear of them. She could see he was new to this scene and, he thought, using her animal sense, recognised his virgin state at a hundred paces. She did not to drink as much as he, but while by his side she never stopped talking, except when she needed her face and mouth to leer at him. Her breasts seemed to be attached to her torso by ball bearings. As the evening wore on she appeared to be able to rotate them at him, either together or individually, like a pair of spinning tops.

He was new to the local beer and had totally misjudged its strength, or perhaps he had simply drunk more than was his custom. It was, after all, still very hot and humid even though midnight was approaching. When they left he negotiated his way to Brian's car without too much difficulty but it was not until they reached the main road that Matthew realised Mary was sitting close to him on the back seat and vigorously massaging the front of his lightweight trousers. Even though involved in the clothing trade, she had apparently found his trouser buttons beyond her. In the next scenario he was in a room he assumed was Mary's—at least a sewing machine was on view. He could hardly see her from his position on the bed, partly because of his intoxication and partly because the only lighting consisted of a low wattage bulb painted blue. Some of this paint had flaked away allowing minor slivers of light to pierce the room. In his inebriated state Matthew saw these as the beams of a fragile searchlight seeking out the escaped prisoner or an enemy aircraft. Mary was removing her outer garments. For some reason she needed to turn her back to him as she loosened her bra, the straps of which were buried into her fleshy body. At this point Matthew slumped on the bed and fell into a drunken stupor. Time did not register for him on that evening and so he could never afterwards recall how long he spent in that dingy room, nor what took place there, nor when he emerged. Mary helped him downstairs where Brian, who appeared to be rather more skilled in these matters, produced some money for her and his own girl, then drove his companion back to the Railway Compound as dawn was breaking.

When Matthew was able to view the events of the night in a careful and sober manner he became fairly certain he had been so drunk that no services had been rendered which warranted any payment, but he did refund the expenditure incurred by Brian on his behalf. However, this did not stop him worrying for a few weeks about whether he might need to refresh his memory of the film on the subject of VD, which had been shown to him as a new recruit during his short army career.

After their marriage Isobel continued to work for the Federal Government, now in the Ministry of Mines and Power, but at this time she also began in earnest her life-long association with the Girl Guide movement. When in the Cameroons she had helped with a local Brownie pack and so, back in Lagos, it did not take long for the Guide headquarters to seek her out. By the time she became Mrs Cresswell she was also the Captain of a large unit of Guides at Queens College, the premier girls' school in Lagos. Before Independence Day, on the first of October 1960, when the guest of honour was Princess Alexandra, the Guides prepared a float on a lorry borrowed from Raymond Habib to take part in the parade and Matthew was conscripted to help with the decorating. Perhaps, he thought, this was repayment for the number of times he had had his shoes cleaned by Brownies assembled at their house keen to perform the tasks required for the Homemaker badge. The celebration of Independence was a great success and, although the ceremonies were somewhat low-key, Matthew felt optimistic that the course of the new Nigeria was set fair and pleased that his adopted country had reached this important milestone. He was amused by an account he read subsequently concerning UK journalists covering these celebrations. They had needed to file their articles three hours before the midnight lowering of the Imperial flag—articles that referred to happy Nigerians dancing in the streets. Unfortunately, as they drove through the streets of Lagos at midnight they found only orderly groups of citizens wending their way home, whereupon one journalist shouted from his car: 'Dance, dammit! You're meant to be dancing.'

Matthew was involved with the Nigerian Girl Guides only on the periphery but there was one leisure activity both he and Isobel enjoyed and that was amateur dramatics. After *The Paludrine Show* he had thought his stage days were over but Isobel was more keen and she was a good natural actress so they joined the Festival Players, so named because they had been founded in 1951 at the time of the Festival of Britain. Matthew painted sets, acted as front-of-house manager or ran the bar, but on one occasion he was persuaded to perform on stage. The play was Terence Rattigan's *Harlequinade* where the principal parts are those of a domineering theatrical man and wife based on the Lunts—or Donald Wolfit. As it happened, the Festival Players contained such a pair in George and Mavis Welsh so the casting of the main roles was not difficult. They performed the play on four nights at a school hall in Lagos. On three of those nights the male Welsh, in a fit of not unusual ad-libbing, cut out of the performance the two lines Matthew had been entrusted with. Isobel had a similar experience. On this occasion she had a small part in a minor thriller by Emlyn Williams and it fell to her to deliver the last line—'We must call the police.'—before the final curtain. However, at one performance the stage manager lowered the curtain before she could speak. Friends of hers in the audience remained in their seats assuming there was a further act because, as they agreed amongst themselves, 'Isobel hasn't said her line yet.' All of this was light relief compared with the real-life drama just over the horizon.

Both Isobel and Matthew liked Dorothy, Peter's wife. She came from Abakaliki in Eastern Nigeria and worked as a nurse at the Creek Hospital in Lagos. Matthew was the best man at the wedding and although the bride and groom had lived in Lagos for most of their lives they had a large extended family and, for this reason, the marriage took place in the capital of the Eastern Region, Enugu. This was the first time the Cresswells had met so many Ibos under one roof—in the church and at the hotel where the reception was held—and, like most jamborees, where more than three

Nigerians are met together, it was a noisy affair; in fact, a very noisy affair with two hundred of them.

Social gatherings in Nigeria, be they Ibo or Yoruba, generally follow a pattern of disorganised formality. There has to be a Chairman but he is not allowed to begin his duties until the 'Presenter of the Chairman' has introduced him, often in a speech of inordinate length. There is frequently on the agenda something known as the 'Chairman's Special Item', which is usually the opportunity for a collection of cash to be made for the bride and groom, or the widow, or the new parents.

When the Cresswells attended Herbert's wedding this event was preceded by two speeches, one from a member of the Herbert family clan, the other from someone on his wife's side. These extolled the respective virtues of the happy couple but one of the speakers managed to make some disparaging remarks about Herbert, or Jacinta, which produced a minor riot and the Chairman's Special Item was hijacked. Result—no cash. During the wedding of Peter and Dorothy, the meal served after the ceremony included goat meat that still showed evidence of the animal's fur. Dorothy told them, with a twinkle in her eye, that her home town of Abakaliki had been infamous in the past for cannibalism and therefore the fur was left on to prove that the stew on their plate was really goat and not human flesh, known in the vernacular as 'long pig'. Nigeria never failed to fascinate Matthew.

He had not yet visited his sister in South Africa. Anyone with evidence on their passport of a trip to that pariah nation would be refused entry into Nigeria. It was possible to overcome this problem, however. The UK Government was prepared to issue a second passport if required and the South African authorities would sometimes agree to place the stamps of arrival and departure on a separate sheet of paper, loosely inserted into the passport for this purpose. Matthew did not resort to any of these devices; he was anxious not to jeopardise his position in Nigeria, but he and Jenny were good correspondents and he felt he was well informed on the differences between her habitat and his, particularly in respect relationships with black Africans. He understood that in South Africa this was limited for some to those they met in the kitchen or while observing the cleaning of the swimming pool, but in Nigeria the situation was totally different. It was a country run by a Government elected by Nigerian voters and even if that state of democracy had now been replaced by military rule, the military was wholly Nigerian. Non-Nigerians in the civil service were few and far between and, more and more, commerce and the professions were being indigenised. However, there was still a considerable expatriate population who worked side-by-side with Nigerian colleagues, or bosses. Although the intercourse between the two was therefore considerable, even in the late 1960s and 1970s there was still a social divide. Black and white met at official parties and just occasionally a white host would invite the likes of Rotimi Lawson as a guest, but there were few Nigerians on the golf course at Ikoyi and most of the Festival Players' audiences were white.

It was against this background that Matthew analysed his relationship with Peter. He knew it was not unique, but it was fairly rare. There were a number of inter-marriages—many of them happy ones of long standing—but few expatriates would be able to claim a Nigerian as their closest friend. Matthew wondered if this was more to do with his background than any special qualities in Peter, but he dismissed this notion. He may have an Anglo-Indian mother and have spent his infant years in India, but Leicestershire society and a prestigious public school had ensured that he was, in adulthood, as typical an example of a middle-class Englishman as it was possible to find anywhere. He was perfectly at ease with the senior echelon of expatriates in the commercial, professional and diplomatic worlds. He played squash with an Australian architect and he and Isobel dined with their near neighbours from the Belgian Embassy, but the chemistry between him and Peter was special.

Neither time nor marriage had mellowed Michael Green. After nearly ten years he still had contempt for Nigeria and the Nigerians, contempt that was fuelled by his new wife. They suited each other: she was as unsympathetic towards them as he was. Even so, his chances of obtaining a posting to Rio or Nairobi or Singapore seemed as remote as ever. In some measure Matthew could understand Green's attitude, as a number of the Nigerians they dealt with could be difficult and devious, but what he could not accept was that Green chose to ignore the positive aspects of their work. The guidance they were able to give to young ambitious Nigerians was, in Matthew's view, invaluable. As time went by he was able to see the fruits of his labours as young people who had been on UK courses, sponsored by the British Council, returned to Nigeria with prospects of a brighter future. However hard the education system in the country tried, it faced a formidable task. In many cases schools were overcrowded, teachers dispirited—sometimes having to wait weeks for salaries to be paid—and premises dilapidated. Matthew therefore saw that any help the British Council could provide was thoroughly worthwhile and he relished the challenge of assisting as many youngsters as possible. Peter's attitude was similar but in 1964 they both decided they needed a change of scene. The negative attitude of their superior was partly to blame for this, but Peter could see there was an arena they could enter where they might be able to achieve more than with the limited resources and narrow outlook of the British Council. During a coffee break one morning, Peter and Matthew's new venture was born.

'Segun Oludemi came to see me last week—you remember him, a bright kid from Abeokuta. No father, and mother a "lady of the night". We managed to get him to the UK and he's back with two good A-levels.'

'Yes, Peter, I think I remember him. Spent hours in our library if I recall.'

'Well, he's been back in Lagos for six months, staying with a cousin, but he can't find a job anywhere. He is willing to do virtually anything but with his background he knows no-one. No "long leg".'

'And he is not the only one; even that Ibo girl we got some nursing training for is having difficulty finding a place.'

'The problem is of course we can, within limits, provide training for those who will benefit from it, but when they get back here talent, brains and application isn't enough. They have no work experience and in most cases they do not understand how the Nigerian system works. It's like your class thing, Matthew: not what you know but who you know. Well, with us it is not the old school tie, it is what tribe you are or which family you come from.'

'Or can you pay the bribe.'

'Yes, that too. It's a tragedy for these youngsters who thought that qualifications were the key, and it is a waste for the country as a whole to have talent that can add to the national good left on the waste-heap. But I've got an idea. With our experience, why don't we see if we can set up a business where we are retained by enlightened employers to give bright youngsters some sort of lower or middle management training to make them more attractive in the labour market. I also wonder if we could get the Government to subsidise such an effort.'

'But we don't know anything about running a commercial enterprise. We are virtually civil servants with an assured salary cheque coming in every month. And even if it is feasible—and as I speak I'm beginning to warm to the idea—where do we get the start-up capital?'

'I'm sure my father would help, but what about your friend, Raymond Habib—he's got lots of money and might like to be a sleeping partner if we can prove it makes economic sense.'

The two friends discussed this idea with their wives. Both were in support and Isobel immediately assigned herself the position of office manager. This encouraged Peter and Matthew to spend time together putting some flesh on the bones of the idea and then prepare a business plan. Peter had a contact within John Holts who expressed interest in supporting this kind of training and Matthew had a similar positive feedback when he talked to Frank Jones, who was now the manager for Personnel and Purchasing at the Nigerian Tobacco Company.

Initially, Habib had dismissed the business plan. It was, he said, full of good ideas—or more accurately—ideals but short on detail as to how the service was to be delivered. However, they eventually put together something that seemed workable, and possibly profitable, and he agreed to join them. He loaned the new firm sufficient funds to get started and found them office premises in one of the family buildings at a concessionary rent. The three partners could see that in the future, enterprises of this nature would need to be at least majority owned by Nigerian citizens, but for the present it was agreed to appoint Peter as Chairman with the shares divided equally. The name decided upon was Central Management Services (CMS), even though for most people in Nigeria the acronym CMS stood for the Church Missionary Society. Peter conjectured that perhaps that was what they were to be—missionaries in a heathen commercial jungle. The new firm selected a handful of likely candidates from people they had known during their British Council days and found them positions in commercial organisations to obtain work experience. They then kept a close eye on each individual and arranged extra training sessions held in a room at a local hotel where they were able to persuade local businessmen to be involved in lectures and seminars. Getting their concept accepted was hard work to begin with, and Matthew wondered in the first six months where the money was to come from to pay the grocery bill at Kingsway Stores, but local commerce seemed pleased with the service they were offering and by the end of the first year they were breaking even after paying themselves modest salaries.

At the beginning of 1967 the firm acquired a new client in the form, indirectly, of the UK Government. One of the aid packages provided by Britain included specialist training for Nigerian military personnel at the Nigerian Defence Academy and CMS were asked to tender to oversee a small part of this. The UK already had extensive experience in military training for Nigeria as they had provided advice when this Academy was first set up in Kaduna in 1964. It was now thought that this establishment was failing to provide middle ranking officers with management skills of an administrative nature when dealing with the commercial world, particularly in the area of purchasing and procurement. Although not of strategic importance, both the Nigerian and UK Governments acknowledged this deficiency and so the latter agreed to finance a trial scheme to provide suitable training in this area for a small number of officers.

The Defence Advisor at the British High Commission, Brigadier Gerard Lakey, was the person given responsibility for overlooking this experiment. When CMS found that their tender had been accepted, he spent some time with Peter and Matthew adding more detail to the outline proposal. It was then decided, within the firm, that Matthew would be responsible for this account and as a result, and over time, he and Lakey became close friends. It was at first sight an unlikely friendship, but possibly the genes of Charles Cresswell were more prominent in Matthew than anyone, to date, could have considered. This was a new experience for Matthew. Unlike his father who, despite his years in the commercial world, was steeped in the military from his teens until his death, the only contact Matthew had had with soldiers, other than his brief National Service experience, was with the lead ones he played with as a boy. Until the January 1966 coup he, like almost everyone in Nigeria, native and expatriate alike, hardly knew there was an army presence in the country. He and Isobel had occasionally visited the Army Kinema at Yaba barracks but as to contact with any soldiers, there was none. There were barracks and he thought a few members of the EB Club were army officers but he had not really registered any notion of an army in Nigeria—or at least one of any consequence. When it mattered, he looked into it. Before 1966 the Nigerian Army, as such, was a part of the Royal West Africa Frontier Force which included the armies of Ghana, Nigeria, Sierra Leone and Gambia. At this time, there were only eight indigenous Nigerian officers in the entire force; the rest were British. The role of an army in a developing country was not fully appreciated by the nationalist leaders struggling for Independence and so there was no effective pressure on the British Government to train Nigerian officers in preparation for such Independence. The first Nigerian to command the Nigerian Army, Major-General Ironsi, was not appointed until 1965, five years after the British flag was lowered.

Gerard Lakey did not wear uniform while occupying this post but he hardly needed a costume to display his military persona. He was a slim, tall man in his forties with a receding hairline. Although graceful in movement, he stood more straight and erect than other men and Matthew wondered how he tied his shoelaces and whether he was any more supple when in bed with his wife. Even in the heat and humidity of Lagos he was never less than immaculately attired and had a wide variety of regimental ties, apparently one for each day of the week. He had served in Malaysia but prior to his arrival in Lagos had been desk-bound in Whitehall. As Nigeria now had a military Government under General Gowon, his position within the High Commission had become increasingly important. In 1955 Lakey had lectured on guerrilla warfare at the Eaton Hall Officer Cadet Training School in Cheshire when Gowon had been a student and the camaraderie of the army became a useful diplomatic tool, even though the situations were now almost reversed. In his role as a military attaché, Lakey was always circumspect when discussing local politics with Matthew, but he was able to confirm what virtually everyone else in the country knew—that Nigeria was becoming very unsettled indeed.

Matthew's letter to his mother in June 1967 contained some

worrying news. It proved only the preface to a situation that, as the months went by, became more and more alarming.

I am enclosing some snaps of John. As you can see he has made wonderful progress since Christmas. It is always said that young children thrive in this climate and he only goes to prove the point. We had to change his nanny but the new girl, Grace, looks after him splendidly and they are great friends. She is married to the brother of Tobias who is a gardener for people who live in Apapa. Isobel and I suspect that he might soon be moving back to his home village and if that happens no doubt Grace will go with him? Unknown at the moment, but yesterday Herbert received a telegram from his brother to say that their mother is very ill and he should come home. We are suspicious about this and believe it is a coded message for him to quit Lagos and return to Ibo-land while he still can. If he goes we shall miss him of course but we do not want to persuade him to stay if his people are going to be subjected to the atrocities that happened in Kano and elsewhere in the past. He is both cook and a steward at present because Tobias, who is the oldest son, has already gone back to Amichi. He didn't appear to have any alternative. His people seemed to be able to pull him back home as if by juju. Herbert manages all right with extra input from Isobel but Tobias had developed into a very competent cook and I do hope we hear from him soon. You remember I told you about him. He has been with us ever since we got married. Before then he worked as a cook at the Hill Station Hotel in Jos. Not quite Mahabaleshwar but fairly posh all the same. What he failed to tell us when we took him on was that he had been the cook for children's teas only. However, his roast beef is now on a par with his famous fancy cakes.

The most important news, however, concerns Peter. He is probably not yet under threat and, although not convinced about Ojukwu's tactics, he feels he must support the Ibo cause and is desperately torn. Does he follow his patriotic conscience or does he cherish more the friendship with me—and our business? I have suggested that as we have a number of clients in Port Harcourt why not set up a branch of Central Management Services there so he is on the spot, as it were, to witness the fate of the new Republic of Biafra. When we talked again about this last night I got the feeling that he had decided this was a happy—wrong word—pragmatic compromise and, as Dorothy and the children are already in Aba, I think he will decide very quickly. What a situation. As you know, the business is prospering, obviously we have tailored our product to fill a gap in the market, but without Peter it will be more difficult to deliver—and I certainly do not relish being on my own. We have some good staff but no-one can replace him in the firm, and certainly not in my heart. I know that sounds exceedingly sentimental but it is true. We think alike and, as I realised the other day, he seems to have many of those characteristics of tolerance and fair-mindedness that we as children saw in our father—and appreciated even more from your descriptions of him. I know he would deplore the prospect of civil war in Nigeria, just as he was so apprehensive about the tribal/religious differences in India and where they were leading. How right he was to feel that way. I still hope sense will prevail but Ojukwu is a stubborn man and he could yet lead the Ibos into disaster.

It is a tragedy to see the impact the current situation is having on Peter—and on all the family. Even after two military coups, Isobel and I have always felt safe here but if there is going to be a conflict on Nigerian soil—Ibos versus the rest—I can see our sense of security evaporating very quickly. There are already stories circulating of expatriates shielding their Ibo servants when other Nigerian busybodies appear on the scene. I don't think there is yet an organised campaign to root them out. What will they do with them? Lock them all up? But we are beginning to feel very uneasy—so different from when Isobel and I first came. She was recalling only the other day that in her 'wild period' she and other friends would often go down to Bar Beach after a party and swim during the early hours of the morning. Equally, in my 'nightclub days', I never thought there was a problem driving through Lagos in the middle of the night and even when we were 'courting' we walked around Ikoyi at twilight with no thought that we might be robbed or assaulted. Perhaps we were just young and foolish but it is going to change, if it has not already done so. Look what they use the Bar Beach for now. I just hope and pray that Peter doesn't put himself into danger

What a mournful letter. Sorry, but this is the position we find ourselves in at present. I hope we can get some UK leave before the end of the year, but we shall have to wait and see.

Have not heard from Jenny for a few weeks—have you? Isobel and John send their love.

Matthew Cresswell was to spend more than twenty of his adult years in Nigeria and from this time emerged the two most important relationships of his life: his marriage to Isobel and his profound friendship with Peter Okonkwo. The first of these was robust enough to withstand the sacrifices that this friendship demanded or, more accurately, what Matthew thought was required of him in its name. Although his wife advised caution on a number of occasions, she understood why her husband needed to pursue the course that he did and so, even when she saw the dangers as clearly as he did, she stood by him. Theirs was a strong marriage, and it needed to be. If it had been less than that, Isobel could easily have seen his friendship with Peter—and its consequences—as an insuperable barrier to their relationship.

'Your Honour, I cite as co-respondent Peter Okonkwo who has alienated the affections of my husband in that he seduced him into supporting a lost cause, an unattainable goal.'

In reality such flippancy had no place in the story as it unfolded. Matthew agreed with the path his friend took—and actively participated in his fight—because he believed this path was the only option if he was to be true to himself. Peter said later that he would have fully understood if Matthew had remained on the sidelines during the Biafran War, as the majority of non-Nigerians did. Matthew's decision, however, was as much forged by the events in Amritsar in 1919 and the fabric of his upbringing as they were in the fires of friendship.

Chapter Two

Charles

He was in Amritsar on the 13th of April 1919 and this changed the direction the remainder of his life in India was to take. When he arrived at the officers' mess it was already dark. He had been on duty with his platoon without a break since early morning and was therefore fully aware of the state of unrest in the city, but when details began to emerge of what had happened at the Jalianwala Bagh, he was bewildered and unable to participate in the feeling of triumph that was beginning to emerge amongst some of his colleagues. He took his glass of gin and bitters and moved through the open French windows into the solitude of the Indian night. He was not a reflective person. Hitherto, the progress of his life had moved forward on well-oiled wheels along paths determined by the established routines of school and the army, but as he balanced his glass on the dwarf wall adjoining the tennis court and lit his pipe he had a premonition that things were about to change.

He loved India at night. There was now little noise from the town in contrast to the disturbances of the last few days and he hardly noticed the familiar chorus of cicadas and bullfrogs. The sky was clear and decorated with stars which, at the end of this particular day, seemed less bright than usual. Even the moon had a sickly hue but what registered most forcibly on that eventful evening was the smell of India. When he had arrived at Bombay the previous year he had entrained for Lahore to join a contingent of his Regiment recently dispatched to the Punjab with, so he was led to believe, an active campaign in Afghanistan in prospect. It was during this journey that his love affair with India began. He had spent most of his youth in one of the prettiest shires of England, a vivid contrast with the desolation of the French and Flemish war-scarred landscapes where he began his military career, but from the outset he had felt a special affinity with the country that was to be his home for the for the rest of his life. One of his most powerful impressions had been the special aroma of India, first experienced during that long journey to Lahore. It seemed to him in those early days to represent the very essence of the country. He remembered the fumes of smoke from the innumerable wood fires, the special odour transmitted by the night-time heat and the many different spices that were the main constituents of the snacks always available to purchase at every station en route, however small. Occasionally, this was reinforced by the scent apparently emitted by the giant Banyan trees planted to give protection from the sun as it relentlessly attacked the corrugated iron used to roof most of the minor station buildings in India. Those railway stations. The population of India was large but most of them lived, not in the slums of Bombay and Calcutta, but within thousands upon thousands of small village communities scattered over this vast land—except for those who eked out a precarious existence at railway stations and where they had taken up residence. Charles, who for the last two years or more had known the British army en masse, had never seen such a density of humanity as encountered at the gothic Bombay railway station. There must be some gigantic trains if these are all passengers, he thought. A census would have been revealing. Mrs Pandit Shah was travelling, second-class, to visit her mother on the occasion of an eightieth birthday. The daughter was accompanied to the station by three of her servants, needed to carry the two baskets she intended to travel with, plus her husband and their seven children, who were not travelling. He could not get away. If he left his jewellery shop for even ten minutes those shop assistants would eat all his gold. This coterie could hardly be distinguished from all ten members of the extended Sahgal family, third class, and bound for Amritsar to beg assistance from wealthy Uncle Rami. There was, however, a very discernible difference when it came to all of the solar-topeed memsahibs travelling first class for reunions with their husbands stationed at strategic locations throughout India. Each of these ladies was accompanied by at least one bearer and one maid with an assortment of luggage ranging from a set of matching leather hat boxes to a portable wash basin. These, and all the other passengers, were to board the waiting trains and leave behind the remaining fifty percent of the throng who were sheltering under the Victorian arches, either because they had nowhere else to be, or were plying their trade as barbers, sellers of sweetmeats, shoe cleaners or tailors and seamstresses. Not everyone was in movement. There were scores of recumbent station inhabitants wrapped up in cloth with heads covered but feet on show, in contrast to the many pi-dogs, never still, as they roamed the precincts sniffing for food. The goods varied from the bizarre to the basic. Different sellers sold different water to the thirsty, depending whether they were Hindu or Moslem; cigarettes and the betel nut came from the same vendor; hot, sweet tea was dispensed by the char-wallahs. Unfortunately, the largest contingent of all was the beggars. These were a distinct class in India: short of one or more limbs; the aged blind permanently attached to their young guides (boy or girl) by the wizened hand on the bare shoulder of the sighted companion; showing evidence of leprosy or smallpox with suppurating sores. Quiescent and aggressive; individual or in packs, particularly the ragged children. Most were totally ignored but there must have been sufficient annas thrown at them to justify their presence at the station—or so Charles assumed. There are a lot of flies in India but these wretched people attracted more than their fair share, particularly around the sightless eyes, the running noses and the lesions of the body. In microcosm this jumble of humanity was repeated at every station en route. Charles was astounded and seduced. Many of his colleagues on the train, particularly those to whom India was familiar, ignored these scenes, but Charles was fascinated. The noise was new: a hotchpotch of cries and exhortations in a variety of languages and dialects. The colours also—predominantly a grubby white, shot with vivid reds and blues; and the smell was new—the smell of India. Not just the tang of unwashed bodies or that resulting from the absence of an efficient sanitary system, but something unique. Charles remembered his first days in India most vividly and this evening the aroma of the Indian night seemed even more evocative.

The lights of the city were subdued, which matched his mood. Details of General Dyer's actions were at this stage somewhat hazy but Charles found it difficult to recognise or accept the connection between the General and the death of hundreds of unarmed civilians. As he looked out into the dark grey sky he heard footsteps on the terrace and turned to wave his pipe at George Meredith, with whom he had served in France.

'Well, Charlie boy, a momentous day, eh.'

'What do you mean?'

'Well, we've shown this lot that we are in charge and it has needed a real soldier to show how it is done.'

'Oh, is that so, George? Do you think it is "a real soldier" who kills so many unarmed men and women?'

'You don't know they weren't armed. From what I hear that mob was plotting the next Indian Mutiny. You know what the Punjab has been like recently. Yes, we had to take a stand. A firm hand was needed.'

'That may be so, but I think we both need to wait until we hear all the facts. However, I have a gut feeling that what has happened today may have stopped a mutiny but has started a sequence of events that will see the end of us in India.'

'Rubbish, man. Our role in this country will see me out.'

'Perhaps, but I just wonder whether the British Raj deserves to rule if this is what we do.'

'Charlie, what has happened to you? You're a soldier. You survived Ypres and all that, and now you talk like this. "Ours not to reason why . . ." etc. We are a small number. There are millions of them. They're savages.'

'Well actually, George, I think you might be surprised at how sophisticated they are. Their civilisation goes back a long way. When your ancestors were painting their faces with woad, these "savages" as you call them were building the most exquisite temples. Buddha was around some centuries before Christ, you know.'

'Good heavens, Charlie! Where do you get all this from?'

'It is what I've read. I'm not just a uniform you know, much as I love wearing it.'

'Oh, come in and let me get you another gin.'

Charles refused the offer and George went back into the mess which was now more animated as other officers were relieved of their duties in the city. Charles felt a blanket of sadness smothering him. Why could he not re-enter that world of soldiers' camaraderie he had so surprisingly discovered in the wretchedness of the Western Front and that had continued in the very different theatre of India. From the chatter distinguishable at the edge of the tennis court it was apparent that his colleagues were not exactly in a celebratory mood. They had all experienced a difficult day dealing with the unrest, but it was evident that few felt the increasingly disturbing disquiet that he did.

His exchange with George had depressed him even more. Surely, after all they had been through together in France, he had not joined the 'don't blame the Generals' brigade. Although Charles had not had any contact with the senior architects directing the British effort in the 'war to end all wars', he was not alone in the immediate post-war years in condemning their strategy, or lack of such, that had resulted in the futile deaths of so many millions. Was he now, he thought, to bear witness to further pointless deaths, and were these deaths more to be mourned than all of those in Europe? The carnage of 1914 to 1918 had been perpetrated by two opponents of more or less equal strength, which meant that casualties were maximised but, as he saw it, today's insanity was of a totally different kind. Charles had deplored the tragic loss of life in the war; too many men who had become like brothers to him had been killed, but there was something in his character, perhaps hidden until now, that told him what had happened at Amritsar was another matter altogether. However pointless had been the deaths resulting from the quest to secure control of a few acres of French, Flemish or Turkish soil, they had been incurred on both sides within a bizarre set of the 'rules of warfare'. Charles thought this was reflected by events such as the Christmas truce of 1914 when troops in opposite trenches had met and shared drinks and chocolate during an impromptu ceasefire, but what rule of war permitted the murder of defenceless civilians? He was not to live to know of Lidice or Sharpeville, but for the moment, and during the weeks and months that followed, he could find no excuse for what had happened in the sunshine of that Indian afternoon.

The General involved in what Charles was already defining as 'a catastrophe' was Reginald Dyer, a man now in his mid-50s who was born in India into a family long resident in the country who ran a brewery near Simla. Charles had not met him but one of his friends had been temporarily attached to Dyer's staff and described him as the type of soldier ideally suited, with his up-bringing and fighting experience, for service in India. The disturbances of the last few days in Amritsar, and in the Punjab overall, were indicative of the sense of restlessness that was growing throughout India. One and a half million Indian troops had served during the 1914–18 war and, after the victory to which they had contributed, it was thought that this should earn them a measure of freedom. But it was not to be. When the war was over the authorities quickly extended the sanctions of the Defence of India Act. Against a post-war backdrop of acute inflation and an influenza epidemic, this led inevitably to displays of civil disobedience. Charles did not yet fully understand the political nuances involved but he was aware that his job as a soldier was to lend assistance to the civilian authorities and the police to ensure that peace and order were established and maintained.

The facts as they emerged were these. Two influential members of the All India Congress and residents of Amritsar, Doctors Kitchlew and Satyapal, had joined Gandhi's civil disobedience movement. As a result of the activities of these two doctors the authorities decided, on the 9th of April, that they be deported from Amritsar and interned in another district of the Punjab. By the following day, as news of the deportations became known, many shops in the city were closed and angry crowds began to gather. Agitation escalated. A number of major buildings in the city were attacked and burned down and at the branches of two overseas banks three British managers were murdered. Another incident that was to have far-reaching consequences involved a Miss Sherwood, a lady missionary, who was attacked and severely beaten while bicycling along a narrow street. By the 11th of April General Dyer had arrived in Amritsar from Lahore and took over responsibility for the security of the city. The following day a number of arrests were made in connection with the uprising. Then, on the 13th of April, Dyer went through the city to have read out at several locations a proclamation restricting meetings and movement by the inhabitants. Despite this he heard that a gathering was planned for that afternoon at the Jalianwala Bagh. Accordingly, he proceeded to that location where he stationed fifty troops overlooking the crowd gathered there. Without giving any warning to disperse, Dyer ordered his troops to fire. The barrage continued for ten minutes; one thousand six hundred and fifty bullets were used, leaving approximately three hundred and seventy-nine people dead and probably as many as three times that number wounded.

Charles' career as a soldier had its origins at Uppingham School. The school had set up a Combined Cadet Force in 1889 and during his time there he became enthusiastic about 'playing at soldiers' as the rugby set described their activities. He was joined in the corps by Herbert Spencer, a West Country boy, who became Charles' best friend and a welcome guest at the Cresswell family farm for some of the short holidays from school. In the summer of 1916, just as Charles was approaching his eighteenth birthday, they were released from the cloistered life of Uppingham School to come face-to-face with the reality of the war in Europe. It was not, therefore, surprising that they joined the army as soon as possible, though according to law they had little choice. In 1914 Britain's regular army was small and scattered about the Empire, one third of the force being in India. When war was declared volunteers swarmed to enlist to serve in what was expected to be a short-lived campaign. Indeed, Charles heard his headmaster at speech day in 1914 declare: 'If a man cannot be useful to his country, he is better dead.' These words might well have come back to haunt him. Out of the sixty-six boys who were in the year senior to Charles at Uppingham, seventeen were killed in the war. By the time Charles and Herbert became eighteen the Military Service Act of January 1916 was in force. This required all unmarried men between the ages of eighteen and forty-one to join the forces; there was to be no more voluntary enlistment. Charles might well have been able to obtain deferment if he had joined his father on the farm as, until that time, agriculture had been an essential occupation, exempting such workers from military service, but this did not enter into his thinking. He was probably unaware that, after the initial surge of patriotism in 1914 when numbers were swelled by those looking for a wage and three square meals a day, by the following year enthusiasm was waning and there were now more jobs available in the civilian world. By the time Charles was in uniform the British Army was necessarily composed of a mix of long-term regulars, territorials and reservists, the Kitchener New Army and then the conscripts. He was to find that these differentiations mattered little when in the trenches. With their public school education and CCF experience they were commissioned on entry. Charles and his father had wanted the Sherwood Foresters to be his regiment, but Herbert had more than one relation in the Somerset Light Infantry and so, after spending Christmas and the New Year with their families, the two young men met in February 1917 at the Regiment's depot at Taunton. Four months later they found themselves on their way to the front.

Arriving at Brigade Headquarters at Ypres, they encountered an air of expectancy; even the battle-hardened soldiers thought that, as a result of the success in June at Messines, the offensive now being planned might be decisive. An end to the war might be in sight. Charles was given command of a platoon, most of whom were regular soldiers. They had seen action the previous year on the Somme and inevitably treated Charles with a degree of scepticism—many of them had been through the initiation of a new platoon leader many times before. Infantry subalterns did not last long at the front. On average, one in four would be killed within three months and the others wounded, one seriously enough to mean that he could not be returned to the front. It was accepted that subalterns would be posted to experienced small units in order for such units to train their officer so that he could, in due course, effectively lead them. A two way process. Charles was quickly inducted into the spirit of his group of soldiers, his first experience of the remarkable fellowship that seemed to thrive best when conditions were at their worst and danger was near. Despite the impression that an element of urgency was being injected towards the next move, the battalion spent more than a month at Headquarters trying to occupy their time with fruitless drill parades and games of football while listening to the sounds of shellfire just a few miles away. The British artillery bombardment during the last ten days of July was massive: three thousand guns and over four million shells. Charles and his men were not deployed in the first infantry attack but on the 3rd of August orders to move forward finally came.

It was still dark when the men were directed to assemble. As instructions were relayed down the hushed lines of great-coated soldiery, Charles could see that there was a certain degree of order amongst this indiscriminate grouping of silent men. As they rose from their crouched or seated positions their shapes became distorted by their kit bags so that in the half-light they were transformed into lines of grotesque hunchbacks. There was no air of a military parade. Cigarettes were extinguished and rifles slung over shoulders as sergeants and corporals could be heard issuing, *sotto voce*, the familiar orders. There was no murmur of the army marching songs that had become such a feature of this war. They were going, or going back, to the trenches. It was not something to sing about.

The track to their destination ran between intermittent lines of wizened trees, many decimated during earlier conflicts, but even without these sporadic boundary markers, their path was well delineated—the mud saw to that. Although midsummer, the rainfall in that part of Flanders had been the heaviest in thirty years and had soon converted the terrain, including the roads, into a quagmire. Each step the soldiers took seemed to consume the same physical effort as a one hundred yards' dash on a cinder track. In places the well-trodden ground was more than twelve inches deep in a light-brown, evil-smelling slime. As they plodded on their squelching boots, like obscene musical instruments, contributed an accompaniement of fart-like squeaky notes to the strangled curses of the heavily-laden men. These profanities reminded Charles of the songs he had first encountered during his training-camp days, when the men, mostly unaware of the dreadful reality of what lay ahead, were encouraged to display their vocal talents to the full. He had learned many of the lines by heart; they were, he thought, the army's catechism. He mouthed extracts from some of his favourites as he laboured on.

I don't want to be soldier,
I don't want to go to war,
I'd rather stay at home,
Around the streets to roam,
And live on the earnings of a lady typist.
I don't want a bayonet in my belly,
I don't want my bollocks shot away,
I'd rather stay in England,
In merry, merry England,
And fornicate my bleeding life away.

Another ditty he recalled had a particular relevance to the moment:

Far far from Wipers, I long to be,
Where German snipers can't get at me,
Damp is my dugout, cold are my feet,
Waiting for whizzbangs to put me to sleep.

There was no more time for musical reminiscences; they had reached their destination, trenches before Westhoek. By 1917 trench building had become more advanced. It was not possible to eliminate the curse of the mud, nor were the builders able to keep out the cold and the rain, or the lice which caused the dreaded trench fever. The other scourge that could not be avoided was the stench from the fumes of cordite overladen with cigarette smoke and the smell of the unwashed men who occupied these pits of horror. Although men were relieved at frequent intervals, ablutions in the trenches were difficult. After a while, however, these malodorous creatures got used to the smell of themselves, and each other. Nevertheless, efforts had been made to convert these holes-in-the-ground into more well-organised places from which to wage war, or at least to provide more effective protection for life and limb. At the Ypres front an elaborate network of these trenches had been established connecting the most forward firing point with Company and Battalion Headquarters at the rear. It was easy to get lost even though some of them were signposted; their names could be anything from Crater Alley to Oxford Street. There were a number of diggings between the front and the rear no longer in use, cul-de-sacs or overgrown positions that meandered over the landscape like furrows made by a drunken ploughman. At the second line of defence the men had dug out rough sleeping quarters, divided from the trench itself by walls of sandbags. The sandbags were ubiquitous. During periods when there was no engagement with the enemy, and these were often long and tedious, it seemed to Charles that the men were continually occupied, at least during daylight hours, with the filling of them. They were essential; they were the building blocks that kept the trenches intact. Mud and earth walls were reinforced with them, firing positions formed with them, shell holes repaired with them. They were everywhere. Not, thought Charles that they had a lot to do with sand. 'Ashes to ashes, dust to dust . . .' These indispensable bags of protection were usually filled with what was available, namely the very earth or mud that confronted the soldier on every side: before him, under him, in his eye-line, adhering to his boots and smeared all over his face. The trenches at Ypres were also the access point to a series of ambitious tunnels under enemy lines, employed for subterranean explosive attacks. This labyrinth was a massive undertaking. British, Canadian and Australian tunnellers had been engaged on the project for more than six months. One of the shafts was two thousand feet long and the deepest a hundred feet beneath the German trenches.

It was in these trenches that Charles began to familiarise himself with the members of his platoon. He was surprised to find that it did not take long before this relationship developed to an intensity he had never experienced before. He could recall the affinity he had with some of his schoolmates—and in particular in middle school with the members of his dormitory—but in this trench that was to be his home for weeks to come he felt something special. His sergeant, Bob Turpin, had been with the Somersets as a boy soldier in the Boer War. He was a typical West Country man whose brogue never ceased to intrigue his platoon commander. They were surrounded by a certain level of chaos. Although Charles appreciated Headquarters' mammoth task of keeping the fighting troop supplied with food for the men and bullets for their guns, the supply chain could be erratic. Sometimes there was an excess of bully beef over hand grenades, or just the opposite; provision of the rum ration rarely failed but there were days when there was a shortage of water; a requisition for blankets might materialise as a box of groundsheets—and so on. Charles felt decidedly uneasy; his experience of the army was very limited but whenever there seemed to be an element of disorder creeping in, comfort was provided by Bob Turpin who, from within his spare frame, emanated a perceptible air of calm and confidence. He was a strict disciplinarian but cared for the men like a mother hen. Feet were his particular preoccupation, and understandably so. No-one wanted a return to the conditions experienced earlier in the war when trench foot could lead to gangrene and amputation. 'Keep your socks as dry as possible.' 'Change them as often as you can.' 'Keep boots properly laced.' 'No foot-rot for this lot.'

'Well, sir, where be home for you?'

'Leicestershire.'

'Isn't that where all the pretty girls are supposed to come from?'

'No, that's Nottingham, although why that is so I don't know.'

'Joined up straight from school I'll be bound, but why didn't you join a local regiment? The Leicesters or the Sherwood Foresters? They're not a bad bunch, either of them.'

'Yes, straight from school. I was there with Lieutenant Spencer and he persuaded me to join your lot.'

'Good choice, if I may say so.'

'Bollocks!' was the response from Private Stanley (Smudger) Smith, the wag of the platoon who had just entered the dugout with some message or other. 'You'd be better off with any other mob but ours. We're always pushed up front before anyone else. The Somerset mugs, that's what we are—and I don't mean those things we drinks our tea out of. If there is any.'

'You watch your lip, Smith', Turpin interjected, but the smile on his face seemed to indicate that he was proud to be one of those sent into battle before anyone else. 'You need to get your knees brown, young Smudger, before you starts sounding off.'

'Some hopes in this dump. I haven't seen any sun for days and not too much bloody daylight either buried in this hellhole. We're not soldiers, we're bloody moles. Look at my eyes, Sarge—aren't they becoming like slits—like those of the moles? And we're about to be gassed—just like how my old dad used to get rid of them when he was gardener at Skipton Hall.'

Charles thought how acute this young soldier was. It was the confinement that he himself found so difficult. He would have welcomed a spell in a deckchair with the sun on his face.

Turpin responded, 'Oh, put a sock in it, Smudger. What do you know? You've only just left your mother's breast.'

The sergeant's last remark led to a discussion about the absence of female company, whereupon Charles switched off and thought about the offensive of the morrow, and again how lucky he was to have found himself with such a platoon. Perhaps it was claustrophobia, or perhaps he had drunk too much rum with his breakfast, but in the heat of the moment he said, very much to himself, 'I love them all.'

Charles tried to find an appropriate word to describe the bunker where this conversation was taking place. A 'retreat'? No. Anything further from the image of monastic silence and solitude would be hard to find. A 'refuge' might be a better word, a temporary hospital for the wounded or a place where men *in extremis* could retire after too much duty in the trenches; but there was no question of solitude and the sounds of war could be heard wherever the soldiers were. This extension of the trench, just about big enough to cater for half-a-dozen men, had been walled and roofed over with crude planks of sodden timber. It was ostensibly the Command Post for this section of the front line trenches but it was also part auxiliary cookhouse when the catering staff were unable to get to the front with hot food. It was also the office where Charles attempted to keep his paperwork, such as it was, up to date. Messengers from Company Headquarters presented themselves through the supposedly effective gas-curtain doorway, as did members of the platoon with reports for Charles. Further planks had been laid in an attempt to provide a dry floor but this was a hopeless task. The mud in the Command Post was not of the concentration found outside in the actual trenches, but it was impossible to deny its entry into this 'sanctuary', brought in on soldiers' boots and putties and oozing up from subterranean depths to force its way through the hopeless plank floor defences. A measure of daylight filtered past the curtain at the entrance but for most of the time the room was in a state of semi-darkness which two inefficient Tilley lamps were unable to improve.

In the gloom Charles read the latest orders, just delivered, as Turpin and Smith returned to the trenches to see what was afoot. He followed them. Nothing was happening; there was a lull. The morning bombardment of the enemy lines by the British artillery was over, as was the daily exercise of rifle cleaning, an essential activity that was rigorously enforced. Those men not on watch-out duty crouched or stood in the mud smoking and complaining, or trying to write letters home, or endeavouring to read. One of the banes of army life was the waiting and for those who were readers this was alleviated by the possession of books or magazines. Most of these were passed round the platoon, becoming very grubby in the process, and works of fiction, of whatever quality, were usually read more than once. Charles was always short of suitable material, even though his mother and his sister sent books to him when possible. He and the men welcomed the few editions they saw of the *Wipers Times,* the most well-known of the trench magazines published by soldiers on active duty. This paper was produced by the 12th Battalion of the Sherwood Foresters who, when stationed at Ypres in early 1916, had come across a printing press abandoned by a Belgian. A sergeant of that unit who had been a printer in peacetime salvaged the press and the *Wipers Times* was born. The paper consisted of poetry, in-jokes and lampoons, and there were often mock property advertisements such as:

'Building land for sale—Hill 60'

or: 'The Salient Estate. Underground residences ready for habitation.'

Reflecting the men's concern with the supply of alcohol, the newspaper ran a serial entitled *Narpoo Rum* which featured Herlock Shomes on the track of the rum thieves. The First World War produced an enormous quantity of poetry, much of which influenced the popular conception of the conflict, and the *Wipers Times* found itself inundated with verse. The fourth edition of the paper contained the following notice from the editor:

'We regret to announce that an insidious disease is affecting the Division and the result is a hurricane of poetry ... The editor would be obliged if a few of the poets would break into prose as the paper cannot live by poems alone.'

One piece of doggerel going the rounds was a ditty about a Major-General called Shute who had been critical of the level of weapon cleanliness amongst his men—and of latrine discipline:

The General inspecting the trenches
Exclaimed with a horrified shout,
I refuse to command a division
Which leaves its excreta about.

But nobody took any notice,
No-one was prepared to refute
That the presence of shit was congenial
Compared with the presence of Shute.

And certain responsible critics
Made haste to reply to his words,
Observing that his staff advisers
Consisted entirely of turds.

For shit may be shot at odd corners
And paper supplied there to suit,
But a shit would be shot without mourners
If somebody shot that shit Shute.

The message Charles had just read gave warning to expect orders for a dawn offensive the next day. He told Turpin of this and then leant against the side of the trench away from the enemy and lit his pipe. In this section he could see from where he was standing twenty or so men, each of whom wore the essential tin-hat. In all cases rifles were either slung over their shoulders or kept close at hand. As usually happened at this time of day, nearly noon, it began to rain. It was not heavy but persistent enough to turn these men, standing or squatting and exposed to the elements, from being damp and cold to becoming wet-through and thoroughly disgruntled.

'How do they put up with it?' mused Charles.

But, having said that, he thought he knew the answer to his own question. It was this most extraordinary phenomenon of 'we're all in the same boat.' Charles thought that if any of them were shipwrecked alone on a desert island that had similar conditions to those endured in the trenches he would not become resigned to such hardships—he would probably kill himself because he was on his own. But in the trenches the man next to him suffers at the same time as he does so he carries on; they suffer together. How does it come about? What is the recipe for this survival cake? There are, no doubt, large portions of 'bloody mindedness' mixed with spoonfuls of pride and not wanting to break down in front of comrades, particularly in the case of the Somersets where most of the men came from the same geographical location and had known each other before the war. They drank in the same pubs, played for the same football teams and courted each other's sisters. Charles knew this was not unusual for county regiments but there were some extreme examples: employees in the cloth industry joined a battalion of the West Yorkshire Regiment and were always known as the Wool Textile Pioneers; the 13th Battalion of the Cheshire Regiment included one thousand employees of Port Sunlight, recruited as a result of a personal appeal by Lord Leverhulme. Pals or workmates before the war did not want to let down the comrades they hoped they would be living with when peace came. But could this be any sort of answer? Were we superior because the strategic thinking of our generals was better than that of the Germans? Was it that we had better weapons than the enemy, more manpower than they, bigger guns, more tanks, better pay? No—all would be of no avail if this indefinable glue that bound these poor, wet, tired and disillusioned men together were to melt. Defeat would be unavoidable. But what about the Hun?

Was this bond exclusively British? He was vaguely aware of talk of mutiny amongst the French troops where, it was said, the dissent had begun after the attack in April in the area of the River Aisne when there had been nearly one hundred thousand French casualties. There was gossip that the French generals were quarrelling amongst themselves, and with the State, as to who was to blame and it was this that had sparked-off a serious spate of disobedience in their army. The Germans were suffering as much as the Allies and yet they fought on. They must have the same glue. (He discovered the truth of this conclusion when he read *All Quiet on the Western Front* in the early 1930s.) His reverie was broken as his pipe went out and Sergeant Turpin came alongside to talk about the push scheduled for tomorrow.

In later life, particularly when he was in India, he was never able to rid himself of the view that this extraordinary comradeship in the face of the worst dangers mankind could devise, was unique to the army. In no other walk of life, in no other circumstance, was this to be found. However, the tragedy in wartime was that many of these important friendships were brought to an abrupt end. Herbert Spencer was killed on the 10th of August during the third abortive attack he and Charles were involved in together. After each of the first two they had been so disillusioned with what had happened that they found themselves unable to discuss their experiences in any detail. On each occasion their platoons left the trenches as dawn was breaking. They were formed up alongside each other, so Charles could see his friend leading his men towards the barbed wire. The first attack was short-lived. Before the men reached the epicentre of the enemy's machine gun fusillade they discovered that the barbed wire, less than one hundred yards from their trench, had not been cut as promised and so the Company Commander quickly ordered a withdrawal. This was successful to the extent that when they re-grouped both platoons were intact, except for seven men who had been wounded by sniper fire. In three cases these injuries led to fatalities and so, as Charles determined, this extremely fruitless exercise had resulted in the death of seven per cent of the personnel of the two platoons. During the second attack, the following day, they were more successful in their attempt to get closer to the German machine gunners, but when they were back in the trenches, deaths by bullets had taken a further twenty-five per cent of their number—and they had achieved nothing.

The third sortie, with the object of pushing back the enemy forces at least five hundred yards, was similarly unrewarding but if the aim had been to improve on the numbers of dead from the first two attacks, it was a pronounced success. As Sergeant Turpin called the roll—the sergeant of Herbert's platoon was not alive to share this task—Charles quickly calculated that over these three days the two platoons had lost more than three quarters of their number. During the third push the last Charles had seen of Herbert was a shadowy figure running through the early morning mist revolver in hand and a tin-hat that had slipped down his head and assumed what, in other circumstances, might have been described as a jaunty angle. Herbert had always been rather awkward. He passed muster as a prop-forward but did not have the body movement or the fleetness of foot to be a wing three-quarter. Charles' last glimpse of his friend showed clear evidence of this. Herbert was waving his men forward as he himself moved doggedly on but Charles thought he could see by the slope of the shoulders that an air of 'resignation to one's fate' had crept in. Or was that how he himself was feeling? Two days later Herbert's body was recovered. The right side of his face had been obliterated and there was a neat pattern of bullet holes decorating his tunic from armpit to armpit. He would have celebrated his twentieth birthday on the 10th of the following month. The wider tragedy was that his fate was duplicated on a scale almost beyond comprehension. In the Third Battle of Ypres the British forces, dead and wounded, amounted to nearly a quarter of a million. On the German side there were nearly twice as many, four hundred thousand. When Charles became acquainted with these facts they attacked his brain with a pain like that of the fiercest toothache. As a result of that one campaign, when the objective had been to advance the four and a half miles to Passchendaele, more than a million parents had lost their sons. He wondered bitterly if the mourning of Bishop and Mrs Chavasse had been alleviated by the fact that their son Noel earned his second Victoria Cross, posthumously, during the campaign in which Herbert had been killed. They lost another son on the same battlefield.

Ten days after Herbert's death Charles was to collect further evidence to support his growing conviction that it was only the armed forces that created a fraternity which could not be fully understood within the limits of normal human behaviour. Best friends, he thought, will throw themselves into raging torrents to save their brothers. Those in love can make astonishing sacrifices for each other. Parents will neglect themselves for their children. But in these trenches Charles was to witness, time and time again, a disparate group, who only weeks before had been virtual strangers to each other, repeatedly prove his theory. Although accompanied by much moaning, soldiers would give their last cigarette to the man at the next firing point; the clumsy one who spills his rum would, with a show of reluctance, be offered a mouthful from someone else's mug. The wise counselled the foolish—even if such advice was sprinkled with large dollops of sarcasm—and the strong helped the weak. Charles was not so naive as to believe that in this hellhole the men were creating a little Eden. There was the usual measure of insubordination, mockery of the slow-witted and criticism of all and sundry from Earl Haig to the cook, but Charles could not rid himself of the impression that he was witnessing something most extraordinary. Whatever happened, the glue seemed to hold.

The oldest member of the platoon, and the tallest, was Private Wilfred Greatbanks. He was seven years older than Charles and, at six feet three inches, nearly six inches taller than his platoon commander. He had been a legal clerk before volunteering, holding a senior position in a firm of solicitors in Taunton. No-one called him Wilf or Fred. As a number of the men had some acquaintance with the Magistrates Courts, he was either addressed as 'His Honour' or 'Beanpole'. He was not a natural soldier, being rather slow of movement and the men joked about this, but no-one ever doubted his commitment—nor, as time was to tell, his courage. Because of his age and professional background all sought his advice on matters legal or otherwise. He was particularly sympathetic with his fellows who had marital or other concerns at home and was able to temper the response of those who received, or thought they had received, what were known as 'Dear John' letters. However he was regarded, as wise man or a fool, it was Smudger Smith who was in charge of the campaign to make fun of 'the old beanpole'. Smith could hardly read or write—he had been a gamekeeper's dogsbody before joining up—but he had a natural way with words which he used to the full in sending up Private Greatbanks. His favourite trick was to pretend he was asking a genuine question on an involved legal issue. The law expert always took this seriously yet still managed a weak smile when it was revealed that the whole thing was just a piece of nonsense. Perhaps employing his limited knowledge of rural affairs, the tormentor often drew opinion from Wilfred on the law of trespass.

'What happens, Your Honour, if a landowner takes a partridge from his neighbour's property and is found with the bird in his left-hand pocket when he is astride the boundary between his property and next-door and his left foot is on his own land? Could he not claim that, although his right foot might be trespassing . . .' Smith always stressed the second syllable of this word, turning it into 'arse'. ' . . . the partridge is his because it is on his land?'

In such instances Wilfred would just grin at Smith and carry on cleaning his rifle.

During September the platoon was engaged in an attempt to remove a nest of German snipers who were well bedded-in, guarding parts of the British line of advance towards Polygon Wood. Charles and his men had managed to reach a number of shell craters about one hundred yards from the snipers where he ordered the use of hand-grenades before attempting any more ground advance. He and Sergeant Turpin were not sure whether any of the grenades would reach the enemy lines but they agreed that at least they might provide a diversion before the troops moved up. The proposed plan was that, rather than attempt an 'over the top' routine, the best shots in the platoon were to leave their refuge as secretly as possible, move into whatever cover was available and get some rounds into the bed of German snipers. Smith was one of these designated marksmen. Charles happened to be in the same shell-hole with his sergeant and therefore had a grandstand view of what happened next. When the men were ordered to throw their hand-grenades, the awkward Wilfred removed the pin and, as he drew his arm back, the grenade slipped from his fingers and partially buried itself in the mud behind him. Typically, Sergeant Turpin, who was standing next to the culprit, calmly removed the grenade from the mud and, with supreme insouciance, tossed it in the direction of the enemy, muttering under his breath, 'Butterfingers!'. For some reason this incident excited Smith into action. He rose to his feet, shouted, 'Charge!', and disappeared over the rim of the crater before Charles or the sergeant or anyone else could react—except for Wilfred. Because of his height he was in even more of a crouched position than the others but as he saw the soles of Private Smith's boots disappear he had most of himself over the edge of the hideout before the platoon had registered what was happening. By the time Wilfred was out of sight rapid staccato rifle fire could be heard. This was followed by a cry of pain which sounded as if it came from Smith. Charles gave the command for the platoon to 'stand steady', then he and Turpin, tin-hats to the fore, peered into no-man's-land. Smith was prone about twenty yards away partly obscured by the bent frame of 'the beanpole' who was scampering to left and right in a vain attempt to avoid the German bullets. The action seemed to be taking place in slow motion. The rescuer's right leg had been hit that made his movements even more awkward and angular; he looked like an absurd khaki-coloured praying mantis flitting over the ground. The observers saw that his rifle had fallen—presumably another shot in the arm or shoulder—but now he had reached his goal, where he draped his rangy body over the recumbent Smith and rolled both of them into a convenient shell-hole which was partly filled with water. Charles heard the splash as he ordered the platoon to exchange rapid-fire with the enemy. This was continued in both directions for some minutes before silence descended. The German snipers did not intend moving and Charles and Sergeant Turpin decided that the operation to remove them by force should be postponed for the day. Except for the sound of distant shellfire the silence became quite eerie and so intense that the noise made by two bodies slurping through the mud like two antediluvian snakes seemed almost cacophonous. Wilfred dragging Smith behind him must have been a tempting target for the German snipers but for some reason no attempt was made to fire. Bravery, thought Charles, is being given full recognition on both sides of the fence.

Miraculously, Smith had been hit only twice, both times in his left leg, but 'His Honour' was more seriously wounded. His pale face displayed a slightly surprised look, as much as to say, 'What was I doing?' but it also showed signs that he had lost a lot of blood. The German armistice continued as the platoon retired to their home trenches whence the hero was first treated at the Regimental Aid Post (RAP) and then shipped back to the Divisional Casualty Clearing Station, accompanied by a chorus of, 'Well done, you bloody old fool!' Smith, patched up at the RAP, accompanied his rescuer to the Clearing Station. Charles had severely berated Smith for his impromptu action, but then informed him that in view of the circumstances no further measures would be taken, provided Smith made sure that whisky be procured from within the hospital environs with which to toast Private Wilfred Greatbanks. Charles fully expected Smith to succeed in this—he was the platoon's arch scrounger—but he intended that a more substantial act of recognition should also be organised. The lanky legal clerk recovered well but did not return to the platoon. He was eventually found a job in the Adjutant's office where he wore his Distinguished Service Medal with modest pride. Charles asked his sergeant if he understood why Greatbanks had acted as he did. After all, it was Smith's own action that took him into danger—and Wilfred and Smith were hardly the closest of buddies.

'Smith is like a firecracker. He can explode at any time and that little incident with the grenade was just like putting a light to the blue touchpaper. Not that this is any excuse. I know you've dealt with him Sir, but he is going to get such a bollocking from me when he gets back he will wish he'd stayed looking after the pheasants.'

'Yes, I understand that, and sometimes we need the volatility that Smith has, but why did our oldest member act as he did?'

'Well, Sir, like it or not, he's a soldier and that's what we do.'

Charles thought this explanation was too glib but as he himself was not able to understand this action, nor its part in the whole schema of the 'soldiers' fraternity', why should he expect his sergeant to be able to explain it?

Before the end of the year Charles' company, brought up to strength, was involved in the third major British offensive of 1917, the objective being the city of Cambrai and the territory beyond. A quarter of a million British troops faced an equal number of Germans across a six mile front. Thanks to the use of tanks, five miles were gained on the first day. It was the first time in the history of warfare that tanks had been used as the main weapon in a thrust. However, this initial advantage was soon reversed. Cambrai was not to be reached and by early December a winter line was established and everyone was back to the stalemate of trench warfare. This short, but violent, campaign resulted in minor territorial gains around Flesquières for the loss of forty-four thousand British and Canadians killed or wounded. For the Germans the tally was fifty-three thousand. As a result of this winter stalemate Charles was granted ten days' leave over Christmas. He then remained at this front until he left France.

Despite the futility, as Charles saw it, of his first year and a half of soldiering, the friendships he had made during that time were a significant factor in his decision to make the military his life's career.

Two months before the Armistice, he was offered the chance to join a Division of the Somersets that had been in India during the whole of the war. In the early twentieth century, India still exerted a considerable fascination for the British middle class. Charles was no exception and the prospect of being able to continue a career as a regular soldier while serving in India was very appealing. The Somersets, stationed at Lahore, were seeking to add young soldiers to their numbers from those who had successfully served during the war in Europe, particularly as their skills might soon be required in Afghanistan. It would seem that the call of Empire, that had attracted adventurous British youth for centuries, was still strong enough to pull Charles away from his hearth and home. Kipling was still a potent influence.

He had served bravely and survived the Third Battle of Ypres and the Cambrai offensive. These circumstances, and the speed with which he had become a very effective platoon commander, had led to this opportunity. He was therefore returned to the depot at Taunton and granted leave. His parents were delighted to see him but despite the success he had achieved as a soldier his father was bitterly disappointed that his son's future would not be on the family farm. The Cresswells had been farmers for generations and John could not comprehend why anyone would want to exchange the independence he was able to offer his son for a regimented life where there was always someone in a position superior to yours. Charles repeated his argument about the affinity with others that soldiering provided but, naturally enough, the farmer could not fathom this. Nonetheless, when it became clear that Charles had made his decision, his parents accepted it gracefully, the friendly family atmosphere returned to the farmhouse and Charles had an enjoyable time, consuming large quantities of home cooking and renewing acquaintance with old friends, such as had survived the war. Rumour had it that as many as half-a-million British soldiers, and three million French and German had died in the hostilities. He visited the family of his friend, Jimmy Rogers, whom he had known since elementary school and who had been killed at Gallipoli. While there he was surprised to discover that the younger sister, Mary, was now a most attractive young lady. At their last meeting, before Jimmy had gone to be a soldier, she had made no impression on Charles but during those autumn days he found himself drawn to the Rogers' house at Melton Mowbray on more than one occasions. His mother asked what the attraction was, but Charles was too shy, and Mary too young, for either of them to acknowledge the budding affection.

Charles may have been uncertain about his feelings for the young Mary Rogers, but he was fully convinced that his decision to remain in the army was the right one for him.

On the 14th of April Charles and his men resumed the duty of guarding the station that had been their task since arriving in Amritsar. The city was quiet. After a delegation of local residents had been to see Dyer, permission was given to bury the dead and for shops to be reopened. The General was convinced that his action of the day before was justified and he retained this conviction for the rest of his life. One disquieting rumour concerned the alleged rape of a number of Sikh girls by British soldiers at the station but Charles was able to assure his commander, by a message sent through military channels, that this story was unfounded. As he explained, his men had searched the male escorts of these girls because they were carrying the traditional dagger, the *kirpan,* but no-one had been molested. With the return to normality, Charles was content to leave his sergeant with the men for an hour as he felt he must visit the scene of yesterday's disaster. He did this as unobtrusively as possible. The dead and wounded had been taken away by the time he reached the Jalianwala Bagh but evidence of the massacre was not lacking. Items of discarded clothing, much of it bloodstained; detritus of all kinds, indicative of a hasty withdrawal from the scene; bullet damage to walls and buildings. As Charles gazed over the area, now virtually deserted, he sensed an air of despair, of shame, hanging over this 'valley of death'. It was shunned, a place of evil. In later years he returned to the scene a number of times, but at each visit he experienced similar feelings, even after a trust set up in 1923 by the Indian National Congress had purchased the land.

Jalianwala Bagh means 'a garden belonging to Jalla', deriving its name from the owners of this piece of land in Sikh times, but by 1919 it was an unoccupied space, an irregular walled quadrangle approximately two hundred and twenty-five by one hundred and eighty metres, used mainly as a dumping ground. On the fateful day a large number of people, mostly Sikhs, had come into the city from surrounding villages and many of them attended the meeting at the Jalianwala Bagh called for 4.30 in the afternoon. General Dyer arrived there at about 5:15 p.m. with fifty riflemen and two armoured cars with mounted machine-guns. The cars were too wide to gain access to the area owing to the narrow entrance, so he deployed his riflemen on a piece of high ground near that entrance.

Charles' disillusionment with General Dyer was aggravated by what became known as the 'crawling order'. The street where the missionary, Miss Sherwood, had been attacked, the *Kucha Kaurhian-wala* lane, had been closed on Dyer's orders. At the site of the assault, a triangle was erected on which those responsible were to be whipped. Pickets, one of them commanded by the sergeant from Charles' platoon, were stationed at each end of the narrow and dirty street. Any Indian, who decided to enter the lane was required to crawl on all fours. During this time about fifty Indians suffered this indignity including an elderly lame man and a blind beggar. Charles was present when the triangle was put to use. He satisfied himself that he needed to consult his sergeant, but after visiting the Jalianwala Bagh he could not resist going to observe what he was already labelling as the second of Dyer's mistakes. Six young Indians, said to have been involved in the abuse of Miss Sherwood, were brought to the scene. They had not been tried for this offence but each was sentenced to thirty blows with a heavy cane for insubordination to the military. After a few words with his sergeant, who clearly thought that what was about to take place was justified—Miss Sherwood was, after all, a white woman—Charles looked on in disbelief as one after another of the six young boys was stripped naked and beaten. A number of them fainted after a few blows, only to be revived with water so that the full punishment could be administered. As Charles watched the blood streaming down their backs and staining the cane red, he became more and more grim-faced. Is this British justice, he thought, or is this the red they paint their maps with? At that time Amritsar and the Lahore districts were subject to Martial Law regulations which extended the authority's powers to administer corporal punishment. Even so, to Charles, these indiscriminate beatings were an extension of the madness perpetrated the day before. He recalled the friends he had lost in the last war. However fruitless, their cause had been clear: they were representing their country in a war against a defined enemy—but where was the enemy in India? The Indians themselves? They who had fought alongside us against Germany? Charles was quickly coming to the conclusion that as a result of what was happening in Amritsar the sides were changing. The British had administered the vast population of India for centuries with only a handful of men but would this be the position in the future? He left the scene with a heavy heart that was not lightened when it became known that a spate of public floggings in the region was to follow. In Kasur, people who failed to salaam every white man were flogged and made to rub their noses on the ground. In another area, the biggest six boys were chosen from each school for flogging. Martial Law Commissions were set up to hold trials of serious cases and these included the examination of the Amritsar citizens said to be the instigators of the uprising. These defendants came from a cross-section of the city's society, from the wealthy Dr Kitchlew to ordinary traders. Kitchlew and Satyapal were sentenced to transportation for life but London was now anxious to end the bitterness. King George V issued a proclamation of amnesty: 'I direct my Viceroy to exercise in my name and on my behalf my royal clemency to political offenders in the fullest measure which in his judgement is compatible with the public safety.' Dr Kitchlew, Dr Satyapal and many others were released.

After leaving Amritsar, Charles made further enquiries about what actually happened on the 13th of April. He was told that Dyer and his officers travelled to the scene of the massacre in open cars with two policemen on horseback in the front and the two armoured cars bringing up the rear. The convoy was completed by a body of ninety soldiers, half marching at the front, the remainder behind. To add to this show of the Raj's might, an aeroplane had circled the area. The foot-soldiers were marched into the Jalianwala Bagh through a passageway just over seven feet wide. On entering, fifty of the men with rifles were deployed, twenty-five each side, while the remainder, who were armed only with knives, stood behind. Within seconds of these positions being taken the order was given to fire on the crowd gathered there. Understandably, when the soldiers were seen a number of the throng squatting on the ground rose to their feet. Some had children on their shoulders. People closest to a speaker standing on a small dais reported that when he saw the soldiers he told the crowd to stay where they were and not be afraid because 'they will not fire on innocent people'. Some observers said that when the firing began the soldiers aimed above the heads of the crowd until ordered by an officer to fire low. To Charles, the Hunter Enquiry, set up in October to investigate the incident, concentrated on evidence from the perpetrator of this tragedy, or his supporters, rather than the victims. However, before the end of the year he was able to read eyewitness accounts by Indians who gave evidence before a separate body, established by the Indian National Congress and chaired by Mahatma Gandhi. Harrowing tales were told. When firing began a number of the crowd threw themselves flat on the ground while others began to run in all directions. One witness said that the shots were directed at those who were running and at the entrances where some were trying to escape. People ran towards the walls seeking exits between the houses surrounding the area, and many of these were shot in the back. A number escaped over walls by climbing over dead bodies while others threw themselves into a well at the Eastern edge of the garden, with the result that a number were drowned because of the weight of bodies on top of them.

A local businessman, Girdhari Lal, who watched what happened with the aid of binoculars from an adjoining roof, told the Congress Enquiry that he later went down to look for a friend amongst the dead bodies:

> There were heaps of them at different places, and people were turning over dead bodies to recognise their relations or friends. The dead bodies were of grown-up people and young boys also. At or near the gates the number was very large,

> and bodies were scattered in large numbers all over the garden. Some had their heads cut open, others had eyes shot, nose, chest, arms or legs shattered. It was a fearful and ghastly sight. I think there must have been over one thousand dead bodies in the garden and then . . . I saw people were hurrying up, and many had to leave their dead and wounded, because they were afraid of being fired upon again after 8.00 p.m. Many amongst the wounded, who managed to run away from the garden, succumbed on their way to the injuries received, and lay dead in the streets.

One other distressing piece of evidence which Charles particularly noted related to the impact of the curfew on the efforts of relatives to deal with the dead. This was what the Congress Enquiry heard from a widow who spent the night in the garden:

> I was in my house near Jalianwala Bagh when I heard shots fired . . . I got up at once as I was anxious because my husband had gone to the Bagh. I began to cry, and went to the place accompanied by two women to help me. There I saw heaps of dead bodies and I began to search for my husband. After passing through that heap, I found the dead body of my husband. The way towards it was full of blood and dead bodies. By this time it was eight o'clock and no-one could stir out of his house, because of the curfew order . . . I waited up to 10.00 p.m. but no-one arrives there. . . I had gone hardly three or four steps when I saw an old man smoking and some people sleeping by his side. I repeated the whole of my sad story to him with hands folded. He took great pity upon me and asked those men to go with me. They said that it was ten o'clock and that they would not like to be shot down. That was no time to stir out; how could they go out so far? So I went back and seated myself by the side of my dead husband. Accidentally, I found a bamboo stick which I kept in my hand, to keep off the dogs. I saw three men writhing in agony, a buffalo struggling in great pain; and a boy, about twelve years old, in agony entreating me not to leave the place. I told him that I could not go anywhere leaving the dead body of my husband . . . he asked for water, but water could not be procured at that place . . .

What I experienced that night is known only to me and to God.

At the end of April Charles was back at Lahore from where he went with the Second Battalion to participate in the Third Afghan war, a short-lived campaign. Amanullah, the new leader of Afghanistan observed the anti-British unrest in India and so determined to re-take the North-West Frontier Province lost in the previous century. He attacked British bases without warning but Britain quickly reacted and launched a massive land and air campaign to invade Afghanistan through the Khyber Pass. Some historians have likened this assault to hitting a mosquito with a sledgehammer. By the end of May the war was over but Charles saw sufficient action to demonstrate once again the special bond he believed existed within the military community.

After many years of campaigning in the North-West Frontier, the tactics of the British army were well-established. Although in this action there was the added factor of air-support, the tried and tested methods of infantry attack were still essential. Advance must be along a river valley with soldiers sent ahead to occupy peaks and ridges where the Afghan tribesmen might establish themselves to pick off the advancing column at will. Before the end of May, Charles and his friend George Meredith were in charge of an advance party whose task was to position men and to guard the two companies of their battalion which had been commanded to strike into enemy territory at rapid speed. Headquarters believed that a punitive campaign would bring a swift end to hostilities—as proved to be the case—but for the moment the platoon of sharpshooters under the control of the two subalterns needed to keep moving towards their positions as rapidly as the terrain permitted. At a peak of rather more elevation than they had yet come across, the two officers split the force and skirted this height from left and right. As Charles moved forward along the narrow and precarious track he was concerned to find that it began to slope downwards, which made him wonder if this was going to take his unit away from the promontory rather than nearer to it. Well aware of the need to move forward quickly and thinking that he had little alternative, he ordered his men forward along this dubious path. A few hundred yards on he observed a clearing from which a number of routes were available with at least one that tracked up the slope rather than down. At the clearing he halted the men, whereupon he heard a fall of rocks behind his head followed by the appearance in their midst of the twirling legs and arms of a Pathan warrior. As he landed he lay still. He was a fearsome sight: thick black beard with crossed bandoliers of cartridges across his ample chest. Charles looked up to see George on a ledge above him holding his clenched hands above his head like a boxer who had just delivered a knockout blow, which is exactly what he had done. George's men had found their route led more directly to the peak but as they moved forward the advance member of the party suddenly stopped and raised his finger to his lips to call for silence, at which point George saw the turban of the Afghan, about twenty or thirty yards away and below the track. As George was about to order an attack on the sniper, Charles and his men came into view and the hidden marksman raised his rifle. The ground between George and the rifleman was covered in a lush grass. He did not hesitate but moved as rapidly as possible over the grass and, before any of the actors in this drama knew what was happening, had delivered a crushing blow to the back of the Afghan's head with the butt of his service revolver. 'Ten and out!' shouted George triumphantly. When the two friends talked this over in the future in the mess, or when out riding, they dismissed it as a minor incident in the life of a soldier, and a rather amusing one at that, but Charles still liked to view this occurrence as another in his list of similar ones that cemented soldiers together as happened in no other walk of life.

The disturbances in Northern India of 1919 were replaced in the 1920s by a period of calm as a result of Gandhi's philosophy of non-violence. In December 1920 the Mahatma launched his theory nationwide, the *satyagraha,* that freedom could be realised by the force of truth. Charles spent the next two years tied to the barracks at Lahore. During this period he sought permission to take UK leave and, although he had at that time been in India for less than two years, this was granted. His Commanding Officer took into account that, because of the shortage of officers at the Western Front, Charles had served the Regiment since February 1917 with only very limited periods away from soldiering. Charles welcomed this opportunity to take stock of his career away from life in the barracks but when he reached home he found that his obsession with General Dyer and Amritsar was replaced by a much more pleasing passion, namely Mary Rogers. On arrival in Leicestershire he was not slow to pay a visit to Melton Mowbray where the mutual attraction discovered in 1918 quickly blossomed into a full-scale romance. Before he returned to India they had announced their engagement and Mary planned to join him there as soon as he was more certain of his future. Both families were delighted with the news, although sad that the wedding would probably take place in some Garrison chapel rather than the village church.

In addition to this one period of home leave, the tedium of life in barracks was relieved by an association with a number of the citizens of Lahore as a result of his involvement in the local cricket scene. Charles was agreeably surprised to find that, thanks to the thorough grounding in the basics inculcated at Uppingham School, he had developed into a useful off-break bowler, even if his prowess was flattered somewhat by the dry pitches of Northern India. In addition to local cricket tours, he also made a number of visits to other parts of India and these excursions did nothing to tarnish his love affair with the country. The variety of scenery fascinated him but it was the diversity of the people that intrigued him even more.

The vast population of India was effectively governed by a small number of British officials, members of the Indian Civil Service, backed by the police and army. A much larger establishment would have been required were it not for the existence of the mainly self-governing Princely States, some of which were the size of England and sufficiently independent to issue their own coinage. One of Charles' most interesting experiences arose as a result of a visit to one of these. This had been arranged by his Adjutant who, in earlier years, had been seconded as military advisor to the father of the current Maharaja. Charles was fascinated to observe how this separate kingdom was ruled, albeit with guidance from British India officialdom. At the Maharaja's guesthouse he was greeted by the Prime Minister who presented *salaams* on the behalf of the Maharaja. A meeting with the leader of this small territory was arranged for the following day, during which Charles was able to observe at close quarters the Maharaja and his palace. The palace and its people were a mishmash of contradictions, a confusion of splendour and squalor. The Maharaja was a small man, less than five feet in height and no older than Charles. He was dressed in a highly decorated and luxurious long coat, worn over narrow white trousers. The coat was of a rather sickly green while on his feet were a pair of ornate bejewelled sandals. On his head he wore a hat similar to a bowler, but with no rim. This was also green but of a shade which clashed stridently with the colour of his coat. This outfit was not altogether unsoiled. The same was true of the palace itself. The room where Charles was received was referred to as the visitors' parlour. Like its owner, it was ornately decorated and contained an eclectic mixture of rather faded, but expensive, furniture. Charles felt sure his mother would not have approved of the general state of cleanliness and, even as the wife of a farmer, she would not have understood why, as her son entered, a cow was being gently ushered from the room.

The Maharaja evidently welcomed guests from outside his normal circle and Charles was intrigued to find his host well versed in the history of the 1914–1918 war and that he also had some interesting views on the economy of British farming. Charles told him of his experiences in the trenches and of the extraordinary bonds that could be forged between men in such uncomfortable and dangerous situations. The Maharaja found this fascinating, particularly as in his position it was more or less impossible to build the sort of friendships to which Charles had alluded.

'In the trenches, Lieutenant Cresswell, did the common soldier not resent you as an officer? Someone with special privileges.'

'No. In the case of the subalterns we were always first out of the trenches. So in most cases the men trusted us and knew we would do our best to try and keep them as safe as possible. On the other hand, the ordinary soldier, and many of the junior officers, were most scathing about those at the rear who planned the campaigns that took so many lives.'

This comment prompted Charles to recall another of the old wartime music hall songs, sung to the tune of 'John Brown's Body':

They were only playing leapfrog,
When one staff officer jumped right over another staff officer's back.

Wisely, he decided not to share this thought with the Maharaja—rather difficult to explain—but he was able to quote from memory the famous poem of Siegfried Sassoon:

'Good-morning, good-morning!' the General said
When we met him last week on the way to the line.
Now the soldiers he smiled at are most of 'em dead,
And we're cursing his staff for incompetent swine.
'He's a cheery old card,' grunted Harry to Jack
As they slogged up to Arras with rifle and pack.
But he did for them both by his plan of attack.

This halted the conversation for a minute or two. Then the Maharaja responded.

'We sent men to Palestine—lost many.'

'Yes, I know. The Indian soldiers fought bravely on many fronts.'

His next remark took Charles rather by surprise.

'Did you ever thrust your bayonet into a German and see the blood pumping out?'

'No, I can't recall that I did. Sometimes it felt as though we were fighting a faceless enemy. Though we saw plenty of Germans running towards us, or when we were advancing towards them, but most of the time we were huddled down in our trenches firing at each other, or with hands over our ears during an artillery barrage that would go on for hours. I shall probably finish my days sitting by the fire with a blanket over my knees, deaf as a post.'

'Why a post?' his audience responded.

'No idea, your Highness. But let me tell you about one special experience I had with the Germans. I had become lost in the maze of trenches there were at Ypres and as I turned a corner I suddenly found myself face-to-face with a German officer looking just as lost as I was. I had my revolver in my hand but for a moment I forgot that I was there to kill Germans. We stared at each other for what seemed a long time, but was really only seconds. Then, simultaneously, we each did an about-turn and walked away in opposite directions. Do you know, you are the first person I've told that story to. I wonder why?'

'Perhaps because our situations are so different—or is it because I'm a wily Oriental and able to magic confessions out of you.'

The Maharajah laughed teasingly, but Charles could see from this brief acquaintance that he was an intelligent and sympathetic man who wanted to know as much as possible about the world outside his kingdom. He had not allowed the fact that he was from a dynasty that had ruled over many millions of subjects for generations to subdue this interest. His next question was even more offbeat than the one about the bayonet.

'Do you believe in a God, Lieutenant Cresswell?'

Charles tried to frame an answer but got diverted into a discourse on his upbringing in Leicestershire, school chapel and compulsory church parades in the army. For his part, the Maharaja tried to add to the limited knowledge Charles had about the main faiths in India—a dense subject, but one that intrigued him and which he vowed to study more thoroughly in time. When Charles' origins were revealed, the conversation turned the Maharaja's views on English farming practices.

'Your father grows wheat, oats and barley, I presume, and keeps the fields fallow one year in four.'

'You seem to be better informed than I.'

'Does he ever consider other crops? Must be very boring, the same each year.'

'Well, I think he does plant sugar beet. Of course, in the kitchen garden, my mother's domain, they grow all manner of vegetables—and tomatoes under glass.'

'But no mangoes. I will serve you the finest mangoes you have ever tasted when you dine with me tonight—and we will also have some of our special Indian sweets.'

Charles thoroughly enjoyed this visit and in later years became a welcome guest of the Maharaja on a number of occasions.

Charles tended to use Bombay as a base from which to explore the Western part of the country, usually staying at the Empire, a modest hotel on Marine Drive. He travelled extensively and met as wide a cross-section of Indian society as was accessible to a young British army officer, but his most significant meeting was with David Blunt. The Blunts had been in India since the nineteenth century. David's grandfather had initially worked in the tea industry but later moved to Bombay where he had set up a business exporting Indian produce to England and importing Scotch whisky, Bath Olivers and other 'necessities' demanded by the Raj. He had prospered and David and his father had expanded the business to include the export of carpets and other items of Indian art and crafts in exchange for the new products of Europe—anything from bicycles to Staffordshire pottery. David ran the operation in Calcutta and during his visits to the firm's head office in Bombay he also tended to stay at the Empire Hotel. When he discovered Charles was a soldier he rather mocked him and engaged in some light-hearted ribbing. However, this became more serious when it was revealed that Charles had been in Amritsar in April 1919.

'What were you chaps playing at? I know we need to exercise a firm hand but that idiot Dyer has probably made things a sight more difficult for the likes of me.'

'Oh, how do you make that out?'

'Look, our hold over the Indians is really very fragile. They tolerate people like the Blunts because we add something to their economy but what do you do when you're not putting bullets into them.'

'I resent that. We've been here a long time keeping order. But I do agree: Amritsar was probably an aberration.'

'Aberr . . . what? Look, old chap, I hear all over the place that the establishment are trying to justify what he did.'

Charles said nothing.

'Do you know what he said to that tribunal? Who was the chairman? Oh yes, Lord Hunter. Dyer said he fired without warning on those "brown" people—those natives—not merely to disperse the crowd but to "produce a sufficient moral effect". There was no question of "using undue severity". I repeat his words verbatim. I was so disgusted with the whole operation I have learnt them by heart. And do you know what he also told the Committee of Enquiry? He said that if he had been able to get his armoured cars down the narrow alleyway, he would have used his machine guns. For heaven's sake, who did he think he was facing? Shaka's Zulu warriors, a horde of Cossacks or a crack German infantry regiment? This was a crowd of Indian men, women and children sitting on the ground, some listening to a speaker advocating freedom for India but most of them talking amongst themselves—or asleep. Makes me sick to my stomach.'

Again Charles did not respond.

'Listen, I was born in this country. The Indians are no better than any of us, but they could teach us a thing or two about humanity. We don't like their caste system but what about class with us? Does your father's farm labourer still touch his forelock when they meet in the cowshed? Do you think members of the ICS see me as their equal? I'm in trade, for God's sake. Of course, the military is a hotbed of class. I play cricket with some army people back home and one of them told me a story of an incident that occurred during one of the Somme offences. A Company Commander at a rear depot overheard an ordinary soldier addressing a Lance Corporal by his Christian name and for this heinous offence the Lance Corporal was demoted and the "familiar" soldier subjected to some sort of barbarous field punishment—chained to a gun carriage or something like that. They probably lived next door to each other in civvy street—and this contravention of "Good order and military discipline" was played out against one of the bloodiest battles in history.'

Charles sighed. He had heard the same story when he was in France but did not comment as it was clear that David was in full flow.

'You think I'm biased. Well, perhaps I am. Blunt by name and blunt by nature. But I'm telling you, Lieutenant Cresswell, that man Dyer has opened up the floodgates. If it wasn't for Gandhi the country would be up in arms now crying for Independence. But it is going to come, that's for sure. I've got three of my staff, and two of them are from the Punjab, who served in the Great War—volunteers, just like you. And what did they come back to? Another insensitive idiot, High Court Judge Sidney Rowlatt, and I speak from experience—my father met him once. Typical upper class idiot who had no idea what the Indians were hoping for. Lived the cloistered life of a King's Bench judge. My chaps say they joined the fight to free the world of the Kaiser's tyranny but what about freedom for them? This man Rowlatt heads a committee that, in effect, re-introduces the 1915 Defence of India Act. Any minor disturbance can be judged by the police or the executive as seditious in nature and clamped down upon with no recourse to the law. No warrants needed to search and arrest people. Special courts. No right of appeal. No Magna Carta. Can you blame them for getting agitated? Dyer tried to justify what he did by referring to the proclamation that had been read out all over Amritsar forbidding meetings and assemblies. Yes, I've got a copy of the actual proclamation at home. But, of course, what he probably didn't know, or bother to find out, was that at that time the annual horse and cattle fair, the Baisakhi, was due to be held in the city, which meant that thousands of villagers from the surrounding countryside came into Amritsar on that day. They wouldn't have heard the proclamation and many of them were within the crowd which gathered at that 'killing field'. Nothing can equal the catastrophe at the Jalianwala Bagh but many of my Indian friends condemn Dyer just as much for the 'crawling order'. The Raj might excuse it by saying that nearly four hundred deaths is the correct figure to equate against one white woman but did you know that it was a group of Hindu shopkeepers who saved her life and that under cover of darkness that night it was they who took her back to her home in a cart, hidden under a pile of blankets? Thank God for Winston. He put things straight. You must have heard what he said in the House in July. I was so impressed I can just about repeat what he said word for word. "An extraordinary event, a monstrous event, an event which stands in singular and sinister isolation. Frightfulness is not a remedy known to the British pharmacopoeia." Somebody needed to say it.'

Little of this was new to Charles, but he said nothing, merely ordered another drink.

'The man is unbelievable. At the Hunter Enquiry he admitted he directed the firing at people lying on the ground and that he made no attempt to help the wounded. And do you know why? He said that he would have been prepared to help them if they had applied! "Applied"—his very word. He then said that they did not "apply" for help because if they did they would have been arrested for being at an unlawful assembly. A man, or woman, lies dying, leaking blood into the sandy earth of the Jalianwala Bagh, but refuses to ask for assistance because he or she does not want to be taken into custody. Incredible! As you know, those in charge didn't really know what to do about him. He was actually promoted for a short time from command of a Brigade to that of a Division. I'm not a military man but if I found one of my staff stealing from me, I'd get rid of him. I certainly wouldn't promote him. And this man wasn't stealing cash, he was taking lives. I know that eventually he was relieved of his command and retired on half pay, but the House of Lords exonerated him and funds were collected in the UK and in India to compensate him. For what! Do you know some of the ladies at the church I sometimes attend at home took up a collection for this monster and asked me for a donation. I told them I couldn't oblige because I had already sent my money to the fund set up to help the victims. They were furious. I'm not much more of a literary man than I am a soldier but it seems to me the Indian who had the Nobel prize displayed the right attitude. Tagore. I believe he was the first Asian man to get a Nobel—well, his reaction to Dyer was to renounce the knighthood that had been presented to him by the King Emperor."

Charles felt obliged to try and defend the action of the military. He agreed with most of what Blunt had said but thought that the other side of the coin should be presented, if only to determine whether his own hard and fast views were still justified.

'Don't forget that prior to Dyer's action the mob had killed three bank managers and two other white men. It is all very well for you in your cosy commercial world to criticise but when you are faced with an angry mob that outnumbers you a thousand to one, action has to be taken. I can tell you I was scared during those few days in Amritsar. I'd seen off the German army with their machine guns and mortars but when you stand in front of a handful of troops and you don't know whether they are going to stay loyal, facing a crowd of people each with a knife in one hand and a lathi in the other, your knees do tremble a bit. The Government believed that a full-scale uprising was in the offing, otherwise they would not have declared Martial Law. And in the event this proved to be successful as, generally speaking, quiet was quickly restored to the Punjab.'

At this stage Charles ran out of anything else to say but he did think that if he was not acting as 'Devil's Advocate' he might have raised the point about whether it was strictly legal to back-date the imposition of Martial Law, as had happened in this case. Surely, he thought, retrospective legislation is hardly justice as we know it. Blunt muttered something about whether any of this gave Dyer the right to put on his killing boots, whereupon they both went in to have dinner.

This rather one-sided conversation took place over two evenings when, except for the hovering waiter, Charles and David Blunt were the only occupants of the hotel lounge. The talk ranged over a number of topics. Dyer was not totally centre stage and, in any case, in one shape or another, Charles had in the past been involved in innumerable discussions of the Amritsar event, many where he had taken a similar line to David's. However, the strength of feeling expressed by someone who knew India well had a significant impact on Charles. This meeting was not to be his epiphany but he had been ruminating for months about his future and in later life he tended to believe that it was largely because of David Blunt that he eventually reached the decision he did.

The Hunter Report was published in 1920 but, as far as Charles was concerned, this only confirmed his understanding of the affair from information gleaned from some of the soldiers who had been at the Jalianwala Bagh, added to his own personal knowledge and observations at the scene of the disaster. He would never be able to erase from his mind the impression those days in April 1919 had made on him, but it took nearly two years to absorb this impact fully and make a choice. This period was agony for him. He used his frequent letters to Mary to try and analyse his feelings and, as time went by, these were crystallised into 'three loves'. The first was Mary. Whatever happened, and whatever action he decided upon, she was to be his wife. She concurred on this point. The other two passions were the military and India. Charles was not trained like a psychiatrist to plumb the depths of his consciousness but he did conduct, over the months, a searching analysis into the conflict in his mind about his role as a soldier. He was well aware that, since joining the Army four years ago, the military had been not just his home and his career—it had formed his character. It was not the active, and often inactive, life of the soldier that was the attraction. It was not the uniform and it was certainly not the pay—without assistance from his father Charles would hardly have been able to pay his mess bills, let alone any other expenditure. Nor was it about patriotism, or at least only in small measure. No, Charles loved the army because it bred, in his opinion, the unique form of comradeship that he had first encountered in the trenches and which had blossomed and strengthened since then. It gave him a warm feeling; it had formed him into the man he was today. But, as a result of those weeks in Amritsar, the fire was going out. It was not rekindled by a report that Dyer had allegedly said, 'For me the battlefields of France and Amritsar are the same.' Charles thought he could probably have survived what happened in April 1919 but what had begun to weigh him down was the truth that within this special companionship he was beginning to become isolated from his fellow soldiers who, in the main, supported what Dyer had done. This was the crucial factor. After a further sharing of thoughts with Mary, through the medium of their letters, he informed his Commanding Officer that he intended to resign his commission.

Once he had decided to leave the army, he was left with the need to determine how he could arrange his future life to satisfy his third love. Two people solved this problem for him. Mary, realising the position, made it clear that she was more than prepared to begin her married life in India and make a commitment that this should be their home for the foreseeable future. The other person involved was David Blunt. A warm friendship had developed since their meeting in Bombay; Charles had been to Calcutta to visit and they had also renewed their acquaintance when David had business in Lahore. As soon as the businessman was aware that Charles intended to leave the army, and that he and Mary wanted to live in India, Blunt offered Charles a job in his firm. Both men realised that military experience was of little worth in the commercial world but Blunt believed that the soldier's affection for India and its people could be a valuable quality. He also perceived that Charles was an intelligent man with people-skills learnt in the army who would be useful when dealing with staff and customers—and he would no doubt be a positive addition to the firm's cricket team.

In his room at the barracks, Charles sat at the dressing table putting it to use as a writing desk. Hanging on the wall face-to-face with him was a rather indistinct photograph of Mary Rogers that had become even more faded as a result of the Indian sun. Slim, medium height, dark hair cut short and eyes that sometimes displayed a hint of a wistful bewilderment that contradicted a steely resolve. Her father had been the Cresswell family's GP before moving to a larger practice in Melton Mowbray and Mary, so she told Charles, had ambitions to follow in her father's footsteps. Dr Rogers encouraged her in this but finding a training place was not easy. During the war more women had gained access to the medical profession where they were, by and large, accepted for their contribution in the war itself and in examining workers in Government factories, particularly those making munitions. However, in the 1920s a number of medical schools that had taken women in wartime closed their doors to them and the idea of sexual equality in the medical world in Britain took a step back. The appearance of Charles on the scene also had an impact. She was only nineteen years of age when they became engaged and as it looked likely that her married life, at least the early years, would be spent in India, she abandoned medicine for marriage. When she accepted Charles' offer she was fully aware that this sort of decision would need to be made. She did not lightly decide on the domestic life over one in a hospital, but she was a down-to-earth, pragmatic character—and she did love Charles, who fully appreciated what she had done.

He took particular care with his letter to her after finally handing in his resignation and receiving the offer of a job from David:

> I have bitten the bullet—no doubt the right phrase for a soldier. I saw Colonel James yesterday morning and told him I had decided to leave the army. I couldn't make out whether he had any inkling of what I was planning to do, he is a wily old bird, but he immediately became both stern and fatherly at the same time and told me 'not to be such a bloody fool' and go away and think again. It took me half an hour to prove to him that I had made up my mind and he then had no alternative but to give in, which he did with good grace and exercising his formidable charm at the same time. I shall miss him—and the others of course. What I am very grateful for is that he didn't enquire too deeply into my reasons. I think I would have felt a bit of a fool if I had told this brave soldier that my love for the army had been extinguished, over time, because of the singular actions of one man. I have a funny feeling that the Colonel may not be too far away from my thinking on the Dyer subject but I am still glad I didn't have to explain.
>
> I did, dearest, also partially use you as an excuse—reluctance to begin married life not knowing how long we might remain in one station—new wife with no army connections whatsoever—home girl never been away from Blighty before—etc. etc. I'll retract all of these calumnies when we're together, promise. I did tell him that I was likely to be offered a job with the Blunts. He couldn't understand the attraction of a future 'stuck in some warehouse or other', as

he put it, but then he has been a soldier for more than twenty years, and most of those in India.

My interview with the Colonel has of course re-opened in my thoughts the debate I have been having with myself for nearly two years, and with you over the last few months. Am I really going to give up the career I love because of what happened at Amritsar and what that did to my concept of the role of the soldier? A thought I had today, and it has been buzzing around in my head for weeks, is that if only Dyer had said, loud and clear, 'I made an error of judgment', I might have been saved. Sorry to go on so, but you will know that yesterday was a momentous one in my life. I hope I, and both of us, will not regret it.

On a more cheerful subject, I am going to see what David thinks about us getting married in the UK (me and you that is not me and David!). If we have our honeymoon on the boat it will only delay my start date with him by about six weeks. Don't say anything to the folks yet but I am sure David will be sympathetic because, in the dusty warehouses of Blunt and Sons, romance is in the air. Ironically she is the daughter of a soldier. I haven't met her yet but David seems to have been caught at last.

The other news is that my new employers have bought a dilapidated bungalow at Malabar Hill in Bombay. It was the home of a Standard Bank manager but in recent years it has become surplus to their needs. The Blunts have not yet decided whether to renovate the property or build something else but there is a one-bedroom cottage in the grounds that David says we can use. It is only small but it is in one of the best and prettiest areas of Bombay. I'm very excited. Me with a house and a wife—sorry wrong order—me with a gorgeous wife and a humble dwelling—an old soldier who has lived out of a kitbag for the last five years.

I should have written this last night but after I'd seen the CO, George and I had a rather liquid evening together. I've told you about George Meredith, he took over Herbert's platoon at Ypres and we came out to India together. He and I rather fell out when we were in Amritsar but over time, and as he has got to know more about India and the Indians, the differences between us have closed and we are back to the friendship we had in Flanders. He's the only one in the mess I've told about my interview with the Colonel. George thought that by dosing me liberally with gin he could persuade me to return to the office this morning, hat in hand as it were, and withdraw my resignation but his only success was to ensure that I had a sore head when I woke up.

As an aside, and we may have spoken about this before, alcohol is a real problem for lots of expatriates here. My Maharaja, whom I have told you about, is very well read and it was he that told me of a saying by Gladstone: 'Drink is the curse of the working man.' Well, for many of the white people here it is 'Work is the curse of the drinking man', as a lot of them, particular the ladies, don't have enough to do and so they drink. They blame the climate—and the bugs—and the servants, etc. etc. Of course there are a lot of hard workers as well; we wouldn't be here but for the dedicated labour of the ICS. Anyway, enough about that. I enjoy my claret and a gin before lunch but I think I can avoid the 'devil drink' catching me although I do sometimes recall nostalgically the draught Bass Jimmy and I used to down at the Kings Arms.

Your letters mean so much to me and your last one was particularly wonderful. I enjoyed the verses. Really very good, and I should know since I met Wilfred Owen once in France! I have a theory as to why this war produced such splendid poetry. I believe I have told you that when I first crossed the Channel I frivolously thought that the troops' marching songs were the only item of culture that the war spawned, but looked at more seriously, it cannot be denied that what did emerge from that horror were many examples of sublime verse. Anyway my theory is this. There was of course the most vivid of subjects, the carnage all around, but also these poets had time. Where possible the powers-that-be tried to arrange duty in the trenches on a cyclical programme. Although there wasn't a lot of home leave granted, after a few weeks in the front-line men were moved into support trenches and then back to the reserve, where they inevitably had time on their hands, before returning to the battle area. Even there, in addition to the other scourges, boredom was a real problem. Many of the men spent hours writing home and a few tried to keep a diary but obviously for those with a literary spark within them they could use up those hours to satisfy their muse. And don't laugh, I also got caught and from Ypres onwards kept a journal. The entries are a bit spasmodic but I'm glad I started it. I've kept going in India as well although when I have my nose down to the Blunt's grindstone, I shan't have as much time to prove my literary genius (ha ha) as I did when in the military. I also wrote some poetry that you can try and help me with when you are here, but to show you what a difficult, if not impossible, task this will be, I enclose an example of my doggerel.

I think of you all the time. You might retort that you rather doubt that with all the activity I have been boring you with, but it is true. As I stood in front of the Colonel yesterday the sun was streaming through the windows straight into my eyes, but I could see very clearly an image of you in the top right-hand pane—and you seemed to be smiling at me and giving me the confidence to go on. I know marrying me means you will now never be your father's partner but I need you to doctor me and I hope you will not be too disappointed. Most of my friends will tell me I am mad when they know what I've done, so as you can see I urgently need a brain specialist—and you are as special as they come.

The enclosure to the letter contained these verses:

Man and mud, as I remember,
Not a girl in sight.
For we're at war, as I remember,
But did we want to fight?

Cold and wet, as I remember.
Relief tomorrow, thank God.
One more day, as I remember,
To kill the other sod.

Goodbye to all that, as I remember,
So said the poet Graves.
But if you're dead, as I remember,
Words are bread upon the waves.

Them and us, as I remember,
Brothers under the skin.
For we're together, as I remember,
To fight through thick and thin.

The smell of gas, as I remember,
Filled us all with dread.
Those hopeless masks, as I remember—
A1 the general said.

The ceaseless guns, as I remember,
Our ears are fit to burst.
The shot and shell, as I remember,
Always does its worst.

Over the top, as I remember;
Automated fools.
The dead are cold, as I remember.
There are no Queensberry rules.

Mary's reply included the following:

Thank you darling for your last letter and, hooray, hooray, for your telegram. I shall be at the quayside to meet you. I am jumping for joy. In case you have forgotten what I look like, I shall be wearing my new hat. It is blue and yellow and Daddy says it is ghastly but it is unmissable. However, before we meet I feel I must tell you that I thought your poetry was rather crass and the rhyming somewhat forced. There, I've said it, but then you always told me that it was my independent spirit that made you fall in love with me. Also, I'm afraid, darling, that as you are soon to give up being a Captain to be just plain Mr, you will find it even harder to order me around. I'm only jesting of course. You will be allowed to visit your club on your own once a month!

One of Daddy's patients served in India, in the ICS I think, for many years and his wife has been most helpful with advice on what clothes I shall need, although whether married to a mere trader I shall have quite the social life that she had is to be seen. However, it has been a wonderful excuse to do lots of shopping and I hope I shall be a credit to you. I presume you will keep up your contacts with the Military?

I am of course nervous about the future. Daddy, as you can imagine, is concerned about health issues and I say to myself if we have babies, where will they be born? There, that has shocked you. Aren't I a forward modern girl to be writing such things to an unmarried man. It is good news that we shall be living in a nice neighbourhood. Shall I bring some curtain material? But I realise you will not be able to reply to this as you will be embarking by the time you get my letter.

Everyone is excited about the wedding, me included, and it seems that your sister has taken charge. I love her dearly and I suppose someone has to see to the practical arrangements, and Mummy is only too glad to have Edith as her Adjutant. See—I'm in the army too.

I won't write any more except to say about your verses, sorry to be so rude, but we will have the rest of our lives for me to try and improve your lyrical ability. At the moment I'm rather glad we are thousands of miles apart because remarks like that would have you throwing cushions at my head, or worse.

Chapter Three

Jenny

'Well, Miss Jenny', said Aunt Edith, 'now that the Matthew is fixed up at Uppingham we must find a nice boarding school for you.'

Adele nodded.

'Not for me thank you. Who would look after Rosie if I'm not here?'

'Come on, Jenny. Do you want your brother to better you?'

'That'll be the day! I reckon he needs to go—might liven him up a bit—but for me, some of my friends are going to commute to school in Nottingham and I would like to do the same.'

Even at the age of thirteen Jenny Cresswell had calculated that the restrictions of boarding school would limit her increasingly active social life, particularly amongst junior equestrian circles. Adele, who was not the type who considered the education of boys more important than that of girls, spent some time trying to persuade her daughter of the benefits of continuing her education away from home but Mrs Cresswell, seeing how determined Jenny was, soon capitulated. As for Aunt Edith, she was quietly delighted that 'jolly Jenny' as she called her, would be staying at The Old Vicarage—when not involved in gymkhanas or point-to-point meetings. Jenny's decision proved to be a good one, particularly as she was fortunate enough to be accepted as a pupil at the Nottingham High School for Girls. This had been founded in 1875 and some of their early pupils were amongst the first women to obtain university degrees and enter the professions. In this atmosphere Jenny excelled, even though she was passed over as head girl, a position she had seemed destined to hold, because of the incident on the train.

By the time she found herself as a school prefect in the Lower Sixth her high spirits and sense of fun, that had until then been kept within reasonable bounds, broke out and there occurred the train escapade which, when it became public, had the whole school abuzz. After some years, Jenny was well acquainted with everyone who regularly travelled on the 8.07 train from Market Harborough to Nottingham and the 5.16 p.m. in the opposite direction. In particular, she became very friendly with a small group of boys of her own age who attended various grammar schools in the city. One of them, Dave Brighton, was nearly as irrepressible as she was, and the two of them encouraged each other to the extremes of admissible behaviour. This young man was not able to explain how his satchel had suddenly shot out of the carriage window, narrowly missing the Station Master at Long Eaton, who had just seen the train safely away from his care. When the owner of this missile was later taken to task, he could provide no reason why Jenny had hurled his bag so unceremoniously off the train—but he had provoked her more than usual. It was alleged that, tired of hearing her boast of her equestrian exploits, he had said that all that time sitting on a horse was making her bottom bigger. Not only was this remark impolite, it was far from accurate. Jenny was a good-looking girl and both she and Dave Brighton knew that. However, this minor incident was soon forgotten by the authorities and the participants but the next time these two went into action, British Rail felt obliged to send notes to the boy's headmaster and Jenny's headmistress.

To alleviate the boredom of the 'oh so familiar journey', as Jenny described it, she suggested that Dave, who at the age of seventeen and a half was already nearly six feet tall—and, so he said, needed to shave his cheeks every Saturday morning—should pretend to be a ticket collector and she a traveller attempting to avoid paying a fare. Tickets were usually shown at stations, not on the train, but occasionally an inspector would appear to ensure that the station checking system was working properly. Jenny's idea had only germinated because she knew that the relevant costume could be acquired because the Great Bowden Dramatic Society, in which Dave's mother was an enthusiastic member, had recently produced *The Ghost Train* at the village hall. It was, therefore, not too difficult for Dave to raid the society's costume hamper. To add to the effect, he was also able to find some modest whiskers to hide his adolescence. As soon as the train left Market Harborough Dave changed into his costume, much to the amusement of the other schoolchildren who, as usual, occupied the rear compartment, next to the guard's van. The impostor then proceeded along the corridor with Jenny in his wake and, trying his best to avoid the regular travellers, began to inspect tickets with a careful rigour. Jenny played her part in the double act, grimacing and making faces at her friend behind his back to the amazement of passengers. As the train neared Nottingham, Jenny slipped ahead and found a seat in a compartment of strangers. When Dave arrived she refused to show her ticket and a fierce argument ensued, the substance of which had been well rehearsed by the accomplices. As exchanges became more heated, Jenny threatened to pull the communication cord and stop the train. Unfortunately, she overdid her characterisation of an affronted passenger and really did pull the cord just as the train was entering the station. Their escapade may well have gone unreported but for this mishap. As it was, however, Dave was severely rebuked at school and at home, and Jenny's name was removed from the list of potential Head Girls.

Matthew did not display any evidence of his mixed-blood ancestry but his sister was fashioned more in the mould of her mother, both in features and character. Adele was taller and slimmer than her daughter but both had a hint of an olive complexion and slightly high cheekbones although Jenny's hair, unlike the black sheen of Adele, was a pale yellow inherited from her father. The twins had left India at the age of five and had never seen their father again but Jenny had a clear memory of him pushing his over-long hair out of his eyes during the tearful farewells, tresses lighter than hers bleached by the Indian sun. The mixing of blood often resulted in Anglo-Indian women being strikingly beautiful and Adele was certainly that. Her daughter's beauty, however, was more English rose than oriental. Adele had grown up in a world where the whole gamut of class existed in its widest form, from the 'Untouchables' to the Brahmins in the Indian caste system on the one hand, to the rigorous class system within British society. Jenny was aware of these differences but she had always been secure in her middle-class skin—and with her middle-class looks and accent. She had lived in Leicestershire for most of her life and when she eventually met Isobel, who became her brother's wife and who had been brought up in the same part of England, she saw a mirror image of herself. Something in the soil, she thought.

She and Dave Brighton met at family parties, cricket matches and other social occasions. Despite trading insults on the train, they were fond of each other and so Jenny agreed to go out with him; this included visits to the cinema in Market Harborough. She was relaxed in his company and perfectly content for him to manoeuvre his hand under her blouse when they were both in the dark anonymity of the cinema's back-row. He did not venture any further than this adolescent fumbling and if he had Jenny would have brought him up short. Invariably they would end their evenings on the bench next to Stanton church where, in the shade of a luxuriant willow tree, they would exchange kisses while Dave conducted a further exploration of her underwear. However, when their brief liaison came to an end as Dave left for university she was still a virgin. She was not worried about this and in due course dealt easily with the teasing she received from her Cambridge friends. 'You must be the only one in Girton—except for the Mistress of the college' was often thrown at her, but she would always respond with a knowing smile as she hummed, like Snow White, 'Someday day my prince will come.'

When she left school she expressed some interest in following in her grandfather's footsteps. Enquiries were made about attending the Royal Agricultural College in Cirencester but as, at about the same time, she had been able to convince Girton College that she was a suitable candidate for admission into their all-female midst, she decided to accept their offer and read English. Jenny and Cambridge suited each other very well. After the first year in Hall, she and three other students rented a house and they stayed friends for the remaining two years of their time at university. However, the most important friendship she made while there was with a young man who was to be partly responsible for the course the rest of her life took.

It was an excessively wet day. The rain had been incessant since dawn punctuated, at regular intervals, by more violent downpours that taxed the efficiency of Cambridge's surface water drainage system. No little boys would be playing marbles today in these gutters. Being close to the shortest day of the year, the hours of daylight available were so shrouded in rain clouds that the margin between night and day, the dark and the light, was hardly discernible. Perhaps for this reason the public bar at The Mitre was more populated than usual for a Tuesday evening but even here the all-pervading wetness was evident. New customers came in with so much rain on their shoulders it immediately poured onto the linoleum and these pools of water were soon supplemented as umbrellas were dismantled and shaken. However, this dampness and the gloomy wooden interior of the pub did little to dissipate the fog of smoke from Craven As and Woodbines, the obligatory accessories for the assembled drinkers, except for the few earnest looking male students or junior dons who favoured a pipe. Many of this minority had not yet become sufficiently accomplished to be able to keep their smoking implements alight while using them as a debating tool to reinforce opinions declaimed loudly. There were no female pipe smokers, but nearly all of the ladies present accompanied their half pints of bitter with a cigarette and two of the more sophisticated were using bakelite holders—'For my health, you know.' Jenny felt very much at home, even though she was one of the few who shunned the noxious weed. She did not object to having herself and her drink engulfed in smoke—it was an indispensable feature of the pub scene of the 1950s. In the main, the students who formed most of The Mitre's clientele were not affluent, but beer was cheap and some, who were subsidised by parents, could occasionally afford to add a glass of whisky to their intake of Mitchells and Butlers. Jenny was one of these and being, as she described herself, a modern young woman, she had just ordered a large scotch and soda each for herself and the young man standing very close to her at the bar. Unusually, the three girls she shared a house with were together that night which resulted in some measure of boisterous behaviour as the quartet insinuated itself into the tightly packed crowd at one end of the bar. In consequence Jenny caught the elbow of the young man in question just as he was raising a pint glass to his mouth. Most of the beer it contained decorated his tweed jacket and flannels but before he could berate her clumsiness, she had ordered the compensatory whisky. She did this in the loudest voice she could command, even though she was inwardly shaking with laughter at the sight of the beer-drenched buttonhole her new companion was sporting in the lapel of his now extremely damp coat.

'Sorry about that but it is a bit of a crush. What's the flower for?'

'I don't think that's any of your business, young woman—and who do you think you are ordering a drink for me.'

'Well, if you don't want it Maggie here will down it in a flash.'

'Not so fast. I rather like scotch but don't get much chance to indulge these days. Cheers!'

'I really am sorry about knocking into you but I don't think beer can do too much harm to that coat.'

'What do you mean? This is genuine Harris Tweed, I'll have you know, but it looks as though I shall have to go and change it before dinner.'

'Going somewhere nice?'

'Yes. It is a small dining club I belong to for Africans.'

'Well, I can hear you have a funny accent but you don't look African to me.'

'Not all Africans are black, you know.'

Despite enjoying the whisky, he was about to turn away from her and resume conversation with the girl on his left when Jenny, without thinking, said, 'Why don't you take me with you? By the way, I'm Jenny Cresswell.'

He spluttered into his drink as he introduced himself and told her that, even if guests were allowed at the 'Safari', he did not think she would be a suitable candidate. At this he drank up and left but not before Jenny had expressed her opinion of his boorish behaviour to her friends, loudly and with some choice epithets.

Joseph Marks was a South African Jew, three years older than Jenny, engaged in postgraduate research on an aspect of international commercial law that she never fully understood. They bumped into each other outside King's College a few days after this first encounter. He smiled at her, apologised for his rudeness and told her that after dry-cleaning, his jacket was restored to its customary grandeur. It had cost him seven and six he said, to which Jenny replied that it would have been much cheaper if he had gone to Sketchleys. As they stood there, perfectly at ease with each other, it seemed natural that they should go to the Copper Kettle and order the dish of the day.

Jenny had been in love more than once, or so she thought, but the possibility of such an event occurring 'at first sight', as the saying goes, was a totally new phenomenon for her. Ten days later she wrote to her mother:

Before I pass on to the more mundane of my happenings, let me tell you straight away I think I am in love. I know I have told you this before, but this time it is different. He is a South African Jew (at least his father is Jewish) not particularly handsome or even very witty but he has the most beautiful steel-grey eyes. All right, I can hear you talking this over with Aunt Edith and saying that your frivolous daughter has fallen for 'a pair of sparkling eyes', but I am not that flippant. He really is nice; he seems so much more grown-up than any of my other beaus. I've only been out with him three times since we first met in The Mitre but I know you will take to him and I would like to invite him to Stanton as soon as possible. You and he are, after all, both colonials!

As a result of Jenny's enthusiasm for someone outside the set of eligible Leicestershire bachelors, Aunt Edith quickly moved into action and, with a display of old-world courtesy that Jenny found irritating yet admirable, wrote to Joseph Marks inviting him to spend a weekend at the Old Vicarage at the end of the summer term. With a similar display of politeness, he accepted the invitation in a dignified, semi-formal letter which Jenny made fun of. Her friendship with Joe, as she now called him, had blossomed but she joked that unless he changed his name their relationship had no future, for who could take seriously a couple called 'Joe and Jenny'? 'Sounds like a pair of children featured in an early reading primer,' she said.

Despite the slightly aggressive tone of their first conversation in The Mitre, Joe was very like Matthew, careful and reticent in contrast to the flamboyant Jenny. He was the third generation of Marks to be born in South Africa. His great-grandfather had left London's Whitechapel in the 1870s for the diamond fields at what was to become Kimberley, but the family had been resident in Johannesburg since the early years of the twentieth century. Joe's father was also a man of law, running a small practice that specialised in property and commercial matters. His mother, who was not of the faith, taught chemistry at a private school for girls which meant, as Joe explained, he was not really Jewish. In any case his father had ceased to practise the faith before his marriage to a Gentile. Jenny was able to point out that she was hardly a blue-blooded Brit and so they had something in common.

Jenny had been correct when she said that her new friend and her mother would get on well together. Adele could see signs of thoughtfulness and sincerity in this man that reminded her of her own son. Aunt Edith's view was that, although he was a foreigner and a Jew, she appreciated his courteous manners and was pleased to inform all who would listen that, in her opinion, he was, 'a gentleman'. Jenny showed him the best features of the Leicestershire countryside, and took him to a local point-to-point meeting, but the highlight of the visit was the party Aunt Edith arranged for Saturday evening. Ten people sat down to dinner, cooked and served by Mrs Collingwood. The guests included Father Claude Donovan, the local Roman Catholic priest, who was partnered with Olive Rogers, the spinster sister of Charles Cresswell's first wife, and George and Sarah Dolby, farming neighbours of the family, a couple of years older than the twins and particular friends of Matthew. The party was completed by two of Adele's oldest friends who were also staying at the Old Vicarage. Henry Travers had worked for Adele's father with the Indian Railways. He and his wife Elizabeth had left India at the same time as Adele and settled, in retirement, in Bath. Matthew was not at home—some duty he had at the University, he said.

With a South African as guest of honour it was to be expected that the evening's conversation would sooner or later turn to the subject of apartheid. Most of the guests were aware in general terms of the political situation there, particularly as the news of the adoption of a Freedom Charter had just been announced. Joe explained the significance of this event and was able to tell the assembled company that the preamble to this Charter stated that South Africa belonged to all who lived there, black and white, and that any Government must be based on the will of the people. This, said Father Donovan, was going to be very difficult to achieve.

'I spent a few years in your country from just after the National Party came to power in 1948 and it was clear then that there were going to be serious problems reconciling that party's policies with the aspirations of the majority of the population.'

Before Joe could comment, Adele tried to compare the situation with India in 1947.

'I know there are differences with India, Joe, but as I understand the situation, one of the main problems is that if with a universal franchise life becomes impossible for the Afrikaners they have nowhere else to go. Well, it was the same for the Anglo-Indian, but of course on a much smaller scale and we never had anything like a position of power. Fortunately for me, I married an Englishman who had the most generous sister in the world,' a slight bow of the head towards Edith, 'and I know that Jenny and Matthew do not feel that Britain is anything but home for them. But, Joe, if there was black majority rule in your country, would your family stay?'

'We all understand that, Mummy,' from Jenny, 'but does anything justify the way the black people are treated—and those who are of mixed race?'

At this Sarah Dolby, who had been at school with Jenny, chipped in.

'Like you, you mean. With respect, Mrs Cresswell, all that mischief Jenny got up to at school was probably due to her mixed blood.'

Jenny scowled and was about to bombard her friend with a pellet of bread when the steely gaze of Aunt Edith stayed her hand. Joe had still not been given the floor.

'What I find difficult to stomach is that the Afrikaner manages to use his religion as a justification for his politics,' observed Father Donovan. 'They evidently believe they have a covenant with God that requires them to occupy South Africa and civilise the barbarians. And their Dutch Reformed Church appears, in general, to approve of the policies of apartheid. The other justification they use, or so I'm told, is the theory of the empty land. The argument presented by the Afrikaners is that when their forebears first arrived at Cape Town, then expanded further east and north over the next two hundred years, there was very little indigenous population, suggesting that the Afrikaners did not displace the Africans but were there before them, or at least arrived simultaneously. Is there any truth in this argument, Joe?'

'I think most people dismiss the empty land view but let me make this point. I do not want to excuse the National Government but I must remind you that apartheid has a long history in my country, some of it originating with the British. My great-grandfather worked in the diamond fields in Kimberley. The British miners discriminated against the blacks and were paid more than them for the same labour. But let me tell you what I foresee. Inevitably, there has to be a one-man one-vote situation, though whether this can be achieved without dreadful bloodshed is anybody's guess. What we do know is that the National Government has the largest army and police force in Africa, backed by a determined Security Service, and this today is one of the worst aspects of life in South Africa—who can you trust? There are spies everywhere.'

'Just like Russia', Jenny said.

Joe continued.

'Early on, the Afrikaner understood the tensions created by denying the franchise to South Africans who were not classified as white and came up with a kind of solution, the creation of the "Homelands". This concept maintained that the black population had their own tribal roots and that they should leave places like Cape Town and Johannesburg and the rich farming land and return to the areas designated as Native Reserves. This goes back to the Land Act of 1913, well before the National Party came to power. Of course, this did not solve the problem because what was allocated as reserves was the poorest land in the country and the percentage of the land mass given up was totally inadequate, and unfair. The whites are 20% of the population and they enjoy more than 80% of the land. Archbishop Tutu likes to tell a joke that has an edge of bitter truth to it. "When the white man first came here he had the Bible and we had the land. Then the white man said to us, come let us kneel and pray together. So we knelt and closed our eyes and prayed, and when we opened our eyes again, lo!—we had the Bible and he had the land." '

Joe paused but everyone was listening intently.

'You are well-informed young man,' said Edith.

'Not at all,' Joe replied. 'Most educated whites are fully acquainted with these facts.'

'I know the majority of people in your country live in poverty, deprived of proper houses or running water or sanitation, but so do many people in this world. However, non-whites in South Africa are also deprived, I believe, of their identity. Is that a fair statement, Joe?'

Olive Rogers continued without waiting for an answer.

'Unless they are standing on the barren soil of their "Homelands", as you have described them, they are not recognised, except as units of labour. Even in the hierarchical system of India the poorest has a place in that hierarchy, or is that an exaggeration?'

Joe nodded in agreement.

Henry Travers was the only one present with experience of running a major commercial enterprise and he quickly saw another flaw in the 'Homelands' solution.

'Right, Joe, if the Afrikaner intends to solve the problem by dividing the country into black land and white land, how does commerce operate in the white areas if there it is to be no black labour living there? I believe that the gold mines rely for their profitability on a plentiful supply of cheap labour, so there's a contradiction.'

'You are absolutely correct. What happens, of course, is that work permits are granted for men to come into the cities or onto the white farms and labour for as long as the white capitalist determines. When they are too old to work, or sick, they have to go back home. The other diabolical aspect of this is that men are separated from their wives and families but many firms allow their workers to return home for two weeks each year, often known as "conception leave". As a result, children are born within these poor reserves and the white man has no responsibility for them. In effect, the next generation of immigrant workers is being produced at no cost to the white capitalist.'

'And there is I suppose another factor,' commented Travers. 'I believe the mixed-blood population is considerable, particularly in the Cape. Where is their "Homeland" and where do they go back to—and surely that applies to those of Indian ancestry?'

'Yes', said Father Donnelly, 'and many of the "Coloureds" I met were very sad creatures. The problem of being neither "fish nor fowl" turned some of them towards drink. Others I met were indistinguishable from white, and many tried to pass for white, but the authorities were often ruthless in tracking down their origins. In my diocese we were forbidden to take into one of our schools two children who the powers-that-be said were Coloured, even though they had fairer complexions than I and both their parents had been pupils at the same school.'

'How awful!,' said Olive Rogers. 'I have been involved in education all my life. We have some problems but I believe the children of those immigrants who came from the Caribbean just after the war are integrating into our society, certainly in our schools.'

'The irony,' said Joe, 'is that most of the Afrikaners have some non-white blood in their ancestry. I read somewhere recently that across them all it amounts to about 7%, but how this is calculated I simply don't know.'

'What a mess,' said Jenny.

'It is,' he responded, 'but let me tell you that, in typical Afrikaner fashion, they very soon after coming to power decided to shut the stable door, as it were, by prohibiting mixed marriages and making sex between the races a criminal offence. They are not unique in this—there is similar legislation in some States of the US. However, I doubt if they can outgun the South Africans in this field. I remember a report I saw in the *Rand Daily Mail* earlier this year about a case which went to the Supreme Court who found a twenty-two-year-old "African house boy" guilty of a crime for writing a love letter to an eighteen-year-old white girl. These laws stemmed from white fears of miscegenation, but they also empowered the establishment to try and bring back into line those white men who had sex with black women. This was more prevalent in rural areas between the white farmer and his black servants, but in addition to the impact on some of the white population, black women were often subjected to harsh treatment where the over-zealous police sought evidence by trying to establish the degree of "bed warmth" found on early morning raids.'

'How do you stay in such a country?' asked Sarah.

'Well, perhaps I'm like the "Coloureds". Where do I go? It is my country. My family have been there for a hundred years and there are some liberals like me who believe we might be able to change things without running away.'

'And I suppose it is even worse for black and "Coloured" women. I can imagine yours is a very macho society, Joe, so the women must be even more disadvantaged,' continued Sarah.

'Yes, but that is not to say they are not part of the protest movement, particularly over conditions in the "Homelands".' Edith interrupted. 'After listening to you, Joe, I think I speak for all of us when I say that we feel—at least I certainly do—a bit uncomfortable that our Government, and we ourselves, have not protested enough. I do have some influence and will speak to Thomson, our local MP, who is a junior minister. Perhaps he can get Eden to put South Africa more aggressively on the agenda. For your benefit, Joe, Roger Thomson was a great friend of Tony, my late husband.'

'And I understand he is a bit in love with you,' Jenny murmured under her breath.

Adele nodded her head, but whether this was to agree with her daughter or with the more serious point raised by Edith was hard to tell. On the question of protest by other Governments, however, she was able to speak with some authority—at least, as far as India was concerned.

'The Traverses and I have more knowledge than perhaps even you, Joe, of the stand of the Indian Government on South African apartheid. They were, of course, mainly concerned about the South Africans of Indian origin, and how they were being treated, but there is some history about this because of the time that Gandhi spent there. His story in South Africa is interesting and very relevant to the freedom struggle in his own country because it was there that he first practised *satyagraha*, non-violent protest. As you will know, he went to South Africa in the 1890s as a young lawyer to represent an Indian trader in Natal and while there he found himself humiliated by the local white people. This experience began his career in politics. He was prominent for many years in South Africa trying to improve the lot of the Indians. As a result, the Indian Authorities agreed, sometime during the early years of this century, not to permit the recruitment of any more indentured labour. What happened initially was that the British settlers recruited labourers—around 1860—to work mainly in the sugar plantations, offering good wages and repatriation after five years or the right to settle in Natal as free men. However, after a while the Indians, as traders or market gardeners, became serious opposition for the white folk. This is where the discrimination against Indians began—and it was not the Afrikaners this time.'

At this point Edith must have thought the conversation was getting too serious and so took the slight pause that followed Adele's speech to suggest the company move to the drawing room.

Jenny, to some extent influenced by Joe, decided that the Law might be the career for her and, with encouragement from her mother and brother, she arranged a place on the Law Society course to commence as soon as her time at Cambridge was over. Sarah Dolby's father ran a small legal practice in Leicester and over the years Jenny had grown to admire him. In his modest way he provided a service to help people involved in what they saw at the time as a minor disaster: a divorce, a family dispute, a serious traffic offence or some other matter involving the police. For all her outward frivolity, she was essentially a compassionate person and believed that a role as a country solicitor might suit her very well. Joe Marks, at least initially, was not involved in this decision. By the time Jenny was admitted by the Law Society he had returned to South Africa and both had discovered that 'love at first sight' could fade as quickly as it began. Adele told Jenny that love could be a complex, yet fleeting, emotion and from memory was able to call on Shakespeare in support:

O, how this spring of love resembleth
The uncertain glory of an April day;
Which now shows all the beauty of the sun,
And by and by a cloud takes all away.

'The Bard' was taught in depth in Indian schools and Adele, in doublet and hose, had played Proteus in *The Two Gentlemen of Verona* during her final year. When Joe returned to South Africa neither he nor Jenny were much concerned to understand these complexities and when, a few months later, he wrote to say that he was about to become engaged to a South African girl, Jenny's reaction was one of pleasure for him. As for her, she was pleased to be offered the chance to serve her pupilage with Clark and Co, where Sarah's father was the senior partner and where, by the end of 1959, she occupied a position as a junior assistant solicitor.

One day in March 1960, Jenny did not drive into Leicester according to her normal routine; she had a local assignment. Alison Jones, the headmistress of the village school was about to retire and she had asked Jenny to give her some advice about a will. Jenny had not visited the school since she had been a pupil there and she was looking forward to seeing it again. As she left the Old Vicarage she thought how pleasant it was to walk through the village where the advent of spring was fully evident. The ancient oak trees skirting the village green were well advanced in the production of their new leaves and many of the cottage gardens displayed the vivid colours of the latest tulips, daffodils and hyacinths. There was a gentle breeze but it was not cold enough for Jenny to require a top coat. She hummed one of the latest hits, Adam Faith's *What do you want if you don't want money*, and, as she arrived at the school, she thought what an appropriate song it was: she would not change any of this for money. Her opinion was reinforced as she was introduced to the one class of children for whom the school catered. Alison had asked Jenny in advance if she would like to talk to the pupils on a subject of her choice and they were kept enthralled for twenty minutes or so as she told them of Rosie, a favourite horse she had had at the age of fourteen, and of what a naughty animal it was. Jenny had known Alison Jones for many years. She had been a popular teacher of English at the Nottingham High School for Girls. In her late forties she had married a widower clergyman and when, in 1958, he had been appointed to the parish of Stanton, she had given up her senior position in Nottingham and taken on the running of the village school. She told Jenny during the morning that she had no regrets; her present role was not a taxing one but she found it just as rewarding as teaching the high fliers at Nottingham. During playtime the legal matters were dealt with and Jenny went on to her office feeling as though her batteries had been most effectively recharged by the morning's excursion. As she turned on to the A46 she thought that perhaps teaching could be the most satisfying profession of all.

After the event, Jenny visualised a South African version of Alison Jones en route to her school on the morning of 21st of March, but in a very different environment. Trees and flowers and tranquillity were in short supply in the Township of Sharpeville, fifty miles south of Johannesburg, and the only similarity with Stanton was the weather: that day in Sharpeville was sunny and warm under a near-cloudless sky. This South African Alison Jones—Jenny envisaged a young teacher named Flora, mother of two boys of school age—walks to school slightly apprehensively. Over the weekend there has been some trouble in the Township and she has heard shooting during the night. Her children left home just after dawn. When she reaches the school she is not too surprised to find it empty as something is clearly afoot. On Seiso Street a crowd is walking towards the police station on the edge of the Township. Flora joins them. When she arrives at the police station there is already a considerable gathering of people who have heeded the call of the Pan-Africanist Congress to assemble at this spot so as to provoke the authorities into arresting them for not carrying passes. Facing the crowd, which increases considerably during the morning, are a line of armed policeman and two Saracen armoured cars with machine guns. At around two o'clock a commotion of some sort occurs at one of the gates to the police compound—Flora is uncertain but she thinks there may have been some stone-throwing. Whatever it was, it was sufficient to spark off the massacre at Sharpeville.

Without warning the police began shooting with rapid-fire and in a short time sixty-nine people, men and women and children, had been killed and three hundred wounded, many of whom had been shot in the back as they fled. Flora could have been amongst them with perhaps a flesh wound in her upper arm. Friends help her to hospital where she stays for two days, but on release she is included with the many others who have been arrested for incitement and public violence. If she had not been hurt, her first move would have been to ascertain what happened to her children and, as she searches through the carnage, there is her youngest boy with his life-blood seeping away into the sand. If her family were unscathed she would have returned home, more frightened than she had ever been before in her life and wondering how many empty desks there would be when her school reopened.

In the aftermath of Sharpeville the authorities banned public meetings in all areas where disturbances had taken place. The response from the ANC was for their President, Albert Luthuli, to burn his passbook. He also declared the 28th of March a day of mourning for the victims, when people should stay at home and not go to work. Many of all races did. The Government's reaction was to declare both the ANC and the PAC illegal organisations; at the same time a state of emergency was imposed throughout large parts of the country, which allowed the imposition of curfews and the prohibition of gatherings. The economy came under severe pressure, foreign exchange reserves halved during 1960 and 1961, and there was a major loss of confidence by overseas investors.

Jenny returned home that evening when Adele and Edith told her of the disaster in South Africa, news of which had been broadcast on the BBC. In the days that followed it was Adele who made the comparison with the shooting at Amritsar and wondered if this latest atrocity might lead to a more democratic South Africa.

Although the shooting at Amritsar was a calculated act, compared to Sharpeville where the firing was the result of a degree of panic by inexperienced policeman, there were some obvious similarities. Both gatherings had been of unarmed civilians, no warning had been given before firing began and the aggressors in both cases did little, or nothing, to help the victims after the shootings. Both tragedies had been condemned around the world, although in the case of Sharpeville the criticism was almost universal on the international scene whereas in 1919 some people had approved of Dyer's action.

Perhaps, Adele said, it was an indication of changing attitudes as *Pax Britannica* moved from its zenith to its nadir.

Jenny and Joe were good correspondents and, as was to be expected, letters post-Sharpeville tended to concentrate on that event. Why had it happened and what would be the consequences? For some strange reason, Jenny became more drawn to the country, as if the 21st of March shootings were exerting, in some eccentric way, a pressure on her similar to that felt by her father over Amritsar. After the South African massacre there was not only a retreat of capital, people left the country as well. Yet Jenny began thinking of a move in the opposite direction. Overnight her Leicestershire life began to pall and when Joe invited her, more strongly than usual, to come and visit, she decided to go in an attempt to exorcise this irrational fixation. Frank Clark could not understand the problem, any more than Jenny could really explain it, but he could see Jenny was not herself and so, in his kindly manner, suggested she take a month's leave of absence. Edith, in her blunt fashion, said it was madness. Who would want to visit that dreadful country and why did the charming Joe Marks not leave and come and live in the UK? Adele was more sensitive and encouraged the trip, although with one of her children already in Africa she rather hoped that, when Jenny had seen the country for herself, she would come to her senses and appreciate what a lucky woman she was to have an interesting job at Clarks and a very pleasant lifestyle. So Jenny wrote to Joe and went.

Joe had emulated his father by marrying outside the faith but in his case it was, for the Marks family, way outside. Emily was an

Afrikaner, related on her mother's side to the Potgeiters—Hendrik Potgeiter had been one of the four main leaders involved in the Great Trek. Despite this ancestry she was extremely uncomfortable in her Afrikaner skin because, as she was to put it to Jenny, 'My blood—and my culture—is Afrikaans, and it is this culture that has created the abomination of apartheid—and I am ashamed.' When Joe married he left the family home in Highfields and moved with Emily to Bryanston. She had trained as a pharmacist but when Joe and his father suggested she should join their practice as the 'administrator and finance officer', as Henry put it, she jumped at the chance. Any concerns that living and working together might put a strain on their marriage were soon dispelled and both Markses welcomed the presence, in their sober working environment, of the dynamic Emily.

The newlyweds were about to get into their car one morning to drive to the office when they saw a GG lorry driving slowly, but unsteadily, along the quiet street outside their house. They were both surprised at this. GG lorries were so named for the letters on the registration plate of Government transport and were more likely to be seen in areas where forced removals were taking place under the Group Areas Act than the Northern suburbs of Johannesburg. Taking a short cut, thought Joe. As the lorry approached it was moving even more erratically and as it passed them the nearside of the vehicle hit the gardener employed by their neighbours, the Johnsons. Moses had been polishing Robert Johnson's car, which he cleaned every morning, and although he must have heard the harsh noise of the diesel-engine lorry, he was not to know that it would swerve towards him. The wing mirror of the lorry connected with Moses' head with such force that it was detached from the vehicle while the gardener was thrown across the bonnet of the Johnson's car splashing blood onto its glistening surface. Before either Joe or Emily could move, the lorry had stopped and a policeman emerged. He was a white man wearing a spotless khaki uniform with insignia that indicated he was a fairly senior officer. He pulled Moses to his feet.

'You stupid fucking kaffir!' he yelled, and administered a sharp blow to Moses' solar plexus.

All this took only a few seconds and before the onlookers were able to reach Moses his assailant had driven off. Joe was muttering under his breath but Emily, who had screamed when she saw what the policeman had done, shouted as the lorry moved away, 'You are an animal.'

As Joe inspected the wound to Moses' head, Emily extracted a notebook from her handbag and recorded the registration number of the lorry, which she had memorised. By this time Robert Johnson had appeared. Having been told what had happened, he wrapped a towel around Moses' head, which was still bleeding, and got him into the blood-stained car to take him to hospital.

When they reached the office, Joe made enquiries as to who might have authorised the use of this particular vehicle and then composed a letter of complaint, demanding an explanation and that action be taken against the police officer and the driver. Emily was all for going to police headquarters in Johannesburg there and then but she eventually accepted Joe's argument that they were more likely to get some response from a written complaint. The Afrikaner authorities, and it was fairly certain that they would be dealing with Afrikaner officials, delighted in the bureaucracy of paper and records and they would certainly prefer a letter to a verbal approach. After the election success of 1948, the National Party had ensured that virtually all employment opportunities in State enterprises, such as the railways and the towering edifice that was established to administer the apartheid system, including the police and security services, were reserved for Afrikaners.

They received a reply in a remarkably short space of time.

> I am in receipt of your letter of the 21st ultimo and would like to thank you for bringing this matter to my attention.
>
> A reprimand has been issued to the driver of this vehicle. He should not have been in the residential area of Bryanston but had been delayed by the traffic on the Pretoria highway and had taken a route through the area where you live to make up time. He should not have done this and please be assured it will not happen again.
>
> On the more serious complaint of injury to a black gardener, the driver assures me that this individual stepped out into the road and although the driver is very experienced, he could not avoid the accident. Captain Swart, who was in the lorry at the time, attended to the injured man but as the contusions he suffered were only minor, and the

Captain was needed urgently at Alexandria Township, he told the man to go back to the house and get his cut dealt with there. Captain Swart, who was sitting in the cab of the lorry, saw this man step out into the road without warning. It is our experience that these natives have no road-sense whatsoever and accidents like this occur frequently. Police drivers are trained to assume that African pedestrians are more likely than not to act irrationally. Captain Swart categorically denies your allegation that the lorry was being driven erratically or, more seriously, that he assaulted the gardener. He is one of my most experienced officers who always complies with the strict code of conduct we have in the police and I have no reason to doubt his word.

I have decided not to pursue the question of who will pay for the broken wing mirror.

If I can be of further assistance, please do not hesitate to let me know.

I have the honour to be Sir
Yours faithfully
Colonel J X Snyman

Before this letter was received, and with the permission of Robert Johnson, Joe spoke to Moses whose head wound had been stitched at the local casualty department and was now back in the servants' quarters at 37, Orchard Drive.

'Moses, I hope you are feeling better. Did they treat you well at the hospital?'

'Yes, Master, but long wait.'

'Now, Mr Johnson may have explained, I am a lawyer and, although my firm does not do court work, I can get somebody else to act for you because I think you should make a formal complaint against the police and seek compensation. Did Mr Johnson pay you while you have been unable to garden?'

'Yes, Sir.'

'Well, do you understand what I am saying about suing the police?'

'I do Master, but no want it.'

'Why not? I will help.'

'Thank you, Sir, but best forget of it.'

'But you cannot do that. It seemed to me that the lorry swerved to hit you on purpose but whether or not, that policeman had no cause to punch you in the stomach.'

'I know, Master, but not hurt too much.'

'That's not the point. He should be punished for that type of behaviour.'

'Master, my family not want to mess with police. Could be very bad for us because of my son, Gabriel.'

'What do you mean? What has your son got to do with this?'

'Let me tell you. He is twenty-plus years of age and has no work. He live in Soweto with his grandmother. He has hot temper. Angry, very angry, hate white-man. Policeman tried to catch him. He was at Sharpeville but not shot. He with others say that after Sharpeville only guns and bombs will work. I am very worried for him, and his mother tell me to keep away from police 'cause of Gabriel.'

Joe was at a loss to know what response to make to this speech. Moses had tears in his eyes.

'Well, perhaps I can help Gabriel. Has he been charged with anything?'

'Don't think so, Sir, but perhaps he listen to you. If you like I go ask him to see you.'

Joe gave the gist of this conversation to Robert Johnson but went through it in detail with his father and Emily.

'We know this is happening everywhere and that there will be lots more like this Gabriel boy as a result of the fiasco at Sharpeville—"No more talking—to get the vote we need violence."'

Henry Marks responded. 'But Joe, it is not our fight, how can we help?'

'Of course it is our fight,' exclaimed Emily. 'Really, Henry, are we going to sit on our hands while this country descends into a bloody civil war.'

From their first meeting Henry had been pleased that forthright Emily used his Christian name and did not call him Mr Marks or Dad or the Afrikaner equivalent.

'All right, we can sympathise and empathise but what can we do in practical terms? If we help with finance we'd soon be closed down. We are not going to plant bombs at power stations, or is that what you want?'

Before Emily could respond, Joe entered the debate.

'There is only one thing we can do: use our skills as lawyers to represent anyone, from whatever quarter, who is falsely accused of crimes against the State, or in cases where the State exceeds its legal authority.'

Both Emily and Henry exchanged glances, as much as to say that this sounded like the right course to take, perhaps the only one possible for them, but Joe went on.

'However, neither you nor I, Dad, have any experience in this field. When was the last time you appeared in court?'

'Well, get someone in who is experienced,' interrupted Emily.

Henry said they would give this some thought but the following day Joe received Jenny's letter the main topic of which was Sharpeville, how agitated this had made her and how she was of a mind to visit South Africa. Madness, said Joe to himself, crazy—but might a Jenny be what they were looking for? An outsider with no preconceived ideas—someone with a feisty nature—not very likely. She would have to be registered locally; that might be difficult, and why would she want to give up her life in Leicestershire to support a succession of what were likely to be lost causes? Although they had never met, Emily was well acquainted with Jenny's personality and characteristics, thanks to Joe's descriptions, but there was no rivalry between them. Joe was hers for ever and ever, so when he talked about a possible role for Jenny, Emily said, 'Why not sound her out? She seems keen to visit so encourage her to come and we can talk to her face to face. But if her face attracts you more than mine, I'll scratch your eyes out, Joe Marks.'

Jenny tried very hard in her letter to Joe to explain her confused state. She took some trouble to find the right words, not so much to give Joe a complete picture before they met, but in an attempt to try and introduce some logic into her agitation. Yes, she had been shocked by Sharpeville, but so had millions of others around the globe and they were not thinking of mounting a white charger and riding to the rescue of the downtrodden South Africans. If, indeed, that is what she wanted to do. She asked herself if she had any qualifications that might prove useful. I am a newly qualified solicitor whose only experience of 'abroad' is the first five years of my life in India and that trip last year for a weekend in Paris. However, her legal training ensured she tried to see all points of view. There could be no excuse for the shooting at Sharpeville, any more than the massacre perpetrated by General

Dyer. However, many thought his action was justified, and if you were a white South African the firm treatment of the remainder of the population could be viewed as a necessity.

After a number of drafts, this was the letter she sent:

You will be surprised to have such a prompt reply to your last letter which I received last week. Your invitation to visit seems to me to be couched in more urgent terms than before so, you poor devils, I am going to call your bluff and accept. And, wait for it, I have been able to persuade my boss that I need a long break and he has given me a full month's leave of absence. So, can I come for that long?

I do not really need an extended holiday; my labours at Clark and Co are hardly Herculean and, as you will expect, I am enjoying a delightful social life. The Farmers' Ball this year was even more fun than usual. Both Adele and Aunt Edith were there and they had a ball, or perhaps that is what you are supposed to do at such a function!

The real reason why I have inveigled a month out of Frank Clark is not because I'm tired—except in the brain. Close to the time of the awful shootings at Sharpeville, I was visiting the village school in Stanton and I cannot now help thinking about the contrast between the pupils I met there and those poor South African children, many of whom were apparently shot in the back. I feel I ought to do something to help, but what can I do? I know it is mad but I cannot help myself. If I come and see you I might better be able to understand that I would be worse than useless in any campaign to help, but if I don't resolve this in my mind, one way or another, I shall burst. Of course, without you, I could just go on chuntering and send a donation to whatever anti-apartheid fund there is, so in the end, it is all your fault. You should never have picked me up in The Mitre that night!

On the other hand perhaps there are differences between me and the average Leicestershire looney—my early years in India, mixed blood and a twin brother already in Africa, although he seems to have an uneventful suburban-type life bringing culture, ha ha, to the masses. I think more crucially my father is most to blame. According to his journals he obviously loved being a soldier, or more precisely it was the camaraderie within soldiering that was the real attraction, and yet he gave it up. He gave it up because he did not agree with what soldiers did in Amritsar—and 'shouldering arms'—I don't agree with what happened at Sharpeville.

I can hear you saying 'naive fool' but if nothing else I really do want to see you again and meet Emily and your father.

By the way I trust you got the wedding present from the family. Aunt Edith had her own ideas as to what was appropriate, but fortunately mother took charge and she has, I hope you agree, very good taste.

As soon as I have booked a flight I will telephone.

Even before she arrived Joe had determined not to treat Jenny as a tourist. From the little he could read in the subtext of her letter, he saw it as his duty to provide some form of crash course in the politics and mores of life for South Africans—and this should be as inclusive as possible. In their social life, and in their legal world, Joe and his father—and Emily in a way—were in no position to act as tutors to Jenny. As he thought about this, Joe realised that, whether by design or accident, the Marks family, like most of the white population of South Africa, only came into direct contact with the black populace when they gave instructions or paid wages to their black housemaids or black gardeners or black nannies. In the case of the Coloured and Indian communities, there was virtually no contact at all. Neither Joe nor his father had ever visited the Townships around Johannesburg; certainly they had never been near Sharpeville. They were not proud of this but Joe saw that apartheid was achieving its object of segregation. Unless liberals like the Marks, for so they saw themselves, actively sought out non-white friends or even non-white clients, the system would win.

Joe and Emily were not unaware that the majority of their fellow countrymen and women were being unfairly treated, but the incident with Moses was, surprisingly, the first time Joe had been a close witness to such treatment. He realised that if they were to explain South Africa to Jenny in all its facets—the good, the bad and the ugly—he himself would also need to be a member of the audience for such a demonstration. Although he could take Jenny to the Townships where they might observe together the physical conditions of the dispossessed, he knew that he needed to be more proactive than that. Joe and Emily had both met Moses' son, Gabriel. Not a particularly attractive young man but clearly intelligent and instinctively political. He could be the starting point in Jenny's education—a useful barometer to gauge the attitude of the young black activists. To appreciate the opposite side of the coin, Joe arranged for them to meet Colonel Snyman, while Emily suggested that she might provide a view from the other end of the Afrikaner spectrum. A final actor was scheduled to appear and that was Father Samuels, a Coloured Catholic priest to whom Jenny had an introduction from Father Donovan. Obviously the nature of the experiment was not revealed to Colonel Snyman, but to the extent that Gabriel could understand what was afoot, or was prepared to cooperate in a frank and open fashion, he was openly recruited to join Emily and Father Samuels as a member of this bizarre assortment of teaching staff.

Soon after Jenny arrived, Joe and she went to see the Colonel by appointment. A reply had been sent to his letter to the effect that Joe would appreciate an opportunity to discuss this matter further and would like bring with him an old Cambridge friend who was researching for a PhD in the field of 'Politics and the police. Race riots in the UK and the USA.' His academic friend evidently thought that knowledge of policing problems in South Africa would provide a valuable tool in conducting her investigations into American and British methods of dealing with racial unrest. This subterfuge had been agreed with Jenny and it seemed to work as Colonel Snyman promised them thirty minutes of his valuable time. The scene was thus set for the relating of four separate accounts—by Snyman, Gabriel, Emily and Father Samuels, and all the storytellers were happy for Jenny to use the small recording machine she had brought with her.

Colonel Snyman was first. After a few minutes of discussion about the incident with Moses, Joe and the Colonel agreed that there were two opposing points of view but if Moses was not prepared to make a formal complaint, they must both simply 'agree to differ'. Jenny then asked Snyman to give his views on policing methods in South Africa where perhaps serious agitation was there just beneath the surface and might erupt at any time, as it had done in the 1950s at Notting Hill and at a number of locations in the USA.

'So you two were at Cambridge together. When I was at Stellenbosch University I went on a rugby tour and we played one of the colleges at Cambridge—can't remember which one, certainly wasn't Girton. *(Hearty laughter)* Anyhow, more seriously. I understand you are new to South Africa, Miss Cresswell. Well, on the one hand, Johannesburg is just like any other major city from the policing point of view. There are burglars and forgers here just as there are in London or Cambridge. We have traffic accidents, domestic violence and family murder but, of course, most crucially we have the problem of the blacks, or, more accurately, a minority of the blacks. You, Mr Marks, may have explained to her that you have to treat these people like children. If you don't watch them carefully, particularly with machinery, you're in trouble. Even if they are able to use it, don't let them near a typewriter or a tractor—they will destroy it in days. But most of them are happy and content. I know they live in terrible conditions but they don't really help themselves. However, it is not my job to worry about their physical well-being. I am only concerned with the small minority who are hell-bent on causing trouble—the agitators. They are only interested in mindless violence, determined to overthrow the State, and in many cases this leads to unlawfulness in other areas. You will not have heard of the *tsotsis*, the gangsters, young men completely out of control, who rob and kill their fellow men and women, whether white or black. But we will win. I have a highly trained force and we are determined to enforce the law. That is the job of our police, as it is elsewhere in the world. We do not make the law; we only make sure that it is obeyed. We need to shield the law-abiding black man from the agitators.

'We have our critics—well let us say the National Party have their critics—but overall the policy they are trying to promote is the best for all concerned. The black people will have, in effect, their own countries where they will make their own laws and those that are here with us to work, they must obey our rules.

'Let's talk about Sharpeville. It was not men of my force involved but it is proper that both sides of the argument should be heard. The police were three hundred in number facing a mob of five thousand that should not have been there. They object to carrying their passes but if they are in order there's nothing to fear. The passes are for everybody's protection, not only ours. If we find someone without a pass they are likely to be a criminal and therefore it is a help in crime-prevention. It was the same at Langa in the Cape. The mob then was six thousand and when the police tried to break it up stones were thrown; the police commander had no option but to open fire. And then what happened? Rioting in the Townships and thirty thousand of them marched into Cape Town on their way to the Parliament—the seat of Government. Thank goodness the PAC local leader managed to disperse them without any more damage being done, but, at the top, Sobukwe is to blame. He should never have told those people at Sharpeville to march on the police station. All right, if the police officer in charge had not panicked there wouldn't have been a problem. We've faced mobs like this before many times in the past without trouble.

'We know who is behind this civil disobedience. It is the Communists. Where my police force may be ahead of yours, Miss Cresswell, is in intelligence. I don't mean the brainpower of our respective constables. No, I mean that element of Secret Service we have. We have lines into all that is happening in the Communist-led agitation movement, whether it is the ANC or the PAC or whatever set of initials they will come up with next. Let me repeat, we shall win. If only everyone would just do their work and behave we could all live together, even with their ever increasing numbers. They do breed like rabbits, you know. But we will fight fire with fire. We Afrikaners suffered for this country. Look at the history, Miss Cresswell. We trekked into the interior to escape the intolerance of the British at the Cape and we fought the Boer War (as you call it) and the Zulus and others for our Independence, and I for one do not intend to give it up now. Let me tell you, I admire Luthuli. The ANC have been lucky to have him, but if he keeps calling strikes and stay-at-home days that respect will soon go.'

Joe and Jenny had agreed in advance to listen to the Colonel without questioning anything he said. Joe had predicted his tone of self-vindication, and Snyman had not disappointed them. The remainder of his monologue was in similar vein, but they saw no reason to transcribe any more than this. Jenny did not know what had happened at Langa, a black Township outside Cape Town mainly occupied by migrant workers. Joe elucidated. As a result of the police fire, two of the protesters had been killed and forty-nine others injured. What Snyman omitted to say was that the local Pan-Africanist Congress man, a student named Phillip Kgosana, persuaded the crowd to march to the police station in Caledon Square rather than Parliament because he was promised an appointment with the Minister of Justice to enable him to air the grievances of the Township dwellers. When he turned up for the appointment he was simply arrested. Joe explained that the PAC had broken away from the ANC in 1958 and that its President was Robert Sobukwe, a lecturer in African languages at the University of Witwatersrand. After the incidents at Sharpeville and Langa, both the ANC and the PAC were declared illegal organisations and Sobukwe was imprisoned for three years on a charge of incitement.

As Gabriel's father lived next door to Joe and Emily (or, to be more accurate, occupied one of the two servants' quarters there—in bachelor status; spouses and families were generally not welcomed by the employers of house servants), they arranged to meet Gabriel at their house. He was careful in his speech, which was understandable. He clearly could not fully comprehend what these white people were after, but he was surprisingly articulate, particularly on the subject of education, and, after some initial hesitation, generally forthcoming. After some discussion of a general nature about his upbringing, and where Jenny came from, Gabriel said:

'Miss Cresswell, how many years schooling have you had? Before university more than ten, I'm sure. Well, in total, I have had but four and a half years in my lifetime and I think we are about the same age. And for me, no university. Some of the time I don't go school because my father could not pay fees, or for books. Other times school was closed. And even when I was there, teacher not good. I've looked into this. The Government spent twenty times more educating white kids compared with black. There were some reasonably good missionary schools that we could go to but then we had that Bantu Education Act. This was brought in so Government could take over all schools. And do you know why? A definite policy to make sure our schooling was inferior. Deliberate policy. The object of the Bantu Education system was to stifle any ambition we might have and to ensure that only training available for us was to become labourer or house-servant. I carry this with me all time. It tells you all you want to know about education for the Bantu.'

Gabriel took from his pocket a scrap of paper.

'When that monster, Verwoerd, introduced the Act he said:

> Members of Parliament, if the native in South Africa is being taught to expect that he will lead adult life under the policy of equal rights, he is making a big mistake. The native must not be subject to a school system which takes him away from his own people and misleads him by showing him the green pastures of European society in which he is not allowed to graze.

'Not allowed to graze! We are to be a herded like sheep and all we need to be taught is how to chew grass. And of course we are herded. Mr Johnson next door is good employer but my father and his family are kept apart and this Verwoerd wants us all to go back to our homelands. What homeland? My father and both of my grandfathers were born in Port Elizabeth but is that our homeland? No. Except for people allowed to work there, Port Elizabeth is for the whites. Well, he and his parents might have accepted the situation but my generation will not. Did you know—ANC be the oldest political organisation in Africa? Set up in 1912, well before they set up their National Party. Since then ANC have tried to better the lot of the black man by peaceful negotiation, but where has it got us? As I've just said, they don't want us to better ourselves. If I could get some more education and pass an entrance examination for university, what university can I go to? In 1959 the Government introduced a new law called the Extension of University Education Act. Nonsense. Had nothing to do with extending university education. It was brought into law to limit number of universities we can go to. Double-speak. I've read *1984* but if Verwoerd has he wouldn't see the connection. He takes away my identity. He will not call me by my name. To white man I am "boy", even if as old as my father—or "John". They go to their church which supports apartheid and pray, but are they Christians? I'm not stupid. I know that we can never chase the white man into the sea. We have to live with him but it has to be on a fairer basis. How would you like it, Miss Cresswell, if in your country there were separate lavatories, separate buses, separate park benches, separate beaches and so on? We are treated like dirt—or like slaves.'

Gabriel's audience made no response except to thank him for being so frank and open and to say that, like him, they hoped things could be improved. After Gabriel left, Emily joined them and they took her 'evidence'.

'I've read the text of what Colonel Snyman said. I'm not sure how much this helps, Jenny. He is a bigoted man but he's both typical, and a caricature, of the Afrikaner. I come from a different strand, what is now being called the "poor whites". Not that my family were really poor. This expression tends to refer to the poorly educated who, if not employed in a governmental capacity, find it hard to get a job within the capitalist system that is mainly dominated by the English South African. The other poor whites are those who left the farm because of drought, or again because they could not compete with the larger agricultural undertakings run by English capital. These people had to leave the land and found it difficult to eke out an existence in the cities. My family could easily have been placed in this category but my mother and father were more resourceful than many who had to leave the countryside. Dad was a good sportsman and they were both employed by a golf club in Pretoria, Dad as a groundsman and Mummy in the bar. Anyway, they did well enough to get both my sister Jonty and me to university but all of us miss the farm—and I still do. We didn't own it. Dad was the farm manager. It was in the Orange Free State—beautiful country. I must take you, Jenny, and show you one day. When we were young Jonty and I played with the black kids whose parents were farm labourers. We climbed the *kopje* and pretended it was Mount Everest, we swam in the dam and indulged in all the other make-believes children get up to. When we played doctors and nurses it was never questioned that one of the black boys would be the doctor to our nurses. We had lessons with Mother but the next farm to us was a big one with a benevolent Afrikaner owner who ran a little infant school that we went to with the labourers' children. Okay, perhaps not typical and perhaps it will be more relevant to your enquiry, Jenny, if you could interview an Afrikaner intellectual, someone from the university perhaps, instead of Snyman at one end of the scale and me at the other. But, having said that, it was from the ranks of the Afrikaner universities that the whole philosophy of apartheid was born. Cronje, professor of sociology at Pretoria, in particular. Whatever, I do know from my own experiences when on the farm that many farmers—you know, by the way, that one of the meanings for the word "Boer" is "farmer" or "farming folk"—treated their black workers like chattels; not much change from the time of the infamous Freek Bezuidenhout. Joe probably knows about this, but let me tell you the story. It's a good indicator of how stubborn and blind to change Afrikaners have been, and many still are. In April 1813 this man, who lived on the banks of the Baviaans River in the Cape, refused to release a Khoikhoi labourer when his work contract expired. This was illegal under the labour regulations that the British had introduced in 1812, so when the labourer complained to the authorities Bezuidenhout was required to appear in a local court. For a period of two years he stubbornly refused to do this. Eventually, attempts were made to arrest him but he resisted the military detachment that came to do this and, after a battle lasting several hours, he was shot dead by a Coloured sergeant. Nothing much has changed since then but, again, what else can the Afrikaner do?

I think that if there is the remotest possibility of you, Jenny, with a bit of help from my conservative husband and father-in-law, embarking on any form of crusade, all you can hope to achieve is to try and counter the more excessive injustices. None of us is going to be able to make any changes "root and branch" as it were.'

Joe fully agreed with this—and then began to plan for the next interview. It was fortunate that Father Samuel's current parish was in Cape Town as this gave an opportunity for Joe to show his guest parts of South Africa outside Johannesburg. They flew to Port Elizabeth where Joe hired a car. He first took her to Grahamstown, the site of Rhodes University where he had taken his first degree. This town had originally been a military post but then became home to some of the English immigrants who arrived in 1820, an event commemorated by the Settlers Monument, built high on a peak overlooking the town. Except for the shanties scattered around the hillsides the town, set in a valley, was an attractive one with wide, tree-lined streets fronted by well-preserved Victorian and Georgian buildings. After this diversion they drove along the famous Garden Route to Cape Town which provided Jenny with a glimpse of some of the most beautiful countryside in South Africa. When they reached Cape Town, one of the most attractive cities in the world and dominated by Table Mountain, Joe pointed out that this city, the site of the first European settlement in South Africa, had another face. The whole of the Table Mountain area to the west of the railway line to Muizenberg had been zoned for white people only. As a result, attempts were being made to move the largely Coloured population from the crowded Townships of District Six and Kalk Bay where some of the families had ancestors who had lived there for centuries—since the time of the Dutch East India Company. Father Samuel's church was in District Six. When they met him he recalled Father Donovan at once; they had for a short time been together in Sophiatown.

'Have you been told about Sophiatown, Miss Cresswell? Well, it was established close to Johannesburg before the 1913 Land Act. This meant that a small number of the black occupants of the Township owned freeholds. Trevor Huddleston and Desmond Tutu lived there—and a sprinkling of gangsters and shebeen owners. This was a new order of black Africans. They were second and third generation de-tribalised city people. Most of them were working class but there was a small and influential black middle class who deliberately distanced themselves from their rural and tribal antecedents. Some very interesting black writers lived there during the 1950s, what the author Lewis Nkosi called the 'fabulous decade', an African version of the Harlem Renaissance of the 1920s. The playwright Athol Fugard used Sophiatown as the setting for one of his earliest plays—which gives me the opportunity to tell yet another story of how, in some cases, the application of the apartheid law is both degrading and ridiculous at the same time. All the characters in this play, as I recall, are black, except for a white clergyman. It was said that Fugard had based this character on Father Huddleston. You will realise that there is just as much segregation in the theatre as in hospitals and railway trains but as a newcomer to our shores you will find it difficult to believe the extent to which these bigots will go to in the name of apartheid. When this play was presented to black audiences, Fugard himself played the priest. It was then agreed that there would be one performance only at the all-white Brooke Theatre in Johannesburg but this audience could not be allowed to see a mixture of black and white performers on the stage, so Lewis Nkosi stood in for Fugard. The audience needed to suspend its belief to accept a black Father Huddleston! Is that not quite the most ridiculous thing you have ever heard?'

The anecdote about a 'black Father Huddleston' prompted Jenny to tell Father Samuels about a similar example from Nigeria, recounted to her by her brother, where the casting of stage parts had been done in a rather more rational manner. Evidently two amateur theatre groups, one with white members only and the other with black, were engaged in a joint production of Peter Ustinov's *Romanoff and Juliet.* To fit the parts to the colours available, as it were, all the Russians in the play were white actors while the American ambassador and his family were black—perfectly reasonable—and Ustinov's Ruritania was relocated to Africa.

Father Samuels continued.

'Of course, the tensions are different in West Africa—there are no settlers. I'm sure you have found other people to describe the hardships suffered under apartheid and you could well ask me what the Christian Church is doing to counteract this. Father Huddleston gave comfort and strength to many while he was here and I can see Desmond Tutu becoming a principal actor on the anti-apartheid stage, but there is a formidable enemy. What the Church does is to bring ease and some possibility of hope to the large congregations of black and Coloured worshippers. Churches in the Townships are crowded but what we can do in practical terms perhaps remains to be seen. I have heard that, as a result of Sharpeville, the World Council of Churches is going to call a meeting to discuss the racial problems in our country. What we all deplore is that this "formidable enemy" I describe has the backing of their own Church, the Dutch Reformed Church, and for them this morally justifies their actions. They are not only formidable, they are stubborn. You may have heard this story, Mr Marks, but it will be new to you, Miss Cresswell. It is said that an Afrikaner pastor came across a black man on his knees scrubbing the floor of his church, whereupon he stopped to compliment the cleaner on the quality of the work but as he walked away he said to the kneeling man, "Very good, but don't let me catch you praying."

I myself am classified as Coloured. As you can see, my skin is as white as yours but they cannot afford to allow any sheep into their kingdom who are not snowy white—there must be no hint of the black lamb. One of my congregation, Coloured of course, is maid to a blind woman. A white blind woman. Recently, there was some emergency and there was no-one else to accompany this woman to hospital, so the maid went with her, but the white taxi driver refused to carry them because it is not allowed to have a white person and a Coloured person in the same car. Is this a Christian country? Despite the complex classification system there are really only two categories: those who are white like you, Mr Marks—and the rest. You may not have heard of another Coloured clergyman like me, but this one is probably politician first and man of God second. Let me read you something he wrote:

> The term 'Coloured' is not of our own thinking, and if we look at the circumstances of the South African situation then you must ask why. We have no peculiar colour, we have no peculiar language and if other people see these peculiarities they see them not because they see them but because they want other people to see them ... I do not want to be labeled 'Coloured' ... all I want to be known as is South African.

'That was the Reverend Allan Hendrickse. I think he states the case for all of us.'

Joe thanked Father Samuel for his time but he thought the priest would probably agree that his exposition would not have added a great deal to Jenny's quest for enlightenment. He began to wonder how successful this crash course had really been. Many of his own circle, born in South Africa, did not understand, or appreciate, the complexities of their country's political system. This was partly because they chose not to delve too deeply, but also because it was complex. For a stranger to absorb it in a month was probably an impossibility. Nevertheless, Joe had known this would be the case and had only begun this experiment because of the faint chance that the new broom might be able to reach dusty corners the more experienced failed, or refused, to see. Both he and Emily answered Jenny's many questions and used their answers to widen the topic to give her all of the information they had within their experience. In addition to the four interviews, Jenny spent some time with Joe's parents, and obtained a view from the older generation. Both Henry and Joe introduced her to as wide a cross-section of their acquaintances as was possible in the time at her disposal. But Joe was still uneasy. Were they pursuing a lost cause? Even if there was any chance of a future for Jenny in South Africa, was this the right course for her? As usual, her overall response was positive. She told Joe she thought she understood the difficulties involved but was not going to come to any hasty conclusions. On the day before she was due to return home there was a mopping-up meeting with Henry, Joe and Emily at the offices of Marks and Co to try and summarise what, if anything, had been achieved.

Henry began.

'Jenny, it has been lovely having you with us and I admire the motives that prompted you to come in the first place, but nothing has really changed. We are a small specialist firm of lawyers and, even if we were passionate about wanting to provide legal help for the persecuted, we cannot. Our hearts might want us to do something but our minds, at least my mind, says no. I am very conscious that this may seem defeatist or selfish, not wanting to lose what we have, frightened—all may be perfectly fair comments but, having said that, here you are. You appear out of the blue and we are not going to ignore this. What remains to be answered is whether you are a good angel, or one that might become a fallen one. Sorry, I'm being carried away. I'm not normally this verbose, but if there is going to be a next step it's important we understand each other.'

'Henry, I appreciate that and am grateful for all you've done, and for your frankness, but it seems to me that you are nearly as confused about this possible project as I am.'

'I'm not confused,' said Emily. 'Henry and Joe are reluctant to change the way they practise at the moment and we can all understand that, but the incident with Moses the gardener has started something and neither of you can avoid this. You could just forget about it and wish Jenny *bon voyage*, then get back to your boring commercial law, but I can see that some grit has got under both of your fingernails and you're looking for a manicurist. Well—I think Jenny would be a good choice. She's got guts, she's got brains, she knows something about the law, and she's a woman. If there is an impossible job to be done, ask a woman.'

Jenny left the next morning with possibilities and alternatives chasing their tails within the confines of her brain to such an extent that she determined to drown these thoughts by consuming all the alcohol on offer from South African Airways.

She explained to her mother and Edith, as best she could, what the situation was but the picture was just as blurred as it had been when she was with the Markses. The files on her desk showed full evidence of a month's absence and she was able to defer any further debate about South Africa by immersing herself in a difficult Trust problem and what looked like a potentially acrimonious divorce.

About three weeks later, just as she had nearly dealt with her backlog of cases, a letter arrived from Joe:

> I have some shocking news for you. Gabriel is dead. Just after you left, Moses came to see us to say that he had not heard from Gabriel for some time and he was worried—or at least as he put it 'bit concerned'—but he did not seem too agitated as this had happened before. Gabriel had not slept at his grandmother's house for more than a week and she did not know where he was. I tried to be sympathetic but what did he think I could do? We do not run a detective agency and I must tell you that at that moment I was rather sorry that our path and that of Moses had ever crossed. If we had not seen that accident outside the house we might have been able to sympathise with you over Sharpeville and then welcome you to visit and enjoy the good things about South Africa. But now, thanks to Moses, we are all at sixes and sevens.
>
> Of course that's not fair. Our next door neighbour's gardener is not responsible for the sea of uncertainty we are drowning in, it is the system, but I hope you can understand my attitude—which I kept well hidden from Moses. Were we being drawn into even deeper water because of his son? Emily volunteered to phone round the hospitals but as you can imagine this was a thankless task and she came to the conclusion that the identity of their patients was not their concern; they neither knew nor cared what was the name of the man in that bed with two broken legs or contusions to the head.
>
> And then last Thursday we had another visit from Moses, early in the morning before we had both left for the office. A policeman had been to see him to tell him to come to the police station at Alexandria Township to collect the body of his dead son. Robert Johnson had evidently given Moses some money so he could arrange this but he wanted us to know. He said the mother and grandmother would be wild with grief but he showed little emotion; it seemed as though

he was resigned to his son's fate—as if he knew it would end like this. He said no more to us but as he walked down the garden path to go back to his bachelor quarters he presented a pitiable figure. He epitomised the downtrodden, apparently accepting the inevitability of their lot. As you recall, his back is bent from years of manual labour, but on that morning he seemed even more misshapen and pathetic.

As we drove into Johannesburg Emily said she thought Moses had come to give us this news, firstly, because we had been kind to him—and Gabriel—in the recent past but, secondly, he must have thought, either consciously or instinctively, that we would take on the task of finding out what had happened to Gabriel. I could only agree with her. At the office I phoned the police station and spoke to the duty sergeant. His report on this specific, now deceased, prisoner was conveyed to me in a polite and efficient manner as though reading from a prepared script. I can just about remember what he said, word for word:

'Gabriel Ntshona was arrested on 2nd July 1960 and charged under the Suppression of Communism Act 1950. He was violent and it required three of my officers to confine him to the cell. Yesterday evening when we checked on him we found he had hung himself. He had made a noose with strips of his shirt. We cut him down and I called the duty doctor who pronounced him dead at 2137 hours.'

And so have we reached our Rubicon? Do I give some *bonsella* to Moses to help pay for the wake and then forget all about it or do I try and find out why and how Gabriel came to this end? But if I choose to investigate, how do I start? Well, being in this halfway-house-stage—am I awake or asleep—Emily and I both had the same thought at the same time—perhaps that's why we married each other—Colonel Snyman. Moses, inadvertently, led us to him in the first place and so would Snyman now lead us to some more concrete facts than I had been able to obtain from the duty sergeant? Again I decided a letter was the best approach, on Marks and Co's best water-marked vellum paper. My missive was polite, but to the point and as soon as I have a reply I will let you know but thought that whatever you decide to do, you ought to be put in the picture—brought up to date.

All send their love and hope your mind is delivering a more decisive message—either nay or yea—than mine is.

Joe sent Jenny a copy of Snyman's reply as soon as he received it.

I cannot go on answering your letters, I have rather more pressing things to do with my time, but as you have shown some interest in the work we do by bringing the charming Miss Cresswell to meet me, I am sending you this reply. I am also prompted to do this because indirectly you are involved with this case. When we discovered that the gardener you championed was the father of Gabriel Ntshona, this was our first breakthrough in an investigation that has been going on for some time. Through this gardener we were able to discover where the object of our enquiries was hiding and although the end result was not what was intended, as they say in the movies, we got our man.

Gabriel Ntshona was a member of a proscribed organisation, the PAC, and, more importantly, we suspect him of being active with a section of that organisation that has as its objective to perpetrate violence against the State. This man was arrested at 0420 hours on the 2nd of July when he was staying with another of his agitator colleagues whom we have also wanted to question for some time. Ntshona resisted arrest in a most aggressive manner and as a result both handcuffs and leg irons were needed. He was taken to the police station at Alexandria where his ankles and wrists were freed. With hindsight that was a bad move but then there was no indication that this young man would take his own life. I admit that we were also remiss in two other areas. He should have been looked at more often than he was and when the officers involved cut him down they were not as careful as they might have been. He was allowed to fall onto the concrete floor of the cell as a result of which his left arm was broken and the edge of the metal bunk, which he hit during the fall, caused severe bruising to his head causing a wound that resulted in a considerable loss of blood.

When this man was arrested he was in possession of a variety of weapons and, more crucially, instructions on how to manufacture home-made bombs of considerable magnitude. I regret the manner of his death but he was a dangerous individual and who knows what damage he might have caused with a parcel of high explosives.

If it was Moses who moved Joe from an initial position of 'sitting on the fence', it was his son who determined Jenny's next step. As a precaution she had already made enquiries as to the procedure involved in becoming eligible to practise law in South Africa. She learnt that the legal system in the country was a hybrid one, a mix of English common law and civilian Roman-Dutch legal principles. While many legal doctrines and the arrangement of the law in general could be traced to a civilian heritage, court procedure owed much to the common law tradition, with adversarial trial, detailed case reports—which included dissenting judgments—and adherence to precedent. With her existing qualifications, she would need to serve a term of pupilage with Marks and Co but it seemed that in practical terms she would be able to appear in the lower courts under the auspices of that firm. Both her mother and Edith were aware of the anguish of uncertainty that had been hanging over her since her return, and so they were not surprised when the decision was made. It was not a totally unexpected event for Frank Clark either. He told her she was making a serious mistake, but there seemed sufficient affection in the way he expressed this to indicate that if this mad experiment was comparatively short-lived, she would be welcomed back into their midst. She telephoned Joe to ask for his imprimatur, which she got instantly. Then she bought her ticket. Six months later she was in court.

On this, her second visit to Court Three at Rivonia in the affluent Northern suburbs of Johannesburg, she was surprised to find every seat in the small chamber occupied. They were a quiet crowd. Most of them were middle-aged or elderly black women and their subdued conversation echoed around the room like the gentle buzz emitted by a small bee trapped in a jam-jar. Their faces were barely visible, eyes directed towards their feet as, Jenny speculated, was their wont; the black people she had met up to now seemed unable to maintain any eye-to-eye contact with her. As she surveyed the scene more closely the strongest impression of the court congregation was of a sea of brightly coloured head-ties, predominantly blue, interspersed with the shining pates of the handful of elderly men present.

She laid her file on the table she shared with three other counsel, none of whom she had met before. She was there to represent the nanny to the children of one of Joe's closest friends who had been charged with a curfew infringement. When Jenny had entered the court for the first time the previous week the Magistrate had been too busy to hear the case, never mind how trivial it might be, and all involved were asked to 'Come back next week.' The crew-cut young man sitting next to her introduced himself and explained the reason for the crowded court. He was there to defend a well-known local agitator—his words—who was being charged with assaulting a policeman.

No-one would know whether the Magistrate felt he had been a little peremptory in not dealing with the curfew case when first presented, but today he called for Jenny's defendant to be brought in so that this prelude to the main event could be quickly dealt with.

'Is this woman represented?'

'Yes sir. My name is Jenny Cresswell of Marks and Co.'

'Thank you—haven't seen you before. You are welcome. Proceed.'

The prosecution was being handled by the police whose representative outlined the case. The nanny had accommodation at the house of her employer but on the day in question she had gone, with permission, to visit her family because her mother was ill.

'You were apprehended by Police Constable Schwartz at 8.10 p.m. on the night of the 13th of October near to the property of Mr Robin Fellows in Bryanston. Is that correct?'

'Yes sir.'

'Were you aware that in that area a temporary curfew has been imposed and you people are not allowed on the streets between 8.00 p.m. and 6.00 a.m?'

'Yes sir, but . . .'

'All right, that's all. Be quiet.'

The Magistrate inclined his head towards Jenny. He was being gracious towards this good-looking court newcomer, although during the examination on behalf of the police he appeared to have been asleep.

'Are you Rose Nwapa and do you work as a nanny at the home of Mr Fellows?'

'Yes, Madam.'

'Where did you go on that day, the 13th of October?'

'I went to visit my mother but, coming back, bus fail and I had to walk some six miles.'

'You knew of the curfew rules?'

'Yes, Madam, but bus fail and I was few minutes late. Very sorry.'

At this point the Magistrate seemed to be about to resume his slumbers, but quickly raised his shoulders and turned to Rose.

'You need to keep time. You're all the same. We do not work to African time here. I could send you to prison for 30 days but if I do I know your charming counsellor will argue that the infringement is a minor one, only a matter of minutes. Oh, let's get on. Fine ten rand. Take her away.'

He smiled at Jenny as she left the court to arrange to pay the fine, but did not notice as she returned and sat at the rear, partially obscured by a pillar, to observe the other action yet to be played out.

By the time she was back in the court, the defendant was already in the dock. He was a small man, rendered even more insignificant by the size of the panelled enclosure where he stood flanked by two policemen, each a foot and a half taller than the accused. He looked an incongruous visitor to these august premises in which the immaculately dressed Magistrate gazed out from his high seat of authority across the handsome courtroom, its walls lined in highly polished oak, high-level windows letting in rays of bright sunlight. The light of justice, Jenny pondered. In further contrast to the smart suit of the Magistrate and the highly creased uniforms of the police guards, John Sobo was wearing a shirt of indiscriminate colour, the collar of which was so torn as to be nearly detached from the garment. His other apparel was hidden by the dock wall but what was clearly visible was a shaven head and face that, in the bright light of the room, appeared to have a chalky hue. One eye was partially closed. The case was opened by the public prosecutor.

'This man, John Sobo, is charged in that on the 29th of

September he was found in the district of Morningside to be without his identity book. Furthermore, when taken into custody he resisted arrest and assaulted a police constable and, Your Honour, he pleads "Not guilty".'

At this the buzz Jenny had heard earlier rose in pitch and one or two of the people in the court exclaimed, but not too loudly, using phrases in Xhosa that she did not understand. The prosecutor continued.

'Sobo has been arrested before. He is well-known to the authorities as a Communist agitator and it is our contention that he flagrantly refuses to obey the law and carry his pass so as to make some sort of futile statement.'

The Magistrate looked across at the table used by defending attorneys, whereupon the lawyer with the crew-cut rose languidly to his feet.

'Why did you not have your pass?'

'I forgot, Sir.'

'Were you abusive to the police?'

'No, Sir.'

'Did they treat you harshly?'

'They beat me.'

At this the defence attorney sat down and the Magistrate intervened.

'Well, what do you have to say for yourself?'

John Sobo did not respond immediately. Then he cleared his throat and tried to stand more erect.

'Sir, I am a law-abiding South African and recognise the need to have courts of justice like yours to administer the law.'

The Magistrate seemed surprised at this articulate opening sentence.

'But I do not recognise the law that brings me here.'

There was a quiet, but obviously positive response from the public at this.

'Nor do I accept that your justice is permitted to use excessive force during arrest. I was beaten around the head on the street where I was apprehended so fiercely that the policeman responsible needed to call for a vehicle to carry me to the police station. I was unable to stand. At the station I was stripped and beaten all over my body before they locked me away.'

At this the prosecutor to rose swiftly from his seat.

'It is policy, as Your Honour will know, always to use police vehicles to carry those arrested to the cells, particularly dangerous men like this kaffir. As to the beatings, does he have any evidence? Doctor's report?'

The Magistrate looked towards the defending attorney, who shook his head. Turning back, he told the defendant he would be permitted to make one further address to the court but he should be warned not to tax the court's good nature by making any more political speeches. The accused looked at the Magistrate—then at his supporters in the court—and continued in a strong clear voice

'The bruises on my body are no longer prominent, and in any case it is well-known that the police will produce evidence in these cases that injuries such as mine are always self-inflicted. We are all falling down stairs frequently, or slipping in the shower. And as all of you can see from my left eye, I walked into a lamp-post of course.'

The Magistrate raised his hand but before he could speak the man in the dock continued more fervently.

'And I am not a Communist. I am a black South African who is denied basic human rights because of this white Government. Morningside is in South Africa. I am a South African. Why can I not walk its streets like you can?' inclining his head towards the Magistrate. 'We do not ask for more—just *equal*—rights. Amandla.'

By this time the watchers in the court were on their feet shaking their arms above their heads as they echoed the man in the dock. The police at the back of the room moved into the body of the court, pushing people down into their seats with what seemed to Jenny to be unnecessary force. The Magistrate called for silence. John Sobo's eyes, at least the one clearly visible, sparkled but he said nothing more. The Magistrate did, however.

'Guilty as charged. Two years' hard labour and ten lashes. Take him out of my sight.'

Outside the court Jenny asked one of the women if any members of John Sobo's family were present. She was directed to one of their number, his wife, who freely responded to her sympathetic enquiries.

'My husband,' said the wife, 'was a skilled bricklayer who worked for a local building contractor.'

Jenny had already formed the opinion that this man was intelligent which prompted her to enquire of Mrs Sobo why he deliberately opposed the law.

'I don't know, Ma. He does not seem to be able to help himself. He is a good father and husband. We have five children all under ten years, but he has been stopped by police so often he finally break. Last time he was in prison six months. His brother look after us. But now two years. I must go back home to King Williamstown and wait for him. But what hope? He will only do it again.'

Until then she had maintained a stoic expression but Jenny's interest began to bring tears to her eyes, and before she had finished her cheeks were glistening with them. Unsure how to react to this, Jenny pressed into the woman's hand all of the rand she had in her purse and her business card. The recipient was loth to accept this gift, but Jenny insisted and went back to the office with a frown on her face.

'This isn't right,' she muttered under her breath.

She was already familiar with many of the myriad articles of legislation that upheld the apartheid edifice and, at second hand, she had seen them at work in the case of Gabriel Ntshona and his father, but this was the first time she had come across the policy in practice. Was she going to be able to provide effective help to people like the Sobos other than by handing out trivial amounts of cash? The apartheid system seemed impregnable. She gritted her teeth and said out loud, 'Bugger it! I'm no quitter. What I can do may be insignificant in the overall scheme of things but I am going to make as big a stir as I can. That poor woman. One of thousands. Something must be done.'

Chapter Four

Charles

The temperature in the waiting room at the Garrison hospital was well over 90° but Charles felt chilled to the bone. What was taking so long?

Mary had been delighted about the baby. They had been married for three years and she was beginning to fret but as soon as Dr Kowala confirmed she was pregnant she was 'joy unconfined'—but efficient with it. She was sensible, gave up riding by month five, and made careful arrangements for the delivery. The midwife was a regular visitor and they were able to indulge in the luxury of having her live in the bungalow with them for two weeks before the due date. This suited Charles. As Mary had given up alcohol for the time being, he quite enjoyed sharing his evening *burra-peg* with Mrs Rawlinson, who was fond of her whisky—'In moderation, my dear.' He had known her husband, a Quartermaster Sergeant-Major in his old regiment, who had died the year before from fever. However, these careful and convenient arrangements came to nought when, at Mrs Rawlinson's suggestion, Dr Kowala was consulted. No cause for alarm, he said, but I think it best she goes to the hospital. As part of the planning, Charles had been able to persuade the Colonel that in an emergency they could use the facilities of the Garrison hospital, with Dr Kowala in attendance.

Charles had accepted the assurance that this change of plan was simply to be safe rather than sorry but he did think, selfishly, that it was a pity he could not spend the waiting time ensconced in his favourite armchair with his favourite pipe. Instead, he was perched nervously on a hard wooden bench in such an antiseptic-looking room that its very appearance signified a prohibition of any indulgence in the use of tobacco. He had been left for two-and-a-half hours already and his placid demeanour was beginning to crumble. His mind wandered . . .

Why are even the walls of this dreadful place made to resemble the rest of the hospital? Covered from floor to ceiling in shiny, six inch by six inch, white tiles; reminds me of the lavatory at the Café Royal, or was it the Savoy?

Floors immaculately clean—no dust in any corner. There are no doubt plenty of squaddies on jankers to improve the normal standard of the Indian cleaning wallah. Memories of days in basic training working on the toecap of his boots—spit and polish. They shone like black silver. You could see your face in them.

What on earth am I raving about? Black silver! No such thing. Why obsessed with reminiscences of cleaning? I'm about to become a father. Shouldn't be musing on such matters—should be dreaming about when I will be buying my son, or daughter, a first pony.

After the wedding—the last weekend in London staying at the Savoy and dining at the Café Royal. The honeymoon on the voyage out. Posh. Port out, starboard home. But surely it depends on where is home. Spent nearly all of my adult life in India. This is home so I'm different—starboard from Southampton. It is not home to members of the Indian Civil Service who spend their working lives in this country but then retire to Bournemouth or Broadstairs. True of the Military as well, although soldiers can be posted away at any time. But, for people in trade like David, and now me, we are in India for the long-term. His father has already purchased the plot in a Calcutta cemetery where he wishes to be buried.

Leaving the Army was difficult and still have regrets but love of India is undiminished. Qualms about giving up the commission are offset, 'in spades', by the happiness Mary has brought to life, made even the sweeter because she also loves the country.

She had been keen to learn as much as possible about her new home. Wondering what working for the Blunts would be like but I can't avoid revisiting the effects of the Amritsar massacre on the direction my life has taken. On this subject, am I being obsessional? Yes. Am I really 'the only one in step'? The Army Council's decision to retire Dyer on half pay for committing an error of judgment was announced to the House of Commons by Churchill. Far from popular in England. In the vote, 129 Conservative MPs entered the lobbies against the Government but the vote in the Lords was in favour of Dyer. Suppose the all-powerful influence of the Raj is just as strong while sitting on the Woolsack as it is in Delhi, or Amritsar, but I cannot erase the memory of those Indian deaths—unnecessary deaths. Understand Dyer has arterial sclerosis and this might have affected his judgment. What will be the next excuse?

Commerce is the best place for me. Beyond the pale for members of the ICS and the Military, but I'm happy. I don't care if they look down their noses at this 'box wallah'. Naturally Mary finds these ramifications difficult to absorb—she has not been brought up to understand the extreme, even laughingly ridiculous, class stratification of the British in India. She could hardly believe the story, said to be accurate, or at least typical, of a Governor's wife who had retired after a splendid dinner party with the ladies, leaving the gentleman to their port and cigars, only to be deeply affronted when she found that someone else had used the bathroom before her. I painted a picture for Mary of a splendidly dressed matron, bedecked in tiara and pearls, rapping her painted fingernails on the bathroom door and screaming, but in a genteel manner, 'I'm the senior lady—I should go first.' You see, Mary, there are priorities for peeing—another of the mysteries of the Orient.

I told her another story. A Governor's daughter travelling on board ship, first class of course, liked the look of a handsome second-class steward. They danced together all night and when she met him next morning—half an hour after they had parted—she ignored him, saying that, in her circle, sleeping with someone did not constitute a formal introduction. Mary did not know whether to laugh or to spit.

He brought his mind back to the present as he paced the room. Avoiding the heavy furniture, it measured seven-and-a-half paces by five. The furniture was typically Indian basic. He thought of the times he had been allocated quarters with what were referred to as 'hard furnishings'; the basic bed, table and chairs, but no linen, curtains or carpets. The furniture in the waiting room was of slightly better quality than usually found in an officer's bungalow. Here it was constructed of solid wooden sections, highly polished by both elbow grease and the clothed backsides of innumerable visitors—including expectant fathers he thought. The main bench in the room looked as though it had been carved from a solid piece of wood, like a dugout canoe.

What is happening?

It was clear that Doctor Kowala wanted Charles to understand fully the cause of Mary's death, and that of their son.

'Mr Cresswell, I am so sorry. There is no way that we could have foreseen this. I regret to tell you that Mary died because of what we call placental abruption. Normally the placenta separates from the uterus and is delivered right after the birth but in Mary's case the placenta tore before the baby could be born and this was the cause of her death. It also meant that the male child she was carrying could not be delivered alive. I suggested that she came to hospital when I saw that there was some vaginal bleeding but not for a moment did I think we would be unable to deal with this.'

Charles was trying to understand what Doctor Kowala was saying. Did these details really matter? Mary was dead. There was no child. Nothing he had experienced in the trenches was like this. Herbert Spencer and he had been like brothers but Mary was a part of his body and it was as if the doctor had just amputated his legs and his arms. He had lost his heart, his mind, his soul. He sat down on the dugout canoe and wept.

Charles had kept an eclectic, but often detailed, journal from the time he was involved in the third Battle of Ypres until he left the army. Thereafter, this had become less discursive—more a litany of business matters. One of the reasons why he had abandoned his more comprehensive jottings was because Mary, without prompting, had taken on the role of recording their life together and, as he often said, she had a delightful way with words and he was just a 'rough old soldier'. To justify this view he often brought up the subject of their relative merits as versifiers. For the rest of his life he would, on occasions, read from the four volumes she had left, one for each year of their married life. Volume Four was incomplete. In the weeks immediately after her death he found solace in reading, often through his tears, some of her descriptions of their life together.

25 March 1922

I had not really thought about it before, but as we moved into the cabin that was to be our home for the next three weeks, I realised that Charlie and I were virtual strangers. What have I done! Neither of us has any clear memories of the times we met as children and I think I only really registered his existence when he came on leave in 1918 and called on Mummy and Daddy to offer condolences over Jimmy. He was so sweet about that, and it helped all of us to accept the loss. We spent more time together during his next leave and we have just had two wonderful days in London after the wedding, but how much time does this add up to in total? I was really nervous—apprehensive—but Charlie has been very kind and gentle and it did not take me too long to realise that for people who are deeply in love, a day can be like a year in any other relationship. And I do love him so!

We are different. He is quiet and even-tempered while I tend to be excitable and talk too much, but he says he likes to hear the sound of my voice. I hope he will think the same when I'm old and grey! I think he has been in men's company too long, although he has tried to explain to me that in some ways this has not been a trial because he has obtained such great comfort from the friendships made in the army. Although I cannot fully understand, it seems that a special relationship blossoms when conditions are at their worst. The more shells are shot at you, the closer you feel towards the man standing in the trench next to you. I didn't feel like that at school. If Mrs Briggs shouted at Rebecca, it did not make our friendship stronger. If anything, I was glad it was not me being shouted at, but this is a foolish comparison. I can't imagine what life in the trenches was like and Mrs Briggs was hardly Kaiser Bill. I suppose Jimmy must have felt the same.

Charlie has made the voyage so pleasant and I'm sure all the other ladies on board are jealous of my handsome husband. When they try and flirt with him he doesn't seem to notice. He's not, as they say, a ladies' man. Not a masher like that Hubert Edith sent packing.

Charlie doesn't talk a lot about the war. He says he is lucky to have come out of it without wounds, but he can't help bringing up Amritsar from time to time. That awful thing has really affected him. I can understand how the horror of it is repugnant to everyone, but for Charlie, who was on the spot, it seems to go deeper than that. So deep that he has given up what he refers to as his first love, the army—although where does that leave me?

I shall have to listen more carefully. I want to share every thought, every fear, and every doubt with him. Must try and keep quiet more often.

10 April 1922

When we arrived at Bombay I could see the site where Charlie said they are going to build a massive arch that would rival the Arc d' Triomphe in Paris. There isn't much to see at the moment, only the foundations. It is being built to commemorate the visit of George V in 1911. In India I understand that the monarch is always referred to as 'King Emperor'. Sounds like a species of butterfly to me but I had better not say that out loud. This arch is evidently going to be called the Gateway to India. I suppose that is appropriate as the port of Bombay is where most newcomers catch their first sight of the country. If there is not much to see of the new arch, the Taj Mahal Palace behind is very much in evidence. I think it is over-ornate but I know I must suspend judgments like this until I know the country better.

I don't suppose our bungalow will be on the same scale. Charlie describes it as basic, but in a pleasant area. He tells me he is sure it will be greatly improved as a result of my 'woman's touch'. I hope he will not be disappointed. Mummy was very much in charge of applying the 'woman's touch' at home, so where does Charlie think I am going to find this item of female mystery?

Charlie says that David Blunt, his new employer, will surely meet us at the quay. I do hope he approves of me.

13 June 1922

It has not taken long for me to realise that I love India nearly as much as I love Charlie. How convenient. He is in love with both, so it would have been a disaster if I had only one love on my side.

20 June 1922

I have realised that, with Charlie so busy, I need to find something to do. One cannot live on coffee parties and ladies' bridge luncheons alone. Daddy's patient who had served in the ICS was able to give me a letter of introduction to Dr Rasjani at the main civilian hospital in Bombay. I went to see him this morning by appointment and found him most charming. I told him that I had grown up with the smell of ether and the sight of blood and, accordingly, could he find me some voluntary work to do in the hospital. I told him I had no intention of becoming a lady of the Raj. He was most courteous and understanding and has promised to see what can be done.

23 July 1922

It has been settled. I shall work at the hospital every morning in the Almoner's department and it seems as though my special duty will be to try and give comfort to visitors, particularly parents, who come to enquire about relatives who are our patients.

3 August 1922

Sami was sick yesterday so I returned Charlie's shirts to his chest of drawers and found, under some old ones he never wears, but won't throw away, a velvety blue case with a medal inside. It was a cross with a purple and white ribbon attached. When I asked him about this he was quite sharp with me. He got it evidently when in France—or was it Belgium? I told him if I'd got a medal for being brave I wouldn't hide it away. He said he did not want to be reminded—too many of his friends died. I suppose he can do what he wants but I think he is a bit mixed up over the war and the army. On the one hand he talks about bonds of friendship and on the other he wants to sweep it all under the carpet. I shall dub him 'Complex Charlie'.

21 August 1922

After some tuition, I last week had the difficult task of explaining to an Anglo-Indian couple what was entailed in the brain operation that was about to be undertaken by Mr Lalkala on their five-year-old daughter. The father works for the railway but had taken leave so that he could visit his child with his wife and that is when they were passed on to me. It was thought that my simple explanation would be less alarming for them than that of the surgeon. I hope I succeeded.

15 November 1922

We had our most serious quarrel last night. Charlie came home tired, some problem with Raleigh bicycles. A consignment of fifty had arrived with only forty-three sets of handlebars. He picked at his dinner but drank more port to make up. About midnight he woke with a start to say he had been bitten by a mosquito and it was my fault because I had not tucked in the mosquito net properly. I said it was probably more his fault, too drunk, and that I did not want to hear the word 'bicycle' uttered again in this house for at least a month. If that's your attitude, he said, I'll sleep in the guest-room, which he did. In the morning he was very contrite, even though badly bitten because the guest-room mosquito net is full of holes.

2 January 1923

The Times of India must have thought they needed to add a little culture so there is to be a poetry competition. I decided to enter. Of late I have been spending one morning every week in a clinic for the disabled. They remain so cheerful but I often think how dreadful it would be if confined to a wheelchair, so I wrote this and sent it in.

The Chariot of the Sick

The large wheels axled at the back
pursue the two small tyres that track
the route this sulky ambulates,
odious chariot that I hate.

Confined restricted and prescribed
my perambulator prison is allied
to comfort—oh, but not for us.
I'd change this chariot for a bus.

With Burns: 'A chair's a chair for a' that.'
But not for the ill who have sat
too long on agony's dire throne,
loathsome chariot of the all-alone.

Profuse with frustration this rickshaw
tries the patient's patience even more.
Joint passenger with deep despair
of this sad monster, the wheelchair.

I didn't win a prize. Too morbid, Charlie said. I suppose he is right, but I do feel sorry for them.

3 March 1923

Mr Lalkala, the brain surgeon at the hospital, is getting married and Charlie and I have been invited to the wedding. Mr Lalkala and his wife-to-be are Parsi and Bombay is one of the few places where there is still a substantial community of them. I have done some research. They practise a religion called Zoroastrian—I hope I've spelt it correctly—and they originate from Persia. They are a rare breed—I believe that in the whole world there are only about 100,000 of them and most of these live in Bombay. They hardly ever marry outside the faith. They have this extraordinary method of burial. No, I surely cannot use the word 'burial'. Parsi corpses are taken to a high place in Bombay known as the 'Towers of Silence' and the bodies left there to be eaten by the vultures. Ugh! But then, as Daddy used to say, 'there's no accounting for taste', or in this case, perhaps that is a totally inappropriate saying. I am told that the reason for this gruesome practice is because earth, fire and water are all considered to be sacred elements which should not be defiled by the dead and so burial and cremation have always been prohibited in Parsi culture. Makes sense I suppose.

10 March 1923

I think David was rather jealous when we told him that we were going to a Parsi wedding. He greatly admires them as very able and honest business or professional people and I think he has a number of Parsi friends, but he has never been to one of their weddings. He told me last night that he was sure it would be a memorable occasion. It was. The ceremony took place in the open air and there must have been over five hundred people there. We all stood around a highly decorated dais where there were two ornate chairs which the bride and groom occupied during the ceremony. They were both brilliantly dressed in Parsi national costume which I will not try to describe but I would like to see Charlie wearing the same sort of hat that Mr Lalkala had on. It was beautiful. We did not of course understand what was being said. The proceedings were conducted by several priests, also clad in the most interesting of garments, but there was an exchange of rings at which point Charlie squeezed my hand quite hard. After the ceremony the guests were seated at lines of trestle tables. I could not understand why chairs were set only along one side of these tables but when the meal came to be served I understood. We sat on one side as an army of bearers came down the other to dish up the food at great speed. It was delicious, but very spicy. Interestingly there were no plates. Each guest had a series of banana leaves upon which the food was placed and we ate it with our fingers. I hate to think what Mummy would have said. Charlie whispered some comment about hygiene but I kicked him under the table and told him not to be so straight-laced and British. As far as I could see the number of wholly white faces amongst the guests was probably less than two dozen, so we felt quite privileged. Neither Charlie nor I had met any of them before but we did meet the bride's mother and father. He is evidently a prominent lawyer, and they were so charming. I do hope that we get to meet them again.

13 May 1923

It was Charlie's birthday yesterday. A quarter of a century. What a lot he has done in that time. I told him I had arranged a surprise—we were to dine at a restaurant he had not been to before—very secret. I arranged a tonga to drive there and he must be blindfolded. We set off and drove around aimlessly for fifteen minutes before returning to the bungalow where Sami, who thought it was a wonderful jape, had set up a table in the garden, now lit up by lots of candles and prepared something special. Unfortunately, as we reached the front gate Bumble barked and I'm sure Charlie recognised it. However, when the head-tie was removed he expressed great delight and surprise and told me I was a little devil—but a lovely one. We had a wonderful evening but the tonga driver thought we were mad.

12 August 1923.

My dear husband tells me that they have just completed their 'year-end accounts', whatever they are, and as a result he is due for a nice bonus. And so I am directed to go to the bazaar and purchase the most expensive silk for new frocks and that I should also order new curtains and cushion covers. It must have been a good bonus. Charlie is not usually this expansive but, seriously, I am so pleased for him. I know he had very serious doubts about his ability to become a successful 'box wallah' (not that this is an expression he ever uses with its connotation of a door-to-door salesman), but the other day when we were playing tennis, Elizabeth Blunt mentioned how pleased her husband was with the way Charlie has adapted. Evidently David had thought this ex-soldier would be valuable in the fields of staff training, recruitment and morale and this has proved to be the case. While David and his father decide on the buying and selling, Charlie is developing the next level of Indian management. David and I get on very well. He is always ribbing me but I think I give as good as I get, at least that is what Charlie tells me. On the question of buying and selling, David told me an apocryphal story the other day that I thought worth committing to my diary. He applied it to his father. Blunt senior had bought a consignment of herrings. After delivery he rang his friend who had sold him the fish and complained that the herrings were bad and inedible. His friend replied that he must understand that these herrings were not for eating, but only for buying and selling. I repeated this to Charlie but he did not think it was very funny, which made me wonder whether it is.

12 October 1923

Charlie has told me lots about what he calls his 'Maharaja', and I was over the moon when His Highness invited us to visit him and stay at the guest bungalow. Evidently some of the Princely Rulers are very much more powerful than others. According to Charlie, the Nizam of Hyderabad has more income than many European countries but his Maharaja rules over one of the smallest of the kingdoms. I'm told that when we meet, don't be surprised if he talks about how poor he is. He will also complain, Charlie predicts, about the Political Agent imposed upon him but in reality they actually get on very well. This proved to be the case.

When we arrived at the guest bungalow we found an invitation to dine with the Maharaja that evening at the Palace. I was very excited, but when I began to worry Charlie with questions about whether my best frock would do, he responded by telling me not to expect too much. It might be called the Palace and it is quite impressive from the outside he said, but do check that your knife and fork are clean before you use them. I rather snapped back at Charlie and told him he was an unromantic bloodless Englishman—had he never read *The Arabian Nights*? We were to dine with a prince in his palace and I for one intended to be captivated.

Charlie was partially right but I still thought it was enchanting. I sat at table between the Maharaja and his Prime Minister and both seemed to be vying with each other to see who could charm me the most, but I was able to dissuade his Highness from passing choice morsels of food from his plate to mine. The other guests were the political agent, Cecil Wright and his wife Edna. Very prim and proper I thought but Charlie says that Wright is good for the Maharaja and keeps him on the straight and narrow. Advises him on finance and keeps him from taking another wife. He has three at present (the Maharaja that is, not Cecil Wright), so I also would have thought that was enough. We dined in a room at the Palace that had silken drapes hanging from the ceiling to give the impression of a tent that would not have shamed the grandest of Bedouin Sheiks. To be fair to Charlie, I could see that the drapes were rather dusty but I thought the effect was wonderful. There seemed to be about ten servants to every guest and they appeared out of the shadows at regular intervals to fill glasses and remove plates. It was rather eerie and yet very romantic, but Charlie complained that however nice candlelight might be he liked to see what he was eating.

The next day the men went on a pig-sticking expedition and so I was left with Edna Wright. She was very kind but my day with her was not the most exciting I have ever had.

13 March 1924.

Charlie came home today with some wonderful news. We are to go on leave and the passage has already been booked. We shall be staying with Edith and Tony, they have such a big house, but Mummy and Daddy are nearby and we are going to have a wonderful time. We have been here for just over two years and I think Charlie deserves a break. He works very hard and even the un-businesslike me can see that he has made a success of his new career.

10 May 1924

We could not have picked a better time for leave in England. The British Empire Exhibition was on at Wembley and we went. Charlie looked very smart in his new blue suit—made to measure at Burton's—and my outfit was also blue but not made by Mr Montague. I said to Charlie that we were a credit to the Exhibition and that we had more to do with Empire than anybody else there. He agreed on that point and said that the other ten thousand people present on the day we went—or however many there were—knew little about the Empire and cared less. Seemed to him they were more interested in the fun fair, that was enormous—much bigger than the Goose Fair at Nottingham that I went to once or twice when a young girl. Privately I think I agree with the mass and thought the Amusement Park was the best thing there but Charlie, being Charlie, was keen to look at the various pavilions, the Palace of Engineering and the reconstruction of the tomb of Tutankhamen. He, more than most, could see that the whole affair was a massive advertising exercise to justify the existence—and continuation—of the Empire, but he rather wondered if it would include India for much longer.

13 August 1924

I am not usually involved with the Casualty Department but one of the surgery patients I had been counselling was moved into that department because of a shortage of beds. While there yesterday a young Hindu woman was admitted. She looked about fourteen. She had a shaven head, was wearing a red sari and was very emaciated. She had tried to commit suicide by slashing her wrists, but the knife used was obviously not very sharp. She was one of the 'Widows of India'. Within the Hindu, widows, if they are not burnt with their husbands, are not allowed to re-marry, but of course the men can. *Sati* has been banned for ages but it still happens. Perhaps you can understand why they'd choose that when they realise what the rest of their life is going to be like. Because there are so many child-brides in India, some of these widows are still very young. They are badly treated and kept isolated. They have no status whatsoever. It is so hateful. If there is such a thing as reincarnation, I pray I do not come back as an Indian woman. So many of them are blighted from birth. The cows are treated better.

12 November 1924

Charlie is not by nature political. His sister is. She never had any ambitions like me to defy convention and enter one of the professions, she has always enjoyed being a county lady—particularly since marrying Tony, and I think if he does not finish up as the Honourable Member for Leicester East, she could well be joining Lady Astor and Ellen Wilkinson. Charlie describes this as more of my nonsense but then he has a different outlook from Edith, a totally different temperament. Notwithstanding, Amritsar has, I think reluctantly, drawn him into a concern for the politics of India. He seems mesmerised by this Mr Gandhi. As far as I can see politics in India are either rather simple, the Indians want

Independence, or very complicated because of those diehards in London who say 'never'. Made all the more difficult on the home front owing to the position of the Princely States but, more crucially, by the disagreements between Hindu and Muslim. Britain has brought in some changes with the Montague—Chelmsford reforms whereby certain things are to be controlled by Indians—like agriculture, health and education—but there is still some sort of veto in the hands of the Governor or the Viceroy. These proposals are known as a 'Dyarchy'. Gandhi evidently said that this was a minimum compensation for Amritsar and others said it wasn't a Dyarchy at all but a Dyer-archy! Charlie does not see any humour in this but he and David do worry about the future. They seem to be kept up-to-date on the Indian political front because the father of Rami, their most senior manager, is well up in the Congress party.

At least Ghandi is concerned about the plight of Indian women.

1 February 1925

Dr Kowala has just, after my dear Charlie, become the man who has made me the happiest woman in the world. I am going to have a baby.

After Mary's death, David Blunt suggested that Charles should take some leave and visit his, and Mary's, family in England but this kindly gesture was, with thanks, firmly rejected. He could not bear the thought of being away from the surroundings where he and Mary had spent their last blissfully happy years. He did not want to hide away or forget. For some time he insisted that Sami should lay a place at the dining table for her. He was not sad or forlorn as he supped his mulligatawny soup opposite an empty chair; he wanted to wallow in her absence—celebrate the memories. He did not want to erase her from his life but however determined he was he could not avoid waking at three o'clock in the morning crying into his pillow as he realised no-one was by his side. As an ex-soldier he was no stranger to death, and in India life for many was often short and brutal. Roadside corpses were not unusual—death from accident or malnutrition—and in many parts of the country infant mortality was alarmingly high. Life was cheap in India, but none of this could reconcile him to the loss of Mary, a loss that had arisen out of a moment that should have been one of profound joy and not of desperate sorrow. He could not grieve for his dead son. He needed someone to blame. But his better nature surfaced as he recalled the delight on Mary's face when she told him she was pregnant. No, he would not blame God and the medics; instead, he would thank God for the years they had together.

The counter to David's offer of leave was purposely to involve himself more and more in the business and this resulted in another offer from the Blunts: would he like to join the partnership and pay for his shares out of future profits?

In this new role his area of responsibility was widened and he became involved in the opening of new branches of the firm in Lahore and Madras, but he also found another activity to fill his desolate waking hours—cricket. When he joined the Blunts in 1922 he quickly found himself Captain, Secretary and Selector for the firm's team, which played in a local league at a fairly minor level. Charles enjoyed his role and was pleased that Mary was prepared to watch and admire while trying to understand the mysteries of the 'googly'. However, she was mildly irritated when the players assumed that their wives should be involved in supervising the tea-making, a duty normally allocated to the ladies at village cricket matches in England. In India it was performed by uniformed servants. Mary would say, 'I notice the twelfth man makes no effort to ensure there are enough cups and saucers, so why should we?' At this point Charles would offer to get her a refill. However, now he had more time available he found himself also playing for a mixed Indian and European team at a somewhat higher level. The game was important to him and he found the team spirit engendered by cricket began to register with him in the same way as his 'trench fever', the words he used privately to signify the sense of comradeship he had enjoyed as a soldier. His Maharaja was not a fan, preferring pig-sticking, but he did introduce Charles to another Princely Head of State, allegedly some distant cousin, who had joined the ranks of the 'flannelled fools'. This was the Maharaja of Patiala who, at the time, was playing for Northern India. On occasions, mostly during friendly or touring games, Charles found himself bowling to the Maharaja who was a good middle order batsman. In 1911, when the Maharaja was still only twenty, he toured England with the Indian team and when the MCC came to India in 1926 he was co-opted to play for the visitors. Charles thought this was a splendid gesture and made a particular effort to attend on all three days of the game, played in December against the Bombay Presidency. The MCC won by an innings and 117 runs. They had fielded a formidable line-up which included Andrew Sandham, R.E.S. Wyatt, Maurice Tate, and A.E.R. Gilligan. The home side comprised a mixed bunch of Indians, some of whom played for their country, and English cricketers like Bernard Howlett, who was in the army, and Cambridge blue, Jack Meyer. The Indians were passionate about cricket and the enthusiasm Charles found in the firm's team, and with his other club, gave him enormous satisfaction. Mary was irreplaceable but on occasions her grace and beauty were nearly matched by the perfect off-break that took middle stump around the batsmen's legs.

He did not refuse invitations to social gatherings. The Lalkalas were generous with their hospitality and he was in some demand as the extra man at dinner parties, both within the commercial world and the military. A certain amount of match-making took place but Charles attended these social outings not to find a replacement for Mary but because he knew she would not want him to become a recluse. He allowed brief liaisons to develop with two of the ladies put in his way. The first was the widow of an army officer who had been killed in an isolated incident of violence that had occurred in the Punjab at the time of the unsatisfactory Simon Commission of 1928. The other was the sister of a tea planter. It appeared that she was on an extended visit to India with the sole purpose of finding a husband, but Charles was not about to satisfy her quest. Mary was still with him. Once or twice he thought he heard her words of encouragement about one potential swain or another, but on those occasions he was not prepared to comply with her wishes. While alive, he thought, he would have granted her anything she asked, but now, no-one was going to take her place. He often had conversations on this subject with her—in his subconscious—but now and then he thought he could see her pursing her lips and telling him to stop being a romantic fool. 'You were never over-sentimental in the past, so why take it up now?' He tended to react sharply to these criticisms and tell her his mind was made up—he would remain unwed—no further discussion required . . . until he met Adele.

The Social at the Railway Institute was a monthly event and attracted a motley crowd. It was there that Adele Emerson's older brother introduced her to Charles. He politely said he was pleased to meet her and offered the information that he had not been to one of these functions before.

'I was slightly surprised to see how attractive the Institute is inside—rather nondescript from the front but it would not, in fact, shame the Bombay Gymkhana.'

Adele thought this rather condescending and decided the sooner she could lose this man the better.

'My father was a member of the Gymkhana. I used to go to their dances quite frequently when I was younger, but I think this place is better, more human.'

'You may be right. Perhaps the Gymkhana smacks too much of the Raj. Are you connected to the railway?'

'Yes, my father is the Chief Engineer.'

'Would you like to dance?'

'No thanks. Oh, there's Ali.'

She turned away. Charles could not but admire her confident posture as she walked across the room and began to talk and laugh with a tall Indian man who appeared, from where Charles was standing, to have made at least one visit in the recent past to Savile Row.

As he left the main function room for the men-only bar, he muttered under his breath, 'Stuck up hussy!'—but then wondered if he really meant that. She was an attractive woman with all the best of the special features found in the Anglo-Indian. She was as tall as he but, he guessed, at least ten years younger. She was not pretty in a conventional way but her high cheekbones and sleek black hair seemed to Charles to project an air of mystery. He ordered a whisky and speculated about her parentage. Her father was most likely British and her mother Indian, or part Indian, but further thoughts about the lady deserted him as he moved across the bar to join Robert Sherwood and two others, whose names he couldn't recall.

'What you doing here, Bob? Are you a member?'

'Yes, old chap, well-kept secret. The bar prices here are the lowest in Bombay—subsidised by our benevolent friend, the Indian Railways.'

'You always were a cheap-skate, Sherwood, but I see you need a refill.'

As he called to the barman the image of the creature who had just snubbed him came back into his mind and prompted him to ask his friend to put him up for membership.

Charles realised that Ali, he of the Savile Row suits whom Adele seemed to prefer, was someone he had met before. After some mind-searching he recalled that, when last encountered, Ali was not wearing a natty suit but cricket whites. It had been during a league match, a few months ago, when this same Ali had treated his off-breaks with disdain and scored a swift sixty before being run out. This made Charles even more eager to supplant him in Adele's affections, and he began to plan his seduction campaign with all the attention to detail he had once used at Polygon Wood or on the North-West Frontier. This rather surprised him. It was a new state of affairs. He had been wholehearted in his wooing of Mary, but this had not been difficult—they were like childhood sweethearts. The situation with Adele was different. He was older, she more sophisticated—and she did not seem to be attracted to him. He made sure that his application to join the Railway Institute was progressed as speedily as possible so that one evening, as a member, he was able to introduce himself to Ali and remind him of their cricketing encounter. Despite his contempt for well delivered off-breaks, Ali turned out to be charming company. When they were drinking together one evening and Adele joined them, Charles thought he had achieved objective number one of his strategy—friendship with Ali leading to friendship with this desirable lady. He was right. Their relationship blossomed.

They had dined well at the Topaki and on returning to her apartment they both decided another whisky would be pleasant. Adele's parents lived in some style; they had turned part of the ground floor of their large house into a separate luxurious apartment for their only daughter. It included a salon of impressive size, furnished with the best that India could provide: elegant wall hangings, Kashmiri carpets and sophisticated lighting. As they sipped their drinks in companionable silence, Charles pictured to himself what the next hour might bring.

Passion has its phases, like Shakespeare's 'seven ages of man'. The lover, 'sighing like a furnace', had passed him by and any suggestion of venues such as the back seat of a car or a seedy hotel room rented by the hour would simply not do but looking around Adele's quarters he would say to himself, Yes, this is the place for the middle-aged lover.

Her first action is to light a number of aromatic candles, quickly adding a delicate, but evocative perfume to the atmosphere. She lies back with her head on a silken cushion and looks at him with those olive eyes and a narrow smile on her painted lips. He thinks again of the 'middle-aged lover' and plans his response to the allure in her eyes. He is drawn to her both physically and mentally. The weeks since that first disastrous encounter at the Railway Institute have been amongst the happiest since Mary's death—and he is fairly certain she feels the same. He begins.

'I'm out of practice and so, unless you find it undignified or repugnant, I want to make love to you with my body—and with words.'

She looks slightly puzzled but says nothing.

'I haven't adopted this approach before—it has just come into my head as I realise how long it has been since I last contemplated taking off a lady's clothes, but I shall try. And you might wish to respond along both avenues as well and put your feelings into words.'

She seems not to welcome this idea but her breathing is becoming more rapid as she nods her head.

'I believe I have fallen in love with you. Mary is a special memory to me as you know, but I cannot recall feeling like this before, at least not since I kissed my cousin at the age of eight behind the cowshed.'

At this she remonstrates by using her fan to beat a light tattoo on his yellow thatched head which, in the candle light, sparkles with perspiration.

'I must see you naked. I can provide words to describe the imagined you, but why resort to imagination? However, the mysteries of the fastenings to your gown look as though they might be beyond me—the mysterious East.'

She raises her right arm so he can see the zip.

'Darling, this is a useful starting point but however much

I would like to extend this exercise for as long as possible I have a throbbing urge below my waist that means I will have to hurry matters on.'

He has by now discarded his jacket, tie and shoes and, as he stands to loosen his trousers, she shrugs out of her green dress in a flash. This halts him in his tracks. He leaves his trousers in disarray around his knees as he moves closer.

'However urgent my needs, I must remove your stockings. I will roll them down to your ankles as gently as my rough hands can manage.'

To assist she opens her legs.

'I see you are not wearing knickers—reminds me of the cowshed days when that was the rudest word we both knew—or do you call them drawers, or pants. You are wet. Look, I withdraw my hand and you can see for yourself. Your juices are staining your thighs. I can't decide whether it is your legs, and the bottom they reach to, or your breasts that I love the most, but your slip still covers that part of you. I will remove it over your head.'

For a moment she wears the satin slip like a coronet.

'From your tits to a tiara. My shirt follows—and now but for the stockings around your ankles we are both as God made us—and didn't he do a good job with you.'

By now he is in a ferment but still manages, as he kisses Adele on the lips, to ask her solicitously, 'Having come this far, are you finding these words upsetting? Why ever did I start this? You'll hate me.' For the first time Adele responds with her voice as well as her body.

'You silly thing! I've had too few lovers to be fully confident. I think I'm even more nervous than you are. I can understand what you're doing and I think it is beautiful. As we fuck I want you to describe it to me.'

She gags slightly on the word but by this time is half sitting and half lying on the ample settee with her knees apart and her legs bent.

'Since we met, I've held you in my arms on three occasions as we exchanged goodnight kisses, but now I must kiss you elsewhere.'

This activity prevents further words as he gently extends her already distended nipples with his mouth. He then stands over her, his cock rampant. Her response is to grasp it and use it as a lever to pull him down to where she guides him into her and closes her eyes. This initial act of love is as careful and unhurried as they both can manage but, even so, it is fairly short-lived. They look at each other and Adele laughs out loud as she strokes Charles' rounded head.

'I love you, you big dope.'

What actually happened was that, before they had finished their drinks, and without saying a word to each other, they became naked and indulged in a most agreeable act of love on her large settee. Charles felt that lighting his pipe to celebrate would not be appropriate so he accepted one of her Turkish cigarettes. As they smoked, Charles told Adele that while deep inside her he had imagined how this whole episode could have been handled differently if he had described, in explicit terms, what was happening.

'You wouldn't have had the nerve, or frankly the verve,' she said.

Perhaps not, he thought, as he took up his glass of whisky, but somehow the verbal version seemed very real.

The next time they met he asked her to marry him and she accepted. They both felt it should be a quiet wedding in view of their advanced ages; he was thirty-five which, she said with some confidence, just about equated to her twenty-three years of life. 'In the field of human relationships, a female year is more valuable than two of yours.' Charles agreed. Twenty-three and still not married—her mother had given up on her, she told Charles, but now she was delighted to find that her daughter had finally come to her senses. 'A bit long in the tooth but he is polite and not a "Johnny-come-lately" or a "gold-digger".' Her mother tended to use such expressions. She would not consider a quiet ceremony for a moment. On this subject, Mr Emerson's views were not sought. Adele persuaded Charles to accept the inevitable. 'At least we will have a good party,' he told Adele.

And they did.

It had been decided some time ago that Charles, as a partner in the thriving business of Blunt and Son, should move from the bungalow at Malabar Hill, where he had begun his married life, to something more befitting his new position. Initially he was reluctant, but he felt Mary poke him in the ribs and tell him that it was the right thing to do. He could not reciprocate all the hospitality he had recently been receiving with a dining table only large enough for four, or six if the guests were all in favour of close bodily contact. So he moved and it was in these premises that the newly-weds began their married life. Adele was also glad to have better entertaining facilities than her parents' dining room. She and a friend had set up a small chain of fashion shops in the city, which was already proving to be a success, and she was pleased to have somewhere more suitable to receive her wealthy clientele, who came from both the European and Indian communities.

She was more sensuous than Mary. When he teased his new wife about this and credited her oriental ancestors she would ignore him, but if he went further and called her his 'chee-chee mistress', she would send him to sleep in his dressing room. This was a rare occurrence and she usually soon relented and followed him there. He would often say in later years that the twins were conceived in 'bachelor quarters' and Adele made no attempt to persuade him otherwise. News of her pregnancy inevitably drew Charles back to Mary and the image he had of her lying quiet and serene on her deathbed in the Garrison hospital. Adele was sensitive to this but both of them were delighted at the prospect of parenthood, even though Charles pointed out that before their child had attained his majority—both were convinced it was to be a boy—the father would be drawing his pension. It was not a boy. It was twins—one of each. Wisely, both parents kept families well away when it came to choosing names. Adele thought she had heard her mother talking about 'Phineas' and 'Phoebe' or 'Adam' and 'Eve'. Even so, the committee of two had a prolonged debate before 'Matthew' and 'Jenny' were agreed. Charles liked 'Jenny' but wondered whether it ought not to be 'Jennifer'. The mother, pragmatic as always, said 'It will only be shortened, so why not put the lifetime-label on at the start?'

The twins flourished. Adele was an efficient mother and Charles a besotted father but during their early years the twins, as in most similar families in India, saw more of their ayah than their parents. Both of these were involved in their business enterprises but after the children were born, a joint decision was made that, whatever the demands of Blunt and Son or Venus Models, they would get away with the children to Mahabaleshwar for at least six weeks during Bombay's hottest season. This Hill Station was used by the

Bombay establishment in the summer and both Charles and Adele enjoyed their visits there. The station, over four thousand feet above sea level, had many pleasant walking trails and several attractive lookout points that provided splendid views over the plains below and from where, on a clear day, the sea could be seen. Mahabaleshwar did not have the grandeur of hill stations like Simla, where the Viceroy and his entourage spent the hot season, but it provided a welcome refuge for the Cresswell family from hot and humid Bombay. They normally stayed at the Green Acres Rest House where the facilities were antiquated, but there was an old-world charm that appealed and the proprietor was as fond of cricket as was Charles. Adele was less tolerant than Mary about this sporting passion of her husband and would drag him off to take walks with her and the children just as he and Ranji had begun to discuss the timeless test match at the Oval—or 'some such nonsense' as Adele described it.

From the time children were born, European parents in India faced the predictable agony that at the age of five, or thereabouts, they would be parted; the climate of the country was simply not suitable for such children after that age. Adele was confronted, like many other wives and mothers, with the difficult decision whether to leave her husband on his own or go to England with the children. She had been born in India and, although she had visited Europe and the USA for holidays, had lived in Bombay all her life. The children knew nothing of England; India was their home and, indeed, as a result of the close contact with their ayah, they spoke Hindustani before English. It was also necessary to consider who would be legal guardians to the children if their mother stayed in India. Charles' sister Edith had no children and, as soon as she appreciated what was required, had promptly offered herself and her husband as ideal candidates. They had a large comfortable house in an attractive country location. They had servants and horses and there was a good village school. In the event, a compromise was reached. To start with Adele would stay with the children for six months, then, provided they seemed well settled, she would return to her husband's side and they would plan to visit England every eighteen months so as not to lose touch. This was an exemplary arrangement. Tales were told of Raj orphans, as they were called, who were shipped off to Britain at the age of four or five to stay with professional foster parents, complete strangers to the children and to those parents whose terms of service did not allow them the luxury of frequent travel such as the Cresswell's were proposing. Many of these so-called orphans were parted from their parents for many years and it was often a matter of luck whether the substitute mothers and fathers treated their charges well or badly before the children were sent off to boarding schools. Even these could be harsh for children who, for the first few years of their lives, had lived in a degree of luxury—or at least with a loving ayah.

However, something came along to change these best laid plans. Charles had fought in the 'war to end all wars' and now, just twenty years later, the great powers were in conflict again. The declaration of war in September 1939 contributed to the family dilemma. India became a participant, whether it liked it or not, and its army would doubtless be engaged, as in the last war. This would directly affect the Cresswells only if Charles decided to volunteer—assuming the army had any use for him at the age of forty-one. But Charles did not volunteer, and he and Adele turned their attentions to assessing the dangers of a voyage to England. They decided these must be accepted so Adele and the twins were booked on the next available vessel. This arrived in Southampton before the start of any substantial German sea offensive and, so by the end of 1939, Charles was alone in Bombay while Adele and the twins were practising getting used to the sound of the air-raid sirens. A few months later Adele's weekly letter told Charles that the twins had settled into school well, they missed their father dreadfully but their main concern was with whose pony was the better and, 'Mummy, when can I learn to jump over fences?'—this from Jenny. Adele also asked if he had seen the newspaper report about the death of one of General Dyer's most ardent supporters, the then Lieutenant Governor of the Punjab, Sir Michael O'Dwyer. He had been murdered on the 13th of March, shot while at a meeting at the Caxton Hall in London, by an Indian who had been sixteen years of age and living in the Punjab at the time of the Amritsar incident.

Adele decided to return to India before the end of the year and, provided there were no problems with air passages, both parents intended to return to the UK for Christmas 1941 when the twins would be six, going on seven, an appropriate moment to consider their educational futures. Adele was able to fly to Karachi via Durban and husband and wife were reunited in January 1941. However, the tentative proposal to spend the next Christmas in Leicestershire was shattered when on the 7th of December the Japanese destroyed the US fleet at anchor in Pearl Harbour. Another external event that was to determine the fates of both Charles and Adele was the formation of the Indian National Army, the INA.

The 1937 elections, the first to be held since the introduction of the 1935 Government of India Act, had resulted in Indians now running provincial government in the country and seven of the eleven provinces were Congress ones. However, the Bengali leader, Subhash Chandra Bose, was vehemently opposed to the 1935 reforms. He was re-elected as Congress President in 1938 and Gandhi decided to come out of virtual retirement to have him removed; his extreme views were not welcomed. Bose then set up a separate party, the Forward Bloc, and continued to demand the immediate withdrawal of the British, a stance he maintained even after war was declared. He saw the war as an opportunity to forward his cause even more strongly but the British authorities quickly stemmed this ambition by placing him under arrest. He escaped and got himself, by various means, to Berlin where he sought an alliance with the Axis powers to form an Indian Army to attack the British in India. The Germans were lukewarm about this proposal but when Japan entered the war he moved to Tokyo and eventually set up the INA that observers believed reached a strength of anywhere between sixteen and fifty thousand men—together with some women who served in a 'Rani of Jhamsi' regiment, named after the warrior queen who had fought in the Indian Mutiny. Bose eventually took command and this army, mainly recruited from Indian prisoners of war and some of the Indian civilian population of the Far East, was attached to the Japanese forces as they prepared to advance against the Allied forces in Burma—then on to India. The existence of the INA was common knowledge in India, at least for those citizens who had access to a radio, because Bose made broadcasts from both Berlin and Tokyo.

Charles was horrified at this turn of events. He simply could not comprehend that some of the Indian soldiers he had served with would now aim their weapons at the British, or, even more frightful, against their fellow countrymen serving in the Indian Army. David Blunt pointed out that to obtain release from a Japanese prison camp a man would agree to anything, but Charles could still hardly believe this was happening. He and Adele had a series of difficult discussions.

'You know, my love, I have made several contrary decisions in my time. No-one could understand why I stayed in the army after the war. My colleagues were equally amazed that I resigned over Amritsar, and when I did my family were astonished that I decided to stay in India. Now, is this renegade, this traitor, going to compel me to take up arms again? Amritsar forced me out. Is Bose going to force me back in? I know it makes no sense, but I cannot help having these thoughts.'

'Of course it doesn't make sense. It is illogical rubbish. You are talking twaddle. Are you really thinking of deserting David? Are you asking me to become a camp-follower? Not only are you too old, you're mad.'

'True. What is also galling is that I met Bose once and was quite impressed. Also, as you know, I've got a number of friends, or at least acquaintances, with Congress connections and they must be alarmed that an ex-President of theirs is pursuing this line. I know there's been a lot of frustration about Independence, and the way the war has called a halt to the process, but does anyone really believe this so-called army is going to help the cause?'

'I know all about that, but what's it got to do with you rejoining the army?'

'Well, I just have this notion that, with my knowledge and background, I could make some small contribution towards ensuring that the INA becomes the damp squib I think it is, or will be. Look, I'm not going to do anything precipitate. Now the Japanese are in the war we have to think about whether this makes India less safe for you, and how the children might react if there is any suggestion in England that we could be in danger. Whatever happens, I think we should consider whether you ought to be with them at this time if some sort of passage is still possible.'

'The usual dilemma: To stay with you, or be with the children. And this bloody war has made it even more difficult.'

'What I think, before we agonise any more, is that I should talk to Colonel Robertson and see what news he has on Bose, and whether a passage for you back to Blighty can be finessed through military channels.'

Colonel Robertson and Charles had several meetings on this subject, the last of which included the senior intelligence officer from the 114th Infantry Brigade. As a result, Charles was offered the temporary rank of major and a place in the Brigade military intelligence unit. With Adele's reluctant agreement, he accepted. At the same time, enquiries about a passage to the UK via Egypt were successful. Adele now had three alternatives: go to Leicestershire and the children, remain in Bombay but be parted from Charles, or follow him to live in a barracks 'somewhere in India'. In the circumstances, and perhaps not surprisingly, she chose the East Midlands and arrived there in August 1943. She never saw her husband again.

At the beginning of 1944, there was even more confusion than usual within the Indian political theatre. The new Viceroy, Lord Wavell, in direct opposition to the views of Prime Minister Churchill, was attempting to plan the shape of a future Independence for the country while trying to alleviate the suffering caused by the catastrophic Bengal famine which, by the time it was brought under control, had been responsible for more than a million deaths—possibly up to three million. The British Government refused Wavell's request for more grain to be shipped to feed the starving and this, and the little progress towards Independence, led to increasing unrest during 1943 and 1944. Intelligence sources reported evidence of nationalist sentiment of a possibly dangerous sort, but the unit where Charles was to serve was more specifically concerned with whether this might lead to a revolt in the event of a successful Japanese invasion. Would large numbers of Indians swell the ranks of the invader, including those of the INA who, it was assumed, would be marching side-by-side with their Japanese allies? It was, therefore, decided that one area that needed to be carefully surveyed was where any invasion would begin: in North East India, on the frontier with Burma.

Charles was to be dispatched to this region to head an operation charged with infiltrating the local community to gauge attitudes towards the INA. At the start he was uncomfortable as an army spy; his military strength had been, so he considered, leading uniformed men in battle. Was he now to become a latter day Kim? What were his qualifications for this role? During his years in commerce he had become fairly proficient in Hindi; he could generally understand all speech in that language, but his spoken Hindi was not such that the native would assume he was a brother. However, these attributes were seen as positive by the Brigade intelligence officer, Colonel George Slocombe. More importantly, Slocombe had been impressed with the empathy his new recruit had with India, and his contacts within the Congress party. Initially, it had been decided that Charles would use these contacts to add to the Intelligence Bureau's overall picture of that party's view on the INA, but eventually, owing to Charles' limited experience in this field, it was felt he would be better deployed in a specific geographical location—in particular, the town of Imphal.

George Slocombe was younger than Charles. Although not strictly accurate, Charles told David Blunt, that except for the Commanding Officer, every soldier in the Brigade was younger than he. Slocombe, who was a product of Sandhurst and the Staff College, had only been in India since 1940 and Charles quickly discovered that he was not tainted with any of the 'prejudice and protocol'—Charles' words—of the British Army as an integral part of the Raj. What he lacked in long-term experience of India he made up for in the acuity that came from a sharp and clever mind backed up by an interest in Indian history. He seemed to have made a speciality of the Indian Mutiny and Charles was impressed by how Slocombe's analysis of this seminal event took into account the views of the Raj and the mutineers. He was also a realist about the Amritsar massacre. While he did not share the intensity of Charles' antagonism, he was far from condoning Dyer's action. Furthermore, he was unconventional, a valuable attribute for an intelligence officer, and he had agreed that, subject to a reading of the Official Secrets Act, Charles could discuss his assignment with David Blunt, but only in the broadest of details. This came about because both Charles and Slocombe had quickly reached the conclusion that if the new intelligence officer could establish himself with a commercial identity, rather than a military one, the chances of gathering useful local information would be enhanced. David went along with this and agreed that Charles could look into establishing a Blunt outpost in the region, allegedly to investigate whether there was any economic viability in exporting, once the war was over, a particular quality of textile made in the area.

Charles had never visited the North East of the country but David was familiar with Assam because of the tea trade. Neither of them had ever been to the town of Imphal, the capital of the State of Manipur, but Charles was told by one of his Congress contacts that the party's senior man in the town was Raji Narayan, who owned and ran a hotel there. The Lake Hotel had a good reputation in the area mainly because of the quality of the food served. The accommodation was limited to five rooms in the main building and twelve self-contained cottages in the grounds. Charles invariably stayed in one of these when he visited, the first occasion being in early October 1943, when he made his first acquaintance with the town and the hotel's proprietor. In normal times this would have been a pleasant excursion. There were some similarities with Mahabaleshwar as Imphal was surrounded by wooded hills and lakes. Within the town was said to be the oldest existing polo ground in the world but its population of less than 100,000, soon to be swollen by the British and Indian troops pouring into the area prior to an operation against the Japanese and an invasion of Burma, was hardly concerned with any form of sport at this time. He quickly came to the conclusion that, in the circumstances, the fiction about opening a branch of Blunt and Son was simply not credible. So, in agreement with Slocombe and David, Charles based himself in Gawahati where he held a number of bone-fide discussions with members of the tea industry about possible further involvement of his firm in this business after the war. At the same time, and with the approval of his superiors, he extended to the Assam region his operation to gauge the popularity of the INA. From this base he visited Imphal every other week and while there let it be known that his interests were to consider any commercial potential there might be in the town that could be developed after the war. Charles thought all of this seemed fairly specious but no-one seemed to be concerned one way or another: there was too much direct military activity for anyone to worry about any covert operations. Even so, Slocombe told him there was still some concern at Divisional and Corp level about a local uprising if Mr Bose were to appear on the horizon. In the overall scheme of things such an uprising might have an insignificant impact on a major confrontation between the British and Indian Armies and those of the Japanese, virtually all-conquering so far, but, as Slocombe put it, when a lion fights a tiger he does not want to be distracted by a mosquito biting his arse. Charles' task was to find out if the mosquito was in season.

Raji's son, Sanjay Narayan, was not included in those who were indifferent to Charles' presence. This young man, who assisted his father in managing the hotel, was antagonistic to Charles from the start. He and his father were very different from each other. On one of Charles' later visits he asked Narayan senior to dine with him one evening, which proved to be a very satisfactory encounter. For some strange reason this meeting reminded him of that time many years ago when he and David had first met at the Empire Hotel in Bombay. Although remote from the core of Congress politics, Raji was clearly up to date; he told Charles he had been in Calcutta only a few weeks ago for a meeting of branch officials. He was not, however, in any way an abrasive political animal. He had been in the hotel business all his life and it was clear from his easy manner with all under his roof, be they VIP guests or kitchen hands, that he was well suited to such a profession. He was a large man with bad teeth, stained with betel juice, frequently displayed because he was wont to laugh a great deal. This mirth was not forced. He was fond of life, although at the moment somewhat concerned about the effects of a war on his doorstep. His bonhomie appealed to Charles.

'You are to be complimented on your cook—a splendid dinner and glad to have your company.'

'My dear Charles, it is my pleasure. Will you have a cigar? '

'No thanks, but may I smoke my pipe?'

'Of course.'

'I see the usual bunch of army officers are dining.'

'Yes, we've never been so busy.'

'Do you think the Japs will invade?'

'I rather fear so. Nothing has stopped them to date. If Singapore can capitulate so easily, what hope for this part of India?'

'I think I agree. You recall your colleague, Hassan, in Bombay told me you are the Congress representative in these parts. Well, if it is not too sensitive, does the party think like you that the next theatre of the Eastern war is going to be on Indian soil?'

'As far as I know there isn't an official line on this but I believe

I can be frank with you about some Congress matters. I know you have some friends in the party and I also know that you are on our side when it comes to Independence. But let's speak about that before we get on to the Japs and so on. I am a moderate, but if by 1940 your country had not moved on from that miserable India Act towards more or less immediate Independence I should have been buckling on my sword. That is not to say we in Congress do not fully realise the problem with Jinnah. We've lived side by side with the Mussulman for centuries. Sometimes there have been problems, but I don't think they want a separate State and we definitely do not. We will not allow that to happen. The problem has been postponed by Mr Hitler but when this is all over Indians will not accept, as a reward for fighting the Nazis, the same treatment we got after the war you fought in. It has got to be give and take. Both ways. We are giving up our blood and you must give up India. You've lived here a long time. You are not part of the establishment and I can guess that when we run things there will still be a place for 'box wallahs' like you'—he burst into peels of laughter—'as long as we get a fair price! By the way, do you have any Hornby train sets in stock? It is my oldest grandson's birthday next month.'

'Hornby—you'll be lucky! But I sympathise fully about sending Indian soldiers to fight our enemies and then not recognising their contribution. Do you think we might be faced with a situation where some of those soldiers finish up fighting for the Japanese on Indian soil?'

'You're talking about Bose. Very sensitive subject.'

At this moment Sanjay, who had been filling in as the wine waiter, approached the table and his father changed the subject and asked Charles what Blunt and Son's wine stock was like.

'Fairly sparse,' answered Charles.

As Sanjay withdrew, Charles remarked that the young man did not seem to like him.

'Yes, I'm afraid he acts that way to a lot of people. Since his mother died I have tried, but he is not a happy man. He is young, of course, and I just hope he will grow out of it but he mixes with bad people. You started to ask about Bose and the INA. There are some around who think he is a hero but not us in the Congress party. We think, and we are not alone in this, that his army is likely to be a joke—but perhaps a tragic joke. Although he has supposedly recruited a large number, I wonder how many of them are using the INA as a passport to return to India. Unfortunately, Sanjay is one who, in his present mood, would like to join their ranks but I cannot see many of the people of Imphal adding to their numbers. What do they think is going to happen? Bose appearing on a white charger! There is going to be a serious battle if you lot are going to stop the Japanese and there won't be any time, or room, for Bose's rabble to be on display. I may be wrong, but think about it. Are the Japs sure that when these renegade troops have their feet on home soil, and if the British forces get the upper hand, they won't find the rifles handed out turned against them? Probably not. With all we've been through there's not a lot of love for the Brits, but I guess even you are preferable to the demonic Japanese.'

Charles listened but said little. Raji continued.

'I'm not staying around anyway to find out. Although this hotel is as far away from the border as it is possible to be in Imphal, if the fighting gets near I have made plans to evacuate the family and those of my staff who would want to move. A friend of mine is an assistant manager at a tea plantation in Assam and, with the agreement of the planter himself, a refuge is available for us.'

Charles was required to submit reports, using secure channels, on a monthly basis, or more frequently if something of moment had occurred. He had received some training in army intelligence report writing. During his earlier army experience this was not a skill he was called upon to acquire, but now he was intrigued to discover that the British Army had over time developed an English style with hard and fast rules, that were very nearly unique. There were, of course, ridiculous examples of this: 'Underpants—draw-string—green—for the use of'; but he quickly realised that it made good sense to adopt a standardised form and style of writing. In the first few months his reports tended to be little more than lists of the people he had met and interviewed and interim conclusions drawn from information gathered, but in February 1944 his report contained more substance, and included the following:

1 Summary of conclusions

After a total of twenty weeks spent in the designated area (see Note 1 for a detailed log), I present this report divided into two, Manipur and Nagaland linked together and Assam. The brief given to me was:

1.1 To obtain, if possible, concrete evidence of the views of the population of these three States on the INA.

1.2 If it is found that there is some support for this rebel army, how is this likely to manifest itself if this army should invade Manipur and Nagaland, and subsequently Assam?

1.3 Based on an extrapolation of this evidence, to formulate an opinion as to what the nationwide support might be for the INA and whether this might lead to serious civil unrest.

2 Manipur and Nagaland

These will be the front-line States if the Japanese invade, as seems inevitable. After detailed investigation, sympathy towards the INA in these States is difficult to judge. It is a complex issue. Most of the populace are mainly concerned about their homes becoming the latest Far Eastern battle-ground and the ease with which the Japanese have advanced up to now, fills them with alarm. This arises from the prospect of danger to their person and property, rather than a fear of the Japanese. There is a minority of the people that believe a Japanese success will hasten the departure of the British in India and lead to an early declaration of Independence. I stress I believe this to be a minority outlook. Allied to this view there needs to be an assessment of the effective-ness of the INA concept, not as a fighting force, not as brothers marching to the rescue to free brothers, but because of the more subtle attraction that, with this rebel army marching alongside the Japanese, the attacking force are seen as liberators and not the enemy. I am conscious that this perhaps uncertain assessment is one that the Intelligence Bureau will have already formed for themselves, but at the front line this is how I observe the situation.

On the separate question of whether people in these States who support the INA will, for whatever motive, rise and join that army in some numbers, it is, in my view, unlikely. The President of the local Congress party in Imphal (see Note 3.1 for a profile on Raji Narayan and Note 3.2 on his son, Sanjay) is of the same opinion. He is not of the more militant variety and, as the Bureau will be aware, there has often been more concern in the past in these States with tribal and ethnic rivalries than in the 'Quit India' movement.

Some elements may cause unrest and agitation beyond normal if they see the invasion is proceeding well but I cannot believe, except for a small extreme section (see Note 3.2), that there will be any direct action of a military or paramilitary nature to attack British and Indian troops either before or during the impending conflict.

Included in the report were a variety of appendices covering all three States, relating to detailed investigations and conversations undertaken, together with a range of statistics compiled from these findings. For Assam, he conjectured that if there was some early success for the Japanese and the INA at the border there would be an escalation in anti-British activity in this State. However, as he pointed out to Slocombe, such a situation could eventuate throughout India, which again only underlined the danger posed by the image of the INA, as opposed to the reality, if they and the Japanese were not repulsed. He also repeated current rumours that whatever numbers east of the frontier had pledged fealty to Bose, many of these were unarmed, or inadequately armed. As Charles surmised, there was little in this report that was entirely new to George Slocombe but he did pay particular attention to Note 3.2 concerning Sanjay Narayan and made inquiries to see if his name was to be found elsewhere in the bureau's files. It was, so Slocombe sent a message to Charles warning him to keep a special eye on this young man. The essence of Note 3.2 was as follows:

Sanjay Narayan

I was able to make some discreet inquiries about this man with the local police using the excuse that I was considering him for employment with Blunt and Son. The report was not good. In 1942 he was arrested as a suspect in a case of serious assault on a Muslim doctor who declined to press charges—it is thought that drugs might have been involved—but the following year he was charged and imprisoned for six months for riotous behaviour in connection with some local rivalry. The police suspect this involved a form of protection racket but nothing was ever proved. His father employs him at the hotel but seems reluctant to comment strongly on his son's behaviour which, even with guests, can at best be described as truculent, particularly if they are white. From my dealings with him it is clear that he is fiercely, if not pathologically, anti-British, a trait he does not share with his father (see Note 3.1). A third party informed me that the extreme racism within this man has roots in some ill-treatment he believes his mother—now deceased—received some years ago at the hands of a British army officer, but, as a result of careful probing with Raji Narayan, this appears to be more imagined than real. However, what is certain is that he resents British soldiers using the hotel and when his father is not present, he is openly hostile. Friends of his father, and other hotel staff, seem to view him as hot-headed and foolish but I suspect that he might be more dangerous than that and his swagger and bravado could disguise more devious intentions. Despite his father, he was asked to resign from the Congress party because of his behaviour, but I am fairly certain that he is active with one or other of the splinter groups within the party, of which the Intelligence Bureau will be aware.

As you know it was agreed at the outset that my bona fides should be as genuine as possible and, although I have not broadcast the information, both Sanjay and his father are aware that I was a serving officer twenty years ago and that I was in Amritsar in 1919. The head cook revealed last week that Sanjay keeps a scrapbook on the Amritsar affair including newspaper cuttings covering the trial of Udham Singh for the murder of Sir Michael O'Dwyer. As you are aware, Singh has become, or is in the process of becoming, a martyr in the cause of Indian freedom. In view of the above, I intend to keep a close eye on Sanjay. I have never heard him mention the INA but if they have chosen agents in this area to promote their cause, he must have been amongst the candidates. He does not of course have the intellect or the experience of Bose but they appear to have a natural arrogance in common. If there is any information in the bureau files on Sanjay Narayan that can be released to me, the more information I have into his thought-processes the better.

There is a further complication, or contradiction, in that the Narayans are not from this area. Sanjay left Madras with his mother and father when the hotel was acquired in 1936, when he was fifteen, so they are viewed with some suspicion by natives of Imphal. On the other hand, a Hindu like Sanjay could be considered to be effective in inciting differences between local communities, and I believe in his case that has proved to be correct.

By the beginning of March the Brigade had moved to the Imphal area and Charles was now able to report directly to Slocombe. He had some interesting information. As a result of his superiors' response to the note on Sanjay Narayan, Charles decided he needed to concentrate his 'spying' activity on this man and therefore resolved to search the rooms he occupied at the hotel. These were two in number, over the kitchen block and separate from the owner's apartment within the main building. They had been a storage area, accessed from a rough outside staircase, but when Sanjay began to work at the hotel they had been converted into elementary living quarters used only when he was on duty. According to Raji, his son had a share of an apartment in town which he used during his off-time. Days away from the hotel could be extensive as he was included in the hotel's workforce only when they were busy, or someone was sick. Charles chose to make his search during one of those periods of absence. He chose a moment just after lunch when the one or two remaining guests and the staff were enjoying their siesta.

As he mounted the scarred and broken staircase he wondered whether he was about to be involved in another occupation new to him, that of 'breaking and entering', but when he reached the landing at the top of the steps he found the door was not locked. He looked around but quickly realised that, even if guests or staff were not safely ensconced within their mosquito nets, no-one was likely to see him. The staircase was at the rear of the kitchen building and backed on to the slope of dense forest which formed the western boundary of the hotel. All was quiet except for the rustling of leaves and cries of the bird-life in the woods. Charles wondered how long this moment of peace would last. Only days, he thought, before he would once more hear the sound of shot and shell and savour the acrid fumes of cordite. At least this time there would be no gas.

He broke from his reverie and pushed the door; it swung unevenly on its hinges. It was badly warped and impossible to lock. The first room he encountered appeared to be a sitting area—also a rubbish dump. The bedroom was beyond. There were no washing facilities. Both rooms were dirty and untidy and smelled strongly of stale smoke, cigarettes and ganja. What possessions Sanjay had were on display for all to see and even the spare uniform he used for his hotel work was not in the wardrobe but hanging untidily over its door, which proved to be another one coming off its hinges. The bed was unmade, the sheets stained and crumpled. Nearby were a number of empty beer bottles, some abandoned underwear and one sandal with a broken strap. It did not take Charles more than a few minutes to reach the conclusion that his act of criminality was going to reveal little—until he saw the table. It was the only piece of near-decent furniture on show. It was painted white and on it, neatly arranged, was a pad of blotting paper, a notebook and a jam jar crammed with pencils, most of which were unsharpened. Clearly Sanjay used it as a desk. Under the tabletop were two drawers which could well have held cutlery in a previous incarnation. They were both locked.

Charles was well aware that the time for niceties was fast drawing to a close; his stamping ground would soon be a battlefield. He looked around and found a broken kitchen knife which he used to deal with the skimpy locks on the drawers. The first one revealed what Charles assumed to be the Amritsar scrapbook the head cook had mentioned. It was, in fact, an extremely dishevelled copy of a souvenir programme printed at the time of the Coronation Durbar of 1911, held in Delhi to commemorate the visit of King George V and Queen Mary. It was about to fall apart into its constituent pages as the binding had more or less disintegrated. Between each page were cuttings taken from newspapers and magazines. Most of these were loose but some had been stuck to the page with a flour and water paste. It was a mixed bag. Most of them had reference to the Amritsar massacre but there were two from 1940, about the killing of Sir Michael O'Dwyer, that Charles had not seen before. A quick glance told him that the assassin maintained his arm had been nudged while attempting to fire at the ceiling, but in later testimony admitted he had a grudge against O'Dwyer. Sanjay appeared to feel the same. On the front cover of the programme was a picture of General Dyer that had been over-scored many times with lines in pencil and ink. Charles was intrigued to know how this programme had come into Sanjay's possession? Perhaps his grandfather had been one of the many thousands who had attended this event in 1911—seen as the highpoint of British imperialism and the epitome of Britain's role in India. Had Sanjay used this publication for this purpose simply because it was available, or did he appreciate the significance? Charles thought he probably did. This pictorial evidence of a major imperial affair was now defaced by pages torn from newspapers that recorded what Charles considered to be the most inglorious event in India's recent past. It was too bizarre to be a coincidence. What made him shiver was the thought that he could easily have been the architect of a similar record. He thrust it back into the drawer.

Its neighbour contained a number of well-thumbed photographs of the type hawked on the quaysides at Bombay and Calcutta to visiting sailors, together with a receipt issued by an Imphal printing firm for a payment of forty rupees. This receipt had been pinned to what looked like a printer's proof of a handbill, both sides of which had text, one in English and the other in Hindustani. Charles read the English version.

Patriots Arise
Our blessed Saviour Netaji Subhash Chandra Bose
is about to arrive to free us
from the Imperial swine
Freedom is coming
Kill the British dogs and their servants
India for the Indians
Bose our new President

Is this discovery of any value to us, he thought? If these leaflets have already been printed, can we stop them being distributed? But even if they have, are they likely to have any serious consequence? He thought again about Slocombe's allusion to mosquito bites. If this invective could inspire some Indians to hinder in any way the tough job the British and Indian troops were about to face, the destruction of these handbills at source might save some lives. Charles, making no attempt to disguise the broken locks, took the leaflet and the receipt and went to disturb Raji from his rest with the request that the hotel car and driver be placed at his disposal. He delivered his evidence to Slocombe who ordered an immediate police raid on the premises of the printer. They were in time. The handbills had been printed and were parcelled up with string but, so it seemed, none had left the printer's workshop. Everyone on the premises was arrested and their handiwork confiscated. Sanjay could not be found.

'What a close call!' Slocombe said. 'We shall never know, of course, but this might have been just the match needed to ignite Bose's local supporters, or would-be supporters, and cause problems for our forces. Well done, Charlie. An excellent piece of work.'

Slocombe then ordered Charles to return to Gawahati as soon as possible, and by whatever means he could. There would be little call for his services any further in Imphal, so he was advised to revert to monitoring the situation in Assam State, though still in his civilian persona.

The next day the town was full of rumours that the Japanese had crossed the Chindwin River in Burma and begun their advance into India. Raji Narayan told Charles that, whatever truth there was in this gossip, he was planning to quit the hotel by the following day with his son and those members of the staff who wanted to leave. He would have left before but had been delayed because Sanjay's whereabouts were unknown. Raji had not seen him for ten days and he could only assume he was staying at his town apartment. In view of Slocombe's orders, when Raji offered Charles a passage back to Gawahati in the 'refugee lorry', as Raji described it, he accepted and plans were made to depart the next day, with or without Sanjay. Both Charles and Raji were glad a decision had been made and, although hardly an event to celebrate, they shared a bottle of champagne and one of Raji's remaining bottles of claret that evening with their cold supper, all the kitchen could provide. Both pondered what lay in the future. Was this a decisive moment in the Far Eastern campaign and, if the British and Indian forces gathering on their doorstep were finally going to stem the Japanese advance through Asia, was an end to the war in sight?

Although the night was dark, Charles was familiar with the path from the dining room to his cottage. As he traversed this he contemplated the end of hostilities and a reunion with his family. He was pleasantly inebriated. On reaching the porch to his room he seemed to apprehend, from out of the corner of his eye, a shadow appearing over his right shoulder. Before he could properly register this he felt a cord around his neck pulled backwards with considerable strength. He attempted to turn and confront his assailant but could not. He threw his arms behind his head and at his neck in an attempt to ease the ligature now biting deeply into his flesh. As he began to lose consciousness a knife blade pierced the breast pocket of his lightweight jacket and slid between the ribs into the heart.

George Slocombe wrote to Adele:

I know the Brigadier has written to you about Charles' death but as I was his immediate superior I would like to explain in detail the work your husband was engaged with. Firstly, I send my personal condolences to you and the family. In my assessment Charles was a most unusual man. He loved India and treated all who lived here with an equality that few within the British establishment do. However, I do not need to tell you this but I write in this fashion to underline the admiration and respect I had for him, even though our friendship was a brief one.

It is almost certain that Charles was murdered by Sanjay Narayan, the son of the proprietor of the Lake Hotel in Imphal where Charles stayed when he visited there. Unfortunately, this man was not taken to trial because the prison where he was being held was destroyed by Japanese shells which killed all the occupants instantly. However, before then I was able to conduct some lengthy interviews with him. He admitted killing Charles and seemed to enjoy recounting the details of the crime and why he had committed it. I hesitate to tell you this as I am sure you will recoil from the picture of such a man smiling at me as he tried to justify his actions, but after some thought I decided you should have the most complete picture I can provide.

Firstly, I need to go back and describe the activities of Charles in the weeks before his death. You will know that he was acting for us as an under-cover agent in Assam, Nagaland and Manipur where his prime objective was to determine the level of support the INA enjoyed from within the local population. He was able to provide us with extremely valuable information in this regard. It is my view that one of his last actions before he died may have saved many lives. Thanks to his initiative we were able to prevent the distribution of leaflets that could have incited people to rise against the

Indian and British forces facing the Japanese, even to the extent of a bullet or a knife in the back. It is not possible to say for certain that this would have happened, but what is sure is that, thanks to Charles, when fighting began the local people were relatively passive, which might not have been the case if this leaflet had been widely distributed.

It was clear from the three interviews I conducted with the murderer that he did not know Charles was working for us, any more than did anyone else at the hotel or within the remaining civilian population. However, it had been agreed from the outset that Charles' former career in the army would not be hidden and certainly Narayan knew this and that Charles had been in Amritsar in 1919. The prisoner was loquacious, although not always coherent, but I regret to have to inform you that the conclusion I came to as to the motive for the killing was principally that Charles had been in the army and had served at Amritsar. The assassin was involved in a movement advocating violence to acquire Independence for India but Charles' death does not seem to have occurred because of this. Narayan kept repeating that his quest was to gain vengeance against General Dyer and to achieve this he was aiming to kill as many white men as the number of Indians who died in the Amritsar incident. He appears, tragically, to have begun his killing with Charles, probably because he thought he would more easily escape detection when Imphal became a war zone, a situation he knew was imminent.

The awful irony is that, as we both know, Charles was as distressed about what happened at Amritsar as was this demented creature. The tragedy of course is that Charles has become another casualty of that calamity which, in my view—and Charles may have told you I am a student of Indian history—was the beginning of the end for the Raj. Narayan was not to know they were, in effect, on the same side, but even had he known I do not think it would have changed what happened. Your husband survived the trenches of World War I and action on the North-West Frontier. He volunteered to rejoin, and we accepted him beyond the age limit because of his vehemence over Bose. He was determined to do what he could to prevent Indian soldiers fighting each other. Well, Mrs Cresswell, he succeeded. This was not a fruitless death. He was a brave man and we owe him a considerable debt of gratitude. This will be feeble consolation to you and the family but you will know better than I that Charles is probably looking down on us satisfied that he did his bit, and he would be pleased to know that the role of the INA has been negligible in the overall scheme of things.

When this war is over, and if you are prepared to receive me, I would like to visit you and convey my respects in person.

Chapter Five

Matthew

The morning Nigerian Airways plane from Lagos to Kano had landed but the passengers were warned of a delay and asked to remain on board. Matthew could see from his window seat that the BOAC flight from London was still on the tarmac. Must have been held up, he thought, it would normally have reached Lagos by this time. Just as the low pitched buzz of passenger's voices was beginning to become more heated owing to the unexplained delay, reinforced by the increase in the temperature within the grounded plane, the BOAC aircraft began to move away from the parking bay. This coincided with an announcement from the pilot that the Nigerian Airways passengers could now move into the terminal building. Ensconced in the plane the passengers had not heard the rifle fire but as soon as they began to disembark it was obvious Kano airport was not as usual. Two green-painted army lorries were leaving the area where the British plane had been parked and as Matthew and his fellow passengers reached the arrivals hall they could observe a considerable military presence. Since the coups of January and July, Nigerians had become used to the presence of soldiery on their streets, at road checkpoints and guarding selected buildings and airports. As passengers checked in at the Lagos airport at Ikeja, a desultory handful of soldiers were to be seen standing behind the Nigerian Airways staff, as if to shadow their actions. None of these members of the Nigerian army seemed to know what their role was, or what they where supposed to be doing, but for their colleagues at Kano airport it soon became clear they had a real purpose in life—to kill Ibos.

Matthew was met by his client, Leo Brady, the Northern Region manager for John Holts, who looked visibly distressed.

'Matt, nice to see you again, but you have chosen a bad time to visit.'

'Why? What's up? Why all the army? Has there been another coup?'

'If only. No, it has started—what we were expecting. They're after the Ibos and it looks as though this time they mean to kill the lot.'

'What do you mean?'

'They've just dragged them off the BOAC plane and shot them in view of all the other passengers. I couldn't believe it. Horrible, barbarous—I've never seen anything like it. You saw the lorries. They are being used as hearses and they're off to a mass grave I'm sure.'

'Good God!'

'And that's not all. As I've stood here waiting for you I've seen Ibo bar staff and customs men being chased through the airport, hunted down and bayoneted or shot. The Hausa soldiers are baying for blood. You can hear them shouting, "Where are the damned Ibo?" Do you speak any Hausa? *Ina Nyamiri* is their cry. It is awful. You know, Matt, this could be the end of Nigeria. The Ibo and the Hausa cannot occupy the same country after this. I know that sounds drastic, but you wait and see. We live in difficult times but I can't believe what I've seen. I've been in Kano for nearly ten years and, although they're not exactly bosom pals, the Northerners and the Ibo have existed side-by-side for years. Some of them are third generation *sabon gari* dwellers. No more.'

Matthew had visited Kano before in his British Council days but in September 1966 he was there on the business of Central Management Services. Kano differed from Lagos in a number of ways. Being nearly six hundred miles closer to the Sahara Desert than the Nigerian coastline, the most apparent difference was the climate: the Lagos heat was wet while that of Kano was dry. Lagos was both the country's political and business capital and Kano the main centre of commerce in the North. Being the hub of Nigeria's groundnut industry, a familiar sight in the city was sacks of these nuts formed into pyramids fifty feet high awaiting transportation by rail to Lagos. Although both were important industrial centres, the demographics of the two cities were very different. Lagos had always been cosmopolitan, home to many of the tribes of Nigeria, including returned slaves of Brazilian origin and businessmen from all over the world—not forgetting the Lebanese—who were also represented in Kano. However, the Northern city was mostly home to the Muslim Hausa, but with a considerable Ibo population. These Easterners were evident individually in shops, at the airport, on the railways and in commercial offices throughout the town but en masse they were segregated from the natives of the area and confined to their own residential locale, the *sabon gari* (strangers' quarters). In view of what was about to occur, Matthew wondered if they should more accurately be referred to as 'ghettos'? He recalled what had happened in Warsaw.

The conversation with Brady took place as Matthew's suitcase was being recovered and they were walking to the car park. Soldiers were strutting around the parked cars but they ignored the white men. If there were any Ibos left in the vicinity they were either in hiding or dead. To reach the Central Hotel, where Matthew was staying, they needed to drive past the home of the Fifth Battalion, where they were held up as three lorries exited the barracks crowded with soldiers and headed for the town. Brady was anxious to get back to his office. He explained that all of his Ibo staff had been repatriated after the July coup except for Jonas, an elderly messenger, who had been born in Kano and had refused to leave. During the short journey from the hotel it became clear the army participants in this massacre had now been reinforced with civilians, who were out on the streets in force, brandishing whatever weapons they could find. On reaching the Holt's depot, Brady's number two hurried out to the car to tell them the army had already paid a visit but Jonas was undiscovered. They had secreted him in the walk-in safe in the manager's office, used primarily to store the cash dispensed twice a year to produce traders.

It was clear there would be little time spent, on this day of all days, in dealing with the assignment CMS was undertaking for the Holt group. After the earlier visit and the success of using the office safe as a hiding place, the area around the main Holt premises presented an aura of calmness and normality, although those present knew this was misleading in view of what they imagined was happening elsewhere in the city. As the Northern Area manager, Brady had overall responsibility for two other Holt enterprises in Kano, the first being a tannery where in times gone by, goat skins had been used to produce what was known as 'Moroccan leather'; the Kano product had been carried by camel across the Sahara Desert. The other factory manufactured the perfumes and unguents used mainly by Muslim men; it included amongst its most popular products the one labelled *Bint al Sudan.* When told of this Matthew wondered if the popularity of these products had something to do with the paucity of bathrooms in the old city.

Brady determined to visit these two locations to see if there were any problems and asked Matthew to accompany him. Both factories had been searched by the marauders but, as all the Ibo workers had been repatriated weeks before, the mob had left. On the return journey Brady's car was stopped several times by bunches of excited men, and once by a group of soldiers, who peered at the Fulani driver and then waved them forward. These events did not make Matthew and Brady any easier of mind. It was impossible to be other than apprehensive. Would the mob hysteria burst and produce a situation where all non-Northerners would become targets? What was going to satisfy these people crazed by the Ibo blood already spilt? Matthew was reminded of the only other time he had encountered a similar situation, though the outcome had been very different.

When he was still living in the Railway compound, his departure for the British Council was delayed one morning. He could not now remember why. As he approached the offices of the Railway Corporation, close to the main exit from the compound, he was halted by the sight of a neat line of about twenty members of the Railway police force with their backs to him. They all wore protective helmets and carried long police batons, presumably standard issue. In front of them was the senior member of this force, an expatriate Inspector whose name Matthew could not now remember but whom at the time he knew well. He had been in the Indian police before coming to Nigeria and many of his colleagues at the Railway Corporation, and fellow members of the EB Club, found the man something of a bore. He really did not have enough to occupy his time and, after visiting the offices of his busier acquaintances within the Railway expatriate community for a chat, he was normally the first on the scene in the club bar when it opened at noon. However, today he was to be seen in his true light. This is what he had been trained for and this is what he was paid for.

He stood in front of his men who, although at attention, fidgeted with evident nervousness. Their leader, who was wearing his peaked cap—no protective helmet for him—and his customary khaki shirt, shorts and long socks, paced easily up and down in front of them. Opposed to this group of policemen were about three hundred men—Matthew could not see any women—some with sticks in their hands. They were not making a particularly loud noise—it seemed to be more of a chant—but they were advancing towards the Railway's guardians. As they did the Inspector ordered his men to take five steps forward and the mob halted. As the protesters gained a little more courage they began to move forward again, whereupon the policemen, on command from their leader, withdrew five paces in orderly fashion. This tactic seemed to halt the mob; immediately the command 'Five paces forward' was repeated. One or two men in the crowd began to throw stones at the police. At this the small unit was ordered to charge with batons at the ready which, surprisingly, and despite the disparity in numbers, had an immediate effect. The mob turned and disappeared out through the gates, except for one or two of their number who lay on the ground suffering from baton concussion. All of this was closely observed by Matthew. As he moved forward he saw two policemen carrying one of the victims away from the scene and he asked where they were taking him.

'To de railway hospital. He has bang for head.'

Curiouser and curiouser, thought Matthew. The police bludgeon this man so that he falls to the ground. They then sheathe their batons and carry him away for medical treatment.

Matthew said aloud to himself. 'This is the Empire—how we have controlled half of the world with a handful of white officials that exude such confidence the odds do not need to be taken into account. That boring Railway police Inspector, with not enough to keep him occupied, epitomises this. When needed, he showed his mettle. Must buy him a drink next time we meet.'

The disturbance Matthew witnessed in the Railway compound was between authority and disgruntled railway workers who had been refused a pay increase, or a perquisite they thought they were entitled to, but the rabble on the Kano streets was not simply a dissatisfied group. These people were bringing to a savage boil the ethnic stew that had been simmering for many years. They did not think about a 'one Nigeria'. They were not concerned with democracy or military rule. They had no thought for where the oil resources were located. The envy and dislike of the successful Ibo within their midst was now transformed into a fury, blind to any sense of reason or human principles, whether founded on the Bible or the Koran. What had been the spark that had set off this madness? Something that had been festering for a long time? Who could tell? The July coup had tipped the balance of power towards the North; the Hausa felt they were now in control. But was this an adequate excuse for wholesale slaughter?

When he returned to the hotel later he was told that the most successful killings of the day had been at the railway station where one hundred Ibos, waiting to leave for the East, had been executed. The hotel had been staffed largely by these unfortunate people but Nigeria Hotels Ltd, which ran The Central, had, like John Holts, repatriated most of them. This did not prevent Matthew from witnessing one particular act of brutality. Unknown to the management, one of the Ibo cleaners had been living in a store room located on the fringes of the main hotel buildings. He may have been undetected by the hotel staff but a band of eight or nine young Hausa men had rampaged through the premises, inspecting every nook and cranny, and, as Matthew stood at the main entrance, this man and his son, who looked about eight years old, were hacked to death in front of the child's mother. As the boy fell to the ground the mob severed his head from his body and presented it to his mother. One of the perpetrators of this horror spoke to the wailing woman in broken English.

'Go, take this back to your East—to your Ibo place.'

This moment was decisive in the direction Matthew's life was about to take. Forever after he could not explain how it was that he had been frozen to the spot. He did sometimes try to excuse himself by saying it had all happened in a flash—deaths of this kind do not take too long to perpetrate—and truly the incident was all over in minutes. The victims made no attempt to defend themselves and the powerful aggressors had sharp weapons. But this would not suffice. Why had he not intervened? He was not the only bystander. The others were equally ineffectual. Muttering exhortations of 'No!' was the best any of them could manage. Futile, to say the least. When recounting this horror to Isobel, Matthew had attempted to excuse his failure to intervene by describing the uncontrollable frenzy that had seized the assailants, a state no-one watching was prepared to challenge. Extraordinarily, as soon as the Hausa men had left the woman seemed to have acquired an enamel bowl and her son's head was resting in it. Other hotel staff took her away and Matthew went to his room. He sat on the bed but found the tears behind his eyes refused to fall, probably due to the shock and the sense of shame and anger that shook his body. Where was the notion of a united country called Nigeria when one set of Nigerians could act so barbarously towards their fellow citizens? He thought of Peter. If they had decided the contract with John Holts had required both of them to visit Kano, would he still be alive? Matthew cut short his visit and flew back to Lagos the next day.

As a result of this experience he began to realise that, over the next few years, Nigeria was bound to be involved in the fate of the Ibo nation. How and why had this come about? Firstly, the diaspora. The land in Eastern Nigeria occupied by the Ibo was the most densely populated region in Africa, after the Nile Valley, but it was also the most developed, with more schools, more roads and more business enterprises than anywhere else in the country. The people were hard-working, adaptable and fiercely determined to provide the best possible education for their children. Others saw them as the Jews of Africa, unscrupulous and devious in business. But they needed to be resourceful; their over-crowded land would not allow them to live simply as subsistence agriculturists. For this reason many of them had sought their fortunes elsewhere and, until this time, the Northerners, and the non-Ibos in the West and Lagos had accepted their presence amongst them. In 1966 it was estimated there were more than one million Ibos living in Northern Nigeria. This situation was about to change. By May, the Hausa became more and more convinced that the January uprising had been part of an Ibo plot to dominate the politics of the country, as they had tended to dominate commerce, and this led to hundreds of them being killed in Kano, Kaduna and Zaria, followed by the July coup which many observers had seen as inevitable. This precipitated the wholesale slaughter of Ibos, mostly in Northern Nigeria, part of which had been witnessed by Matthew. Some authorities said ten thousand perished in these genocidal killings; others contend the number was closer to thirty thousand. Peter heard of a mother arriving at Enugu railway station with a child's head in an enamel basin which event, together with these thousands of deaths, become a major *casus belli* throughout the East.

At about this time Isobel gave birth to a boy at the Newstead

Nursing Home in Apapa. They named him John—both parents had grandfathers with that name.

After the July coup those officers and men of the Nigerian army of Eastern origin were immediately at risk and there was a spate of unlawful killings at barracks in many parts of the country. These murders went on for weeks until those Ibo soldiers who had not been killed retreated, in one way or another, to the East, leaving the Northern military in control, first in the North, then in the West and Lagos. A number of attempts were made to restore order in the country but, after the atrocities that occurred in barracks and on the streets of many towns in the North, Ojukwu and the Ibo people became convinced a united Nigeria was no longer possible. Thus, the State of Biafra came into existence.

Matthew's assumption that Peter would open a branch of CMS in Port Harcourt proved wrong. Dorothy and the children were being looked after by her father-in-law who had sufficient resources at hand, at least at the beginning of the war, for Peter to feel confident as to their safety. He had also naturally calculated that Port Harcourt would be a prime target for the Federal forces. If he had moved there, how long would he have been able to stay? Matthew understood his concern but pointed out that the town was also essential in Biafra's cause and would no doubt be defended resourcefully.

'Yes, I'm sure it will but it is not really an Ibo town you know. That's what Gowon will say, though there is no doubt its prosperity is due to the efforts of the Ibo. No, I hesitate to run because, despite the atrocities in the North and elsewhere, I'm still not fully convinced Ojukwu has done the right thing.'

'Was there an alternative? If I read it correctly there was an acceptable agreement at Aburi but, thanks to a colossal misunderstanding, it came to nothing.'

'Just so, and I think the opportunity lost is going to have disastrous consequences.'

'You are probably right. Nevertheless, I do not think it is safe for you to stay here.'

'Look Matt, I've lived in Lagos and the West for most of my life. Why should I be forced to move?'

'These are not normal times. Anyway, let's see what happens.'

Peter continued to work at CMS but Matthew became increasingly concerned as Ojukwu and Biafra came under a sustained and fierce attack, both in the media and on the ground. However, it was a Biafran triumph that finally persuaded Peter to leave. Early in August 1967, 'S' Brigade of the Biafran army commanded by a Yoruba, Brigadier Victor Banjo, took the Federal forces totally by surprise as he crossed the Niger at Onitsha and moved into the Midwest. Benin was quickly occupied and by the 20th of the month the Ibo forces had advanced as far as Ore, only one hundred and thirty miles from Lagos. This caused a certain amount of panic within the capital and there were rumours that General Gowon had a plane standing by to fly him to Zaria, but it was also said the British High Commissioner and the American Ambassador at the time persuaded him to stay. The Biafran army advanced no further and, on the 12th of September, Banjo, without authority, ordered a withdrawal from Benin and moved his forces back to the Niger. This was not a tactical move, there was a more evil motivation. Banjo had initiated dealings with some of the Western leaders, including Chief Awolowo, as he had decided on a plot to assassinate Ojukwu. On the 18th of September he reported to his leader in Enugu, taking with him an armed escort but, most foolishly, he had talked about his plot to a number of people and Ojukwu was well-informed as to Banjo's intentions. The only reason a Yoruba had been given this command was because he was a personal friend of Ojukwu, which made this plot all the more despicable. Banjo was arrested and, together with three other ringleaders, sentenced to death for high treason. All were shot at dawn on the 22nd of September.

As this became public in Lagos, Peter, for perhaps the first time, became really concerned for his safety and decided he must leave and join his brothers in Biafra. He had a passport and he might well have been able to buy a ticket and fly to London but there was a real possibility that if he did that he would be arrested at passport control at the airport—and, as he said to Isobel and Matthew, he was not going to be able to help his people if dead or incarcerated somewhere. It was Isobel who came up with a solution. Before John was born, Isobel and Matthew had often visited Cotonou in neighbouring Dahomey to stay at the Hotel de la Plage and enjoy the French cuisine. These weekends had provided a welcome relief from Lagos, particularly when the food supply chain within the country provoked remarks like, 'Oh no, not chicken again.' To sample the oysters and *Filet Mignon* on the hotel's menu under the heading *Par Avion* was for both of them an extravagant delight.

'Why don't we go to Cotonou next weekend?' said Isobel. 'I could do with a break from all this war talk. We can leave John with the Richards.'

'You must be joking—at a time like this?'

'Yes—and I think on this occasion we should take a driver, so it won't matter if you drink too much French vino.'

'What on earth are you babbling about? A driver?'

'Peter. He can then discard his peaked cap and fly out of Cotonou and you can have the pleasure of driving back.'

'What an ingenious idea. You're brilliant, as I've often told you. But do you think he will he agree?'

In the past the only drawback to those weekends away was the hassle suffered by all travellers at the border crossing. This was at Idiroko, about fifty miles from Lagos, where both the Nigerian and the Dahomean customs officers and immigration people enjoyed making things as difficult as possible for all travellers. Matthew always refused to mitigate this experience by distributing items of currency, be it of a Nigerian origin or the CFA Franc that was used throughout ex-French West Africa, but both he and Isobel could see that, with Peter involved, this would be a special case. At this point Isobel suggested they consult Raymond Habib to see if he would like to come with them; they could treat him to a good dinner on the other side to repay his recent hospitality and he would be more skilled at dealing with the border officials than Matthew. In addition, as Isobel pointed out, if they went in his brand-new Mercedes, a driver would appear more natural and the grander the vehicle the more cooperative underlings tended to be. Raymond thought this a most satisfying plan; he loved cocking a snook at officialdom but, he threatened, he would be expecting champagne to be served before the anticipated gourmet feast.

At this point the participants in this scheme gathered together and acquainted Peter with what was proposed. He was very reluctant. He had no problem with his dignity—he could act out the part of the servile driver with the best—but he was concerned about whether such an escape would leave his friends in jeopardy. What if the border people recorded the number of people in the car and noted the discrepancy on the return? He realised he could not use his own passport, but how could he acquire a travel permit of the sort carried by Nigerians who would not normally have a passport? What if they were searched and his passport was found? Raymond took charge. He assured Peter he could help him out with the travel permit and if there were questions on the return journey they would have a story ready about how the driver became ill and had to be admitted to hospital, or how he had run off with a Dahomean damsel, or had been arrested for speeding and the party intended to return next week to arrange bail. We can all, Raymond said, spend the journey seeing who can come up with the best excuse.

Peter made enquiries about Ibo contacts in Cotonou and the party left on a Friday to give credence to its being a weekend jaunt. Matthew and Isobel were tense as they approached the Nigerian border, while Raymond chatted to them over his shoulder; he was in the front seat. Peter, clad in a slightly scruffy white uniform and hard peaked cap, tried to look unconcerned and surly at the same time. The first check was passports, where they joined the usual queue of varied vehicles. There were a few private cars but the Mercedes was held back mainly by a medley of lorries, mammy wagons, overloaded mini-buses and even two mopeds, each being used by a pair of passengers who were attempting to carry over the border baskets containing fruit, packets of sugar cubes and other items that might have extra value in Dahomey. All the passengers of these transports were familiar with the procedure and had left their seats ready to be quizzed and harassed by the officials. Raymond's gleaming grey car was called forward but Peter needed a steady application of the horn to be able to weave his way through the impatient throng. The predictable question was asked: 'Why are you travelling?' The border official hardly bothered to listen to their reply; he appeared to be half asleep from boredom—or perhaps drunk or drugged. Whatever, he waved them through, hardly glancing at their documents, held by Raymond in a fan formation. Indeed, as they moved on, Raymond flapped them around to try and agitate the hot and humid air which entered through the open window and interfered with the air-conditioned interior. When they reached the Nigerian Customs, Peter became centre stage.

The officer ignored the passengers but, in harsh and guttural tones, ordered the driver, 'You, get down and go open de boot.' Peter did this, whereupon the customs man disturbed with his swagger stick the two small weekend suitcases and the paper bag—which ostensibly contained the driver's spare belongings—without asking for anything further to be revealed.

'You can go,' he barked at Peter, who returned to his post and drove to the equivalent operation at Igolo on the Dahomey side. When they reached this point the queue was even longer but nothing was happening because the Dahomean officials, in true French fashion, had closed the border down for two hours—it was lunchtime.

The officials returned to their posts after the mandatory siesta but none of them looked particularly refreshed. No-one asked to see passports; they were unconcerned about people because the car was more important, an indication, thought Matthew, of the materialism of the age. Raymond was required to produce the registration papers for the Mercedes and the insurance certificate, together with the additional endorsement which allowed the vehicle to be taken out of the country. The serial numbers of each of these documents were recorded in a substantial ledger alongside the registration number of the car which was underlined in red ink. To do this the official used, with some care, a black ebony ruler, cylindrical and as thick as a big man's thumb. It looked more like a weapon, thought Isobel, but this was its sole purpose: to underline 'XP 451 LAM'. No record was taken of the number of persons travelling in the car.

On arrival their first point of call was the Monoprix department store where they bought clothes for Peter. They then checked into the hotel and went for a walk on the beach to sharpen their appetites for dinner. This was served in the courtyard of the hotel under palm trees. The lights hanging in these trees and the candles on the tables produced the atmosphere of ease and calm which the travellers welcomed. All enjoyed a delightful meal, including the champagne demanded by Raymond. They left Peter in Cotonou on the Sunday and returned to Lagos. The border crossing was uneventful, but equally tiresome; no-one was concerned about a lost driver.

At a later date, when Matthew related to Jenny the story of the bogus driver episode, she told him of some parallels in her adopted country. The playwright, Athol Fugard, was starting to make a name for himself. He lived in Port Elizabeth and had set up a black drama group there, viewed suspiciously by the authorities. Two of its members had decided to give up their factory jobs to become full-time actors. Such positions for black people in South Africa were not recognised, so one of these aspiring thespians was registered as Fugard's gardener and the other as his driver, even though Fugard did not have a car at that time. Rather more seriously, before he was sent to Robben Island, Nelson Mandela used a chauffeur's uniform as a disguise on more than one occasion.

Except for the soldiers involved in the conflict, and for the Ibo and other minority peoples under siege, most of the country was unaffected by what was happening in Eastern Nigeria. This was also the situation with CMS. Despite Peter's absence, the business considerably expanded during 1968 and 1969. It was becoming more and more expensive to employ expatriates, so they were being replaced by senior Nigerians, mostly promoted from within organisations, leaving vacancies for middle-level managers. This was CMS's speciality and Matthew met the increased demand for their services by employing a number of British businessmen on short-term contracts, some with extensive Nigerian experience in commerce or the civil service who had retired early. In the case of the latter many had been required to leave their posts as the Federal Government indigenised the civil establishment. This provided a short-term solution but Matthew, looking to the future, wanted more Nigerians in senior positions in CMS. To this end he was often able to cherry-pick from the people they were training—gamekeeper turned poacher. It was during this expansion that Femi Oloronshola was employed to fill a new position as Finance Officer. Until then Matthew, with help from Isobel and the accounts clerk, had been able to look after the financial affairs of the firm, but it now became necessary to employ someone at a more senior level. This new appointee had been recommended by Rotimi Lawson. CMS had done work for a British paper company with factories in Lagos and Port Harcourt, as a result of which Matthew had met one of their non-executive directors who had a long Nigerian history. He had served as a District Officer before World War II, but during that conflict had been stationed in Lagos in charge of food rationing. It was he who introduced Matthew to

Lawson, who was one of the first Nigerians to qualify as a chartered accountant, and with whom Matthew became firm friends. His firm were auditors to CMS.

Rotimi Lawson was a Yoruba but one of the few Nigerians Matthew had ever met who had no tribal bias. Because of this, and his commercial ability allied to an easy charm, he was treated with the utmost respect by all in the Nigerian business community. He was a director of a number of major companies and his firm acted as auditors for a wide spread of the commercial world with interests in the country, be they local or international. Unusually for a Nigerian, he also appeared to be apolitical. He deplored what was happening in his country, and what had happened since Independence. Matthew often thought that what Nigeria needed was someone like Rotimi running the country rather than greedy soldiers or self-serving politicians. He acted for many of the major Ibo companies that had a national business, one of which was owned by Peter's father. From his Onitsha trading base, Chief Okonkwo had set up, or was involved in, a number of enterprises throughout Nigeria and he had some substantial property holdings in Lagos. During the war, Rotimi Lawson and Partners continued to look after Okonkwo's affairs. Any monies that were received from these investments were kept in the Lawson Clients Account—clearly they could not be remitted to the East—but Matthew could well imagine that every penny would be meticulously accounted for. Although Rotimi distanced himself from the political scene, with his standing in society he was inevitably well known to many of the ministers in the first civilian government and to members of the opposition, including people like Chief Awolowo and traditional leaders in the West and the North.

Matthew soon heard from Peter. After a tedious journey via London, Lisbon and Sao Tome, he was finally reunited with Dorothy and the children. This reunion was cut short when he was given a message to join his father in Umuahia as soon as possible. On reaching what was now the capital of Biafra, he found his father, who had been a great friend of Ojukwu's father, had been given the role of food commissar within Biafra. His terms of reference were to facilitate the distribution of local produce to those parts of Biafra where the threat of starvation was most serious. He was not involved with distributing whatever food aid was brought into the country, but he quickly brought Peter up to date on that front.

By April 1968 the Ibo forces had been pushed out of the Cross River valley. This had been a major source of food and reports from the Red Cross and others being transmitted to the West from the considerably reduced Biafra contained warnings about the increasing spread of *kwashiorkor*. Outside the medical profession, this condition, usually found in children suffering from protein deficiency, was unfamiliar until the advent of world-wide television reporting. The image of pot-bellied children standing on stick-like legs, usually with black or brown skin, became recognised all over the world as a sign to write out a cheque for Oxfam, or Caritas, or another similar organisation. Regretfully, Biafra provided many examples that brought tears to the eyes and a loosening of the purse-strings. All the major aid agencies found themselves well-funded to provide the relief that might save the lives of these children, but getting the powdered milk from Copenhagen or Amsterdam into Biafra was another matter. A number of proposals had been made by governments and agencies involving land corridors and water transport but Federal Nigeria was less than cooperative and Ojukwu was concerned that if this donated food passed through the hands of his opponents it would be tampered with. By the middle of 1968 an Oxfam representative reported that if substantial supplies of food were not brought into the country within six weeks or so four hundred thousand children could die of starvation. He had estimated the supplies needed were three hundred tons per day. This was eventually achieved, but not before many had died. The airlift into Biafra of both arms and relief supplies became a central saga within this conflict. Indeed, the aeroplane, whether used to kill or to succour, played a major role in the Biafran war. Aircraft attacks by Federal forces were indiscriminate and often inefficient, and the bombing of civilians greatly influenced public opinion in the United States and the West. On the other hand, many of the pilots on the Biafran side displayed considerable courage and resourcefulness when flying in both arms and aid.

Father and son were delighted to see each other although the parent was unhappy that his son had delayed returning to Biafra for no reason that made any sense to him. However, he had interesting news for Peter: Ojukwu wanted to see him—he had a job for him. Peter recalled what he knew about the Biafran leader. Colonel Emeka Ojukwu had been born into wealth. His father amassed a fortune from transport and property but he did not live to see the part his son was to play in the future of Nigeria; he died in September 1966. Peter was pleased he was now going to be able to form a view about Ojukwu the soldier after meeting him face to face, but he was apprehensive about taking on any assignment when he was still not fully convinced the break from the rest of Nigeria had been unavoidable.

'Why did you stay in Lagos? Aren't you a true Ibo?

'Your Excellency, it is complicated. You ask a very straightforward question and I will try and reply in the same manner. Yes, I am very much an Ibo but I also want to be a Nigerian. We could be the most important country in Africa and I thought we would show the world we have the will, the brains and the resources to face the imperial powers as equals. It is partly because of imperialism that we have today's crisis. A divided Nigeria. Different peoples who were just as different when the borders were established those many years ago. I so desperately wanted to see if we could reconcile things with the Hausa; I wasn't sure secession was the only course available.'

'You are a very brave, or perhaps foolhardy, somebody to say that to me—but go on.'

'Even when the attitude taken by Gowon, whom I now see is only a puppet for the Northerners, seemed to indicate you were right, I still had this crazy idea that perhaps I could do some good in Lagos and change people's minds. Of course, that was an idiotic notion. Outside Biafra, almost everyone sees us as rebels.'

'I'm very glad, for your father's sake, to hear you have come to your senses and realise what opposition we face. There are too many luke-warmers, or traitors around, and I didn't want to see you as one. So you are now firmly in the family?'

'Yes, Sir. You have a massive task and I want to help.'

'Good. I have an assignment for you, my friend, never you worry. You wouldn't be sitting here taking up my valuable time if I didn't. I respect your father. He tells me you have a sharp brain. We shall put it to use. I want you to work with Cyprian Okere. He will brief you.'

Without further ado, Peter was ushered out.

When he next met Matthew he tried to explain to his friend what impression Ojukwu had made at this first meeting. The most surprising characteristic was the voice. Although he had a council of advisors around him this man was, in effect, the supreme leader with sole responsibility for millions of people, all of whom faced an uncertain future. And yet he was as calm and soft-spoken as a general practitioner giving medical advice to a patient in a perfect bedside manner. For a Nigerian the voice was exceptionally low and he spoke in slow and measured tones. He was heavily-built with an ebony black beard, cut short. His eyes were piercing, seeing, Peter thought, into the very recesses of men's minds.

'Nonsense of course,' he said to Matthew, 'but I must tell you he impressed me greatly. He was always said to have the best brain in the army and now I can well believe it.'

Cyprian Okere had been a senior executive in the Nigerian Broadcasting Corporation but was now a member of the crucial team set up to present the Biafran image to the outside world.

'Let me tell you what this department is doing. As you know, Biafra has been recognised by a few countries, very few unfortunately, but for most of the world we are dissenters engaged in an African bush-war. At the start the UK in particular paid little attention because they thought it would all be over in a matter of weeks.'

'Yes, just like World War One—a conflict that resulted in more than ten million deaths and which the British said would be over by Christmas.'

'Exactly. What Britain and America fail to realise, or are not prepared to understand, is that this situation is one we couldn't avoid. The Northerners have made it clear they are going to run Nigeria and, what with that and the slaughter of our people on the streets, what alternative did we have?'

'Yes. My partner was at Kano airport when those criminals dragged people off the BOAC plane.'

'It makes me want to spit in anger. Well, of course the British soon discovered we were not going to be finished off in days, but instead of adopting a neutral stance they have now come out fully on the Feds side, supplying arms and manipulating the media to portray Colonel Ojukwu as an egotistical monster deliberately leading his reluctant people towards death or starvation. I may be exaggerating but it does sometimes read like that.'

'I've only just come from him and although I have not met him before he seems very sincere to me.'

'Without him we would be nothing. We are now getting responsible British journalists visiting us and touring the country to see for themselves how we go suffer. One or two are writing accurate reports but there are still those who send in their copy from the comfort of the Lagos hotels without even bothering to look at Biafra on the ground. I think, as the world's general public are now seeing pictures of our hungry children, the media will become less biased, but none of this seems to have any effect on the intransigence of the British Government. We are still rebels who need to be subdued, whether by guns or starvation.'

'Yes. I could see that when in Lagos and, before you ask me, let me tell you I stayed away from home thinking I might be able to help from the other side of the line, but that was a foolish mistake. My little voice was certainly crying in the wilderness. What I find sickening is that Gowon, and the people behind him, are deliberately using starvation as a weapon, and the British Government seems prepared to connive at this. How can there be a "One Nigeria" in the future? You probably know the Federal slogan is, "To keep Nigeria one is a job that must be done." Well, it now seems to me the watchword for the unspoken subplot is, "One Nigeria *sans* Ibo". Not because we are separated from the rest of the country but because we will be exterminated. All right, another exaggeration, but what else are we to think?'

Peter soon realised he was more likely to make an effective contribution to the Biafran cause in an intellectual capacity than with a gun in his hand and he therefore welcomed his new role. He found Okere an intelligent man, fully conscious of the difficulties of the new regime. He was not one of those blind patriots who were convinced his people would win because their cause was a 'righteous one'. He knew the logistics told a different story. Despite the best efforts of the Biafran leadership, and of the bureau of which Okere was a key member, the small number of countries that had recognised the new State was insignificant in world opinion. In particular, despite early indications of support from the general public in Britain, their Government was a staunch supporter of the Federal camp. As Okere pointed out to Peter, the headquarters of Shell was only just across the river from the 'Mother of all Parliaments'.

Peter was given the task of analysing the British press reports which dealt with the conflict but, after about six months, he was also charged with acting as the main point of contact within the administration for visiting London newspapermen. Initially, he wondered why he had been singled out for these duties. His father obviously had more influence than he realised, but he soon found that Okere would not have left him in this position if he had proved less than able and dedicated. Peter also believed working alongside Matthew had sharpened his ability to deal with the vagaries of the British mind, particularly as displayed by hard-bitten and sceptical reporters.

One of the reporters Peter dealt with during the early part of 1969 happened to mention that the Defence Advisor at the British High Commission in Lagos was still Brigadier Lakey, and went on to say he appeared to have considerable influence in Lagos and, he thought, in Whitehall. As a result of this information Peter began to wonder if something could be made of this in the Biafran cause. He talked it over with Okere who showed interest.

'Using this Lakey somebody might be a waste of time, but I will try anything. Is he anti-Ibo?'

'No, I would say not. Ironically, as a military man, he deplores this war. He has said to my partner, Matt, and me that there are clean wars and dirty wars. The first is when you are fighting for an unambiguous cause. He fought in Burma against the Japanese. They wanted to dominate the Pacific, as Hitler wanted to see a fascist world created in his image—things worth fighting against. Even Korea to an extent—to halt the spread of communism. He's not sure about the Spanish Civil War but he is clear about our conflict—a very dirty war indeed. Of course, these are his personal views—under the table as it were—but if you think we can provide him with an angle, or facts not common knowledge, to help our cause, I believe we could persuade him to pass such information up the line and try and penetrate the Whitehall brick wall.'

'Splendid. Just what I wanted to hear. It is your partner he's most friendly with, is it not? We could try and get you back to Lagos and talk to Lakey but it sounds to me, if you agree, we will get a better result if the messenger is one of their own. Do you think Cresswell would do it for us?'

'I'm almost certain he would, and not just because of our

friendship, which is very strong, but because of what he has seen being done to the Ibo.'

'Good. This plan seems to be developing some legs. What we need to do is to get your friend over here so he can see what conditions are like, and how our people are suffering. Then, if he does act as a go-between with Lakey, he will be speaking from first-hand experience. Will he come, do you think?'

'Probably yes. Presumably you have channels to get messages to Lagos?'

'Yes. I can get a letter from you into his hands in less than a week. In the meantime, let's see if we can assemble the most potent catalogue of facts for our new agent to take back, hopefully to number ten Downing Street.'

Shortly after Okere and Peter were engaged in formulating this plot, Gerard Lakey unexpectedly asked this potential new agent to come and see him at the offices of the High Commission in Kajola House. Matthew wondered what this was for. Any matters concerning the contract for the Military Defence Academy were usually dealt with by Lakey visiting CMS; visits in the opposite direction were rare. Lakey looked grave. He moved towards his visitor and made sure the door of his office was properly closed.

'Matt, this conversation never took place. Understand?'

'No. Frankly I don't. Sun got to you at last?'

'It is no joke. I have the feeling you might be planning to visit Peter. If so I want to ask for your help.'

'How do you know what I am going to do? Surely you're not keeping tabs on me?'

Lakey, in conventional style, tapped the side of his nose.

'Don't worry; we know a lot more than people think, but what is important is that HMG wants you to help.'

'Is that the Queen personally?'

'Don't be flippant, you idiot. This is not a subject for jest. We need to know reliably what conditions are like in Biafra.'

'Hold on. You want me to be your informant? Am I being recruited as a spy? What's the stipend like?

'None of that. I don't think we are getting a true picture of what life is really like. I'm not asking for a report on the military situation, because frankly that's not too difficult to judge. The Hausa soldiers charge down the main roads firing at shadows while the Ibo uses the bush, near perfect guerrilla country, to harry the enemy and attack with their fiendishly effective homemade rockets. It might make a good subject for a research paper at the Staff College. "Has there ever been a modern war where so much ammunition was wasted?" And what galls me, part of it is supplied by us.'

'Well, why don't you stop supplying arms altogether?'

'It's not that simple. The UK arms industry is part of the UK economy, provides employment, and as long as we believe they are going to be used in a proper way, then Nigeria is simply a customer.'

'Proper way—for Christ's sake Gerard! Is it proper what's happening over there?

'Just between you and me, I don't much like the situation either but back to the subject at hand. If you do go, will you report to me what your impressions are?'

'I'll think about it. Now, aren't you going to at least offer me a cup of tea?'

Matthew received Peter's letter and decided he should go.

The interior of the plane was in darkness from the time of take-off to landing. Most of the aircraft capacity was taken up with packing crates clearly marked with the logos of the Red Cross or similar sister organisations, but at the front of the plane were two rows of seats. Conversation with the other passengers, a mixed bag and all strangers to Matthew, seemed inappropriate in the inky blackness; so he pondered. What was he doing on this aeroplane flying into darkest Africa? Was he seeking his Kurtz? Some people in Lagos might see Ojukwu in this enigmatic role and would Matthew agree with them after this visit? Was he taking an unnecessary risk travelling into this twentieth century 'Heart of Darkness'? Isobel was understandably nervous but she had seemed able to articulate a convincing reason for his action before the more slow-thinking Matthew had provided a conclusion for himself. She pointed out he did not support the action being taken against the Ibo and he did not agree with the tactics being employed by the Federal forces. In addition, if the continuation of this horrible conflict could not be halted, she knew he would want to do what he could to persuade the British Government to be more neutral in approach. She then came to the crux of the argument: Peter. He had been somewhat lukewarm about secession but had now written in such passionate terms Matthew had felt compelled to respond in the name of friendship. He would embark on this mission, perhaps a perilous one, because of Peter. The letter had been guarded; short on detail but vividly clear in its sentiments. Matthew could help his friend and his friend's new country. He had the opportunity of being cast for what might turn out to be a prominent role in bringing this war to an end—so please help. Matthew could not see he was in any way fitted for such a task but he was prepared to admit to himself he was mildly excited about the prospect of being centre stage instead of in his usual position as assistant to the assistant stage manager. His father had chosen to be a soldier and, despite his reticent nature, had seen real action on a number of fronts, even under-cover for his last act of all, but Matthew, until now, had been firmly located in the rear. The most adventurous thing he had undertaken to date was to apply for a job in Nigeria and take a trip to Cotonou. Was this about to be changed in the most dramatic fashion?

The plane droned on. Surprisingly, he found he was able to detach his thoughts from war, politics and starvation. He thought about air travel and its state of unreality. It is out of this world; it is illusory, he said to himself. The cocoon within the aircraft flying at many times the speed of a motorcar, at thirty-five thousand feet above the earth, creates this sense of fantasy. There are sound mechanical explanations for the existence of these isolated pockets of rarefied air inhabited by a few hundred strangers, but as they attempt to eat a unique brand of food while confined to a space only twenty inches wide it is easy to wonder, where are we? On a train or in a car or on board ship the travellers can connect to their own world, the earth or the sea. The latter may appear unrelated to normal life but oceans change and items of landscape can be seen, but in the air we are enveloped in nothing, or at least nothing we can relate to. All that can be seen is tightly contained within a space that allows for no escape. The desperate can plunge from a moving car or train, or dive into the adjoining sea, but until this mechanical monster returns to Mother Earth all are trapped. Parachutes and ejector seats are not for these drones huddled together in their A300s or DC10s. In an extraordinary way even the return to earthly reality is distorted. Just occasionally, Windsor Castle can be recognised on the approach to Heathrow but, for the most part, those who bother to try and regain their material selves before the wheels touch the tarmac will scan, with little success, the urban landscape below to try and determine whether that is the River Thames or that shape really Table Mountain. More often than not the detachment is complete, right up until they first place their swollen feet on *terra firma*.

Matthew recalled this sense of the unreal from his first flight to Lagos those years before. If anything, he mused, the bar of the Stratocruiser, hung below the aeroplane, exaggerated the feeling of extreme detachment. He had flown many times since then and Lagos and its environs had become very familiar but he had often peered through the window as the aircraft descended and invariably could not tell whether the landscape of unkempt huts below was part of the suburbs of Agege or those of Ondo or Ikorodu. However, the flight into Uli, Biafra's makeshift airfield, was of a totally different calibre. There was none of the feigned luxury of the commercial airliner. The DC3 carrying Matthew from Sao Tome to his rendezvous with Peter was cold and noisy. There was even more of a contrast when the plane came into land. Matthew was not given the opportunity to guess from the geography of the runway where they were because the approach was taking place in almost total darkness. There must have been rudimentary lighting to guide the pilot, but the passengers exchanged the pitch-black of the cockpit for an invisible runway. Uli—Biafra's airport metropolis

Peter was there to meet him and they hurried away from the airport as quickly as possible to a nearby village where a bedroom had been made available for Matthew. Dawn was approaching as he reached his lodging but the condition of the people, both adults and children, was not difficult to perceive, both alongside the road and beneath the window of the room where he was destined to sleep. Here was a miscellaneous group of children and adults squatting on the ground. Nothing Matthew had seen in the newspapers or on television could have prepared him for this horrific tableau. In the thin morning light it was difficult to separate one person from another, or adult from child. It seemed to be a near inert mass of human flesh torn from the tormented world of Hieronymus Bosch. As Matthew peered more closely he could see an old woman whose eyes were open and staring at him but whose body was withered and dreadfully emaciated. There were two other adults, both women, one of whom had a child at her breast. Their eyes were closed. The five children crouching at the base of this parcel of sickened humanity automatically extended their hands towards the white man, palms towards heaven and the God who had deserted them. Matthew also; he had nothing to give them. He then realised that no-one amongst this group had uttered any sound. These were Nigerians, who worshipped noise and were never at a loss for something to say, but now these people were so traumatised, perhaps so close to death, even the supplicant children could only go through the motions. None of the usual, 'Please massa, I go beg you.' He sat on the rudimentary bed and swore under his breath. How had this been allowed to happen?

By the time Matthew woke the sun was high and the people camped under his bedroom window had gone. There had been early morning rain and the air smelled fresh. He told Peter of the people who had been squatting so close to him while he slept.

'Yes, I caught a glimpse of them. You will discover this war has bound the Ibo people together in a way no other event could, but we are still human beings, with our own frailties and failings. There has been an amazing cooperative effort, particularly on the fighting front, but if I can scrounge a bit more gari than the next man I'll do so. The result is inevitable. The strong and resourceful survive better than the weak, particularly if the male members of the family are dead or away fighting. This is not Utopia you know. The army gets priority in the food stakes but there are sure to be some unscrupulous people elsewhere who are able to bribe, or coerce, in order to get more than their fair share of the aid-supplies. You won't remember my young cousin Joseph. He was at the wedding. When the fighting began he was still at Nsukka University but he was soon in the army and by the time he was nineteen he was said to be the youngest Captain in the Biafran forces. Well, he seems to be well fed.'

'Are these supplies getting through all right? There were problems at the start, were there not?'

'Yes. Everything still has to be flown in but the shipments are regular and the overall position is much improved.'

'Thank God for that. But I suppose there must be a major refugee problem.'

'Yes. This obviously makes the food situation more difficult but there is also the question of accommodation. I don't know what the statistics are but we are probably housing the same number of people in a land area one quarter of the pre-war size. You know what was the Eastern Region stretched from Nsukka and Ogoja in the North up to the Cameroon border in the East and all of the Delta around from Calabar to Port Harcourt and beyond. Not all occupied by Ibos, of course, but the Efiks and Ijaws and others are no supporters of Gowon and, as their land was taken, they retreated into the much reduced Biafra.'

Before the meeting with Okere, Peter had been instructed to spend two or three days with Matthew showing him conditions in the country. The disparity between the hungry and the well-fed soon became obvious but what particularly stayed in Matthew's memory was the visit they made to a refugee camp on the outskirts of Umuahia. This had formerly been the Public Works Department depot for the city. Many in this camp lived in tents or hastily constructed shacks but near the centre of this overcrowded area was a fairly substantial building that had previously been the office block. The yard and offices no longer saw the daily comings and goings of trucks, cement mixers and loads of concrete blocks, nor the gossip of carpenters, bricklayers and labourers gathered for their mid-morning tea break and smoke. What was now in evidence was a mass of bedraggled humanity punctuated at regular intervals by cooking fires; noisy children ran in and out of tents and ramshackle huts. There were no animals. In the office building were seven separate rooms occupied by seven families who shared the office cloakroom, where there was a WC and a wash basin but no bath or shower. A communal lean-to kitchen had been added to one end of the building. The maximum number in any of these rooms was four adults and five children but not one of them contained fewer than four people. Matthew calculated that what would have housed the small desks of seven supervisors or typists or clerks, plus one or two messengers, was now home to more than forty people.

As he made these calculations, one of this number emerged from the cloakroom with a threadbare towel in his hand. He was a thin man of middle age wearing spectacles, the frame of which had been repaired in two places with flesh-coloured sticking plaster. He greeted Peter and Matthew with a friendly salute.

'Can I help you?'

'Sorry to intrude. This is my colleague, Peter Okonkwo, and I am Matthew Cresswell, visiting from Lagos.'

'I see. How is the big city?'

'The same. Chaotic as usual. You know it well?'

'No. I have visited it a number of times but until the war I was at Nsukka.'

'Were you at the university there?'

'Yes. I was a professor of African history.'

'Oh. I did history at Nottingham.'

'Researching Robin Hood, no doubt. Excuse my frivolity but these days I need to exercise my sense of humour.'

'We understand. Do you have your family with you?'

'No, my wife went back to our village south of Aba while I was still at the university and we have not managed to make contact since then. As you can imagine, I'm very worried.'

'Yes. Children?'

'Three. She took them with her.'

'Are you here on your own?'

'No, my steward stayed with me in Nsukka so, when we had to leave, we all came together.'

'All?'

'Eke and his wife and three children. We have one of these rooms divided by a curtain.'

'How do you put up with it?'

'I have no alternative. My home is not this place and I have no friends or relations to go to. We are lucky to get what we have.'

'Where does Eke come from?'

'He was born near Nsukka, so his home has now no doubt been taken over by the soldiers.'

'Are you able to work? Sorry to ask you all these questions but the more I know about how people like you are faring—oh, I don't know—perhaps I can stir people up in Lagos to finish this whole bloody affair.'

'I don't mind. Makes a change to talk to someone where the topic of conversation is not food or, to be more precise, the lack of it. Yes. They've got a school going at the large refugee camp set up down the road on what used to be a Boy Scout camping ground. I go there most days to teach but it is hard for the kids to concentrate when their stomachs are so empty.'

'What a tragedy this all is. Is any of it worth while? Was Ojukwu right to secede?'

'I don't know. We hear so many rumours about him—not listening to advice. They say we could get more food in if he would agree to daylight flights, but he won't. He's a stubborn man.'

'Wish I could offer you some real help. What do you need the most?'

'You'll probably be surprised. I'd love a bottle of cold beer and a large pot of pepper soup but, at the moment, what I really crave is soap. I hate not being able to wash properly.'

Peter said he would see what he could do and both men thanked the professor for talking to them. They shook hands in formal fashion. As he left Matthew could only, once again, deplore what casualties this war was responsible for. This intelligent man could at any time die by bomb or bullet, or starvation, but what he most hated was not being able to maintain the standard of hygiene he was used to. Would he and Peter feel the same way in similar circumstances?

During the tour of the area, Matthew tried to assess what the impact of this conflict had had, or was likely to have, on the differing participants. The Federal army, mainly composed of soldiers of Northern origin, was no doubt being paid well and fed well, but it was general knowledge that they were reluctant soldiers. Their leaders were no doubt quite clear as to why lives were being put at risk, but did the man at the front, or his mother, follow this? At the highest level it was obvious that the former Eastern Region could not be permitted to secede, for it was where the oil was to be found. Although oil prospecting in Nigeria had a long history—Shell D'arcy were on the spot in the 1930s—it was only in recent times that the size and economic potential of Nigeria's oil fields was being realised. This valuable resource belonged to all, not just to the Easterner. Matthew was sure Ojukwu was fully aware of this but, considering what had happened over the last few years, he was equally convinced oil was not the primary motive for the split. He could not erase from his mind the picture of a boy's head sitting in an enamel bowl. That child was not killed for the sake of oil riches.

The soldier facing the Federal army had a clearer notion of what he was fighting for. His homeland was being invaded—he was engaged in a war for survival, although tales were rife about the methods of conscription employed by the Biafran commanders. No male was safe from being forced to bear arms. However, whether by compulsion or a voluntary sense of patriotism, many had died and many more would suffer the same fate. Peter took Matthew as close to a combat zone as was possible but it was not clear to either of them in which direction rifles were pointed, and whose rifles they were. Matthew recalled what his mother had told him of his father's experience in the trenches during World War I. Sometimes for months, if not years, the opposing armies did not move, but faced each other over the same piece of no-man's-land. Here, the action was, to say the least, fluid. As the Federal forces overran a village, the villagers and the soldiers vanished into the surrounding bush; as their opponents moved on, they moved back, even though there may not have been much to move back to. For the mass of the people caught up in this horror, it was not just their lives but their material being that was affected. The refugees; would they ever see their homes again? And how would they reconstruct the life they had, their houses, their schools, their farms and their businesses? They were going to need a lot of help, thought Matthew, and when this devastation is caused by a civil war, where is help to come from? He was a reluctant witness to this tragedy. The events at Kano were etched into his mind. Less than ten years after Independence he had seen, at the PWD refugee camp, men, women and children living in utter squalor and poverty.

Before the scheduled meeting with Okere, he told Peter of his interview with Lakey.

'Is it fate? Am I destined to be the classic double agent?'

'What do you mean?'

'One side wants me to paint a picture for the Brigadier to see if the colours can change any minds in London and your lot want me to do the same thing, but commissioned by Colonel Ojukwu.'

'For the moment, I can't see a problem.'

'If I were a lawyer you would ask me who I was acting for. Is there a conflict of interests?'

'No. You simply don't tell Lakey you are acting for both sides.'

'That would be the obvious course but I think I might get a more sympathetic hearing, at least in Whitehall—at a distance as it were—if I come clean and become what I want to be, the honest broker acting in the best interests of both parties.'

'Is that possible? I'm not sure. Let's see what Okere thinks. But whatever happens you must make sure the Feds don't find out what you're up to. You are hardly going to be an international spy. I don't think Len Deighton would be interested in you, but that lot can act illogically and I don't want to be visiting you in Kirikiri when this war is over.'

'No danger of that. I'm sure Gerard is secure so from where else can they find out? As far as the office and our friends are concerned, I've travelled to the UK on business. Unless Isobel should decide to trade me in for a younger model.'

'Do not jest, my friend. This is serious stuff.'

They spent an hour with Okere, who established a relaxed atmosphere from the start.

'I do appreciate you agreeing to take this on, Mr Cresswell. It might be a complete waste of time, but you never know. By the way, I think we've met before. Were you in the Festival Players?'

'Yes. Or, more accurately, my wife was; she's the performer. I just do the labouring jobs.'

'May I call you Matt?'

'Fine.'

'Well, Matt, I was involved in the arrangements the group made with the Nigerian Broadcasting Corporation when you made a recording of Dylan Thomas's *Under Milk Wood.* I sat in on the first rehearsal to make sure the mikes were working properly.'

'What a coincidence. Peter told me you were with the Broadcasting Corporation. We had great fun over that recording. Even I had a part.'

'I was also with the Lagos Players for a short time.'

'Oh. I think the Festival players did a joint production with them before our time. So you would know Jab Adu and the Olusolas. Of course, Winnie was in your business, working for the *Voice of America.*'

'Sure. Good friends of mine—which only goes to show how sickening this war is. Yes, they're my friends, Yorubas, but now we face each other over a firing line. What a tragedy!'

Peter intervened.

'I couldn't agree more. The classic civil war situation: friend killing friend. This is the leitmotif of this sorry state of affairs. Although few of us have many Hausa friends, I am not antagonistic to them individually. It's just that at university, and even in our business life, we get to meet so few of them. But with other Nigerians in the South, it is nearly like brother fighting brother. As I told you before, Cyprian, I had the temerity to tell the Colonel at the time that I wasn't sure cessation was the best move. Oh dear, what a mess!'

'Most of us here,' said Cyprian, 'feel much the same way. But did we have a choice? Anyway, let's get on with the task in hand. Matt, you look anxious to say something.'

'I've already told Peter this, but there has been an interesting development. Just before I left Lagos, Brigadier Lakey called me to his office to ask if I was planning to visit Peter and, if so, would I report back on what conditions were really like in Biafra. You probably know that in London and Lagos they believe your people in Geneva have been too successful and what we read and see on TV is Biafran propaganda—pictures of starving children stage-managed by Ojukwu himself.'

'That's interesting. What did you say?'

'I was noncommittal. I joked about how ludicrous I would be as an informant. Kept it light and cosy and asked him if the pay was good, but I know he was deadly serious.'

'Well. We now have a situation here. I need to think this through and consult my colleagues. Whatever do we do next?'

'Having talked to Peter about this dilemma, if that's what it is, what I would like to do is to come clean with both sides. If Lakey knows what I am presenting to him comes with your seal of approval—I mean both sides know what I'm doing—then the UK might be more convinced of the authenticity of what I tell them.'

'Look, you two, let's meet again this afternoon. My first reaction is that our best bet is to be totally honest. Hands on the table. I'm sure there is an Ibo proverb to cover this situation, and even more sure there is a Yoruba one, but "nuttin done come to mind" for now. I'm getting quite excited.'

In the event, Okere sent them a message that he could not see them until the following afternoon so they decided to occupy the morning by visiting Amichi. Since his departure from Lagos in May 1967, nothing had been heard from their former cook, Tobias, but Matthew had an old address and he and Peter thought it worthwhile trying to see if he was still alive. They found the village without too much difficulty and, as seemed to be the norm in this densely populated land, the third person they asked knew of Tobias and exactly where he was staying. Both men were astonished at his appearance. Tobias was clearly not sure who Peter was, but he recognised Matthew immediately. The man standing in front of them, clad in a single piece of a faded cloth tied around his waist, was thin but appeared reasonably healthy. A purple scar meandered from his shoulder and down his left arm nearly as far as the wrist, but what had momentarily obscured his identity was his hair. It was still thick and curly but as white as snow. Matthew saw this even more closely as Tobias fell to his knees and took Matthew's hands into his. His first words were barely audible.

'Massa, you done come oh. How is Madam?'

'Tobias. Thank God, you're still alive. You look very thin. Are you chopping well?'

'Yes, sir. We now get food but before we very hungry. It is good see you. What of Madam?'

'She is well. We now have a baby son.'

'Ah ah. Wonderful.'

'Is your brother living nearby? Is Grace still alive?'

At this Tobias burst into tears and fell to the ground. Matthew pulled him up.

'No, sir. Both dead.'

'I'm so sorry. What happened?'

'Last year. Five soldiers come and they abuse Grace and shoot my brother.'

'How awful! From the Federal army?'

'No, Massa. They be Biafra armyboys.'

'No! Can you tell us what happened.'

'Just before evening time, these men burst into room we sharing. All have those *atamoti* guns. They shouting and swearing. Very drunk or drug taken. They told us stand up. Point gun at me and my brother. Pull wrapper from Grace and throw her to de ground. One man sit on her head. Others stand on her arms with big boots while first soldier pulled down his trouser and take out his thing and push between Grace's legs.'

'You mean he raped her?'

'No, Sir, all of them do it. Take turns. Then turn her over and first man he do it again—in anus. My brother and I is screaming but gun pushed into our bellies. He can stand no more. Put hand to soldier's throat and spits in his face. Where he got spit from I no know. My mouth like skin of coconut. Shoot him. Five bullets. I run. What could I do? They no bother follow me.'

'How horrible! What happened to Grace?'

'I very scared. Stay in bush three nights. When comeback, Grace dead. People say she lose much blood.'

Matthew was speechless. Peter asked Tobias if he was sure they were Ibo soldiers. He replied that he knew they were. They spoke the Ibo tongue. When he was asked if he had reported this to the police, he shrugged his shoulders, a gesture that spoke volumes.

'Even if I done find policeman, what they go do against soldier boy'.

Matthew gave Tobias what money he had and promised to come and see him again soon. During the drive back to Umuahia Peter and Matthew said very little. Matthew tried to picture the scene just described to them but for some reason he could not—all he saw in his mind's eye was an image of the head of a child nestling in a blood-stained grimy enamel bowl.

The journey from Amichi was not without incident. When they were about twenty miles on their way, they heard a plane overhead. Peter slowed down, then pulled into the side of the road to park. Before either of them could leave the vehicle they heard a deep crunching sound like the note created by the most bass of all bass drums followed by an orange flash and sound of people screaming and wailing. More casualties, they thought, as they drove forward. The road was still intact but a small huddle of huts alongside was on fire—the straw roofs providing first class incendiary material. They stopped and were told that, by a miracle, no-one was hurt. When the bomb had fallen everyone, including children, had been assembled under the traditional palm-oil tree where village meetings were held.

'What a relief!' said Matthew. 'I have just about had enough for today. If you had driven a little faster, Peter, we could well have found ourselves a more productive target for that bomb.'

At the final meeting with Okere, Matthew discovered that he was to be drawn rather more deeply into the political scenario than he had at first expected.

'Matthew, I've had prepared a brief for you to present to Lakey.

He may well be apprised of most of what it contains but there are some facts in this that may help our relationship with your Queen. However, with the approval of the boss, Peter's father has come up with an idea and we hope you will agree to help.'

'After what I was told yesterday, I will do anything I can to stop this awful conflict'.

'You had better hear what is involved. I know your heart is in the right place but you will need to use your head with this one. Could be perilous.'

Matthew said nothing.

'Chief Okonkwo and Rotimi Lawson are old friends, as you probably know, and you could say the same for our Commander-in-Chief and his father. They both admired Lawson—a man of great integrity and honesty, respected by many. At the last Council meeting a view was expressed that the Yoruba might be nearly as antagonistic to the Northern soldiery, and the Northern hierarchy, as we are. After subduing the Ibo, will the Hausa seek to impose their will on the Westerners? Far-fetched perhaps, but it did begin a process of thought that led to the idea of trying to contact some of the Yoruba leaders to see if they could influence Gowon and his backers to find a way to a peace with us and some fair dealing in the future.'

'Where do I come in?'

'It was Chief Okonkwo's suggestion that we contact Rotimi Lawson and see if he would act as a go-between with people like Chief Awolowo and some of the Obas and we ask if you would be prepared to see Lawson when you get back, explain what we have in mind, and deliver this personal letter written by Chief Okonkwo, with the authority of Ojukwu. You can add your own account of this meeting and, even more importantly, what you have seen on the ground during this short visit.'

Matthews' face became contorted with a mixture of apprehension and grief as a picture flashed into his mind of the interior of the hut where he had met Tobias. Okere continued.

'No-one will condemn you if you say no. This could be dangerous. If Lawson agrees, but the Yorubas are not as discontented as we think they are and report this approach to the Federal Government, the messenger—you that is—could be in some trouble.'

'Yes, I see that. Is it worth the risk for something that is probably a forlorn hope?' Again Matthew recalled Tobias' face with tears running down his cheeks. 'But what the hell! Nothing ventured, as they say. Sure, I'll do it. And I'll tell you why.'

He was about to relate Grace's fate but realised, once more, that, although he fully sympathised with the lot of the Ibo people, his involvement in this unhappy conflict was just as much about that extraordinary bond of friendship he had with Peter as it was with what he had seen over the last few days. Charles Cresswell would have understood this, so Matthew said nothing other than to express how keen he was to make any contribution that might lead to a peaceful settlement.

On his return to Lagos, and before seeing Gerard Lakey, he called on Rotimi Lawson at his house in Ikoyi. He later told Isobel that he came away from that meeting uncertain of Lawson's reaction. He had been somewhat surprised to find Matthew acting in this role but he had read the letter from Chief Okonkwo with some care and listened attentively to Matthew's background explanation. He appeared to be sceptical that an approach to the likes of Chief Awolowo would yield any results but he did agree to put out some feelers and do what he could. However, he became more positive as he warned Matthew to keep this entire affair as secret as possible and that he could be in real trouble if anyone in the Federal Government found out about his role. If there was to be an involvement with the Yoruba establishment he, Lawson, would be at the centre but his position in society might save him from any severe retribution. Not so Matthew. He would be seen as an interfering foreigner and, as Rotimi said, the last thing he wanted was to be sending food parcels to Kirikiri prison. Naturally, this did nothing to ease Matthew's anxieties.

He then moved on to his next task, to visit Lakey. He took with him the report Okere had given him, which included a paper by a medical group set up for the purpose, recording the improved overall level of calories being enjoyed by the Biafrans since the aid supply chain had been improved. However, this made for disturbing reading when compared with the intake accepted as the necessary minimum for a healthy populace. Details were also provided of approximate casualty levels since the start of hostilities and an attempt had been made to divide these between civilians and soldiers, firstly killed or wounded by air raids and then similarly at the front. The figures also gave deaths said to be due to malnutrition. No mention, Matthew thought grimly, of women killed by their own soldiers. In addition to these papers he went to his meeting not only with his direct experience of conditions on the ground in Biafra, but with another card he intended to play at an appropriate moment—if necessary—Aunt Edith. For security reasons he had kept her letter locked away at home but today it was hidden from view in his inside coat pocket ready to be shown to Lakey if he so decided. The Biafran papers were in his briefcase.

> What an amazing boy you have turned out to be. Neither your mother nor I was too surprised when Jenny became involved in politics but you—what a turn-up for the books. First of all you go and find our dear Isobel, you then father a child who I can see already is going to be just like daddy and now you're about to enter onto the international stage. If they make a film about your exploits you should insist that Michael Caine plays Matthew Cresswell and that nice Sydney Poitier will be Peter. Michael Hordern for your friend Lakey?
>
> You will be surprised at your stiff old auntie engaged in such frivolity but your doings have left everyone at the Old Vicarage in a bit of a flutter. Mind you, we needed it. Your mother and I are getting staid. Must be when the event of the year is our trip to Cheltenham, but I do hope we are not going to be changing a visit to the races for a trip to The Tower!
>
> Let me tell you what I have done. Thanks to your uncle, God rest his soul, I have always been close to Conservative MPs in the Midlands. Not that the local man was much help in the early days about the anti-apartheid campaign, but he has introduced me to one of his colleagues who is a member of one of the Foreign Affairs Committees in the House. Well, I say 'introduced'—when we were dinner guests together recently I realised I had met him before. Anyway, for security reasons at this stage, let's call him Mr X. No names, no pack drill. Where on earth does that come from? I'll get Adele to look it up. Must be an army saying, so just her thing.
>
> Having broken the ice, and when he was visiting locally, I managed to get him to lunch at home two Sundays ago—just

him, your mother and I—and we made him sing for his supper. Goodness, another stupid saying. I doubt if the man can hold a note and it was luncheon, not supper. I first swore him to confidence—Chatham House rules, or something like that—then I told him the whole story. About your business and friendship with Peter; how you were in Kano when British territory was invaded, i.e. the BOAC plane. I rather liked the gloss I put on that dreadful incident. I then told him how simultaneously you had been selected by the Biafrans and HMG to report on conditions there and finally what your report is likely to say.

Mr X, as you would expect from the Opposition, does not have a high regard for the Ministers in charge of our foreign policy—Southern Rhodesia, for example—but he admits he doesn't know too much about Nigeria. He has been to Ghana so West Africa is not a complete mystery to him and he is sensitive to the fact that it is our bullets that are being fired and he is not alone in the House in wanting to see an end to this Nigerian problem. You were in Nigeria in March for the Wilson visit. According to my Mr X, Wilson has apparently been defending his stance since last year against stiff opposition in the Cabinet and even more in the country. A Gallup Poll showed between 70 and 80% of the public were in favour of the UK sending help to Biafra. Mr X doesn't altogether blame the Prime Minister who has stuck to the basics, i.e. Gowon heads Nigeria's legitimate regime—Britain has traditionally been the country's arms supplier and if we don't sell, the Russians will—and this could make things worse. However, I understand a number of senior members of the Government are unhappy. Wilson therefore decided on the visit to try and deflect this opposition and pacify public opinion. As you know, Ojukwu wouldn't meet him. Do you know why? But it seems to have done the trick on the home front and at the moment in some quarters Federal Nigeria is back in favour. None of these shenanigans help the beleaguered Biafrans of course, but let's see if an old woman in Leicestershire and a brave young man on the front line can do something to change that. This means, as I read Mr X, that if there is anything he can report to his Committee that might bring this about, he will try. He is a typical

Opposition politician and if he thinks he can be in possession of facts not known, or not understood, on the other side of the House he will not hesitate to use them. Sources protected of course.

Do let me know how the meeting with Lakey goes.

Love and kisses to Isobel and little John.

Lakey looked at the papers Matthew had brought but, before he could comment, his visitor made it clear that he had told the contact in Biafra, the person who had supplied this information, that he had been approached by the British Government, through Lakey, and therefore both parties should see him for what he was—a messenger boy. He explained he did not want any misunderstandings; he was not acting for Biafra and he was not acting for HMG. Lakey did not seem surprised.

'Rather expected this would be your attitude, old chap,' was his comment. He then looked more closely at the information in front of him.

'I suspect we've got most of this already but at first glance there is some interesting stuff and I will get it back to my masters in London and see what they make of it.'

'Will it help to bring the war to a quicker conclusion?'

'Who can say? But I rather think that, although we all appreciate your efforts, and I know how passionately you feel about getting it finished, it is going to fizzle out of its own accord. The Feds seem to have lost heart, even though their opponents are on their knees. Anyway, well done, but let me warn you again: whatever happens, don't let the authorities here in Lagos know what you've been up to, even if it might prove to have been fruitless. They are quite capable of blowing the least thing completely out of proportion.'

'Thanks. I understand all that but let me tell you something not in these papers and which only makes me even more desperate for the war to be over. This must be for your personal information, although you may have heard similar stories.'

Matthew then told Lakey about Grace and her husband.

'God! Isn't it awful? War. An excuse for all decent human behaviour to be abandoned. That really is so horrible for you when you know the people involved. I'm so sorry. I came across things like that in Malaysia—but you never get used to it, at least I never did.'

As instructed, Matthew made no reference to his part in a possible role for Rotimi Lawson nor did he tell Lakey about Edith. Her letter remained in his pocket. Nor did he mention that he had copied the Okere papers and sent them to someone who was clearly revelling in what she liked to describe as her 'Mata Hari' role. Evidently, Mr X was most intrigued as to how she had come by this information but she delighted in telling him she could not possibly 'reveal her sources'. Although Matthew knew Lakey would make the best use possible of the information just given to him, he had no qualms about approaching the problem from another angle via Edith. He was later able to read reports of the committee of which Mr X was a member and see that during the last two meetings in 1969 a more pro-Biafran sentiment had emerged. However, the war did just fizzle out, as Lakey had predicted, whereupon Matthew was able to welcome Peter back and be pleased that the peace process was, in the end, a relative success.

Matthew was never able to assess whether his minor role had had any impact whatsoever on the final outcome of this sorry affair. Both parties to the conflict, one much more than the other, simply got too tired to carry on. Ojukwu left his short-lived kingdom and flew to Abidjan in the Ivory Coast. During the last month of 1969, however, no-one could be sure the end would be so soon. However, what was for certain was that Matthew was invited to present himself early in the New Year at Dodan Barracks to be interviewed by the Federal Government Security Services. This invitation, one not be refused, was delivered at his office just before Christmas by a somewhat disreputable looking individual, not uniformed but wearing a brightly coloured shirt worn outside a pair of greasy check trousers, who seemed incapable of coherent speech. Nevertheless, he was sufficiently articulate to be able to inform Matthew he should 'Go for Dodan Barracks six p.m. on five January' to see Inspector Dawodu. It was, naturally enough, this invitation that sowed in Matthew's mind the seeds of concern which soon blossomed into panic. He tried his best, but it was not a particularly 'Happy' Christmas.

Under the civilian Government, from 1960, the country had been administered from the offices of the Prime Minister on the Marina in Lagos, formerly the Governor-General's office. These premises were now used by a number of ministerial departments because, after two military take-overs, the seat of power had moved into barracks, Dodan Barracks to be precise, in Obalende, where the new leaders could feel secure. General Gowon lived and worked behind high walls and barbed wire, closely guarded by soldiers and an armoured gun-carrier. Over the last four years these premises had taken on a character of their own, both sinister and symbolic of the regime. As Matthew drove to his rendezvous he feared he could be in good company. Wole Soyinka, who had only recently been released after twenty-two months behind bars, had probably made a similar journey. He may well have been aware that his summons was to do with the anti-war speeches he had made, as well as his writings, but Matthew could only wonder whether they knew about the papers he had delivered to Lakey or, even more worrying, the letter to Rotimi Lawson?

Nigerians were amongst the world's most patient 'waiters'. The more senior the man, the more people there were waiting to see him. Matthew had witnessed this phenomenon over his years in Nigeria, particularly when visiting his Nigerian clients at their homes. It was not unusual to find between twenty and thirty people squatting patiently in driveways and in halls, waiting for the 'Oga'—the big man—to hand over coins or notes, or promises to intervene in a dispute, or to sign a piece of bureaucratic paper, or to find a job for the supplicant. They waited for hours, sometimes for days. Matthew, like most expatriates, was adept at avoiding being one of the 'waiting masses'. You do not go to the bank yourself but send a clerk or messenger to stand in the queue. The same was true when it came to renew a driving licence or passport, or register a birth. Hospitals were to be avoided at all times. But now Matthew had no alternative but to sit and wait, as patiently as possible, until the Inspector should deign to see him. The wait lasted for nearly ninety minutes.

When he was eventually ushered in he was asked to sit on what appeared to be an unstable wooden chair, one leg of which was shorter than the others, and face three men sitting at a table littered with empty Fanta bottles, stained tea mugs and two overflowing ashtrays. As the sun was now well over the yardarm, all three had moved from Fanta and tea to Star beer. Three half empty bottles were on view. They looked unrefrigerated to Matthew. There were no glasses. He was not introduced to any of these men, no names were offered, nor were any uniforms or insignia on view; all three men were dressed in similar fashion to their messenger. Matthew never discovered which one was Inspector Dawodu, if, indeed, he was any of the trio. Two of the men spent the whole period glaring at their quarry through half-closed eyes. They never moved their gaze from him, except when lifting beer bottles to their lips, and uttered not a word. The third man was the spokesman. Was he Inspector Dawodu? Whether or not, he conducted the entire interview.

'You are Matthew Cresswell?'

'Yes I am, and you are?'

'You know Peter Okonkwo?'

'Yes.'

'When you last meet with him?'

'A few months ago.'

'Where be dat?'

'In Biafra.'

'Ah, you go visit the rebels?'

'I went to see my friend and partner. We are in business together.'

'How can you be in business with Ibo man?'

'As I have told you, he is my friend and he still owns shares in the business.'

'Oh, you send him money?'

'No. There is no way I can do that, but if we make any profit he will get his share when this awful war is over.'

'Who say you can go Biafra?'

'I'm a British citizen. Why can I not go to Biafra? In any case, what is this all about?'

'You have work permit for Nigeria?'

'Yes, of course I have.'

'Who issue work permit?'

'The Government.'

'Is it Ibo government?'

'No, of course not.'

'You know we can withdraw any time?'

'I suppose so.'

'You know what is undesirable person?'

'Yes.'

'Are you one?'

'No.'

'What job you do?'

'My company provides training courses.'

'You training Biafrans'?'

'No, how can we?'

'When you go Biafra, what you take to them?'

'Take to them. Nothing, except presents for my friend's children. Toys you know.'

'You bring something back when you go return?'

'No. There's not much left in Biafra to bring out.'

'You sure?'

'Yes. Now again, what is it you want with me?'

'Give me your passport.'

'I haven't got it with me. I don't carry it. Is there a law which says I must?'

'Never mind O. So you support these rebel dogs?'

'No. I think this war is appalling. You should stop it "one time". When I was there I went to visit our nanny. She is dead and her husband. So many die. For what?'

'Blood is on Ojukwu's hand. He start this. He wants to keep Nigeria's oil. "To keep Nigeria one is a job that must be done".'

At this the other two members of the tribunal seemed to be about to repeat the slogan, but did not, and relapsed into their half-awake and surly-looking pose. One of them began to explore his right nostril with a stubby fore-finger.

'*Must* be done? If it results in all those deaths?'

'Why you really visit rebels. Are you a spy?'

'Don't be ridiculous. Do I look like a spy? I have been in Nigeria since 1958. I was with the British Council before setting up my business. I'm really just a teacher.'

The interview continued along these inconsequential lines for another fifteen minutes or so.

'Well, teacher, next time we call you, bring passport. One last ting. You know Femi Oloronshola?'

'Yes. He used to work for me.'

'You can go.'

An innocuous examination. But what did they really know and why the reference to Oloronshola? Three months ago Matthew had found discrepancies in the firm's accounts and asked Rotimi Lawson to do an emergency audit. This showed a number of accounts unpaid that had actually been settled but cheques never banked, although as far as the client was concerned they had been cashed. There appeared, therefore, to be a clear case of fraud. Oloronshola was the only member of staff who could have committed this but, knowing the difficulty and delay experienced in Nigerian courts, Matthew, in consultation with Rotimi, decided not to report the matter to the police. Oloronshola was questioned and denied any wrong-doing but he could not explain the missing cheques. At this he was dismissed and asked to leave the office immediately, which he did with exceedingly bad grace. It was only later that Christopher, the firm's long-serving clerk, told Matthew that Oloronshola had a brother in a senior position in the police force.

Except on the purely business front, it was unlikely Oloronshola had known of Matthew's dealings with the British High Commission, but it was clear he wanted to create as much mischief as possible and Matthew knew that, if they wanted to, the Nigerian police could easily expand an unfounded allegation into a case of sedition. As he drove home he became more and more apprehensive. By the time he and Isobel were sharing a drink, his head was spinning and he was considerably agitated. Isobel told him he was over-reacting.

'I can't help it. I know they can't really do much to us, but I'm scared.'

'That's not like you.'

'I know it isn't. When we were on our way back from that ghastly meeting in Amichi we were only minutes away from being bombed, but somehow I wasn't frightened then. Nor when standing next to those murdering butchers outside the Central Hotel. But now . . . It is something to do with Dodan Barracks. It has such a sinister reputation. It represents all that is evil about a military regime. Clandestine, behind closed doors—or behind high walls and barbed wire. People shot there and no-one knows anything about it. Even the man who interviewed me—not very bright—but he managed to convey an uncomfortable degree of menace.'

There were no further calls to Dodan Barracks but Matthew still occasionally woke in the early hours imagining he heard army boots climbing the stairs to his bedroom. However, as the weeks went by and Dodan Barracks appeared indifferent to Mr Matthew Cresswell, he regained his composure and sense of proportion. If the war had not ended as abruptly as it did, and the authorities had discovered more about his trip to Biafra, his concerns might have been justified. On the other hand, they could well have considered his activities, such as they were, insignificant, if not slightly ludicrous. He was never to know.

Matthew had never considered himself a Richard Hannay or a George Smiley in this affair. Many of the things he had seen and experienced left no place for heroes and he certainly did not cast himself in the role of one. On the other hand, who were the villains? The decapitators in Kano and the rapists of Amichi, for starters. But what about the principal actors? For the few years Yakubu Gowon remained Head of State he invariably displayed the easy-going personality of a man who was fair and reasonable. Perhaps he was exactly that. Matthew came to meet him through the auspices of the Nigerian-Britain Association and always found him modest and charming but, as was to be shown, it was the inherent weakness behind the smiling face that was the problem. The increase in oil output was startling; from twenty thousand barrels per day in 1960 to two million in 1973. By 1976 oil provided 93% of export earnings, compared with 11% only ten years earlier. Tragically, this led to increased opportunities for corruption which Gowon did little to clamp down on. In October 1974 he announced the indefinite postponement of a return to civilian rule, which added to the discontent that led to his being deposed, while out of the country, by the bloodless coup of July 1975. If Gowon could not be classed as an out-and-out villain, was Ojukwu such a one? Will hindsight show that, without his forcefulness, the Ibos might have accepted the genocidal killings of 1966 and looked to survive by other means than a declaration of secession? We cannot know, Matthew thought, whether Ojukwu gambled that the Federal Government would accept this without going to war, but if he did, it was a costly gamble.

During the decade of the 1970s many businesses in Nigeria flourished as the country's oil revenues increased and CMS was no exception. Peter and Matthew agreed that, provided talent came first, they would structure their company in the future to reflect what was being called 'the National character' and so, by a process of careful selection, they reached 1980 with four more working shareholders. One of these was from Benin, another a Yoruba and two from the East, an Ibo and a man from Calabar. There were still no suitable candidates from the North. They worked well together and even Raymond Habib was impressed with how the value of his shares had been enhanced. As a result of the indigenisation decree, Matthew had needed to reduce his percentage holding but this had given him no concerns.

He and Isobel had recovered their composure after the Biafran traumas and now had a daughter to add to their pleasures. On the personal front all was well, but in the country at large one crisis followed another. December 1976 saw an abortive coup, during which Murtala Mohammed was assassinated to be replaced by Brigadier Obasanjo, another soldier but committed, like his predecessor, to a return to democratic rule, which was duly achieved in 1979. The military came back in 1983 with the avowed intent of ridding the country of the corruption that had boomed during the civilian administration; the new head was General Buhari but he was deposed by yet another military coup in 1985. Politics and the state of the nation did not improve for Nigeria thereafter. Power, whether in the hands of the military or the civilians, led to the Nation's wealth being dissipated; the country's poor got poorer year after year.

It was clear to Peter and Matthew that Nigeria was heading in the wrong direction. The optimism at Independence in 1960, and the sense of relief felt by almost everyone at the way the peace process of 1970 had been handled, proved small beacons of hope in a catalogue of disasters. Both men agreed that the beginning of the end was the discovery of oil—or, more precisely, the expansion in the production of Nigerian oil to the position where the country became the seventh largest producer in the world.

'I know the Ibo will be judged in the future as an unpatriotic Nigerian who sought to secede because nearly all of the oil resources are in the East—and there is a considerable element of truth in that—but we both know the cause was much greater. You will see—domination by the Hausa and the North is inevitable.'

'Yes, Peter, I agree, but there have always been tribal differences and always will be. We aren't doing too well in Northern Ireland.'

'OK, but I still think if we had not found oil we would have been a happier nation. Poorer perhaps, but has the oil wealth really benefited anyone except those at the top? The trouble with oil is it is too easy. We used to be the largest producer of groundnut oil in the world and now we import it. No-one bothers to plant cocoa on the scale we used to. Why? The farmer, and everyone else, sees oil as the lucky accident that means they do not have to work anymore. Black gold.'

'And, as a non-Nigerian, the worst tragedy of all is that oil has changed the whole character of a nation in not much more than one decade. It is not to just the economic results—the old adage that as the rich get richer, the poor get poorer—but the psychological harm that can probably never be reversed. The happy smiling Nigerian I met when I came here in 1958 has, on the whole, been replaced by a specimen diseased with corruption whose only response to the ills he or she sees everywhere is to chant, "What of me? Where is my share? I want a piece of the National Cake, but I'm not prepared to work for it—at least not honestly." Sorry to sound so depressing but I know you agree with me. Do you remember the first time Isobel and I visited your family in the village? I'm sure I must have told you. I think it was in 1964. We were using the Peugeot 404, like most other motorists in the country, when, about twenty miles from your home, the car broke down. As usual, the vehicle was quickly surrounded by a number of a budding mechanics who appeared out of the bush all eager to help. However, their joint skills hardly required exercising as they pointed out to me that three of the four nuts holding down the carburettor head were missing and petrol was leaking into the engine. As you know, I am totally un-mechanical, but before utter despair set in a similar Peugeot pulled up behind. When the owner saw my predicament he offered to help. He did this in a very practical way: he took one of the nuts from his carburettor and fastened it to mine; his car would still run and we were able to carry on to Aba, where I arranged for a more lasting repair to be carried out. That Nigerian did not stop and help this white man for reward. All right, I gave him a few quid but his actions came from his nature. He was proud of his ingenuity. That was his real reward. But would that happen today? Of course not. If anyone had been prepared to stop they would have made the same repair and then stolen the car.'

'Yes, and left you in the bush minus your watch and your wallet,' responded Peter. 'Oil and corruption. There is a story going the rounds about dishonest regimes elsewhere in the world that I can imagine originated here. You may well have heard it already, but it bears repeating. The Nigerian Minister of Works visits his counterpart in Venezuela—it needs to be another oil-rich country—and is impressed with the luxury of the Minister's house. When asked how he can afford such opulence, the Minister takes his visitor on a tour of the capital, points to a brand new highway and tells him it cost two hundred million US dollars. He then bangs his clenched right fist to his left breast, as a US patriot does when the *Star Spangled Banner* is played, and says proudly, "25% to me". The visit is reciprocated. The Nigerian lives in even greater splendour. How do you afford this? Next day the Venezuelan is taken to see the great River Niger. His host points to the river and asks him to marvel at the wonderful new bridge spanning a gorge at the widest point and costing the same two hundred million US dollars. When the puzzled visitor says he cannot see any bridge, the Nigerian repeats the gesture of the patriot and exclaims, "100% to me!" Nonsense, of course, but if we go on as we are it might one day be true.'

Chapter Six

Jenny

Marks and Co acted for the Peires Press, a small firm of specialist publishers, in matters of copyright and intellectual property. These clients did not normally deal with fiction but had approached Henry Marks for advice on a work submitted to them which they believed had some limited literary merit. What had aroused their interest, however, was the apparent mystery surrounding the origins of the piece. Andreas Peires and Henry Marks were old friends and, over the telephone, Peires explained the circumstances.

'We were sent the first few pages of a story that might be set in South Africa but that's not made clear and in fact the writer, or writers, go to some lengths to create obscurity. The alleged author, whom no-one in the trade has ever heard of, is said to be one Cornelius van Dyke and we assume this must be a *nom de plume.* He also mentions a firm of publishers, Howards and Co., also unknown to us. The only address we have is a Post Office box. Normally we would ignore semi-anonymous offerings of this kind but one of my partners started to read it and became intrigued. It employs the hackneyed technique of using someone else's letters or diaries to relate happenings from the past. In this case there are said to be some tape recordings. This may be a familiar device but it has been handled skilfully—and in what appears to be a deliberately furtive manner. If the remainder of this work is of a similar nature, we could be interested in publishing it as a one-off to our normal list, but I need your advice as to whether you think it might contravene the existing law.'

'Send it in, Andreas, and we'll try and measure it up against the Act. It's all very subjective but that's the trouble with censorship. One man's meat is another man's poison. I'll get our new associate to read it. She did English at Cambridge.'

Jenny welcomed this assignment as a relief from the almost daily court appearances that now occupied her time. Once it was known within the legal fraternity that Marks and Co had a lawyer who actually wanted to represent defendants in Magistrates' Courts for minor apartheid law offences, she had soon been inundated with cases. It was 1964. Jenny had no regrets about moving to South Africa and was now fully engaged in the work that she and the Marks family had envisaged for her, even though decisive victories in the Johannesburg courtrooms were rare. Her reputation as a hard, but fair, advocate for the oppressed underclass grew but the wall of apartheid was difficult to breach.

Until now Jenny had not come across the Publications and Entertainment Act of 1963 and so, while waiting for the script to arrive from Peires, she began to research the legislation. Under this Act all publications and objects could be put up for review and banned if found harmful or offensive to the interests of the State and its citizens. There were six categories of undesirable material. Jenny concentrated on the first four.

> A publication or object shall be deemed to be undesirable if it or any part of it
>
> (a) is indecent or obscene or offensive or harmful to public morals;
> (b) is blasphemous or is offensive or harmful to public morals;
> (c) brings any section of the inhabitants of the Republic into ridicule or contempt;
> (d) is harmful to the relations between any inhabitants of the Republic.

The South African Government did not refer to censorship—it could be said that they 'censored' the word—preferring 'publications control'. Publications could mean virtually anything; not only books, magazines and films but T-shirts, key rings and even shop signs. Anything could be deemed 'undesirable'. It was said that control over the written word in the Soviet Union engaged some seventy thousand bureaucrats investigating seven thousand writers; in South Africa informed sources thought the ratio was greater than ten to one. To Jenny, South Africa seemed paranoid on this subject; it saw coded messages opposing the State in all sorts of areas. As she became more interested in this subject she was to come across a number of farcical examples. For instance, in one classic case a local playwright was required to replace the word 'fart' with 'anal wind'.

The manuscript duly arrived at her desk and she took this up with keen anticipation.

EVE

Introduction by Cornelius van Dyke.

The origins of this story come from the spoken word. Howards and Co., my publishers, acquired a number of audio tapes and asked if I would explore whether a transcript of these recordings could be worked up into a viable piece of fiction, or 'faction'—no-one has yet bothered to explore how true this story is. Howards themselves do not wish to be involved because, as you know, they only deal with scientific textbooks. It was sometimes difficult to catch every word; the machine used must have been an old-fashioned recorder and the tapes were nearly the size of a paperback book. Nevertheless, Howards and I thought what was recounted was so unusual, and yet so commonplace, it would be worth the effort of transcribing these words into a written form. The story is poignant, funny and tragic all at the same time and accurately reflects one of the dilemmas of the society we live in. The method I have adopted is to let the two actors speak for themselves with interruptions from me only when deemed necessary for continuity purposes. I have tried to convert the vernacular into reasonably grammatical language without destroying the charm. I am sending you only the first part of the story until I know whether this work is of interest to you. The man speaks first.

Man

When I made enquiries I discovered she had been working at our Northern branch for three years. As I had visited the shop at least once every week, why had she not registered? Her name is Eve. The first woman! To understand the extraordinary—or was it in fact 'very ordinary'—story that resulted from Eve, I need to describe myself to you, the reader, and extend this to a psychological examination for my own benefit so I can try to understand how this example of magic was wrought. Magic? Well, after you have read my account, do you have a better word? Is there any more persuasive explanation? And because of the *dramatis personae* engaged in this domestic comedy—if I might be permitted to describe it as such—I am not in any way referring to black magic, unless the chocolates. And even then the image is lost. The tagline in the advertisement was—'all because the lady loves Milk Tray'—not Black Magic.

The last few sentences may have persuaded you that I own a sweet shop, or am a philanderer or just a mite whimsical. Wrong on all counts—but half a mark for shopkeeper. My family sell electrical goods in four shops within the city. Refrigerators, cookers, toasters and irons for pressing clothes. I am second generation in this game and act as general factotum to my older brother who is the Managing Director, although we are equal shareholders. Dad was very fair about that. Whimsical? No-one could call me that—blunt and unimaginative perhaps—whimsical, no. Plaintive sometimes when my voice is added to the rugby songs sung in bath and bar after I have spent eighty minutes trying to kick the shit out of the opposition's hooker—but hardly whimsical. Philanderer? Ask my brother, who plays prop, and the other thirteen; they would laugh you out of court. They do not know of that infamous encounter on holiday at the coast. Infamous—or, more accurately, inadequate, inglorious, even humiliating. I cannot even recall what she looked like. I think she wore a blue dress. Are you getting the picture? A full-blooded, but apparently emasculated male, with a boring occupation both in the electrical retail world and on the rugby field. By the time I get up from the scrum all the excitement, if there is any, is going on twenty-five yards from me and I don't see the wretched ball again until I get to throw it in. A nose that has been broken twice does little to improve my appearance. My ginger hair stands up like the early shoots of corn, as do the strands of my moustache, although this is of a different colour from the hair on my head. All the male members of our family—and, I always thought, my paternal grandmother—sport the moustache, however unsightly. My ears are very large and, to add to the attraction, one is larger than the other. When I open my eyes wide, not a regular event—it only happens when I find Hofmeyrs are selling the Hotpoint at a lower price than we are—they resemble the slits in the helmet of an old-fashioned suit of armour.

Don't get me wrong. I like women, at least those I know reasonably well which, when I add it up, amounts to my four sisters, my sister-in-law and the washerwoman who launders the kit after every Saturday. I live at home with the family. Why not? It is comfortable and the food is good. I'm getting fat. Still, all hookers seem to be shaped like me—rugby ones that is. Intellectual pursuits? Hobbies? I have loved taking photographs ever since a boy and have become quite skilled at it. I like to go to the pictures, preferably cowboy films. I swim every day and sometimes get picked for the water polo team. I am threatening to learn to play golf when there is no rugby so you can see I lead a full life. No time for romance or anything like that—but then I encountered Eve; she entered my prosaic world. Three years and no conscious sighting of her. Was she always hidden away somewhere, making the tea or unpacking boxes or avoiding the attentions of Dirk? No, the fault was in my eye. She was invisible; I chose not to see her, just like the hero of Ralph Ellison's novel. The guy that plays scrum half, who is brighter than me and a bit of a liberal, persuaded me to read it. I thought most of what I read—did not get to the end—was nonsense, but noted this at the beginning: '. . . invisible because people refuse to see me . . . When they approach me they see only my surroundings, themselves, or figments of their imagination—indeed, everything and anything except me.' At least this is one explanation. She was part of the background. Unlike the white goods we sell, the decoration of all our shops inclines to a nondescript brown or an indifferent beige. So what happened? You will be astonished. It was the feet. Packing some upper shelves—with a four-slice toaster I think it was—with no shoes on. I had never seen anything so beautiful. The ankles above were slim and the bone that protruded from this elegance was perfectly shaped like a little hillock—a *kopje* as they say in some parts. The nails were cut short and unpainted—no adornment was necessary.

In the dim light of the shop these feet seemed to glow—they were multicoloured. I could not see the soles but I imagined them to be pale like a winter moon. Forgive my poetic language, but that is what she does to me. When she went to the storeroom for more toasters, I asked Dirk who that was and what was her name and how long she had been working for us. Junior shop assistant, Eve, three years. He is a man of few words.

I looked up her details in our files. Information rather sparse: single, a year older than me and educated up to Standard 6. The address was even less valuable; I have no idea where Tolkington Street is. The next time I visited the Northern branch I made some attempt to tidy my hair, difficult task, only to find she was off sick. What was the matter with me? I had a clear impression etched in my brain of her feet, but what of the rest of her. Had I taken in any other features or was this a foot fetish? As I said before, it must be magic. What type of a man is attracted to a woman by her feet? It is supposed to be the smile, the laugh, the hair, the tits, the arse—but feet. Give over. Are attractive feet enough of a foundation for a fulfilling relationship? As I said to myself, yes, foundation for the body, we could not stand up without them—but would those two delicious objects satisfy any real man? I made my memory work hard. Slim legs, what I saw of them. Curly hair. Bosom? No idea—the female frame hidden by those hideous uniforms we supply but I believe that, because she was standing on a step ladder, I saw an unusually slight behind. Somewhat surly of countenance, or do all our shop assistants look like that?

CVD

I listened carefully and am fairly certain Eve's posterior was described as 'slight' and not 'tight'.

Eve

I looked over my shoulder to see if he was trying to look up my skirt but no, he was staring at my feet. What a strange man. He must have been playing that stupid game at the weekend. He has a black eye, although in his case it is of a purple colour. When I returned from the storeroom he said

'Hello'. I replied 'Hello'. He then left. He is shy, but very ugly. Very strange in men, at least amongst those I have known. The next time he came to the shop he smiled at me and asked some questions about which electric kettle was the best seller. I told him that I thought Mr Dirk could best answer that but he continued to smile. He gave me a boiled sweet and then left. What am I to think? He is a boss man while I am only a junior in his shop. With anyone else I would have said he wanted to get me into his bed. That has been my experience so far with all the men in this wretched town, from whichever side of the tracks they come, but he seems different, even diffident you might say. When these words are repeated as print upon paper, if they ever are, the reader should not be surprised at the excellence of my English. I did not get much in the way of quality education (I must try and describe my schooling later) but I have read the books of Jane Austen and those of two of the Brontë sisters so I am well aware of what constitutes a 'well-made sentence'. Will I ever write, in my diary or my own fiction, 'Reader, I married him.'? Jane was confronted with similar problems to mine. Class and arrogance—a Byronic hero mocking an unhandsome girl. I too am plain, at least I think so, and the gradations between men and women in our stratified society could be said to be even more strangulating than in nineteenth century England—and the consequences of moving from one division to another can be more dire. At worst Jane could have finished up back in the orphanage or in the workhouse, but for someone like me, it could be much worse.

He visited the shop twice last week. It makes Mr Dirk even more irritable.

Man

I cannot get her out of my mind. After practice last week I left the bar after only one beer. The lads said I must be sickening for something but, whatever I had, they hoped it wasn't catching. What would they have thought if they knew that I had driven out of town thinking that on the outskirts I might randomly find Tolkington Street? What an idiot! Dangerous too—some tough hombres out there. Randolph

Scott or Alan Ladd would be more decisive. Perhaps I am more like James Stewart: naive, a blunderer—but without the charm, or the looks. Should I write her a letter? Hand it over in the shop when no-one is looking? But what to say? It is really quite simple. I am attracted to you, I know there are differences—major ones—but I would like to get to know you better. However, on reflection and in the circumstances, no letters. I hope you do not think it is creepy or underhand but in the end what I did was to follow her when she left the shop one night. I parked around the corner. She caught the yellow bus. There was a lot of traffic but I was able to keep close enough to see when she got off. I had my rugby cap pulled well down over my eyes so I am sure she did not recognise me as I drove past her and turned into a quiet street at the next junction. I walked back and 'accidentally on purpose' bumped into her at the corner. 'Good heavens!,' I said. 'Fancy meeting you, Eve. Where are you going?' I think she laughed in my face but glided past and wished me goodnight.

Eve

He is weird. He followed my bus home in his dilapidated Volkswagen and then pretended we had met by chance. He must be mad. I must be careful not to encourage him but cannot be too offhand; I do not want to lose my job. If he was one of my own kind, but with the money, would I give him a second thought? No. I've been through that with the rich and the not so rich, even though I suppose that is where my destiny lies. From within his own kind would I bother? Probably not. I've had no experience in that direction but with all that is involved there has to be something more than the rent-free tenancy of a flat and a visit three times a week. As Eliza said, 'I'm a good girl, I am.' Well, I may not be spotless, but I crave something more than a position like that or marriage to an insensitive male from my lot. I know that is the future all of my kind face, a mother for their children and a home for their circumcised cocks, but does it have to be so? Does anyone talk about love? 'The real thing' as it is called. We romanticise about film stars and heavyweight boxers. We read the glossy weeklies and revel in the so-called bliss of prospective motherhood. I suppose in the end what we all want is security. But what is the reality? Old before our time. Too many children. Competition between home and bar. Physical cruelty. No joy, no hope, no self-identity.

Let's see where it goes with the shopkeeper. Could be a lot worse.

CVD

It is not, of course, possible to transfer to paper a tone of voice but during this speech there seemed to be a realisation on the part of Eve that her future was uncertain, to say the least, but equally there were no indications that she was about to deliberately encourage her swain.

Man

I still thought the staged chance meeting was the best approach and the next time I bumped into her, not literally, was between the shop and the bus stop. There were not too many options for us but she agreed to walk with me towards the park. It was dusk and as soon as we were away from the shopping district there were few observers in the half-darkness. We progressed slowly, but awkwardly, side by side. I did not hold her hand. What happened next was not planned on my part. Within the park are the rugby playing fields and what I have forgotten to mention is that in addition to being the hooker I am also the Secretary of the club. As a result, I have a key to the pavilion which is kept on my key ring. I talked to her about rugby and asked if she would like to see where we play. I pointed out the pavilion. Not very comfortable or romantic, but at least private. I told her I had a key and would she like to see inside. She said 'Yes' and when there asked what the smell was. I told her it was the liniment players rubbed on tired limbs. She was fascinated to see the baths. At her house, so she said, they use a metal tub with the water heated on the stove, and then only on Friday nights. Not that the pavilion baths were anything to write home about: large concrete boxes, big enough to hold eight or nine mud-spattered men. On the other hand, compared with what she was used to, there was a more or less constant supply of hot water. She asked if she could have a bath. I said

'Yes'. She said, 'Find me a towel and then go away.' I did both. When she came into the changing room, she looked different; it must have been the wet hair. She asked if I would like to kiss her, which I did. She then said that she must hurry to catch the bus and she would prefer to go on her own. She left me sitting on the bench under my coat hook. I wondered what was going to happen next. Was this wise? I threw the damp towel into the laundry basket and went home.

CVD

Was the request to use the bath a provocative action? I cannot tell, but from the tenor of the man's voice I assume it had been totally spontaneous.

Eve

Mr Dirk notices the frequent visits but I am so careful I think he does not know the cause. He seems more active than ever before—must think Head Office is on to him. I know they have a system of staff discounts but doubt if this extends to the whole family, including his mother-in-law and her brothers. It certainly should not cover Miss Hortense who takes her reduced priced goods with a twinkle in her eye for the manager and a scowl on her face for me. It does not seem fair that I should have to carry her boxes to the car but I do not seem to have any option. Now Mr Dirk thinks they have found him out he virtually jumps to attention when He walks in and is so involved with ingratiating himself he hardly notices the glances in my direction. We met outside the shop—well, actually a few streets away—and he asked if he could drive me home. 'Save the bus fare,' he said. I told him I thought this was not a good idea but asked if he had the key. It is only a piece of inanimate, shaped metal but it began to loom large in our lives. We went there and this time we had a bath together. He is a funny shape, even unclothed; he is as shy as a kitten. Not that I in any way encouraged him or flirted. He said he was overcome to see the naked me and that was enough. He then asked if he could see the colour of the soles of my feet. So strange. We kissed again before I left by myself to walk to the bus stop.

Man

Her skin is like satin—or even smoother. Not that I did much touching. The bath is big enough for there to be a lot of space between us. What a contrast. I have evidence of a teenage appendectomy, a six inch scar on my right shoulder where that dirty bugger Peter V dragged his studs and I think there is still evidence on my back of those two nasty boils I acquired a year or two ago. And that's only above the groin. The various battle scars on my legs are out of sight, obscured by the amount of body hair I grow. Like Esau, I am a very hairy man. On my legs it is a dirty orange colour, several shades darker than that on my head. My feet are exposed. I have lost the nails on three toes—cannot recall where or when. The hot water shrivels my old man so it is out of my sight due to the size of my belly.

Eve

He told me he has been made eyes at by a nice girl at the bank. She is called Miriam. Must be something about Old Testament women, he says. I know he is only teasing me but I believe him when he says that he seems to have become more desirable to women since he met me. I told him that's because he now has his hair brought under control and he's lost some weight—but I know it is more subtle than that. I don't know whether it applies both ways but our relationship has done something to him. Softened and yet more confident. For example he asked if he could take pictures of me without any clothes on. I was about to smack his face but then decided to suggest that if he wants to photograph me in the nude, I should do the same to him, particularly the area below the waist, after he has finished. Not a pretty sight. This stopped him in his tracks but I know he wasn't being prurient. He didn't want the photographs for erotic reasons. I believed him when he said they were to be for 'his eyes only'—just something to remind him of me.

Man

However keen I might be on photography, the idea of using her as a model was a stupid one. We are both very vulnerable, but she more than me. But I would love to have been able to exercise my skills on such a subject. Her widest part is at the hips, her breasts are small but, unlike me, with her the hot water extends her nipples that are as purple as blackberry juice. Even when wet, her hair everywhere is still curly and thick. I do not have a mental picture of the biblical Eve—didn't pay proper attention at Sunday School I suppose—but I now know exactly what Venus looked like. I am being a romantic.

Eve

He has told me, more than once, that he loves me but I have not responded one way or the other. How can I? He is not very practical. However, I eventually decided I needed to be more proactive and told him that if he liked I would leave home and take a room somewhere between his part of town and mine where we could meet. It was his look of horror at this suggestion that finally made me realise that I loved him just as much as he loved me. Very sentimental, Mills and Boon, but if you could have seen us together you would have said more like 'Beauty and the Beast'—or do I flatter myself? We were a gross, even pathetic, pair wallowing about in an impossible situation. I painted for him the picture of where we stood, which of course he fully realised but he was trying to avoid the awful truth.

Man

When I got to the ground today, the washerwoman—I really must find out what her name is—was late in bringing the kit so there were a few players waiting outside to get into the pavilion. I did the honours and when I went to have a pee I saw something that made my heart jump. Over the row of wash basins is a long mirror so crazed that when using it we all look distorted, like in those crazy houses at the fun fair. Well, across the middle of this glass was inscribed I LUV U. In red. Proved to be lipstick. The boys already there started to accuse each other of using the pavilion as a love nest but no-one pointed the finger at me even though they know I have a key. Says a lot about me and my reputation as a ladies' man! What was she doing? Not like her at all.

Eve
When he told me I pointed to my lips and told him I used a colourless balm and have never owned a stick of red lipstick in my life. A mystery. Did the washerwoman have a secret passion for one of the prop forwards?

Man
Where else are we to go? We couldn't go to the pictures together, or to a bar, at least not in this part of town. There was, she said, a drinking den near Tolkington Street but that I would probably not like it very much. So the pavilion became our love nest. I was careful not to put on the lights, except in the bathroom which had no windows. Was it furtive or romantic? Whatever, she has bewitched me. No, that's not fair. She has made no attempt to draw me on. In many ways she is as demure as one of those Jane Austen ladies she talks about. What a change of fortunes. I'm the boss and she's a shop girl but she is educating me. When mother found me reading *Wuthering Heights* she told me it had nothing to do with mountaineering and hoped I wouldn't be too disappointed. But she has not forced her love of books onto me. It seems natural to be interested in what she is interested in. Perhaps that's what is meant by being in love.

Eve
I tried to picture him at the Palace Bar. He would certainly have stuck out like a sore thumb. But does it matter if for the time being we are only allowed to sit holding hands in the dark and imbibing the masculine aroma of that changing room? It is a comfort just to be with him.

Man
We are both fully aware of the problems involved in any long term relationship. If nothing else, my brother, who is a mason, is very careful of his dignity and of that of the family. We are of substantial middle-class stock but Dad was able to buy an electrical goods shop from some man who drank the profits, and that's where it all started. A long term something with a shop girl, or, horror upon horror, a permanent

relationship, would make my brother more than hopping mad. He would be violently furious and Dad would be rotating in his box. Brother's wife is worse. Her father worked for the railways and so she could be said to have married up, out of her class, and this has made her even more conscious of her status. Like they often say, the converts become the most assiduous Catholics. I have not yet mentioned this to Eve but I have begun to wonder whether we should quietly leave the country and set up, as a properly married couple of course, in a more benign world. I pinched this word 'benign' from yesterday's weather forecast—liked the sound of it.

CVD
The light-hearted aside about the weather forecast did not disguise the agitation in the voice by the time the saga had reached this point. I have listened to the remainder of the taped story, considerably darker than the first half, but await a response from you before transcribing any further.

Jenny, under Henry's supervision, wrote a brief opinion to Andreas Peires.

Both Henry and I have read the story thus far but you must be the literary judge. For me, I can only describe it as quirky and charming. But would anyone buy such a book? I am sure you can extract from the work as well as we can those references, or inferences, that the Publications Committee might see as an indication that the locale for this love story is South Africa, and that the girl is black, or 'Coloured'. If they think it worth their attention, which is doubtful in our opinion, they could say that the law is contravened under the public morals clauses and that it is a description of an activity illegal under the Prohibition of Mixed Marriages Act of 1949 and the Immorality Act of 1950, as amended in 1957. What mostly concerns me is that if the tapes are not a device, or even if they are but the stories are factual, there is the danger that a submission to the Committee might expose these two people to action being taken under the legislation referred to above, if they can be located. In previous cases of

> this kind, guilty parties have been jailed and often the black or 'Coloured' transgressor, particularly if female, gets the longer sentence. Taking this into account, it is our opinion that an application under the Publications and Entertainment Act of 1963 would be premature at this juncture and potentially dangerous for the two people whose lives are possibly revealed in this account. We can review the position if, and when, further instalments are received. It is for you to decide whether you should encourage Mr van Dyke to produce more.

Peires acknowledged the opinion sent by Jenny and agreed to take no further action unless and until they decided to ask for further instalments to be produced. Some months after this, Jenny returned unusually late to her office from the courts. Her case had been the last on the calendar and the Magistrate was anxious to complete before the court rose for the day because he was off to Plettenberg Bay next morning. It was not a complicated case but a delicate one, perhaps one of the most interesting Jenny had handled to date. It stemmed from a rent boycott. In Johannesburg, and some other municipalities, there had been a history of bus boycotts, resorted to by low-paid black workers in response to rising transport costs, and now, in isolated incidents, tenants in some of the Rand Townships had refused to pay the increased rents demanded by the Johannesburg City Council. The police had been called in to evict non-payers but as a result of their overzealous action the daughter of Thabo Iromze had been partially blinded. Jenny was acting for this girl, through the father, in an action against the police for compensation. At the end of a hearing spread over three days, the Magistrate had finally decided that his court was not the right place for a case of this kind and had refused to pass any judgment other than to refer the matter to a higher jurisdiction. The grieving parents, the blind girl and Jenny had to begin all over again. Consequently, the advocate was not in a receptive mood when her clerk, well after office closing hours, said there was a woman in reception who wanted to see Miss Cresswell. Jenny left her office to see who it was. Her caller was dressed in the modest black suit, white blouse and sensible court shoes which was the uniform of female office workers. She said her name was Eve and that she was sorry to trouble Miss Cresswell so late, but she was in serious need of help. Jenny ushered her into the office and told the clerk to go home.

'Why have you come to see me?'

'I know you have read my story, and I will tell you later how I know that, but for now, a policeman came to see me today at my place of work. He asked if I had a white boyfriend but before I could answer he instructed me to report at John Vorster Square tomorrow morning, without fail. If they really know something, why didn't they arrest me straight away? I am frightened about going to that place. One hears such terrible stories.'

'What do you want me to do?'

'Will you listen to my story, or at least the essentials of it, and then consider coming to the police with me.'

'I am very prepared to hear what you say, but tomorrow I have two defendants in the Magistrates court at Sandton and I must be with them.'

'I understand. At least it will be a relief if someone else knows what has happened to me. I am both Eve and Cornelius van Dyke. These names are presumably familiar to you because Peires and Co. wrote to my Post Office box and told me they had requested an opinion from you as to whether what I had written raises any legal issues. My name is Miriam Johnson and under the Population Registration Act I am classified as Coloured. My father, and his father, worked at a wine estate near Paarl. The owners, the van Dykes, whose name I appropriated, have always been good to my family. My father, now retired, developed into a skilled viticulturist. He and my mother are both Coloured, remote ancestry unknown. The van Dykes believed in home education, so they employed a series of tutors for their children and, most of the time, I was included as a pupil. I am so fortunate. I had the sort of learning few people in my circumstances in this country ever enjoy and, as a result, I found a good job at a Cape Town bank where I was trained as a typist. Three years ago I was transferred to the head office in Johannesburg and am now the secretary to the Chief Loans Officer. I am twenty seven years old and not married. My best subject was English literature, as you might guess from my literary references. My co-author, if I can call him that, would only know of Ralph Ellison if he were a member of the Pumas, or the Lions, or some other similarly named rugby team. That's not to say he did not contribute. The record of his feelings and actions are, for the most part, accurate. Our relationship was, of course, doomed from the start. When it came to the crunch it was class as much as colour that led to its failure. I will explain the details later. We were intimate eventually, in that smelly old pavilion, but an escape over the border was just a pipe dream. I do not regret what happened. Within the restrictions of his upbringing he was a special person and he saw me in the same light. He was not naive but somehow the colour difference did not seem to matter to him, at least not until he came to face the long term. Do not get the wrong idea. He was definitely not a man for a one-night stand; he was just not able to see through to the inevitable conclusion. It was that inevitability, and the frustration that love like ours cannot be even a remote possibility in this country, that decided me to write this story.'

'I can understand that, but did there have to be so many convolutions?'

'I know it seems odd, but what do you think would have been the reaction if a black or Coloured girl submitted such a manuscript to Peires Press? Would they have got past the first paragraph? I just wanted to tell my story. Nothing to do with my ego—seeing my book on a library shelf—nor is this a crusade; nothing I say or do is going to alter the facts. People like me cannot ride on your buses or sit on your park benches but at least in the realms of romance we are more or less equally disadvantaged. The black cannot love the white and the white cannot love the black. Simply because of the Afrikaners' fear of miscegenation, you, Miss Cresswell, and I, are not allowed to fall in love with whomever we like. That's why I chose the name Eve. The first woman—and in love. But your Government demands our essential nature be destroyed. Moreover, in my case, my whole race is classified as a mistake, an illegality. If sex between black and white is not permitted, the very fact of our existence is denied.'

'Well, actually it is not my Government. I am not a South African. But as a woman I can fully empathise with what you are saying. Look, why don't we go back to my flat and have a glass of wine. It is a great pity I cannot come with you tomorrow but, as soon as the police have finished, do let me know what happens.'

In the more intimate surroundings of Jenny's comfortable flat further information was forthcoming. When asked how the police might have got wind of the affair, Miriam could only point to one of the groundsmen at the park whom they had seen loitering about the pavilion on more than one occasion. She had typed the manuscript on her office typewriter, after hours. There was only one copy which she had sent, with a stamped addressed envelope for return, to four publishers but each in turn had rejected it. Peires Press had been her fifth attempt. By the second glass of wine they decided the embryonic story needed a title and Jenny had suggested, in somewhat jocund mood, *The Love Pavilion*. As they talked on about this, both realised what an inappropriate title this was, particularly after Miriam described the building in more detail.

'*The Love Pavilion*. Sounds like something in a Chinese or Indian romantic fairy story. It would be approached by a curved foot-bridge over a sparkling stream. Clad in orange blossom and painted a delicate pink. There would be a conical roof and the interior perfumed with the scent of roses. It was far from that, I can assure you.'

'Yes, I can imagine. I sometimes used to go and watch a former boyfriend of mine play rugby. Most of the pavilions he used were of a grubby white and I can just imagine the smell inside.'

'Yes, that's about it for our love nest—badly needing a coat of paint outside, and inside nearly indescribable. Even though it may not have been inhabited in the last few days by thirty or more sweaty males, their aroma lingered on. In fact, the smell of liniment was welcome to cut through the powerful presence of their body odour. To add to the glamour, there is nothing in my experience as disgusting as a discarded jockstrap. I know the bath scenes we described sounded rather romantic, but there always seemed to be a scale of scum across the base of those concrete boxes.'

'Awful. I can imagine it, but where else could you go? I suppose being together wiped out all those images.'

'You are so right.'

Miriam then returned to her reasons for writing the story in the first place.

'When I said I did not have ambitions to see my book on sale I believe I was being less than totally honest. For someone like me to be recognised as a writer would be an astonishing achievement. However, that is most unlikely ever to happen, but I wanted to have, if only for my own satisfaction, an account of how this country attempts to manipulate human nature, our genes, our emotions, into a pattern that they decide upon. And this manipulation can be so completely unobtrusive. They do not need to send any security policeman to knock on our bedroom doors; they have injected their control into our minds. I felt it in that pavilion. It is like the Thought Police in Orwell's *1984*. We are continually under surveillance because we believe it is so. I am taking these images from an extraordinary play by a man named Athol Fugard. Have you heard of him? I was able to see his play some years ago. In it two 'Coloured' brothers make themselves believe that they will be jailed for life, or something worse, simply because they enter into correspondence with a pen-pal and then find out she is a white girl. There is no-one else on stage. No policemen. They police themselves. So perceptive.'

Jenny said she had heard of Fugard, then asked Miriam about the man in her case.

'His name is John Streger. Full-blooded Afrikaner. His family own the electrical goods shops trading as Marshals. You will know of them I'm sure. We met in the bank where I work. The book accurately describes him as he is. Except for the rugby, he is far from a typical Afrikaner. He is gentle and considerate and I suppose we are still in love, but when we both reached the point where we knew we would have to get out of the country if we wanted something more permanent, something more than furtive meetings in the all-male preserve of a rugby club changing room, he just could not do it. I did not blame him, he had too much to lose, but I told him that we must break it off completely for both our sakes. He understood and it is now nearly a year since we parted.'

'How sad. But why do you think the police have only just become interested? You don't think he could have said something?

'I'm sure not. I cannot explain. Perhaps John recently annoyed that groundsman in some way and he has decided to get his own back.'

'Well if that's it, I wonder if your John has been seen by the police?'

'Who can say? But, as you know, in cases like this they tend to target the black party, and the groundsman sees me as no threat, whereas a disclosure about a white man could be more dangerous.'

Miriam failed to appear on the morrow, or the days soon thereafter, and Jenny became concerned as to what had happened to her.

In the meantime, and much to the annoyance of all concerned, the case brought by Thabo Iromze and his daughter had been returned by the Justice Department to the Magistrate who had avoided a completion so he could go on holiday. He was not very pleased. When the parties were in Court, he began by saying that the evidence given before would stand and since all the witnesses had been heard, the respective counsels should now present their closing statements. The lawyer acting for the police was brief. He regretted the injury suffered by Bisi Iromze but he went to great lengths to show that this had resulted from her participation in a criminal act, namely resisting the police in the course of their duties.

Jenny began, in indignant tone.

'I have listened carefully to what the police attorney has to say but to describe the actions of my client as criminal beggars belief. Criminal act—firstly I ask the Court to consider the word "act". What act? Has there been any evidence produced to support the contention that this unfortunate girl was herself involved in the *fracas* that occurred at 17 Southern Way on the 20th of September? If you will permit, Sir, I would like to try and paint as accurate a picture as possible of the events of that day, and what led to the police brutality. The girl's father has never been in any sort of trouble until now. He has been a tenant at this property for the last fifteen years and has always paid the rent promptly and in full. He has kept the property in good repair, even exceeding his obligations in this regard, when the landlords have failed to honour theirs. His tenancy agreement does not require him to undertake structural repairs but last year he replaced the roofing sheets which were blown away during the freak storm that hit Johannesburg. These sheets were so damaged they could not be reused. He had to buy new. The landlords refused his request to reimburse his costs. He has decorated the outside of this property at regular intervals, despite the fact that this is included in the agreement as a landlord's covenant.'

At this point, and much to the Magistrates' evident irritation, the police counsel interrupted, *sotto voce*, to point out that an obligation to pay the rent was also a covenant in the agreement. Jenny continued.

'When the city council decided last year to increase rents by an average of more than 10%, my client had a letter sent to the landlords objecting to this unwarrantable increase and saying that he could not afford to pay. The irony is that he was, until the boycott, working for the Council in their maintenance department as a painter and decorator and his wages had not been increased for the last three years. He was reluctant to withhold his rent when the city-wide boycott began, but in the circumstances he was persuaded to do so. As is well-known, the reaction to this concerted action was an extensive campaign of eviction and I am told there was a deliberate drive to target every tenth house in each street and move out the occupants by force. Fortunately, before this thoughtless and cruel exercise went too far, the Johannesburg City Council reduced the rent increases to more reasonable levels and the boycott was called off.'

'We know all this, Miss Cresswell,' said the magistrate. 'Where are you getting to?'

'With your leave, I need to remind the court of the background to demonstrate the enormity of what occurred on the 20th of September. Tragically, the family of my client were targeted before the police action was called off. Bisi's father was at work and the only people at home were Bisi, who was not at school owing to sickness, and her mother. When the police came on the scene, Mrs Iromze locked all the doors and windows. Her husband had fitted some very secure fastenings and, when the police found they could not immediately force their way through the front door, they used a make-do battering ram. I understand that in some cases battering rams are standard issue for police units but on this occasion a piece of timber was used—a 'four by two' as it is called. Four inches by two inches, usually employed for rafters or floor joists. This length of timber was to be used to break a window at the front of the house. At that very moment this ten-year-old girl, who was even more frightened than her mother, went to this window to see what was happening. The ram hit her full in the face, forcing glass into her eyes and cheeks, and breaking her nose. She has lost all the sight in the right eye and 75% in the other. Counsel for the police has apologised on his client's behalf but maintains this was an accident. Accident! How did this so-called accident come about? If I ran my car into someone I did not see, that might be termed an accident, but if I was driving unreasonably, if I was driving in a manner outside that of normal civilised driving behaviour, would that still be an accident? I therefore submit that the injuries this young and innocent girl suffered were not the result of an action properly taken within the law. No-one denies that police forces the world over have an obligation to uphold the law and to take such action as is necessary and reasonable to ensure that all citizens comply with the law, but the action that took place on the 20th of September at 17 Southern Way was not necessary and certainly not reasonable. The police were not there to arrest hardened criminals. They were not there to arrest saboteurs or bomb throwers. They were not even there to apprehend political activists. They were really only acting as uniformed bailiffs to obtain possession of property in lieu of a debt. Bisi and her mother, the only people in the house, are not criminals. They are not murderers, or arsonists or bank robbers. This is a housewife and a ten-year-old girl who locked themselves in the house because they were frightened. And by what? The aggressive behaviour of the police who then, to compound their attitude, employed a make-shift battering ram. I repeat, a battering ram, to gain entry. What was this? The siege of Troy? Not only that but they used this unnecessary weapon in such a manner as to cause the tragic accident I have described. Bisi is a bright girl. She was doing well at school and now for the rest of her life she is going to need support. My plea to you, Sir, is that you will see your way to finding against the police and award my client damages in the sum of a minimum of R500,000 which will be used to set up a trust fund for this girl to provide the help she will need throughout her life. In addition, I contend that the award should include an amount for the cost of teaching Bisi how to use the Braille method of reading so she can continue her studies.'

'An impassioned plea, Miss Cresswell,' responded the Magistrate. 'Firstly, let me say to all concerned in this case that I am sorry it has taken so long to reach this stage. I still believe this matter should have been heard in a Court of higher jurisdiction but as I have been overruled on this point I must determine the verdict myself. I regret that much time has been lost but I still need a little longer to consider and contemplate. I will deliver my decision in writing within seven days but at this point I must tell both parties I am inclined to agree that in this particular case the force used by the police was excessive and I shall take that into account in determining whether the payment of compensation is justified, and if so, in what amount.'

The Magistrate was true to his word and ten days later Jenny received a copy of the written decision which awarded damages in a substantial sum. They were not as much as she had hoped, but Thabo Iromze was more than satisfied with the outcome, although nothing could bring back his daughter's sight.

Jenny was to discover that Snyman was at least accurate on one score when he said that Johannesburg was home to plenty of criminals, never mind political activists. She thought about this. Are they criminals because of the politics? If the thief had the vote would he give up thieving? What can be said, with some level of certainty, is that the disadvantaged underclass—the black people—is more likely to descend into dishonesty, either to survive or as a violent reaction to being consigned to the scrap-heap of nothingness. If you are not allowed to labour legitimately, what is the alternative but crime?

Joe helped Jenny with the law relating to general and punitive damages. He thus met Thabo Iromze and was included in the invitation to celebrate Bisi's twelfth birthday, which occurred shortly after the news of the damages award. Joe was concerned about a trip to 17 Southern Way but Jenny said it would be discourteous to refuse. However, on the day Jenny went by herself, since Joe needed to stay with Emily who had a severe toothache.

When Jenny was about three streets away from the Iromze house, and just before it was becoming dark, she pulled into the side of the road to consult her street map. Like most of the Townships, all the houses looked the same: identical concrete boxes distinguished only by the amount of rubbish accommodated in the front garden, if the strip of land between the house and the street could be so described. The estate slavishly followed the dictum of a town planner obsessed by the grid formation, which made directions easy to follow, provided you correctly counted the number of intersections to your destination. As she picked up the map, the offside rear door of the car was opened and she heard, in guttural and peremptory tones, 'Don't look round. Drive on.'

Her first thought was what a fool she had been, firstly to make this trip alone and secondly not to lock the car door. Joe was going to be very angry with her.

The back-seat passenger said nothing more. He did not smell very nice but Jenny knew she was in serious trouble. Car theft was prevalent and all drivers were exhorted to take care. The silence was broken by the command to turn right. Jenny tried to think how Ida Lupino would have dealt with a similar situation. She did not know if her passenger was armed. Could she brake suddenly and escape the car before he recovered? Run into a lamp-post? Make erratic swerves to put him off? As she considered these possibilities, her nervous driving produced its own solution. She could see nothing of the man in the rear-view mirror so she decided to half turn her head towards him but before she could do so her hands slackened on the steering wheel and the car came to a shuddering halt with the nearside wheels in a shallow roadside ditch. The passenger reacted more quickly than she did. She was not hurt, just dazed and disorientated. By the time she had recovered her senses, he was dragging her from the driving seat across the adjoining waste ground towards a bunch of unkempt trees that looked as though they were habitually used as a rural lavatory. She was pulled to her feet. Her shirt was torn from her shoulders as the assailant used it to tug her along the ground. She now had her first glimpse of him. He was a short black man, probably in his twenties. His hair was long and dirty and several of his front teeth were broken. His mien was deadly serious but he also looked as though he enjoyed his work. In an instant Jenny thought, what is he? Thief, or rapist, or both? As he released her momentarily she tried to gather her torn shirt around her bare shoulders. He scowled and stared at her bra, which was pink and decorated with small flowers. Jenny was fit. She rode most weekends and played a lot of golf. Could she manoeuvre enough space between them to be able to kick him in the groin effectively or would the use of fingernails to the eyes be the better option? She did neither. She spat in his face. There had been no conversation between them until then.

'White bitch. You'll pay for that.'

He tried to drag her closer towards the trees, this time using her hair. As she hit him in the mouth, he began to shout and she was thrown onto the sandy ground next to a pile of fresh excrement. However, as she looked up, she saw two men looking down at her—the short ruffian and a much larger, older person.

'All right brother, leave her to me. You've got the car. Why not make a run for it while you can? I'll see to her.'

The short man mumbled that he didn't need help from anyone but, seeing the bulk of his companion, decided to take the advice. As Jenny got to her feet she saw her car being driven away, the ditched tyres creating a cloud of dust that virtually obscured the departing vehicle. Was she now in an even more difficult situation? She might have been able to avoid the clutches of 'shorty' but this man was in an entirely different league.

'It is Miss Cresswell, is it not?'

'Yes, do I know you?'

'Well, we all look the same to you white people, don't we? But you're too pretty to forget.'

Jenny's heart sank. He went on.

'I was in court. They gave me you as my lawyer. I had destroyed my passbook. You didn't get me off but you tried hard to show that my act was against an iniquitous law. "No defence," they said. My name is Jacob Moto. Just finished two years in prison—actually, would you believe, commuted to fifteen months 'cos no more room in the jail. They are becoming so efficient at locking up the blacks they can't build the lock-ups quick enough.'

'But what are you doing here? Yes, I think I remember you. I talked to your daughter before the case came up. An impressive girl, if I recall.'

'Yes, she is now a nurse.'

'But how come you are here?'

'Pure coincidence. Just going to work. I'm a barman at Auntie Alice's shebeen. Come on, let's go to the bar and you can telephone from there. Are you all right?'

'Yes, just a bit shaken. What a saviour you are!'

'That's as maybe. But you shouldn't be by yourself. Where were you going?'

Jenny explained. She and Jacob became good friends thereafter. He proved to be a useful confidant when she was looking for information, from the black man's point of view, when preparing a defence.

Only a few days later, an unexpected letter arrived on Jenny's desk. It had reached her safely because the cheap brown envelope had her business card attached to it by three pieces of grimy sellotape. A fourth had been lost in transit. She applauded the postal system of the Republic. Inside the envelope was a sheet of lined paper torn from a school exercise book. The message, written in pencil, read:

> Can Madam remember me? I am Mrs Sobo. You were kind at court when he got sent to prison. They are letting him out soon, but I very worry. Will he continue to protest? You are kind somebody. Can you see him and tell him to look to his family and not bother police more. We are coming back to Johannesburg. Address above is my brother. Will you see my husband? Tell him no more foolish? Please.

Am I a lawyer or a social worker? thought Jenny. She discussed it with Henry and Joe.

'Well, my dear, none of us knew what we were getting into when as a firm we decided to try and help the dispossessed and when you, as an individual, made the extraordinary decision to move to South Africa and be our instrument of mercy. By the way, are the fees coming in satisfactorily for those cases when you are appointed by the courts?'

'Don't be mercenary, Dad. We can afford some subsidy.'

'Henry, you are right to raise that point but I think you will find I am just about paying my way. When I'm employed by commercial firms to defend key workers who have transgressed the apartheid law, I make sure they pay the full scale and, as you know, I am being asked to give written opinions when there are borderline cases. Nevertheless, back to my original point. Am I to be a social worker? You see the pathetic letter from Mrs Sobo. I can't ignore it. I doubt I can do much good but I'll see if I can get the husband into the office. A cup of tea and a biscuit in these august surroundings might do the trick.'

John Sobo stayed out of trouble. Like so many of the more militant, the clampdown by the Government after a spate of bombings made them realise that if protest in the past had been futile it was now a near impossibility. Mainly as a result of Sharpeville, and the other disturbances of 1960, there had been a dramatic change in ANC policy. Until then they had been committed to reform by non-violent means but it had now been concluded that, unlike India, where passive resistance had on the whole worked, in South Africa more decisive action was required. Both the ANC and the PAC set up militant wings. During the early 1960s these were involved in over two hundred bomb attacks on post offices, Government buildings and other strategic targets. The Government's reaction was to introduce further legislation. By the General Law Amendment Act of 1962, usually referred to as the Sabotage Act, the State was granted virtually unlimited powers and a whole raft of individual rights and liberties was consigned to the scrap heap. However, by 1964 this limited violent resistance was over and Nelson Mandela and other leaders were serving life sentences on Robben Island. Jenny defended a number of people involved in these actions, but in only one case was she able to prove that the accused was not involved.

A month after her first appearance Miriam re-appeared at Jenny's office. She no longer wore her business suit. Her apparel was now jeans and a shirt, but the most startling difference was in her appearance. She seemed to have developed a twitch to the right side of her face and the hair visible under the torn baseball cap she wore was untidy and dirty. She sat opposite Jenny in silence for some time as if she was trying to catch her breath, or collect her thoughts. Jenny broke the impasse.

'I have been worried about you but I didn't make any enquiries as I thought at this stage they might only make things worse. So, what did they want to see you about?'

'Well, it seems fairly certain that they know nothing about the book. They didn't say, but it must have been an informant—probably that groundsman. When I arrived I was seen by a fairly junior policeman who interviewed me in a room adjoining the main reception area. I think this indicates they were not really too concerned about my actions, but when I refused to answer his questions other than to say that whom I chose as a boyfriend was no business of his, he became quite angry. I was then escorted to a room on the fifth floor. I think it was the fifth. It had no windows, just a desk and three wooden chairs. I know it is unreasonable, even stupid, to think like this, but I was glad there were no windows. Stories are told about prisoners jumping from upper storey windows. My first interrogator was no longer involved. In the room were two men in uniform, presumably more senior, certainly more sinister. They called me "Sisi" and asked why I wouldn't answer one simple question. "Are you fucking a white man?" They scared me, but I still said it was no business of theirs. The reaction to this was not anger but an exchange of smiles. They seemed to know exactly what to do next—as if it was a practised routine. One of the men took off my jacket and my shirt and pulled me up to the desk. The other took off my bra. By now I was screaming at them. They ignored this and as one held me tight the other forced me to bend over a drawer in the desk so that one of my breasts would hang into it. He then slammed the drawer shut so that my breast was squashed. They did this three times—to each of them. I was not asked any more questions but some lewd remarks were passed as they left the room. After I had replaced my shirt and jacket the first policeman came in and took me downstairs. I was then locked in a cell. The pain in my breasts was agonising and there was a nasty discharge from both my nipples but I kept thinking that it could have been worse. I could have been raped. But do you know, Jenny, I felt as though I had been raped. My femininity had been violated.'

'How horrible! What a monstrous action. How do they devise such tortures? And you say you don't think you were the first. This is awful. We know they have tortured men in a variety of ways but this must be unique in the abuse of women. What happened then?'

'The next day I was taken back to the same room but this time there were three of them, the third man with more braid than the other two. He did not say a word but looked at me with a leer on his face. He seemed to concentrate his gaze on my breasts; he must have been fully aware of the desk drawer technique. I was never told the names of the two men who had violated me but as the senior one left I am sure I heard him addressed as Colonel Snyman.'

'Snyman. Oh, we've crossed swords before. Sorry to interrupt but I'll tell you about him later.

'There's not much more to tell. The two brutes asked if I had slept well and then told me I could go. As I got to the door I heard one say to the other, "What she needs is a real man. She'd know it if she got my six inches." I felt sick. I could almost believe the whole exercise was a subterfuge to get a good look at my tits. I did not come back to see you straightaway. I was in shock and, as I've been dismissed from the bank, I've been looking for another job. One visit to John Vorster Square, for whatever cause, and you're immediately *persona non grata.* I'm probably unemployable. Can you imagine the reference the bank would give? "Excellent worker, but not sure about her security status" or something like that.'

'You poor thing. We can't allow this to happen. This is supposed to be a civilised country. What about John? Have you seen him? Have you told him what occurred?'

'No. I don't think he is relevant to any of this.'

'Nonsense, of course he is. Let me speak to him.'

'Please don't. I'm so ashamed. I can only tell you because you are a woman.'

Jenny did not insist that John Streger be told what had been done to Miriam, but now that Snyman's name had been mentioned she thought Henry and Joe should be brought up to date. Emily insisted she too be included.

'Our Colonel Snyman has re-appeared on the scene. You know about our mystery book. The author has turned up. She is a really nice person whom I have now met on two occasions and I am so furious at the way she has been treated, I can hardly speak.'

Jenny related Miriam's story with an added comment as to which part of the Colonel's anatomy she would like to trap in a desk drawer.

'This matter began with a piece of literature. Now I have met Miriam I admire what she has written even more. So I have come up with a plan, taken from literature—directly from Shakespeare. Do you all know *Measure for Measure*?

Heads nodded, some more decisively than others.

'The bed trick is central to that story. Could we plan something like it? If we could obtain evidence of Snyman in bed with Miriam we could use it for all sorts of purposes. The wonderful irony of it. The brutality of his men arises from an alleged sexual liaison. If we can show he is guilty of the same so-called crime, what a revenge!'

It was Emily who showed that her memory of the Shakespeare play was the best.

'Not sure I'm altogether with you at the moment, Jenny. If that Snyman is to be Angelo, who gets to play Isabella?'

'Oh,' said Jenny. 'I've cast myself in that role already.'

She decided to put Henry and Joe out of their misery.

'Angelo lusts after unmarried Isabella. If she will sleep with him he will pardon her brother Claudio who has been sentenced to death. She refuses, but then contrives the "bed trick". She tells Angelo she has changed her mind on condition that their first meeting takes place in complete darkness. He agrees. Isabella's place is then taken by Mariana, to whom Angelo was betrothed but reneged on his promise. The union is consummated, in the dark, and by this act he is forced to marry her, something Mariana desires. There is, of course, more to the play than the bed bit, but do you get the picture?'

Henry scratched his head.

'You want to arrange a marriage between Miriam and Snyman—or are you to be the lucky bride?'

'No, of course not. He's already married with grown-up children but that makes it all the more delicious. I may be wrong, Joe, but I got the feeling that when we met him the first time—and since—he rather fancied me. Keeps bringing up the Cambridge connection. I'm going to seduce him.'

'Dad, you're working her too hard. She's gone mad. Stark staring bonkers.'

'It does sound mad and it won't work if I fail on the feminine charm front but if I can get him to think I find him attractive enough to want to go to bed with him, and he's arrogant enough to believe such a fantasy, let me paint the picture. Quiet little hotel in the suburbs. Candlelit dinner for two before retiring to the four-poster upstairs. One last drink, into which I have slipped a powerful sleeping draught. Undress the brute and resist the temptation to place his penis on the window sill under an open sash window. Miriam enters, stage left. As he wakes to find her, clad in a sheer negligé and draped over his awful carcass, a photographer appears. He does his work and Miriam escapes before Snyman has fully woken up and realises what has happened. It does not take him long to see that he has been set up. He is reluctant to meet with us the next day, but soon sees he has no option. Joe and I then show him what a gruesome sight he is *au naturel.* Gosh, I've just thought of a super twist. When we get upstairs I suggest, as we take our pre-coital drink, that it would be very sexy if we wore masks. In his drugged state we can arrange some further pictures—needs a good photographer—of the great man without his mask. Miriam can use it. He is in bed with two unrecognisable women, neither of whom is his wife. One black, the other white. The mind boggles.'

'You'll never get away with it.'

'Listen. You know how strait-laced these people are. I believe his wife is a member of one of the most prominent of Afrikaner families and her brother is a pastor in the Reformed Church. Well, that sort are the first to transgress.'

'Possibly, but how are you going to persuade him to go with you to that small hotel you describe so vividly?'

'I shall court him. Where do we start? Do you think he and his wife will accept a dinner invitation from you Henry? I bet they would. He'd love to patronise the enemy. Extending the olive branch. I could start there.'

'But if the photographs do not have the potency you imagine, how will you use them? What is to stop him sending a hit squad around to lock us all up—or something worse?'

'I've thought about that. Sealed envelopes addressed to the wife, the head of State Security and the Prime Minister to be sent if anything untoward should happen to us.'

'But, Jenny, what you are suggesting is illegal.'

'Henry, do you think it legal for a young woman to be stripped to the waist and made to bend over a desk drawer so that those brutes can trap her breasts in it?'

There was silence for a moment. Then Joe, the practical member of this intrigue club, spoke.

'Where are you going to find a photographer who will not expose us all after the event?'

'Oh, I'm so glad someone has seen this possible flaw in the plan, but that is my *pièce de resistance.* John Streger. Miriam says he's an ace photographer. Isn't it delicious? He and Miriam can extract the sweetest revenge of all on this vile representative of a Government that has destroyed their relationship. William, bard of Stratford-on-Avon, I salute you.'

Emily hugged Jenny.

'This is what the fates brought you here for. This will be your finest hour.'

The male members of the Marks family still looked sceptical but Henry agreed that, provided Miriam was completely in favour, nothing would be lost by at least arranging a dinner party and sending out invitations. Miriam, who thought Isabella one of Shakespeare's finest female creations, was as taken with the idea as Emily, but also apprehensive. She did not have the courage that went with Jenny's white skin but, as she had shown so far in this saga, she was far from being an insignificant and invisible black woman. She did not know whether John would agree to participate as proposed—it was way out of character for him. On the other hand, she knew he would enjoy the photographic challenge and he too might like to be involved in obtaining some redress for what had been denied him by the State. It would be impossible for the centrality of Government to be brought to book, but when John was told of what Snyman's men had done, she thought he would be pleased to accept the Colonel as a representative of an evil regime.

John turned out to be an enthusiastic recruit and Joe suggested he be included in the projected dinner party. Snyman was a rugby aficionado and John was friendly with the current captain of the Transvaal first team. Could John secure him as a guest? He would be another attraction to bring the fly into the spider's web. Rugby did the trick; Snyman and his wife accepted the invitation from Mrs Marks. Mrs Snyman proved to be a dignified lady of considerable charm, and wealth. It was her family money that paid for the mansion they lived in at Houghton; the model of Mercedes her husband drove could not have been afforded on a policeman's pay, however senior his rank. It soon became clear that she rather disapproved of her husband's profession and, partly orchestrated by the hosts, the words 'security', 'sabotage' and 'police' were avoided during the dinner-table exchange. Fortunately, all the ladies present, except for Jenny, were rugby fans but the fact that the country was excluded from the international scene meant that topics were limited to local rivalries, like that between the Transvaal and the Orange Free State. Jenny sat next to her prey at dinner and made sure the conversation enabled the Colonel to be shown in a flattering light. She had half formulated a plan for a follow-up meeting after the dinner party and put the first stage of this into play by requesting to see him to discuss a professional matter. She did not propose this at the Marks' house but phoned him a few days later. She told him she wanted to expand her ability as a lawyer by taking some academic courses on criminal psychology and would be grateful for the benefit of his considerable experience to determine whether such an exercise would be of any value to her and, if so, how to achieve this ambition. Snyman said he was really too busy, but then promised her half an hour on the Friday of the following week. She wore her shortest skirt.

'It is good of you to see me, Colonel, in view of the fact that we are in some respects opponents.'

'Jenny, please call me Jan. I don't quite see it like that. You have your job to do and I have mine.'

'Yes, but you are at the front line of an iniquitous system. Okay, you're now going to kick me out for saying that but on the surface that's what it looks like. However, I remember when we first met, you said that your only concern was to see that the law was upheld.'

'Just so. We do not have to approve of the laws—we police them—but I can understand that someone like you does not approve of what our lawmakers have done.'

'You're right, but I'm not simply a bleeding-heart liberal. I can oppose what is happening because if the balloon goes up, and the streets flow with blood, I can pack my bags and go back to England. You don't have that as an option. Jan, this is old ground. You've heard the arguments hundreds of times.'

'Precisely.'

'I am also beginning to see that it is not all black and white. Oh dear, unfortunate phrase. You know what I mean, it is not so cut and dried as it is made out to be. I defended a black man recently who had been picked up for a passbook offence. Told me he was being continually harassed by the police. They seemed to follow him wherever he went and delighted in locking him up. The verdict was the usual, but by accident I discovered something more about this man. His record for some reason didn't come up in court. Your people are not perfect, are they? Evidently, he is a well-known thief, and a skilful one at that. Targets the house he is going to rob and seems to be an expert in unarmed combat. He has put a number of night watchmen in hospital, I understand. None of this came out and I saw him as just another victim of apartheid, but I also discovered that the previous time he was arrested it was for an assault on his wife. She had refused to press charges. I went to see her. Wouldn't say a word, but not so her neighbour. This man, who complains about the police, is a monster. He beats his wife and children and has a succession of whores whom he takes to his house despite his family being there. As I was leaving, after talking to the neighbour, he appeared and was most unpleasant. I was quite scared.'

'There you are. Criminals.'

'I didn't want to bore you with that story but I just wanted to show that I am less naive than when I first arrived.'

'I'm glad of that.'

'Let's get onto the object of my visit, and again many thanks for finding the time. This case I have recounted has convinced me I need to try and understand the criminal mind better. Where do I begin?'

Jenny gave him a flashing smile and crossed her legs. He noticed. He then spent the next ten minutes giving her the benefit of his experience, suggesting books she might read and giving details of who within the academic world might be able to help. Before she left they came back to politics.

'Do you think there is going to be more unrest? That bomb at the station—is that a foretaste of things to come?'

'No, my dear, that was a one-off, a loner—and a white man, of course.'

'I'm glad to hear that. I like it here. Don't want to leave. For one thing, I find the men so much more masculine than the ones I knew at home. I think this new feminine movement is beginning to emasculate the lot of them.'

Snyman said nothing but grinned.

'Look at that man at dinner the other night—what was his name? John Streger. Ugly as sin—sorry, I shouldn't be so blunt—but a real man, I bet. Another reason why I love this place is the golf. The courses are superb, membership is cheap and I can play all the year round.'

'Oh, I didn't know you were a golfer. Where do you play? What are you playing off?'

'Since I've been here I'm down to twelve. My best in the UK was eighteen. I'm a member at Bryanston, but would love to try out the Royal Johannesburg.'

'Well, I'm a member there. Don't get much time these days but I was down to single figures when I was at university. Why don't you come as my guest one Saturday?'

'That would be wonderful. You are so kind.'

As they shook hands at her departure she applied an extra ounce of pressure. The courting was progressing satisfactorily.

It was necessarily a slow process. A partnership between a fifty-three-year-old Afrikaner policemen and an English girl of twenty-eight could give rise to comment. Accordingly, their first two encounters on the golf course came about when Snyman invited Jenny to substitute in his regular foursome when one member had dropped out. As her presence at the club, and in his company, began to become accepted, she took the initiative and challenged him to a game between the two of them. On the thirteenth she deliberately hooked her ball into a small copse, not out of bounds, but with some grassy undergrowth. As he helped her to find the ball she was able, when bending over, to display rather more of her upper thigh than was normal for the conservative Royal Johannesburg Club. She gave him a good game, but allowed him to win on the eighteenth.

The plotters, with Jenny in command, thought the time was now ripe to let their prey know that this young lawyer was attracted to him and that it was for him, as the male hunter, to make the first to move. All decided the fuel needed to spark his engine was flattery. After their second game together at Royal Johannesburg, Jenny asked if she could again seek his advice on a professional matter and see him at his office. Snyman was now relaxed about their being seen together on the golf course. His wife did not play, so why should he not bestow the privilege of playing at this prestigious club on this relative newcomer in their midst? However, too many appearances at his office could be another thing altogether. Jenny had anticipated this and was, therefore, not surprised when he suggested it would be more convivial if he continued his thesis on the psychology of police work over lunch. He chose a small Italian restaurant in Sandton. Jenny had come armed with a real-life scenario she then adapted into a hypothetical case which included some elements of titillation: an alleged rape. She attacked him with her wide-eyed, innocent, yet sophisticated, look and begged him to tell her what approach should be taken. He thoroughly enjoyed delivering his lecture, and the company. Jenny kept up the pressure and telephoned the man three days later.

'Jan, you will be getting sick of me, but it looks as though the real-life case we talked about last week is coming to trial. It is way outside your jurisdiction, a Pretoria court. If you think there's no conflict . . . well, to tell the truth I'm out of my depth. Henry and Joe are useless in these matters and they've advised me to withdraw, but I feel so sorry for the woman.'

Before he could respond she carried on, somewhat breathlessly, and with a degree of agitation.

'And it is my turn to repay you for that delicious lunch. Please say we can get together soon. The case comes up on Monday.'

'Of course, you know I'm only too pleased to help. As I said before, it is good that you should widen your experience and I don't see a problem about giving advice in the abstract—as long as you don't quote me.'

Jenny grimaced. He had the most unattractive laugh.

'You are sweet. Trouble is there's not much time and, as I know how busy you are, and I'm in court every day this week, would Lucy spare you if we had dinner together? We could eat early, on your way home from the office. There's a good fish place in Morningside.'

'I'm sure she will, for you. You've become quite a favourite, you know. She very much enjoyed your company at the Marks' dinner.'

'Super. It is at 30, Centre Street. If tomorrow night is okay I'll meet you there at six thirty.'

'Look forward to it.'

Over dinner they sat side by side on a banquette, so arranged by Jenny in advance, and, by the end of the meal, they were holding hands between courses.

Snyman drove Jenny back to her flat. She had arrived at the restaurant in a taxi—her own car was being serviced, she explained. She made no attempt to persuade her escort to see her to the front door but accepted a modest kiss on each cheek as she left his car. She entered the lobby of the block of flats, hoping he would still have in his nostrils the aroma of the distinctive perfume she had deliberately employed for this evening's rendezvous. She believed enough seeds had been sown to ensure that the next move would come from him. How right she was. He phoned the very next day.

'I did enjoy last night, but I feel guilty. I don't think I gave you as much help on that abuse case as I might have done.'

Jenny had been slightly concerned when she heard the word

'guilty'. Was the hook slipping? She gave a sigh of relief as he finished the sentence.

'Are you by any chance free tomorrow night?'

'If you have some more wisdom for me, I'll make sure I'm free.'

They dined at a restaurant close to the offices of Marks and Co. Her car was still being serviced, so he drove her home as before. Jenny made sure that the exchange of professional opinions was still in full flood, so it seemed natural they should continue the discussion with a glass of brandy in her living room. The lighting was low, but the conversation continued as master to pupil.

'Jan, you should go. Lucy will wonder.'

'Not a problem. This is her bridge night and she won't be home for ages.'

'As you say, but I still think you should go.'

As he stood up to leave he took a step towards her and she flung her arms around his neck.

'Jan. What is happening to me? Oh, please go.'

'No. I must stay with you.'

'I can't breathe. Not here. In my own flat. Somewhere neutral. Remote. You decide. In the outback somewhere. Please go.'

They kissed and she held him very tight. He telephoned the next day. He had chosen the rendezvous, but she chose the day to give time for the team to reconnoitre the venue. The sleeping potion had been acquired and sequestered in John Steger's bathroom cabinet. Amongst his shop-keeping fraternity was a pharmacist who had been able to concoct the right mixture.

The lovers met at the country inn after journeying in separate cars. Joe Marks and John were already in residence. John was able to obtain a photograph of Snyman as he checked in. Jenny was deliberately an hour late. As she drove to the rendezvous she recalled her acting debut on that train from Market Harborough to Nottingham, and wondered if she was about to be called upon to deliver her finest performance. She was a vivacious and attractive woman but still thought it amazing that a man like Snyman could be so easily seduced. She prayed the dénouement would live up to expectations, banking as she was on the macho-Afrikaner being unable to resist her charms. She imagined his earliest ancestor farming in the Cape. She had read the history.

The stock whence her quarry emerged had its origins in the

men who established the supply station at Cape Town for the Dutch East India Company. These were not farmers. For the first few years instead of supplying the vessels en route to the East or Europe, the local agriculture had to be supplemented by these same vessels in order for the garrison to survive. In an attempt to counteract this, a few of the company's servants were given freehold smallholdings each of about twenty acres. Thus the first burghers of South Africa were created. In time these farmers began to move from the coastal regions further inland where they were deeded leaseholds over land extending to six thousand acres each. For the next hundred years or more the Boers were in conflict, of one sort or another, with the strictures of the company, the indigenous population and the English administration, the British having taken final control of the Cape in 1806. In 1836 many of these Cape Boers took part in the Great Trek, moving further and further away from British control and influence and the constraints imposed by the abolition of slavery in 1833. Hundreds of miles from his nearest neighbour across the veldt, Snyman's great-great-great-grandfather would have sired lots of children from a wife kept at home as a breeding machine. The man was the master. He whipped his servants, and no doubt his children, and slept with whichever of the black or Coloured female servants took his fancy. She knew this was a crude picture of a cruel stereotype. Today Snyman was respectful to his wife; nevertheless, there was enough of the Boer patriarch left in him to have brought him to this fate.

She met him in the bar, out of breath and shaking. He looked triumphant. As she was so late they moved into the dining room and so were not alone until they reached the bedroom. Her overnight bag had been taken there by the porter on arrival. They embraced with a mutual degree of ardour but she told her companion that she was still nervous and asked if they might have another drink. Snyman had indulged before and during dinner, encouraged by Jenny. While he made an urgent visit to the bathroom, she was able to doctor his brandy. The potion was colourless, odourless and very potent. He was slumped on the bed, gently snoring, within minutes. The sleeping draught was guaranteed to work for six hours exactly. Jenny returned to the room taken for Miriam, after reporting to Joe and John that the plan had worked so far.

As dawn was breaking the first set of photographs were taken. John arranged the naked and unconscious Snyman in a suitably sexual position adjacent to the unclothed bodies of Miriam and Jenny, each of whom wore a mask. This is what it must be like working in the porno-film industry, he thought. These pictures were to be the supplementary evidence. Just before the main event, Miriam slightly changed the plan. Instead of a state of nakedness or the revealing negligée she decided that wearing Snyman's shirt as her only article of clothing would be more provocative and, if she made her escape so clothed, he would have further problems when he came to leave the hotel. So it proved. Jenny left the scene as Snyman gave signs that he was about to wake up. Before this occurred, and while Snyman was on his back, Miriam, with John in attendance, lay by his side, the shirt worn high on her body, her head turned away towards the bathroom door. Snyman's night-time tumescence had not yet subsided so that his penis appeared aroused as if by sexual desire. As soon as his eyes opened, the Hasselblad SLR camera was operated several times and John and Miriam, her head still averted, quit the room before Snyman was fully awake. At the last moment Miriam took his shoes with her. They joined the others in the nearby bedroom and remained there until they had observed his departure—in stocking feet and without a shirt—from their bedroom window.

All that remained was to confront him with the evidence. After some discussion it was decided that the most senior member of the plotters would be a better envoy than Joe and Jenny. With some reluctance, Henry Marks agreed.

'Colonel, I received these photographs in the mail this morning. I thought you should see them immediately. I should also tell you that I have been given a detailed report, written by one of your victims, recounting a barbarous action taken by your men involving a woman and desk drawers. If made public, I believe your superiors would find such behaviour unacceptable, particularly from a senior policeman who appears to have had an relationship which contravenes the Immorality Acts.'

Snyman had spent an uncomfortable few days realising that he had been deceived by Jenny and wondering to what purpose. Now he knew. He could hardly implicate her without danger to his marriage, and without revealing the Jenny affair he would have difficulty in protesting that the photographs were a fabrication obtained by trickery. He continued to glare at Henry.

'My informant has instructed me to deliver the following terms. You will write a letter explaining your involvement in that abusive treatment, which will be described in detail, and apologise fully. You will then do what you can to ensure that in the future women in police custody are not subjected to such treatment ever again. Although I have the name of one of your victims you are required to address this letter to, "To whom it may concern." You must then retire from the police force immediately; what reasons you give you can decide for yourself. If these conditions are not fulfilled within the next seven days, I am instructed to make these photographs public. As you can see they also include pictures of what I believe is referred to as "three in a bed". Very unsavoury. I must also tell you that copies of these pictures, together with an account of my meeting with you today, will be placed in sealed envelopes with instructions that they be sent to your wife and the Minister of Justice in the event anything untoward should occur to those you might suspect of being involved.'

By now Snyman was so bursting with rage that tears sprang to his eyes. His body was shaking.

'You won't get away with this, you stinking Jew. I've done nothing wrong. You and your gang are the criminals—particularly that slut, Cresswell. I have extensive contacts in the criminal underworld. I shall hire the necessary assassins.'

'Do not be too hasty. Don't forget the sealed envelopes.'

Snyman spluttered.

'You Calvinists believe in an eye for an eye and a tooth for a tooth. You call us criminals. You, Snyman, are an appalling example of the worst kind of Afrikaner. You abuse your power. You use the protection of apartheid legislation to indulge in sadistic torture. You will not remember this but my son was concerned with a gardener's son, Gabriel Ntshona, who died when in your care. You said he committed suicide. We didn't believe you then and we don't now. I think you should also know that it was that boy's death, together with the police action at Sharpeville, that persuaded Jenny Cresswell to come to South Africa to try and help your victims. I think she has cooked your goose, my dear Colonel, and this "stinking Jew" has just thought of a codicil to our agreement. I expect that, within the next seven days, Gabriel's father will receive, via me, an anonymous donation of one hundred thousand rand. Goodbye.'

Before seven days had expired Snyman had complied with all the demands, except the resignation, but at the end of the month there was an announcement in the press to the effect that Colonel Jan Snyman had retired after over twenty-five years of dedicated service to the South African police force. He had taken this action for 'family reasons'. None of the conspirators ever heard his name mentioned again, nor did they encounter man or wife socially. But then they did not to move within the Houghton set. Joe explained to Moses that they had been able to arrange some compensation for his son's death while in police custody. He was to keep this to himself, but the money would soon be available for collection at their offices. Moses was not disappointed.

Over the next few months Jenny and Miriam became close friends. The budding author no longer harboured ambitions to become a published writer and Jenny had talked to her about coming to work with Marks and Co. She even entertained the possibility that she might study law, until Miriam made her own decision.

'After what has happened to me I bear no anger for John's actions. He wouldn't have been happy away from Johannesburg and I could see, as well as he, that there were few prospects of our having a future together. I think, if it can be measured, he was more in love than I, but I know he'll recover. He was certainly glad to be involved in our adventure. He saw it as doing something for me, to spite that awful man and as some recompense for our having to part. He should not feel guilty. If he hadn't taken the step, I would probably have done so, sooner or later.'

'Yes. In the end I think he has acted very well. He's really quite a nice man. What do you do next?'

'You talked about the law. Well, I agree we can't have too many like you fighting battles for the oppressed but if we cannot change this country there may need to be a revolution, and if it comes to that I want to be involved in the fight. I have been able to make contact with some senior ANC people and, all being well, they are going to smuggle me out of the country and into Zambia for training. They say people with some bit of brain is what they are looking for.'

'Oh dear, Miriam. Are you sure that is the best choice?'

'Yes. I shall miss you. You have been more than just a good friend. What you went through on my behalf was wonderful.'

'The added bonus of the cash to Moses Ntshona was the icing on the cake. Well done Henry. He's not such a dry old stick after all.'

It was no surprise when Miriam disappeared—the recruitment had obviously been effected—but what was a surprise concerned John Streger. One day he rang Jenny and asked if she would like to go to the cinema—there was a Gary Cooper season and *High Noon* was back. 'Why not?' she said. Over the next few weeks she even went to watch him play rugby—it was some cup final or other. She was not sure about the game but enjoyed the party they went to afterwards. His team had won. She had been pleased to receive word from Miriam with a return address and wrote to her, using Adele as an intermediate post office.

> You are not going to credit this. Your John has asked me to marry him and I have said yes. Can you believe it? He's nearly twice my weight but only stands as tall as my ear lobes. He has not become any less ugly, but what's in a rose! You were really good for him. He had the best teacher in the world and you can be proud of your pupil. He is no longer clinically shy. He has developed the most charming manners. He becomes less of the stereotype Afrikaner day by day. He adores me. I have never met such a polite man. And I find it all so attractive. We think the same way about apartheid. He loves South Africa but knows they cannot go on like this. I once told my family I'd like to go to Nigeria with my brother because I wanted to find myself a real black man. Well, I've failed in that but I have found an African and he is real. Very real. The Markses think I'm mad. They thought I would be more likely to go for the Richard Burton type, but they are sensitive souls and see how genuine this is. I'm so excited. Goodness knows what Aunt Edith will make of him, although, on second thoughts, she might well see the streak of gold that I do. She may be a great snob, but she's no fool.

Wouldn't it be wonderful if I could take you to visit my mother and her? When might that be? I do despair sometimes. How long are you and your people to be a subject race?

I'll try and send you some wedding photos. And, if possible, a piece of cake.

Chapter Seven

Adele

At the age of seventy-one, Nelson Mandela has today walked through the prison gates. He has spent over ten thousand days in jail—twenty-seven years. Jenny phoned me to say they could not get to Cape Town to be amongst the welcoming throng. She joked that he has just put her out of business—to which I replied, 'I hope so'—but then she has taken on more of the firm's traditional work since Henry retired. Jo is at a bush hospital in Zimbabwe doing her medical elective stint but I am sure the Cresswells will have been represented because Robert is still at the University of Cape Town. Wish I could have been there. What an amazing man! An inspiration to the whole world. When did I last visit South Africa? Must be nearly three years ago. No sign then of what was to happen; in fact, John felt the strife in the country was worse than ever and people were still forecasting a blood-bath. Today's news has opened a floodgate of memories.

I have not thought seriously about it before but I suppose I am in essence an 'Empire woman'. I have lived in the heart of rural Leicestershire since 1943 but so much of my spirit has been in India and Africa, even if most of it was only experienced second-hand. I was seriously concerned when I heard that Matthew had been into Biafra. That mild and gentle boy, head always in some book or other, had become a spy. What a disaster Biafra was: civil war, the worst of all conflicts. I remember when I was at St Joseph's there was a map of the world on the wall with the British Empire coloured in red and all the other countries in a dull brown. Bartholomew's, or whoever were the map people, must have made a fortune; the same maps were on display in every English-speaking school throughout the world—or do I mean the Empire? The tragedy is that those bits of red I know best have been coloured crimson by the spilling of human blood. The Hindu and the

Muslim. The Ibo and the Hausa. The Boer and the Xhosa. Amritsar and Kashmir. Kano and Umuahia. Soweto and Sharpeville. That 'Wind of Change'—did it blow good for anyone?

I am nine years older than Mandela. If he is the current success story of what used to be the British Empire, I look back to the failures, or half failures, that I and mine have been involved in. After this century's many examples of 'man's inhumanity to man' it might be difficult to understand today the horror of the Amritsar massacre. Less than four hundred people were killed compared with the Holocaust millions, the Khmer Rouge and the Russian purges, but from my perspective it had a life-changing impact on the man I was to marry; within my compass it was the first of those examples where the British Government was, to say the least, ambivalent. What I mean by 'ambivalent' is that they sometimes said one thing and did another. To some extent I can speak with more direct knowledge of the Independence finally won by the Indians. Even with hindsight, I am not sure Whitehall could have done anything to avoid the disaster that was partition. You might say the same about the Biafran débacle. From what I have heard and seen of the Nigerians they are perfectly capable of making a mess of things without any help from anyone else, but I agree with Matthew that the British Government might have been able to alleviate what happened—the thorny question of the sale of arms of course. With my other 'sphere of influence', South Africa, there was a lot of rhetoric from the West about the evils of apartheid, sanctions and so on, but I do not believe that anything they did really helped the oppressed. I know there were economic pressures on de Klerk and his predecessors but I believe, in the end, it was the passive resistance by the black and Coloured people, exemplified by Nelson Mandela, that gave rise to what happened today in Cape Town. It was Edith—she kept a sharp eye on these things—who pointed out that Britain's support for the anti-apartheid movement had not prevented Harold Wilson agreeing to a £20 million sale of aircraft to South Africa, despite a supposed embargo on arms sales. She believed that in the past the UK often appeared hesitant about strongly opposing apartheid. Barbara Castle, who rather raised Edith's hackles, was a member of the Cabinet and a firm supporter of the movement, yet, when Albert Luthuli, the President of the ANC, was awarded the Nobel Peace Prize in 1961 it was said that the Foreign Office was advised not to meet with him because the South African Government 'would not like it'.

I wish Jenny were nearby, but I suppose today's news means they are unlikely ever to leave South Africa now. At least I can visit, provided I stay fit enough and they are very good at coming to see me. Could be worse. Isobel and Matthew could have moved from Lagos to New Zealand, or Alaska, but how lucky I am they are just down the road. They did well to buy The Grange when they did. I miss Edith of course and I suppose I should do what Matthew says and sell the house. It is much too big for me now but it has been nice having somewhere to entertain visitors from 'my empire'.

Who was the first one after Charlie died? Must have been George. More than forty years ago when I was still in my prime—and he wasn't too bad either. I thought I would never get over losing Charlie. I was angry and sad at the same time. Why did the idiot go back into the army? Was it a wasted death? From what George Slocombe said Charlie did not feel it was. He loved India and, just as Amritsar coloured his life, the thought of one Indian soldier fighting another was something he so abhorred he took up arms to try and avoid such a thing coming to pass. George gave me the whole story. I am not sure whether at the time this made me feel better but George himself did go some way towards easing the pain. To me Charlie never looked like a soldier. When I first met him I called him a 'box wallah', and that's what he was. We were not ICS, but the top echelon of the Railway rather looked down on those Britons engaged in trade. When I got to know him better I realised that he was a very good soldier—he never talked to anyone about the MC—and he was passionate on the subject of the comradeship of the soldiery, even obsessive I sometimes thought. If you are looking for an epitaph for his gravestone you could do worse than use the word 'upright'. My dictionary includes the definitions 'honest' and 'honourable'. He was certainly both of those. I think if my love for him had not been so strong I might have responded differently to George's overtures—if that's what they were. Now *he* did look like a soldier. When I met Gerard Lakey much later it was the most enormous fun to compare them. As far as the moustaches were concerned they could have been twins. I was so pleased when Jenny persuaded John to shave off his ugly excrescence.

George Slocombe was heavily engaged with his intelligence

duties in India right up until the 1947 Independence and was not back in the UK until two months after that fateful day of the 14th of August. The midnight hour. I do not think Rushdie has ever equalled his first book—he captured it for me—not that I have read them all. It was so awful. I am so glad Mummy and Daddy did not live to see the catastrophe. Charlie too. He would have been more horrified than I. Half a million dead, they say. No wonder George Slocombe was busy trying to make sense of those last few months. For a while there were some British soldiers left and Charlie would have been interested to know that the last to leave, in 1948, were the First Battalion of the Somerset Light Infantry, his old regiment. It was on all the newsreels: the men parading alongside the Gateway to India before embarking.

When he wrote to me from Imphal he said he would like to come and see me, provided I was prepared to receive him. See me about what? More explanations. More excuses. He should never have exposed Charlie to those dangers. Murdered by some fanatic—and for what? Did the death of my husband make any difference to the outcome of the conflict? But that is the problem with wars and the men who die in them. Each mother, each wife, sees each death as a personal and individual tragedy, but for war itself that death is just one of the many that have to be added to the mass of deaths needed to achieve a victory—or, just as often, to suffer a defeat. When I received his letter I read it, then tore it in half—both anger and grief, I suppose. Edith persuaded me to sellotape it back together again. He wrote again in early 1947—thought he should explain why he had not been in touch. I did not reply. However, when back on English soil he sent me quite a charming letter from a Clapham address and asked if he could finally come and pay his respects. Again I did not reply but Edith, with my reluctant agreement, invited him to visit the Old Vicarage. He was given a choice of three weekends over the next two months and he came for the first available.

Not only was I unsure of my attitude towards him because of Charlie, but I suppose I included him in the establishment that had made such a mess of the handover. I know that was not a reasonable attitude—as usual, the Indians were their own worst enemies – and of course I can no longer talk about Indians as one set of people who occupied the subcontinent. There is now a Pakistan.

He came up from London by train and took a taxi from the

station. I could not understand why such a good-looking man was still unmarried but he had been in India without a break since 1940 and no doubt eligible ladies were hard to come by at that time. I was still reluctant to meet this man who had been so involved in sending Charlie to his death. He had been dead for three years but it was more than four years since we had lain side-by-side. I still sometimes wake up in the middle of the night and am surprised to find he is not there. He always slept on his back, never snored, and invariably had a peaceful smile on his face. I do miss him. I remember vividly the first time we made love at my house when he talked some nonsense about Shakespeare's 'seven ages of man'. Despite what he had been through, surviving the First World War and losing Mary, he was still essentially a shy man, a modest man, and no spring chicken either; he was thirty five when we first met. Now I was to face the man who had deprived me of him. As soon as our visitor was settled in he asked if we could go for a walk, just the two of us, so he could give me all the details of Charlie's last months. In his earlier letter he had said he admired him; I now saw that this was a genuine sentiment. By the time we were back at the house my attitude had begun to soften. He was what is described as 'an officer and a gentleman'. We talked about the tragedy of partition. He was far from being xenophobic but I think he convinced me that Mountbatten and his team had done the best they could in the circumstances. It seems that Jinnah was the unfathomable one. Did he really want a separate State or was he bargaining for a larger say in a united India?

I have often wondered if the swing from dislike or hatred to affection—and love—are more rapid when most extreme. I thought at the time that I must ask Jenny if she has any psychology experts amongst her friends who could research this fascinating topic. Anyway, within twenty-four hours George and I were the best of friends. Edith liked him too and it seemed natural to invite him back to the house a few weeks later when there was some function on. For the life of me I cannot recall whether it was a race-meeting or a dance. On the first night of his second visit Edith was away on WI business and it was Mrs Collingwood's night off so I cooked dinner for the two of us and he opened the wine. We both drank more than was good for us and it was only Edith's return that probably prevented our being naughty together there and then.

That night Edith had woken with a premonition that the kitchen door had been left unlocked. On her way back upstairs, having discovered her fears were groundless, she found George, in dressing gown, standing in the corridor outside the first floor bedrooms. According to Edith he had a quizzical look on his face as, though he did not know which bedroom belonged to me and which to her—or to the children, come to that. She tried to pull my leg by saying he was just about to toss a coin as she appeared—or was he going to knock and see what came up. However, as soon as he saw her he muttered something about a glass of water and disappeared back to the guest room on the second floor. There were no further midnight prowls. He must have been deeply embarrassed by the sight of the formidable Edith and, when cold sober the next morning, I quickly came to the conclusion that he was not really for me and I should not encourage him further. We remained friends for a year or two and met, but only infrequently, until he was posted to Korea. We lost touch thereafter. Edith thought it an enormous joke. 'Intelligence officer,' she would say, 'and hasn't got the brains to find his way into the right bedroom—that is if he had decided which of us he was going to seduce.'

Mrs May Collingwood. She and her husband Ernest lived in the lodge cottage. She looked after the house and he the garden. She was called 'Mrs Collingwood', and nothing else, by everybody, including her husband. All called him Ernie. Even though the Old Vicarage's acres kept him well occupied, his hobby was an allotment. He went to the King's Arms twice a week—Friday nights and Saturday lunchtime. On his first visit of the week he drank three and a half pints and on the second, two. He thought Market Harborough was too noisy and the only time he had left his home county was as a boy, on a Sunday School trip to Skegness. His wife was an incomparable pessimist. If I commented that the weather was fine, her invariable response was that we would pay for it later. All pots to her were half empty, not half full. If complimented on a meal she had cooked, she was always able to find some defect to highlight. 'Them broad beans weren't fresh.'

One side effect of meeting George was that he proved to be a good listener and it helped me enormously to be able to talk about Charlie to someone who was familiar with his territory. George's interest in Indian history also helped; he was a knowledgeable sounding board. He had not the same passion for cricket that

Charlie had but he was surprised when I told him the aged spy thought himself a 'bit of a poet'. Those talks with George were comforting to me. Should I have made more effort? How different would my life have been if I had married him? Both children liked him but it was they who were to become the purpose in my future—not a union with a man who did not set my pulses running as Charlie had.

Before George went to Korea he was kind enough to volunteer himself as a guide on an expedition I had been thinking about for some time. Charlie had always been reluctant to talk about his personal involvement in the tragedy at Ypres but he was, characteristically, less reticent in remembering his colleagues, particularly his school friend, Herbert Spencer. I had made some enquiries and discovered there was a memorial to him at the Ypres Reservoir Cemetery and I was resolved to visit it on Charlie's behalf. Edith was of a like mind; she had met Herbert when he and her brother were at Uppingham School. The sight of all those symbols of unnecessary deaths moved me greatly. Charlie had tried to justify the killings on the Western front by saying that the soldiers on both sides thought they were fighting a just war, as opposed to Amritsar where the opponents, Dyer and unarmed Indians, were not equal. I always thought this was a difficult argument to sustain, and after visiting the spot where his friend was buried I thought it a nonsense. Sorry, Charlie, to be unfaithful to your memory but after seeing those cemeteries—and considering what happened in India at the time of partition—I have become an ardent pacifist. At a later stage I considered joining the Greenham Common protest, but did not.

It was not until after we were married that I discovered Charlie had been awarded the Military Cross for gallantry during the battle for Polygon Wood. Initially, I was angry that he had kept this to himself but later I discovered that, except for some of his army colleagues, no-one else knew, not even Edith. I am not even sure he ever told Mary. When I left India in 1943 I insisted on bringing the cross back with me and, after the visit to Flanders, Edith and I decided it should be framed and hung in the dining room. Was that perverse for a now confirmed pacifist? Perhaps so, but if Charlie would not let it be known how brave he was I was damn well going to do so. Charlie was more forthcoming about his participation in the campaign at the North West Frontier. His exploits amongst the Pathan, allied to his love of cricket, made me think recently of a story in the comic both Matthew and Jenny read when they were young. Was it the *Wizard* or the *Hotspur*? I think the story was called *The Wolf of Kabul*, about an agent for the British Intelligence Corps who always dressed as a native. He took on all comers, which were usually the Pathan, with help from Chung, his native servant, who was lethal with his 'clicky-ba' (cricket bat).

I did not even try to understand why George was going to Korea. A new enemy—Communism. Russia, our former ally. I think, facetiously, the West used it as an excuse to keep the soldiers busy. Verwoerd used it as an apology for persecuting the blacks and McCarthy used it as a reason to persecute anyone in America whom he considered to be an intellectual. I've seen many of the anti-war films—*All Quiet on the Western Front; La Grande Illusion, Paths of Glory* and *Catch 22*—but I think Richard Attenborough's *Oh What a Lovely War* best illustrates the follies men drag us into. Charlie knew a lot of the lyrics from the songs in the film. He loved to repeat one line: 'And live on the earnings of a lady typist.' Never understood what intrigued him about that. I thought Attenborough also made a good job of *Ghandi*. What inspired casting Ben Kingsley was. He had played the Coloured man when Miriam and I went to see Fugard's *Statements after an Arrest under the Immorality Act*. Fugard was also in *Ghandi*. He took the part of General Smuts.

Forgive an old lady. I ramble on.

The lives of my children became an important item in my life post-Charlie, and as they soon began to live in foreign parts travel also became a valuable ingredient in my existence. I did not go to Nigeria until after Matthew was married but as I had met Joe Marks when he was at Cambridge I was on their doorstep fairly frequently. Additionally, there was the pilgrimage to India. Although I had thought tentatively of trying to visit Charlie's grave, it was only after talking to George that this became an unstoppable ambition. He had told me of the Memorial in the nearby town of Kohima commemorating the dead involved in repulsing the Japanese advance into India:

When You Go Home, Tell Them Of Us And Say,
For Your Tomorrow, We Gave Our Today.

When I first heard these words I could not decide whether to ring the travel agency immediately, or abandon the whole scheme. Are they banal in the extreme, or uplifting? I still do not know.

After his death, Charlie's shares in the business had been bought by David Blunt for, as far as I could gauge, a very fair price. There were problems about remitting the proceeds to the UK but David overcame this in time and a large proportion of the monies was eventually sent. However, there were remaining funds in Blunt's accounts and I resolved to use these to finance an Indian trip for Edith and me. It was extremely difficult to obtain permission for non-Indians to visit Manipur and Nagaland, but I gave David a long notice of my intentions and eventually he was able, through his many contacts, to arrange this.

On the whole I think going back to India was a mistake. It is now the largest democracy in the world but I found the corruption difficult to stomach. David was wonderful and entertained us like visiting royalty, but when I found how much it had cost in bribes to obtain a permit to go to Kohima I was shocked. It is a very isolated area, in parts most beautiful, but not like India at all, at least the India I knew. In Bombay the vestiges of the Raj are still there—the Cricket Club for instance—but it is not the same. How could it be? At least it is relatively peaceful, but I found I was more comfortable with my children's territories in Africa.

I still try to walk as far as the church each day but the bones creak a bit. I remembered the walks Charlie and the children and I took, all those years ago when visiting Mahabaleshwar. In Stanton it was chilly, but bright, and the air smelt fresh. It must have been something in the atmosphere that prompted those memories. We were so happy—and complete. I determined not to mope. Visits to Arthur's Seat and Wilson's Point to see the sunset; crazy Indians who applauded when the sun went down; delicious strawberries. We also used to visit Panchgani on day trips. Odd, but it was a major centre for boarding schools and Matthew told me he had a Polish friend in Nigeria who had been evacuated from his own country and educated in this Indian hill town. It is a small world.

I have never said so in the past, but I was not sure about Isobel. I thought that if she had to go three thousand miles to find a husband, something must be wrong. Totally illogical I know, and perhaps no girl seems good enough for a mother's son. 'A son is a son 'til he gets him a wife but a daughter's a daughter the rest of your life'. Nevertheless, it was a most successful wedding and, over the years, she has become like a second daughter to me, particularly as they now live nearby. In 1981 she and Matthew decided they needed to leave Nigeria. The business was going well but they both felt they should be back here as the children approached their university years. Matthew, as you would expect, had planned the move back to the UK with some care. He had taken a distance-learning course with the Management School at Leicester University and this, together with his hands-on experience, had secured him a lectureship in the same school. He was content with this—not very remunerative, but he had left Nigeria with some capital and he found teaching satisfying, and not too demanding. What did exercise him, however, was the situation in his adopted country. What a mess they were making of it. If I had thought that India was tainted by the smell of corruption, the stink coming out of Nigeria was overpowering. After Gowon was deposed in a bloodless coup—said to be because he was not being strong enough over dishonesty—the next soldier-leader was assassinated on his way to work only streets away from where Matthew and his family lived. Obasanjo took over, delivered the country back to civilian rule but democracy changed nothing. Those whom the people had chosen—or had they? Nigerians were becoming most efficient at rigging elections—were even bigger blackguards than the soldiers.

When Matthew and Isobel came back to the UK they made contact with Gerard Lakey. who had retired from the army and found himself what he referred to as a 'cushy number' as the Secretary of one of the gentlemen's clubs in London—I cannot remember which one—near to Pall Mall, as I recall. He invited me to lunch there one day—in the ladies' dining room, of course—and I found him charming. He admired what Matthew had achieved in Nigeria as he knew from first-hand experience what a difficult country it was—and still is—but what pleased me most was that he encouraged me to talk about Charlie as a soldier. Two of his father's brothers had been killed in the 1914–18 conflict. Again all I could think of to say was, 'What a waste.' Maggie may have taken us into the Falklands War, but if a majority of European rulers in 1914 had been women, would there have been the catastrophe that led to the death of nine million combatants, and another five million civilians as a result of the passage of arms, or starvation, or disease? Gerard says that this subject is discussed at

Staff College but there can never be a satisfactory answer. I can only be glad that Charlie survived that war. I told Gerard about his reticence over the Military Cross. He was not surprised. 'Exactly what Matthew would have done,' he said.

Isobel was awarded the MBE for her contribution to the Girl Guide movement in Nigeria and we all went to the palace when she curtsied to the Queen. When I say 'all', Matt and the two children were allowed to witness the ceremony but Edith and I had to stay in the car which Matt had driven, with permission, into the courtyard at Buckingham Palace. The Brits do these things so well. Isobel fully deserved this honour. If she ever thought the affections of her husband were being taken over by his regard for Peter, then Matt could have felt the same way about Robert Baden-Powell. Since they came back to the UK she has been even more involved. International Commissioner for the county is now her position, I believe.

Edith died in 1985, just before her 90th birthday. It was a peaceful end. She was a lucky woman. Other than arthritis, she kept well all her life and died in her sleep. We had lived together for more than forty years. She was like sister and mother to me and surrogate mother and grandmother for the others. When Isobel and I were clearing out her wardrobes we found a small leather attaché case that proved to contain nearly one hundred letters to her sometime fiancée, Tony Shelton, and an equal number of replies. The first was dated September 1914 and the last three weeks before they were married in the summer of 1916. We both sat on the floor of her bedroom and felt no sense of prying as we began to read. Isobel was in tears before I was.

'What an amazing old bird she was! Did you know these existed?'

'No. She never mentioned them. She adored him and he her. What shall we do with them?'

'I've no idea.'

'There has been a plethora of stuff published recently about World War I, but these may be too ordinary for that. However, as Edith has been so central to this family—the Queen bee you might say—let's get them printed in book form for distribution within the family and for a few other friends and contacts. Might be good for the grandchildren to know that we old folk also fell in love.'

'What a good idea. I'll get Matt on to it. Just up his street.'

'I think Edith must have had some letters from that Hubert man who was on the scene before Tony, but obviously nothing worth saving. Charlie met him a few times. No-one in the family liked him, particularly not their father. From what I can gather he was considered too smooth for the Cresswells. Used an excess of Bay rum cologne and wore a cravat.'

She would be so pleased to know that John has joined the family firm. I suppose in the end Matt became a good businessman and his son seems to have inherited that. I do not care much for that girl John is squiring. Her hobby appears to be shopping, but at least she is not a drug addict. What they are going to do about Lorraine, I don't know. She decided she needed to find herself and to do that she must trek around the world. They are too easy with her, in my opinion. What will she find out about herself in Thailand that she cannot discover in London or Leicester?

When I eventually met Miriam Johnson I was really impressed. I have no direct experience of the race problems of South Africa but I could relate to her as a result of my early years. These were not exactly in the mould of *Bhowani Junction*, but I was inevitably exposed to some discrimination. I felt I already knew her after Jenny's description but Miriam soon brought me up to date on what had happened since she left South Africa. Such a brave woman. After her experience at the hands of the South African police she had gone into exile, believing that militancy was the only path to freedom for her people. She told me she realised what had been done to her was perhaps minor, compared with others who had been systematically tortured over long periods of time, but that horrid use of the desk drawer had so affected her she felt she had to do something positive to fight. Unfortunately, when she eventually arrived at the *Umkhonto we Sizwe* training camp it was not quite what she had expected. The South African Government was fully aware that these camps existed and did their best to infiltrate them with informers and spies. As a result, everyone, particularly newcomers, were suspect and this atmosphere of distrust and looking over one shoulder all the time quickly disenchanted her. She told me of one man at her location who was a specialist car thief in Port Elizabeth who had been recruited by the South African Security forces and promised immunity for his crimes to act as an informer. He had been discovered and executed by the group she had joined. That was in Angola to where she was posted from Zambia. She persevered for some months but by then began to wonder if the high command of the *Umkhonto we Sizwe* was any more democratic than the South African Government. Her intelligence was respected but she never felt at ease and when she was given a job to courier a message to sympathisers in London she decided to quit. Evidently, Jenny and John were in touch with her and had been able to provide initial finance for her to stay in London, until she found a job. In due course, they were also able to obtain the necessary permission for her to stay in the UK.

Another human tragedy. These black and Coloured people all had the same goal and would you not have thought this would have united them? But it seemed not. The South African Government did their best to foster discontent and distrust, but again the freedom fighters themselves could not always work together. I say black and Coloured, but South Africans of Indian origin were also prominent in the fight against apartheid. They had been specifically discriminated against in Natal, where most of them lived, but they were also involved in the anti-apartheid movement countrywide. Indians were amongst the accused at the Treason Trials of 1956–7 and Mandela was friendly with many of their leaders, some of whom were imprisoned with him on Robben Island.

I told Miriam we had a lot in common—we were both mongrels. I think this shocked her at first but she recovered when she saw what I meant and we had a good conflab about it. She said that in my case I knew exactly where I came from. 'Your mother was an Indian and your father a full-blooded white man.' I thought back. Mummy was a real beauty—all the best of the oriental features. She must have bewitched that young engineer. He was under intense pressure to give her up but he persevered and, even with that so-called stigma, he did very well in the top echelons of the Indian Railways. However, my mother was not of entirely Indian blood. Her father had been an engine driver, one of the thousands of Anglo-Indians who served the railway with such pride and so I said to Miriam, 'I am, on one side at least, as mixed of blood as you might be.' Miriam fully understood all this but made the point that although my people lived in a country where there were strict class and caste differences these were not prescribed by law, by a myriad of laws. She also said that in her case the mixing of the blood went back a very long way. She may have been the result of a relationship between black and white within the twentieth century but such contacts had a long history and she had no way of knowing who her antecedents were. When Cape Town was first settled there was a need for labourers so, while elsewhere slaves were being exported from Africa, the man in charge, Van Riebeeck, was importing them into the continent, mainly from the Far East. The officers of the United East India Company did not generally take their wives to the Cape (I read that in 1663 there were said to be only seventeen white women at the station) and so these officers, and eventually the free burgher farmers, bred from female slaves and the indigenous natives a mixed race from whence Miriam may have been spawned. In the first twenty years of occupation by the 'white tribe of Africa', seventy-five per cent of the children born at the Cape were non-whites, thus adding to the supply of slaves at little cost to the establishment.

Anglo-Indians were often good linguists, speaking Hindi or other local dialects as well as English, but with the Coloured of South Africa, Afrikaans, as spoken by their oppressors, was also their first language. What a paradox. The original Boer generally spoke Dutch but as they began to emerge as a separate people, the Afrikaner, they needed to adopt a language of their own. To achieve this they sought to counteract the cultural domination of the British colonial regime and to elevate the then Afrikaans language which, in the nineteenth century, was extensively varied between regions and social classes, apart from its association with poverty and 'colouredness'. These variations in dialect stemmed from the origins of the language itself. The lowland Dutch of the seventeenth-century settlers had been mixed with the Malay and Portuguese creole of the imported slaves, to which was added some Khoisan speech, together with further injections of German and French. It was to become the language of violence. The Xhosa-speaking black man picked up by the police is harangued in Afrikaans. What a mess!

I do not know to what extent John helped Miriam because of guilt, or whether it was simply because both he and Jenny were simply acting as good friends. John has turned out to be a great surprise, at least to me. Whether Jenny saw something no-one else did I do not know, but once he was married he began to take a more active interest in Marshalls and it was he, rather than Hermann, that arrogant brother of his, who took them into manufacturing, a move which, within ten years or so, meant my daughter was married to a rich man. The brother—I only met him twice—did not know about the Snyman episode but he had some inkling that John was involved with a non-white woman and I would not be surprised if he thought Jenny was not much better—she had a half-caste mother after all. Jenny was as diplomatic as possible but when John was able to buy his brother out, they were glad to be in a position to have as little contact as possible with the rest of the family. However, before that happened we did have that hilarious dinner party the first time Edith came with me on a visit to South Africa—in 1968. Jenny had described this man, and his wife, as absolutely archetypical of the narrow-minded Afrikaner who despises the black people in the country. When he bothered to notice them at all, he treated them as either half-witted children or hardened criminals. Fortunately, Miriam never had to meet him. Jenny disliked him intensely and so took great delight in setting up the charade to come, in which she wrote the script and was in charge of make-up and costumes. Hermann and his wife—what was her name? Bel I think—were invited to dine with John and Jenny in honour of the visit of the mother and the aunt. The younger Markses were also involved. John had been primed to mention to his brother that he was a little nervous about the visit of mother-in-law—with phrases like 'a bit of a native' and 'hope the police don't pick her up for being in the wrong neighbourhood'. Somehow, he was also able to suggest, at different times, that now he knew her better, he wasn't sure whether Emily Marks might not have a 'touch of the tar brush'. I wore a vivid pink sari. My hair had been darkened with some sort of oil and drawn back flat to my head. I wore the bindi—the red spot between the eyebrows—and an embarrassment of cheap glitzy jewellery. Jenny's make-up was on the dark side with so much kohl plastered around her eyes she looked as though she had just escaped from an Arabian harem or a Calcutta brothel. Emily was, sad to say, not very convincing. Her dark face cream gave her the look of a female Al Jolson. When the insufferable couple walked in they must have wondered if they were in District Six or an Indian enclave of Durban. With Aunt Edith as choirmaster, we all spoke in the most exaggerated English upper-class accents to belie our outrageous dress and complexions. There were lots of phrases like 'how frightfully jolly' and 'spiffing weather we're having', sprinkled with references to Ascot, Buck House and polo at Windsor Great Park. They didn't stay long, particularly as dinner comprised mealie meal and some sort of local stew. I don't think they realised they had been subjected to a theatrical performance, but whenever John had to deal with his brother in the future he was often asked if his 'darkie' mother-in-law was keeping well.

Jenny had been deeply involved in one change of direction within Miriam's life and perhaps I was to become equally involved in another. I had read rave reviews of some new plays from South Africa being presented at the Royal Court Theatre in London. Two of them were collaborations between Athol Fugard and the actors who performed in them, John Kani and Winston Ntshona. However, the play we went to see was by Fugard alone: *Statements after an Arrest under the Immorality Act.* The reviews were mixed. I asked Miriam if she would like to come with me. She knew what the play concerned—difficult not to with a title like that—and she was naturally even more interested because of the affair with John.

I think we were both surprised. Although most of the play had two naked lovers on stage, post-coital, it seemed to me to be distinctly un-erotic. What it did, most forcefully, was to demonstrate one of the fundamental apartheid strictures: you cannot love whom you want. Near the end the man has a long speech saying that he can see, taste, feel, smell, hear, walk, work and think—but he cannot love. Powerful stuff. To me it underlined the real evil in South Africa—the deliberate separation of the people. The man is very interested in the theory of evolution and you could almost believe these two had created their own Garden of Eden. The first half takes place in virtual darkness, epitomising the furtive basis of this relationship and the way the oppressed in South Africa are kept in the dark. Is it credible to see the man as part Caliban—'this thing of darkness'? In contrast, the second half is announced by an uncomfortable blaze of light with the entry of the police and the photographer's flash bulbs that expose the sin of these two people. There then follows the cross examinations. In Fugard's skilled hands these amount, in the main, to monologues by the man and the woman describing themselves and their journey towards the humiliation of the present situation. It was clear that many people in the audience, with little knowledge of South Africa, did not appreciate all the nuances. These two lovers, of different races, are probably the only two educated people in this small dusty town set in the Karoo, the South African desert region. I was fascinated by the Karoo. Jenny and John took me to New Bethesda where they said Fugard had a holiday home and which was the locale for his play *Road to Mecca.* It is not just sex that attracts Errol Philander and Frieda Joubert to each other. They are two people in this isolated town who have interests in common and anywhere else but South Africa they might have formed a long-term relationship, albeit adulterous. Fugard has the Coloured man married, and the white woman a virgin spinster, to add to the problems in this liaison. Miriam, of course, understood only too well. She could so easily have been one of the two people disturbed by that police raid, and she had chosen the name Eve as her *nom-de-plume.* A few weeks after seeing this play Miriam told me that Fugard's work had struck such a chord, and he had so acutely portrayed the reality of her unhappy country, she had finally decided to become a writer. As she says, with South Africa as a background, there is no shortage of subjects for someone like her to write about. I wished her the best of luck and, from what I hear, she has had some modest success.

Edith was not a reader—too busy perhaps, but that is not the real reason. I believe the world is divided into those who read and those who do not. I mean those who read fiction. What a presumptuous statement. Ernie Collingwood reads the *News of the World* on Sundays while his wife is content with *Woman's Weekly.* I now sound even more like a cultural snob. Other than the *Financial Times,* Tony Shelton tended to concentrate on political biographies and I often thought his books were chosen by weight rather than for their contents. For me, I have read all my life and in that Miriam and I are twin souls. During the second half of the twentieth century there has been an extraordinary increase in the production of, and interest in, fiction from what is referred to as the 'Third World'. Sometimes called 'post-colonial' I believe. A goodly proportion of this is by Indian writers and therefore of particular interest to me. As Miriam said, the conditions in her country gave her plenty of material for her writings and the same was true of India. I naturally took an interest in the troubled times of Indira Ghandi and the State of Emergency but the best picture was provided by a novel published in 1985, *Rich Like Us* by Nayantara Sahgal. This had a particular resonance for me. The dedication was: 'To The Indo-British Experience and what its sharers have learned from each other.' I was also taken by something the writer said at a conference last year. She was talking about a form of schizophrenia suffered by many educated Indians—and perhaps this also applies to me. Her father, who was a dedicated advocate of freedom for India and was imprisoned by the British, wept when London was bombed in the Blitz and when Paris was taken by Hitler's armies. Nayantara Sahgal thought that if he had been asked who he was, he would have said, 'I am a member of the human race—and all the rest is rhetoric.' I wonder why this strikes such a bell in my own consciousness.

If the principal women in my extended family were characters in a novel, there would be criticism that on the whole they seemed to be cut from the same the piece of cloth, me included. I never met Mrs Nyman, and John's sister-in-law was an irrelevancy as far as I was concerned, but with the others the facts must speak for themselves. The similarities between Jenny and myself are understandable but the characteristics we share with Isobel cannot be explained by the fact that we, at various times, lived in the same heart of England as each other. I think Isobel is more of a heroine than any of the women in our family story. She could easily have been as provincial as the Collingwoods but at the age of twenty-two she decided to go and work in Nigeria. There was nothing in her heritage that could have determined such action. Although her parents had moved about England—her father was in domestic service—the usual extent of their travel was Great Yarmouth for seaside holidays. Her mother came from a lower middle-class background; a number of her relatives ran their own small businesses—shops or, in one instance, a small transport company. But Mrs Ramsay was a spirited woman who had passed on some of the same to her daughter. Matthew needed an Isobel. She gave him the maximum support when he thought the Government was going to lock him up for his fairly minor role in the Biafran War; in his business life she also proved to be very skilled at what they today call 'networking'. She has made The Grange into a most welcoming home where, I suspect, I shall end my days when I have to sell the Old Vicarage.

Of course, I never met Mary, although I did become close friends with her remaining Leicestershire family after leaving India. Was she built of the same stern stuff as Isobel? It must have been quite an adventure to leave home and the prospect of a career in medicine, to live with a man she knew only slightly—and in an alien environment. When Charlie's things were eventually shipped back to me they included her journals. I knew of them—he never travelled anywhere without them. I felt no jealousy. I understood. But I did not read them until they were in my possession. Unfortunately, all they reveal is that she could also be seen as coming from that same bolt of cloth. On the other hand, is that so strange. The man who was attracted to an Adele and sired a Jenny would, more likely than not, have had a first wife in the same mould. The journals reveal, in my opinion, a woman more sensitive than both Jenny and me. Whether this is reflective of her time I don't know but I can see a softer person—and certainly more of a poet than any of us.

Miriam, of course, grew up in an alien world, light years away from that of Jenny and Isobel but, largely thanks to her luck with education on the farm where she was born, she has survived. She agrees with me that the affair with John had a considerable impact on her development into the assured and competent woman she is today. Is this strange? Perhaps there is an element that says if a black, or Coloured, girl working in a bank in Johannesburg can provoke such a sincere and deeply felt act of love in an Afrikaner, she must have had some special qualities. However, I think it is more delicate than that. I think each gave the other something. Love, the great teacher. She became confident in her femininity—although this was severely threatened by the incident with Snyman and his men—and he less *gauche*, less ugly. Not in the physical sense, but in attitude. As I never stop saying, Miriam fashioned that man into someone worthy to be my daughter's husband. Isn't human nature wonderful? Both Peter and Matt became bigger people because of each other. Miriam drew strength from John, while at the same time she acted as a most effective piece of sandpaper to remove a lot of his rough edges. How thrilled she will be about the release of Mandela.

Emily likewise. Her place in our drama was extremely significant. If it had not been for her intervention with her husband and father-in-law it is unlikely that Jenny would have finished up in South Africa. Although an Afrikaner, she deplored what her people were doing and became as much a crusader as Jenny. She had made the best of the situation, coming from a very poor family, but the tragedy was that Joe and she had no children. I think it was this that led to the break-up of the marriage. As Jenny had discovered when they were together in Cambridge, Joe was essentially a dull man. He was kind-hearted and no doubt affectionate towards Emily, but when that IBM man came into the picture Joe seemed to accept what happened with a kind of resigned inevitability. According to Jenny, he did not put up much of a fight. The story, as told by my daughter, was that Marks and Co had been asked to advise the giant IBM Company on the registration of one of their more obscure patents and this had brought Scott Middleton into their midst. Before this company quit South Africa in protest over apartheid, he had been their legal counsel in Johannesburg and, as the saying goes, swept Emily off her feet—and eventually back to the USA. I never met him but Jenny tells me Joe never stood a chance. Scott was not a typical Hollywood-male type but was full of American charm and confidence. I believe that they are very happy together. And Joe surprised everyone by getting married again, but this time to a local Jewish girl.

I keep repeating myself, something I do quite often according to the grandchildren. When I left India I was thirty-three and so, if my arithmetic serves me well, I have spent, except for excursions abroad, the last forty-seven years living in a part of England that hardly knows there was such a thing as the British Empire. Or if they do recall it from their school history lessons, they could not be less concerned—the fate of the Nottingham Forest football club is more important. Yet I still see myself as a 'Daughter of Empire'. Despite its critics—and in some areas I'm one of the fiercest—there was a plus side. I was nurtured within a system that cared for the generality of the people. All right, the British were in India for their own economic reasons but soldiers like Charlie were genuinely there to keep peace and not to fight wars, and the ICS, however snobbish they were, did administer the country efficiently, if not always as humanely as they might. The people saw the difference under the virtual dictatorship of Indira Gandhi in the 1970s which led to that draconian state of emergency. Except for the fighting in Malaya and the Mau Mau uprising, most of the red colour on that map was expunged by a peaceful transition to Independence. That did not happen in Algiers. There seems to me to be a basketful of contradictions. The Empire created a country called Nigeria of a mixed bag of tribes and religions but by the time they left, there was a sound governmental system in place with a handful of very good Nigerian civil servants. Look at Peter. The British set up Ibadan University, where he studied. Thanks to that education—and, I like to think, the influence of my son—he has built up a major business by hard work and application—and no corruption. If only he and his like were running the country. Did the Belgians create any Peters in the Congo?

I criticise the Government for not being more proactive in the anti-apartheid campaign but I know very well there was not a lot they could do. It needed a miracle, and perhaps that is what has happened. I suppose it can now be seen, with hindsight, that non-violent action, a passive revolution, was the only internal option that had any real chance of success. Urban terrorism would not have succeeded and the sabotage that took place in the 1960s was aimed at targets to create the most publicity rather than to kill white people. The Townships were sealed off from the rest of the country. There was no maze of alleyways suitable for guerrilla warfare, as in Algiers or some of the Balkan towns. The two opponents, the protest movement and the South African Government, were totally mismatched. They had the most powerful security force on the continent of Africa. By the early 1980s there were said to be one hundred and eighty thousand men fully operational, with a reserve force of half a million troops from the conscription requirement for white South African males. In addition to this military muscle there was the rigorous system of control in the form of apartheid. Opponents of this military force were constrained by the Pass system, direction of labour, and other instruments of petty-apartheid, while the National Government's State Security Service had grown into one of the most efficient (and brutal) in the world, as Miriam can testify. Against this military muscle it is not surprising that the armed resistance, despite the support of the Soviet Union, was so ineffectual. The most effective elements within the campaign of non-violent action were strikes and boycotts. The two-day general strike in 1974 really worried the Government as it brought the nation to a virtual standstill: eight hundred thousand people refused to go to work and four hundred thousand students boycotted classes. Rent boycotts were also extremely effective: by September 1986 it was estimated that sixty per cent of the black population was not paying rent. As you can see, this Leicestershire widow did her homework.

No doubt Mr Mandela has no time today to look back over his

life. He has had long enough sitting in a prison cell to do that, but for some reason his release has released a flood of nostalgia in my breast. I know he is a literary man and he has probably read the same splendid South African poetry that I have—I was introduced to it by Jenny. Dennis Brutus was also in jail. He was shot while trying to escape but it was largely as a result of him that South Africa was excluded from the Olympic Games. He wrote while in prison and I recall extracts from one of his poems, *Somehow we survive*:

Somehow we survive
And tenderness, frustrated, does not wither.

over our heads the monolithic decalogue
of fascist prohibition glowers
and teeters for a catastrophic fall;

most cruel, all our land is scarred with terror,
rendered unlovely and unloveable;
sundered are we and all our passionate surrender

but somehow tenderness survives.

Well, the oppressed South African has survived—at least, those who have not been murdered, like Steve Biko, or scarred for life, as perhaps Miriam is. And so have I.

To what extent Jenny's efforts alleviated any of the suffering cannot perhaps be measured, but she tried. Matthew's involvement had no impact on the tragedy of Biafra, nor on the subsequent decline of the country, but, like Charlie, he did what he did in the name of friendship. Nelson Mandela had Winnie at his side today, so perhaps what does survive is the family. Let us hope that as we approach the millennium the concept of the family will flourish, even if the generality of people and nation states continues to disappoint.

I can hear my grandchildren telling me, most politely, that I am just a pessimistic old woman. That could well be the size of it.